D1827163

BECAUSE OF ONE MAN

Barry Waters

Published by Barry Waters

Publishing partner: Paragon Publishing, Rothersthorpe

First published 2019
© Barry Waters 2019, Spain

ISBN 978-1-78222-731-1

Book design, layout and production management by Into Print
www.intoprint.net
+44 (0)1604 832149

Preface

October 2012.

Meg, her blue eyes shining, looked expectant as Louise entered the Nursery, her hungry tummy telling her that it was time for her afternoon snack.

Out of all the tiny residents Meg was Louise's favourite, she looked at Meg warmly, smiling, moving slowly, whispering reassuring words of kindness and encouragement.

Placing the semi warm beaker of milk on the plastic table, along with Meg's favourite bread and strawberry jam, she took a step back.

"Come on little one, eat up."

Although hungry, Meg nervously pushed her small body into the cushioned wall behind her. Louise took a few steps back to sit on a stool in the opposite corner. She watched, smiling, as Meg grabbed at the bread, greedily pushing it into her tiny mouth, eyes alert, not moving from Louise's warm gaze.

As Meg ate, Louise looked on, she wondered as she did most days, what had happened prior to this thin, pathetic sad child, who had been brought to her just over two months ago. Although little more than a toddler she had the strained look of tired desperation, suspicion and even aggression for one so small.

It had taken Louise many weeks of encouragement and patient love and care before Meg didn't panic or scream, when she entered the room, still having one to one attention, unable to mix safely with the other tiny residents.

Louise looked around the colourful patterned room, depicting the cartooned lambs and various other animalistic young. She couldn't help the tearful glassiness that filled her sad eyes.

In the thirty years or more that she had devoted her life to childcare; Meg was without doubt the saddest case in memory. Lots of thoughts filled Louise's mind as she tried to remember the good times, the happy times, and the pleasure that her profession had brought her over the years.

***

April 2012 – 5 months earlier.

The man in the wheelchair pressed the four way switch on the right hand side of the arm rest. His body remained still as the motor buzzed into life, and the chair rotated to the left. His eyes were moving, his paralysed lower body was unmoving. Taking his hand off the control he pulled the hood of his jacket tighter to his head to protect against the wind and rain that was pounding him relentlessly. Through the onslaught of the deluge he looked towards a block of apartments, in particular a window on the second floor. His tear filled eyes stared at the flowered curtains. It had been three years since that day his life had changed forever, three years since his comfortable happy existence, had been turned around in the most violent circumstances. Three years since he lost his beautiful girlfriend, the first and only girl he had ever loved. Three years since he lost everything he had. *Because of one man.*

Due to the severe beating he had taken, a beating that had been ordered, two men waiting for him armed with baseball bats, two men who had been sent to ambush him, the man in the wheelchair had been left in this crippled pathetic state. Over the last three years he had gone through many months of pain. Many months of various operations to part mend various parts of his broken body, then more painful rehabilitation, then more operations. Only to be told that he was still doomed to life in a wheelchair. This wheelchair. He hated this wheelchair.

Another tear as he looked up at the flat. He had been happy in that flat, his flat, the flat he had worked hard for. The one where he planned to live happily ever after, just the two of them, him and his beautiful girlfriend, together forever. Now it was gone, all life as he knew it was gone. *Because of one man.* He had been watching the window for over an hour as one guy left and a few minutes later another one entered. Maybe coincidence, maybe they weren't going to the same flat, but the red light in the window was switched off after they entered and back on again after they left.

Tears streaming down his rain drenched face, he pressed the wheelchair control again, the wheels spun in opposite directions, turning the chair round. He took a last glance at the apartment window then headed away into the night, his thoughts a mix of sadness, regret; *but most of all, anger and revenge.*

2010 Eighteen months earlier.

In a terraced house in Peckham Rye a meeting was being held, a family meeting. A father and his three sons, sitting round an ancient wooden table. The room was an old fashioned kitchen come diner situated at the back of the house. A sideboard along one wall behind the table, the opposite wall accommodating a sink, a fridge and a gas cooker.

It had been eighteen months since the Serbian immigrant called Bojan Duric had received a call from the Kings College Hospital, telling him to get there as quickly as possible. Two of his three sons had been badly beaten and found unconscious behind a nightclub in Peckham. The younger of the two, Dorde, was in a coma and on a life support machine. He was suffering from severe head injuries. His elder brother Aco was in the intensive care unit. His life was not in danger but his legs were smashed and broken in several places. He also had damage to his lower spine. Their recovery had been slow and painful. Many operations and many months later they had been discharged. Aco would never again be able to walk unaided. Dorde, not the brightest of people to start with had suffered multiple skull fractures leaving him more damaged than he was prior to the attack.

Bojan had spent the last year concentrating on his two boys, visiting them every day they were in hospital, talking to Dorde, softly encouraging him to wake up. Eventually, after being released, he and their mother Mila had looked after them as if they were new born babies. Now eighteen months later, Bojan had decided it was time to talk, time to get to the bottom of what had happened that night. Find out who was responsible for their terrible injuries. Bojan looked at his boys; he could not help the tears that glassed his eyes. His thoughts were a mix of sadness and regret; *but most of all anger and revenge.*

July 2012 – Present day.

Roger Scott was bored. Pleasantly bored, but still bored. He looked at his sleeping wife of three years. Still as beautiful as when she first walked into his office many years earlier to be interviewed for the position of his Personal Secretary.

It had been three years since his life had changed in dramatic fashion. Three years since the breakup of his south London empire. Three years since he had tasted true love for the first time in his thirty five year life. Roger moved out of the bedroom, past the Jacuzzi and through into the lounge, padding barefoot through the thick pile carpet. Gazing out of the window he admired the view of London, its famous landmarks starting to appear through the morning mist.

As he lazily stretched his six foot lean muscular frame, he pondered over the last three years. His life certainly had changed in dramatic fashion. The wedding. Their wedding, held at the small but beautiful church in the village of Cliffe, in the garden of England known as Kent. Close to where Roger owned a large country house on the edge of the marshes, close to the Thames. The wedding was then followed by a honeymoon in the Seychelles, followed by a round the world cruise. More holidays were forthcoming. All chosen by Sam, his pretty young wife. Some of the places they visited Roger had never heard of. There were nights at West End theatres, something else Roger had never experienced.

All very nice but was it really his thing? He had spent less time in London and more time in Kent, mainly due to Sam and her horse Penny. Sam thought the world of that horse; it was her pride and joy. She was never more happy than when she was riding Penny across the endless marshes the surrounded their country home. Sam was happy which made Roger happy. He moved away from the window as he cast his mind back to his life prior to Sam, his beautiful wife who had unknowingly been responsible for the dramatic change in him.

Roger had survived a tough upbringing, tormented and bullied by his elder siblings as his drunken mother looked on, his father rarely being around to offer any help or assistance. Until when at the age of twelve Roger fought back. By then he had grown tall and well built for his age. That, mixed with his evil temper and violent ways, ensured that the bullying stopped. Although his elder brothers were more mature in years and physique, they were no match for Roger's vicious temper. During the next few years he became feared in his local area, being able to beat other boys superior in both age and size, never happier than when inflicting pain on his unfortunate opponents. Their cries for mercy and that they had had enough were met with Roger's reply that *"they'd had enough when he decided,"* as he gleefully inflicted more injuries upon his victims.

Roger's early life of mugging and street robbery had developed into protection, prostitution and drug supply, eventually investing in nightclubs and a snooker hall. He had a posse of men on his pay role who were happy through both fear and respect to work for him. All six foot plus, all hard men, except Mary, who despite being the only female in his team, could fight with the best of her male counterparts. Most of them had been with Roger since his early days. He had started small, just himself, and then as time progressed and his businesses grew, he had taken on more people.

Then three years ago it had all changed, the string of massage parlours that Roger owned had been given to his guys and Mary. His drug business was no more. He was now a legitimate, respectable businessman. He still owned the snooker hall and the two night clubs, *"Sam's"* and *"Club Mina."* the former being renamed after his wife. He also owned ten gaming salons containing one arm bandits and the new roulette machines that were becoming popular with his clients to the point of obsession. It was not rare or unusual to see men and women alike lose their entire week's wages in a matter of minutes. Very much a cash business, of which the majority was laundered by his long time friend and accountant, Sol Hindmarch.

Over the years Roger had also built up a property portfolio, mainly flats where he allowed ladies to work, flats with a red light in the window, nothing illegal for a girl to work alone. Most of the clients made contact via a website that showed pictures of the prostitutes, and a phone number to a call centre where three ladies, whom Roger had known for many years, received the calls. Ladies who were no longer attractive enough to sell their own bodies but were happy to be still involved with Roger Scott and his business. The call centre manager was a lady called Mina. Roger and Mina had a special relationship that had been their secret for many years. It consisted of casual sex when the need arose. These clandestine meetings mainly happened in his office behind the locked door.

The telephone calls were taken, the appointments were made, the clients would visit, pay an agreed price for an agreed service. The takings were then collected every two days by twin brothers, Tom and Jeff, who were not only Roger's employees but were also childhood friends. All in all a very lucrative and profitable business, almost legitimate, but Roger was bored. Pleasantly bored but still bored.

July 2012.

In a terraced house in Peckham Rye a meeting was being held, a family meeting, a father and his three sons. They were sitting round an ancient wooden table, drinking tea. A simmering kettle sat on the gas cooker behind them. Bojan Duric had lived in London since 1990. He moved from Serbia with his wife Mila and their two sons, Aco who was five and his younger sibling Dorde who was three. They settled well and after four years another son was born. They called him Rodovan. Mila was happy, her family was complete. They had a comfortable house and had managed to escape Serbia before the wars had started. She was a pleasant friendly lady who enjoyed living in London.

Her husband Bojan was a complete contrast to his amiable wife. He was a fearsome fighter who had an evil vicious streak. Almost immediately after moving to London he set about building a reputation by visiting the local bars, drinking and picking a fight with anybody who looked at him the wrong way. As the years went by he became feared throughout the local area. Various so called hard men from both the local and neighbouring areas would issue a challenge only to come off second best.

In their teens both Aco and Dorde were starting to follow in their father's footsteps. First at school, then in the same bars where Bojan had built his reputation. The problem was, they didn't have the brains of their father. In fact they hardly had a brain between them. Now, as they all sat waiting for four guests to arrive, four men that Bojan had known from his days in Serbia, his mind drifted back three years, to when he had received a call from Kings College Hospital.

It was early in 2009 when his two elder sons had visited a nightclub in Peckham. They stood looking at the inside of the dingy premises. They had decided they wanted more than the small amount of money they were bringing in by offering local businesses protection and debt collection. By now, they were in their early twenties and had grown to the same six foot height as their father. They were also feared locally. When together they would often be the cause of most of the trouble and fighting in the area. On the odd time they came off second best their father Bojan would be there to mete out revenge and retribution.

Thinking they were invincible they had decided to acquire a nightclub. Why not? They were tough, hard as nails. Feared by all who knew them. Now they could take what they wanted when they wanted. They would start with one club and then in a matter of a few years they would probably be running the whole of south London. Then maybe all of London.

After looking around various nightclubs, they settled on a less salubrious looking place in Peckham. *A good place to start*. In their arrogance and without much thought or planning they had entered the premises. After getting a drink from the well stocked bar and taking in the situation, they approached the manager. *This was going to be easier than they thought*.

Colin was an experienced manager; he had been in charge of the club for many years. He had seen the likes of the two brothers come and go many times. So when they made veiled threats to the effect that they were going to take over the nightclub, and that they had a gang of Serbian hard men working for them, Colin smiled, told them it was no problem. He would go and bring the owner. Surely there was no need for any trouble. It could be sorted without any problems. They smiled at each other. *This was definitely going to be easier that they thought*.

Roger Scott listened to what Colin had to say before walking out of his upstairs office and down into the club. He saw the two brothers at the bar, he approached them. Smiling he spoke;

"Evening gentlemen, my manager tells me you want to take over my club. How much are you offering?" Aco looked at Dorde, smiling, he shook his head arrogantly. He stepped closer to Roger and answered;

"Listen you fuckin' prick, we don't buy anything. We take what we want, and right now we taking this shithole whether you like or not. So if you don't want to feel pain maybe you pack bags and fuck off."

Roger glanced around. He could see that his bouncers were taking in what was happening. He turned slightly to his left and then spun back and with lightning speed, his fist flew from the hip, crashing into Aco's temple. As Aco went down Dorde took his eyes off Roger to look at his brother, as he turned back Roger had taken a step forward and smashed his forearm onto the bridge of the Serbian's nose. Dorde felt the bone and cartilage break as his knees gave way and he joined his brother on the floor. Roger turned and nodded to three of his guys who had been watching. They hadn't been worried; they knew Roger always liked to lead from the front, command respect, and that he could handle any situation of this nature. Roger leaned over the two prone figures;

"If I see you two pieces of shit in here again you will be fuckin' dead." He gave another slight nod to his boys and then strolled back upstairs to his office. As the other patrons of the club looked on, the three bouncers grabbed Aco and Dorde by their feet and dragged them to the back of the club, then out through the fire door, which led into an unlit alley. The same three bouncers then set about kicking, stamping and jumping on the two brothers until they were a bloodied, broken and tangled mess.

As Bojan looked at his sons again, a knock at the door brought him back to the present, and the reason they were gathered there. He opened the door and welcomed four men into the room. Anto, Boro, Danko and Vlado, all Serbian Muslims who had been forced out of their homeland by persecution and violence. All had lost family members in the most horrendous way during, and also after the war had finished. They, like many other Muslims had suffered while the world watched, and now they were bitter, very bitter. They were all friends of Bojan, who, although was non Muslim, had helped them to hide from the gangs of mercenaries who were intent on murder. He had remained friends with them after leaving his home country. Then around two years ago, after realising that they would be in danger for the rest of their lives if they stayed in Serbia, and they would be of help, he had arranged for them to travel to England. After the usual small talk and catching up, the discussions began. The four men left one hour later. Bojan had given them clear instructions as to what he required.

***

Emily Austen was celebrating her eighteenth birthday. Her mother Cassandra had wanted nothing more than a family party, at their home in a quiet leafy avenue in Dulwich Village, along with Emily's father James, her twenty year old sister Jane and a few close friends. Emily, with the verbal backing of her elder sibling, had insisted that she wasn't a child anymore. She wanted to go to her first night club with her friends. After all, at eighteen, she was almost a grown woman. Although she was still not in agreement, Cassandra had watched with pride and some trepidation as her two beautiful daughters had walked down the well kept garden, through the gate and into the taxi that awaited them. Their father slipped his arm around his wife in reassurance; she looked up at him smiling a false smile. Mum was worried. It had been different when Jane had turned eighteen. Jane was confident, more grown up and more mature for her years. In her parents' eyes, Emily was still and always would be their little girl, naive and innocent with her baby doll looks. Also the club they were going to had a bad reputation. A policeman had been shot dead there a few years ago.

After a lot of convincing from her husband Cassandra had reluctantly agreed to let her daughter visit the night club, on the condition that she stayed with her sister and left her mobile phone switched on at all times. Emily protested that she was still being treated like a child, but realising it was the only way she would be allowed to go, she agreed.

As the taxi pulled up outside the night club Emily giggled excitedly as she noticed several of her friends near the door, holding cards and presents and waving at her. Fifteen minutes later, all safely inside, Jane watched, smiling as her younger sister gyrated around the dance floor to the throbbing beat of loud music, her plastic sash proclaiming *"Eighteen Today"* flapping around her shoulders. Jane was smiling happily, looking around at the sea of male faces staring at Emily and her friends. She had never been so happy.

As she turned to the bar to pick up her drink a good looking guy had appeared next to her. Maybe around her age, tall, handsome, wearing a white jacket, pressed trousers and highly polished brown leather shoes. He smiled warmly then said hello. Jane smiled back as she returned the greeting. They chatted for a few minutes. His name was Rodovan but his friends called him Rod. He was quite charming without being smarmy. He told Jane that he was

Serbian, but he had lived and worked in England all his life. They chatted for a few minutes more about nothing in particular. Jane explained that she was here to keep an eye on her younger sister. She pointed to the dance floor where Emily was still with her friends. Rod looked at Emily, a little troubled Jane thought, he commented on how happy she looked. Jane thought the guy seemed relaxed but also as if his mind was elsewhere. He kept glancing around the room as if he was nervous about something. She noticed that he had looked at his watch several times during their conversation. Maybe it was just her imagination, maybe it was just the way he was.

As they continued to chat Jane assumed that she really was imagining things, maybe what he was doing was quite normal, and maybe she had her mother's instructions on her mind and was being overzealous. Content that Emily was safe Jane excused herself to Rod, and after asking him to mind her drink, she headed for the ladies. She pushed the door open then glancing at the mirror as she passed; Jane entered the cubicle, locked the door behind her and started to undo her jeans. She would only be a minute, Emily would be fine. She was so happy for her sister, so happy that she had helped to persuade their mother to allow Emily to attend the nightclub. Jane smiled to herself as she sat down. It was turning into a wonderful night, one she and her sister would remember for a lot of years.

It was then that she was startled by a loud *bang* from outside of the toilet door, then more startled by louder screaming. Then the music stopped, then a pause, then even more screaming, desperate painful screaming.

The house brick had gone through the window of *Sam's* nightclub at around midnight. It arced through the air before descending in a shower of broken glass onto the crowded dance floor. Those close by screamed as they were cut and sliced by the shards that rained down upon them. People stopped dancing to look in horror as a five litre plastic container with a burning rag sticking out of it, followed the brick through the gaping hole where the window had once been.

Petrol needs air to burn, so nothing happened until the container hit a young lady on her shoulder, spilling its contents over her and several of her friends in the vicinity. The girl screamed in shock as her hair and clothes quickly caught fire. The remaining petrol pooled across the dance floor as people screamed and tried to flee the flames and heat. Handbags on the floor that had been danced around rapidly caught fire, along with flowing dresses and flimsy blouses. The girl who had caught the brunt of the container collapsed in a ball of flame, her plastic birthday sash melting into her skin, searing and charring as it went. She screamed for a few seconds in terrified agony then lay silent as the flames engulfed her.

Jane opened the door of the ladies' toilet to be met by fire and fumes, panic and screaming. She ran towards where she had last seen her sister, pushing past the black suited bouncers who were attempting to release the contents of the fire extinguishers they were holding. There was a large space on the dance floor where those who hadn't managed to get to the doors had pinned themselves against the walls, staring in horror at what was left of a burning body. The automatic sprinklers finally burst into life and started to douse the remaining flames. Jane rushed towards the centre of the dance floor, the heat and smoke hitting her lungs. She stopped, screamed hysterically then fainted on to the now wet floor as the reality of what had happened hit her. Jane knew that the remains smouldering in front of her could only be what was left of her beautiful young sister.

***

The Silk Road Chinese Restaurant in Camberwell Church Street was unusually quiet for a Saturday night. Maybe because it was after midnight, or maybe just the time of the year. Roger Scott and his wife Sam were sitting at their reserved table. Meal finished, they were sipping the last of their second bottle of Chablis. The food had been excellent and the service of Mr. Winn the owner, and the rest of his staff, exemplary. Sam looked lovingly at her husband, she was as happy now as she had been three years earlier, when he had proposed to her. Sam smiled inwardly as she remembered his futile attempt at being romantic. Roger didn't do romance, he had never been in love before, he had no experience of ladies other than the girls who worked for him.

Sam remembered how he had shuffled around in his seat, not looking at her, for the first time since she had met him he appeared to be lost for words. Glancing around he had nervously placed a small box in front of her, then mumbled quietly; "Want to get married?" Sam had flung her arms around his neck and almost screamed *"Yes, yes, yes."*

Now she continued looking at him as she recalled how her life had changed in such dramatic fashion, how she had gone from being his secretary and living a small flat, to being his wife and sharing not only the penthouse apartment that overlooked London, but also the five bedroom mansion near the village of Cliffe, in Kent. She enjoyed the quiet countryside but most of all she enjoyed exercising Penny, her thoroughbred horse. Penny had been a first wedding

17

anniversary present after Sam had expressed an interest in learning to ride. She had become quite proficient in the saddle and Penny had become part of the family. Not just her horse but also her best friend. Sam was at her happiest when exercising Penny around the endless marshes on the Hoo peninsula.

Gazing at each other lovingly, as if they were the only two people in the restaurant Sam suddenly jumped as Roger's phone rang. He continued to smile at her as he picked it up and glanced at the screen, his face changed as he pressed the answer button and listened. Sam watched as he slowly nodded his head, anger starting to show on his handsome features. Then, his skin appearing to change to white to match the knuckles on his clenched left fist. He pressed the off button and glanced at Sam as he selected a speed dial number and waited for it to answer. He spoke:

"Jeff, Its Roger, need you out the front soon as." He put the phone down and looked at Sam; she could see anger mixed with upset on his face.

"What is it darling?"

"Problem at both night clubs. Got to go."

Roger waved to Mr. Winn, who had been watching intently to come over to their table. He asked for the bill. Mr. Winn sensed something was wrong but having known Roger for many years, he knew better than to ask. He appeared moments later carrying a small plate. Roger took a cursory glance, dropped two fifty pound notes onto the plate then stood. Sam stood with him and they headed for door. Neither Roger or Sam or Mr. Winn noticed a guy sitting alone at a corner table. A guy who was taking an avid interest in the happy couple.

The same guy watched Roger and Sam as they

approached the door; he then picked up his phone and pressed a digit.

Sam thought it unusual that when Roger opened the door he walked outside, instead of holding it open in his usual gentlemanly fashion, for her to go first. He stepped into the night to look along the street in search of the black BMW that Jeff would be driving.

That was when he saw four figures step out of a doorway next to the restaurant. He turned quickly and shouted at Sam to get back inside, before violently pushing her through the still swinging door. He spun back around as a fist connected with his temple. Roger staggered back against the wall behind, then side stepped a second blow that glanced off his face.

He quickly weighed up the situation. Four men, approaching as one, all with venom in their eyes. Roger stood his ground, staring, waiting for their next move. He saw a knife blade flash in the street light. He pushed himself off the wall, lashing out instinctively, his right foot finding its target between the guy's legs, he then head butted the next nearest one, perfect hit, on the bridge of the nose.

Roger was vaguely aware of a screech of brakes on the road in front of the restaurant as he focussed on the two guys moving in for the kill. One stepped forward raising some kind of cosh above his head. Roger saw the cosh at the same time a fist connected with his stomach. He saw it coming, exhaled as it found its target, clenched his muscles, the force of the blow, although negated by his quick thinking, still made him stagger back. He noticed the guy he had head butted slowly getting to his feet.

Then a shout as a large hand grabbed the wrist of the man with the cosh, bending it back, snapping it like a twig.

Jeff, six foot six, broad shoulders, over twenty stone, a neck that roughly matched the size of his head, snarled as he relieved the guy of his cosh before smashing it forcefully into its former owner's head. The guy dropped without a further word as Roger flew into the last assailant. Head first between the eyes followed by both fists blurring into the guy's head, then vicious kicks as he went down, up and down his body, back, neck and head. Jeff had turned and brought his knee into the chin of the guy who was attempting to get back up, his head snapped back as he hit the floor unconscious. Three down and out.

The guy that Roger had kicked between the legs attempted to stagger away. Roger shouted for Jeff to open the car boot as he jumped on the guy's back, his weight smashing the unsteady man's head into the ground. Grabbing him by the collar, while twisting his arm up his back, he dragged the lifeless body to the now open car boot before throwing him inside and closing it. Roger calmly walked back to the three prone bodies; taking out his mobile phone he photographed all three before taking their wallets and their own phones. He handed them to Jeff who was now sitting in the driving seat of the BMW.

Roger looked around, after midnight, nobody about. Passing cars taking no notice, maybe what they witnessed as they glanced away from the road ahead was a regular occurrence. Then he looked back towards the restaurant to see Mr. Winn and Sam starring out of the window. *Shit. She had witnessed the whole event.* He strolled to the door as police sirens could be heard in the distance. Roger turned to Jeff, told him to get Tom there as soon as poss, then signalled for him to leave. The BMW sped away.

Jeff and his mute twin brother Tom had known Roger since their school days, when he had rescued them from a neighbouring gang who were intent on causing them serious damage. They had worked for him since the age of sixteen, first as minders and drug mules then as chauffeurs and personal bodyguards. The twins were loyal employees, not the brightest pair around but they loved Roger like a brother. Both were hard as nails and both possessed a vicious temper.

Roger opened the door of the Silk Road Chinese Restaurant and forced a smile at Sam. He walked towards the toilet door as Mr. Winn scurried after him, apologising; "Sorry Mr. Scott, I thought you were going to get hurt so I phoned the police." Roger turned, glared menacingly then answered;

"Me hurt? I've been sitting at that table all night."

As he glanced towards the table something or rather someone caught his eye. A man, sitting alone in the corner, looking at Roger. Roger stared back, taking in his face, his features. He thought he recognised him. Also there was something not quite right about him. He took a step towards him as the blue flashing lights of a police car filled the room. He turned to Mr. Winn.

"Two glasses of white wine. *Now!*" He turned to Sam and nodded towards their table before disappearing into the Gents. He emerged a minute later and sat opposite Sam without looking at either the police sergeant or the constable who were listening to Mr. Winn, explaining that there had been vicious fight outside; a gang of people had beaten up the three guys who were lying in the street, and then ran around the corner into Datchhelor Place when they heard the police sirens. It was lucky the police had arrived when they did because somebody could have been killed. The two policemen looked at everyone in the restaurant. The constable, a PC Jenkins, looked at Roger who was sitting with his right hand in his pocket while sipping his glass of wine with his left. He gave Roger a slight knowing nod then looked elsewhere. Mr Winn assured them that there had been no damage and that he was merely doing his duty as good citizen when he rang them. The two policemen left as an ambulance arrived. Just another night in Camberwell, the culprits would be long gone.

Sam sobbed quietly as she sat next to Roger in the back of the BMW. Tom was driving, heading to *"Sam's"* nightclub. She had remained calm in the restaurant then burst into tears after she had entered the car. Roger had put his arm around her and tried to soothe her, telling her he had to get to the nightclubs. Tom would take her home. He would talk about what had happened tomorrow. Inside Sam was shaking; she wanted to ask questions, who were those people? How did they know Roger was there? Why did they want to hurt him? Why didn't he tell the police the truth, how could her husband be so vicious then so nonchalant afterwards? *But most of all where was Jeff taking the guy in the boot of the car?*

Roger was having similar thoughts. How did those four amateurs know he was in the Silk Road Restaurant? Was it a coincidence that one of his night clubs had been firebombed and a serious attempt made on the other one on the same night? Who was the guy at the corner table? There was something about him. Roger needed to know more. He picked up his phone and rang Mr. Winn. He spoke;

"Roger Scott, don't talk, just listen. One of my guys will call in to see you later today, give him a copy of the CCCT footage from when I entered the restaurant tonight to when I left. Also if the guy sitting in the corner by himself paid by credit card I want full details of it."

He cut the connection and sat back. Mr. Winn would have what he wanted. He wouldn't want his windows broken or his restaurant wrecked. He paid money to Roger on a monthly basis to ensure that didn't happen.

***

Two hundred and thirty miles away, a man in a wheelchair carefully steered himself through the open door and entered the lounge of the Victorian house that he shared with his two brothers. He cursed as he noticed that one of them had left the TV remote control on a shelf that was slightly out of reach, out of reach of his seated paralysed body. He sat still in the chair, slowly shaking his head. He hated his life. For three years he had been stuck in this motorised contraption. For three years almost housebound, *because of one man*. Three years ago he had run his drugs empire that stretched from his front door to every pub, club, nightclub and backstreet in the vicinity. The whole town and every town many miles north and south of there. Then, three years ago, his drug empire had collapsed. Three years ago, a guy from London had not only inflicted a severe beating on him, so severe that he had lost the use of one arm, but then the London guy had created a war between him, his brothers and a rival gang from Moss Side in Manchester. He had taken a bullet to the bottom of his spine. Hospitalised for six months. *Now destined for a life in this fuckin' wheelchair*. The police hadn't wanted to know. They had sat back and watched. They saw it as a welcome cleansing of their diseased and corrupt streets.

He glanced at the clock above the fireplace. He then managed to manoeuvre the chair towards where he had earlier left a two pronged grabber. He placed it almost touching the remote control and squeezed the handle. The two prongs closed onto the TV remote. He lifted it easily and released the prongs allowing them to drop the control onto his lap. He glanced at the clock above the fireplace again. Just in time. The television news was about to start.

After the usual music and spoken headlines the main news began. He stared impassively as the cameras focussed on a London nightclub. The troubled looking reporter, pointing at the doorway as stretcher after stretcher was being carried out and into a convoy of waiting ambulances, explained that first reports indicated more than one fatality. Witnesses spoke of a petrol bomb being thrown through a window on to a crowded dance floor, where it then exploded, covering everybody in the vicinity in flames. The reporter went on to say that it was thought that the nightclub, known as *Sam's,* was owned by a local businessman known to be called Roger Scott, and the club itself was no stranger to violence. Just three years ago, a London detective had mistakenly been gunned down by one of his colleagues inside of *Sam's,* while on an undercover operation. Police were studying CCTV footage and were also appealing for witnesses. The reporter then turned to a young couple, the girl crying, her partner with his arm around her, gently patting her shoulder;

"This is Michelle and Andy who were in the night club at the time of the alleged attack. Can you please tell us what you witnessed?"

Michelle started to explain in a soft Irish brogue how the club had been full when broken glass landed on a section of the dance floor. She and Andy had been standing near the bar waiting to be served. They had then stood frozen in shock as what looked like a fireball hit a young girl, she and the people around her were quickly covered in flames.

Michelle's voice faltered and shook as she burst into tears again. Andy nodded to the reporter then led his girlfriend away. The reporter turned to face the camera to explain that there would be further news throughout the night, and then gave details of a telephone number for worried friends or relatives.

Two hundred and thirty miles away a man in a wheelchair smiled as he pressed a button on his remote control and switched off the television.

***

Sam screamed in horror and disbelief. Tom had stopped the BMW two hundred metres from the night club, *Sam's* night club. *Her* night club. The night club Roger had refurbished three years ago and then renamed after her. She looked out of the back window as Roger jumped out of the car and gestured for Tom to go. The BMW slowly pulled away as Sam watched the fire engines and ambulances, blue lights flashing, waiting. Police keeping onlookers back. She saw Roger talking to what was maybe a plain clothes officer, maybe a detective, clearly her husband was explaining who he was. Then they were gone. Tom steered the car away, taking a left turn and disappearing out of sight of the mayhem.

Sam sat thinking as the silent Tom took her in the direction of the penthouse that had been her London home for the last three years. She cast her mind back to before her relationship with Roger had blossomed. The stories that friends and family had told her about him being involved various crimes, how he was a gangster, how she should not have anything to do with him. Sam had ignored it all. Roger was a good boss who paid well and treated her with respect. She would make up her own mind.

She then thought about the guy Roger had locked in the boot of the car Jeff was driving. She thought about the violence she had witnessed Roger mete out on the four guys who had attacked him. Maybe it was self defence, maybe he was fighting for his life, but he appeared to be enjoying it. He could have done enough and left it for the police to sort out. He could have told the police the truth. After all, he was the innocent party. Four men had attacked him. Why did he try to cover up what had happened? Were her friends and family right? Should she have given him a wide berth from day one? Found another job? Maybe, but Roger had always been the perfect gentleman. Her loving husband of three years had been exactly that. *A loving kind husband.* They had honeymooned, holidayed, and spent their days between the London penthouse and their idyllic country house near the village of Cliffe. Sam's head still appeared to be spinning with questions as Tom pulled up outside the apartment. Questions only one man could answer.

Two days later.

Roger stood inside of what was left of *Sam's* nightclub. He had just left *Club Mina,* where he had spoken at length to Colin the manager. At around the same time that *Sam's* was being attacked, a house brick had bounced off the frame of one of the ground floor windows at *Club Mina*. It had spun harmlessly into the street, but the noise had alerted one of the security staff who ran outside. He saw the brick first then watched as a man in dark clothing disappeared on a motorbike, leaving behind a five litre plastic container which was full of petrol, a rag hanging from the open top. No harm done, but only because of incompetency. The security guy ran back inside and reported his findings to Colin, who in turn had rung Roger.

Roger looked around *Sam's* and surveyed the damage. Apart from the broken window there was severe fire and water damage. There were still police crime scene tapes around the dance floor where the petrol bomb had landed. Two fire-fighters and a policeman were surveying the scene. After explaining who he was, he walked upstairs past the private lounge and into the office. He switched on the television and went through the CCTV footage from the night of the attack.

Finding the exact time it had happened, he replayed it over and over, then over again in slow motion. The television screen was split into twelve small squares each showing various parts of the premises, from the front door and foyer through to the main dance floor and bar area.

He watched as the fire bomb hit the dance floor dousing the people where it landed in petrol then flames. He then went back to the other views of the interior, the bar, the seating area, the foyer again, looking at each individual area at the exact time the bomb hit. Most if not all the faces showed a look of horror and shock. Roger looked again and again for a face, maybe someone he recognised, maybe someone with a smile, maybe someone with a phone at the ready, ready to capture the tragic events on video. An hour went by, he switched off the TV. He was looking too hard, he would try again later. Sitting back in the chair he went over the last forty-eight hours. Two attacks at near enough the same time, or were they? Could it have been the same person on the motorbike? After all, the two clubs are less than a mile apart. He would check the timing of the attack on *Club Mina*. Standing up he thought about the time of the attacks again. It was only a matter of minutes later that

27

he was being confronted outside the Silk Road Chinese restaurant. Coincidence? Maybe, but he didn't think so.

Roger stared at his desk, four wallets revealing nothing. Not a credit card or a driving license, or a family photo or a memento or anything that could lead to the identity of the owners. Just four wallets, some cash, no help. He looked at the four mobile phones next to the wallets. Three of them had no recent calls, received or dialled out, nothing in the contacts or emails or photos or anything that could help. The fourth one had received a text from a withheld number that simply read; *"Now."* The text had been sent at about the time Roger and Sam had stood to leave the restaurant. Clearly the first three had been cleared of all incriminating evidence before the attack outside of the restaurant. The fourth hadn't, maybe no time to clear it.

Roger turned to his laptop computer. He brought up the mobile phone tracking app. He typed in the first number, then waited for the information to download. He would go into the history of all the phones, find out where they had been, maybe an address, maybe a hotel, maybe a meeting room where they had planned their attack. Half an hour later, nothing. All data cleared. Roger went through the CCTV footage of the nightclub fire one final time. Still nothing to attract his attention, to make him suspicious. He thought about the four amateurs who were waiting for him outside of the Silk Road. They were clearly being looked after, being told what to do, puppets on a string. He needed to go deeper.

Roger inserted the copy of the CCTV footage from the Silk Road restaurant into the CD player. It had been collected by Jeff from Mr. Winn earlier. *Handed over with a smile, without protest.* The TV screen showed a grainy video taken from above the counter area. The whole restaurant was in view, unclear but in view. He pressed the fast forward button then slowed back to normal speed as he saw himself and Sam enter. Roger watched for an hour as they ate their meal. Nothing untoward. He pressed the pause button, then sat back in his chair and studied the rest of the room. In particular the guy sitting at the corner table by himself. The guy who Roger was sure had been looking at him. The guy who he was about to approach when the police arrived. He pressed fast forward again, pausing at the point where his phone had rung. He zoomed in on the guy in the corner, watching him in normal motion as the bill had arrived. Watching as the guy clearly retrieved his phone and pressed a button while still not taking his eyes off Roger. *Something still not right.*

He continued watching as he and Sam had walked outside and then further as Sam quickly returned. Then forward to when they both left for the final time. The guy in the corner watching them as he signalled for his bill. Roger watched further as the guy paid in cash then stood up to move. Slowly, very slowly. He retrieved a walking stick from beneath the table then gradually got to his feet and headed towards the door. Roger allowed a slight smile. He had a start, not much but it was something.

Roger turned off the TV and sat back again. He thought about the last three years, how he had changed. Three years ago those four guys' outside the restaurant wouldn't have got near him, he would have seen it coming, been ready, hospitalised them or worse without breaking sweat. The attacks on the night clubs, would anybody have dared to try that three years ago? His reputation went before him, feared by all who knew him. The Roger Scott of old would have known about the attacks before they had happened. He slammed his fist into the desk. He had gone soft, too comfortable. He had problems and he knew it. He left the nightclub and headed to a small warehouse near Southwark. There was somebody there who was going to give him some answers.

**

Assistant Chief Constable Ted Walton winced as he replaced the phone on its cradle. He slowly sat back in his chair. The pain in his stomach was particularly bad today. He picked up the packet of indigestion tablets and emptied two into his hand. He looked at them before throwing them into his mouth, then resisted the temptation to smash his fist into his desk.

One hour earlier he had received a message to contact a friend from his golf club as a matter of urgency. Under normal circumstances he would have called back later, when he had time, when there were no other more pressing matters to attend to. This was different. The friend who had made the call was more than a friend, more than a close family friend. He was called James Austen, father of Emily Austen, Ted Walton's goddaughter. Ted had heard about the nightclub fire in Peckham. The whole country had heard about it. He also knew there had been casualties. Four dead and maybe more to come, but this hit him hard, made it personal. Emily Austen was a sweet little girl who came from a respectable decent family. They would be devastated, as he was. To make matters worse, it brought back memories from three years ago.

The Assistant Chief Constable went into deep thought. It had been three years since the death of his son. *His secret son.* The son that only he and a lady called Eileen Nixon knew about. A result of an illicit one night stand between himself and his best friend's wife. A son who like himself was the best. The most talented prospect the Metropolitan Police had employed for many a year. He was destined for the top. Scotland Yard. It was only a matter of time. *His secret son…* Detective Sergeant Bill Nixon had bravely disarmed a gangster who was waving a gun around in a crowded night club. Without any thought to his own safety he had wrestled the guy to the floor and relieved him of the loaded weapon. Only to be killed by two bullets from an armed police officer, who claimed it had been nothing more than self defence. *Only to be shot, not once but twice in the heart by an idiotic fame-seeking excuse of a coward, who represented the Armed Response Unit.*

Assistant Chief Constable Ted Walton was still bitter, yes, very bitter. In his opinion his son, *his secret son* was on the verge of a massive breakthrough in the fight to arrest and jail a south London gangster named Roger Scott. Despite his requests, the case against Scott had gone cold. Nobody at Camberwell Police Station appeared to be trying too hard to continue the investigation.

Ted Walton had suffered countless sleepless nights since the death of his son, Bill Nixon. To make matters worse, his best friend and police colleague, Chief Inspector George Richard Nixon was the husband of his secret son's mother, Eileen Nixon. Ted had spent a lot time consoling them both after their loss, after the death of their son… *his son,* while at the same time suffering his own grief. Putting on a brave face as he visited their house on regular occasions, trying not to look Eileen in the eye, in an effort to keep their secret.

Now this. His goddaughter had been killed in the same nightclub as his son. The nightclub owned by Roger Scott. His son died a hero, saved many lives. Emily Austen was an innocent victim. Two people he loved were now dead. *Because of one man.*

He stood and slowly walked to the window, in deep thought as he watched the hundreds of tourists, office workers, taxis and bicycle couriers going about their business. He had less than one year to go before enforced retirement. His reputation was intact, no blemishes on his perfect record. Various decorations and medals had been deservedly received.

He came to a decision. An easy decision. His final few months of employment would be dedicated to finishing what his son had started. To take down Roger Scott.

He winced in pain before picking up the phone again; he ordered a car to be outside in five minutes.

***

Mina and Jana had worked for Roger Scott since the age of eighteen. They had been sex slaves, held in a shed which housed nothing more than a bed and a sink, at the back of a south London carwash, managed by a cruel Serbian named Slaven Villic. Villic had bought them from Serbian gangsters who had kidnapped them as fifteen year olds and forced them to work in a brothel on the outskirts of Belgrade. He had raped and beaten the two girls while plying them with drugs until they had lost all fight. Villic took money from the carwash clients, and while their cars were being cleaned the two girls were being used several times a day.

Late one night after Roger had called into the carwash, he and Jeff had killed Villic, making it look like a robbery gone wrong. After rescuing Mina and Jana he had let them stay in his flat. He had then opened his first massage parlour. They had worked for Roger as prostitutes for around fifteen years. He treated them well. Good pay and time off. They were happy; it was the only work they had known. As they got older the wear and tear on their bodies began to show. They were becoming less attractive to the clients. Although it hadn't stopped Roger from having the odd sexual fling with Mina, bending her over his desk and taking her from behind when the need took him. He loved his wife dearly and would never hurt her, but Mina who had never married was an occasional welcome bit of recreation.

Roger had then moved her and Jana into his call centre to take the phone calls and arrange appointments for their younger replacements. This was where they were now, sipping coffee and chatting between answering the phones.

Under normal circumstances, Tom would have been sitting in the back of the converted terraced house in Peckham which now had an office and storeroom upstairs. The downstairs had been converted into the call centre. Three desks, each housing a computer and telephone. Two ladies working there at any one time. The room at the back which normally housed Tom was a converted kitchen, with nothing more than a table and chair and a small television. Tom was absent today, he was in a small warehouse near Southwark with his brother Jeff, standing over a man who was tied to a chair, hands behind his back, a sock in his mouth held by gaffer tape. The two guys who hammered on the back door of the call centre clearly knew that Mina and Jana were alone.

Mina tutted then looked at Jana as she put down her coffee cup and stood up, mumbling about Tom forgetting his keys. She moved out of the call centre, through the next room, past the table, chair and small television. She grabbed the door handle and slowly pushed it down. It was an old door and the lock mechanism was stiff. Mina was about to pull the door open when it flew back into her face and body. Clearly it had been kicked or hit hard from the outside. The force knocked her across the room. Dizzy but conscious she screamed as two men rushed through the door slamming it behind them. One of them grabbed Mina, pulling her to her feet before hitting her with the back of his hand, shouting at her to shut up. He then roughly dragged her through the door to the call centre where his accomplice was leaning over Jana, fist next to her face, telling her to keep quiet.

Mina and Jana were terrified, they had never experienced violence in the sixteen or more years they had been involved with Roger. They were both pushed to the floor, and while one guy stood over them, the other produced a large hammer and proceeded to smash all the computers beyond repair. He then collected notebooks and diaries off the desks and placed them in a bag. He pulled out the telephone wires and smashed the handsets on the floor. He picked up both Mina's and Jana's mobile phones and threw them to the floor before crushing them with the heel of his shoe. He walked over to where the two frightened women were cowering in the corner and gave them both a hard slap across the face. He growled at them both, telling to stay where they were for an hour or they would be badly hurt. Turning to the door, the two guys walked out before locking it behind them.

Mina and Jana were shaken but not hurt; they had been beaten a lot more and a lot worse during their younger days in Belgrade brothels. Mina had waited five minutes. She then stood and went to a cupboard in the corner of the room, a cupboard with a false back. She removed some reams of paper to reveal a small safe set into the wall behind. Mina pressed a six digit code into the key pad, opened the safe door and retrieved a pay and go mobile phone.

Roger glanced at the black clouds that hung over the small warehouse near Southwark. The weather matched his mood and temperament, as he entered before locking the door behind him. He looked into the gloomy bare space where Jeff and Tom stood over a man tied to the chair. He was still gagged, his eyes were swollen, his nose flat and bloodied. Roger glanced at the twins, a slight nod of acknowledgment.

"Has he said anything?" Jeff answered;

"Apart from *Infidels,* no." Roger leaned towards the guy, there appeared to be little or no fear in his swollen eyes. He spoke;

"You are going to answer my questions, the easy way or the hard way, I don't care, but you are going to answer them."

He gave a slight nod to Jeff who moved forward to cut through the gaffer tape that was holding a sock in the guy's mouth. The captive's eyes widened as the knife moved towards him. Jeff cut through the tape and roughly pulled it away. The guy spat, mouthing obscenities in a foreign language. Roger's fist smashed into his nose. The force of the blow and the weight of the man made the chair tip backwards onto the floor. Tom grabbed the guy's hair dragging him and the chair upright. Roger stepped in closer. He spoke again;

"Who sent you and your three friends to wait for me outside of the restaurant?"

The guy smirked and spat again, shouted *Infidels* again, this time at Roger. Roger turned to Jeff, a slight nod. Jeff stepped behind the captive yanking his head back while stabbing his fingers into the guy's eyes. The man screamed,

35

mouth wide. Tom moving quickly stepped forward; the agonised guy didn't see the pair of pliers until they were halfway into his mouth and closing onto his front teeth. Tom squeezed his hand shut, the crack of ivory, more screams.

Roger circled his prey, wiping the saliva from his face. He spoke again; "Easy way or the hard way, up to you."

As he turned to Jeff, about to issue another order his phone rang. It was Mina.

***

Roger had spent most of the previous day being questioned by two detectives from Camberwell police station. He had answered all their questions in an almost honest manner. *No, he had no enemies that he knew of. No, he couldn't think of anyone who would want to cause him malicious damage.* The police had pressed him about his whereabouts on the night of the attack. He had told them the truth. They said they would check with Mr. Winn at the Silk Road Chinese Restaurant. Roger hoped they wouldn't check too deeply into the events of the night. He hadn't mentioned the attempted attack on *Club Mina*, as he hadn't mentioned the attack on his call centre.

They pressed him further, back three years. The night one of their colleagues had been shot and killed in the very same nightclub. Roger reminded them that there had been no previous trouble or problems prior to that night. He also reminded them that it was one of their own who had been responsible for the tragic death of the unfortunate detective. They left Roger at that point telling him that they would return again to see him.

Now it was 6 am as Roger pounded the heavy punch bag again and again. He had just finished thirty minutes on the free weights and a previous thirty minutes sitting on a rowing machine. His body ached. He ignored it, crashing his fist into the bag harder and harder until he had to stop through exhaustion. He opened a bottle of water. Sitting down on a nearby bench he went over the last three days.

He had sent Sam to his country house in Kent. Suggested she had a break, take her mind off what had happened. Sam had reluctantly agreed. She didn't want to go. She wanted to talk to Roger, she wanted answers. She had tried to talk to him in the brief time she had seen him but Roger hadn't been his usual loving self. The smiling caring husband of three years. He had been abrupt, off-hand. At one point a little frightening. She had raised the subject of him locking a guy in the car boot and Jeff driving him away. Roger had turned quite aggressive, telling her that it was his business and she should mind her own. She should also forget what she saw. Sam was shocked; it was a side of her loving husband that she had not seen before.

Sam steered the Porsche 911 off the A2 and headed towards the village of Cliffe Woods that would take her through to Cliffe, and eventually to their home. Although she was unhappy about being sent there by Roger she was also looking forward to the warm welcome from Mrs. Cowens, their widowed live-in housekeeper. She would leave it for now. Roger clearly had a lot on his mind. She would try to relax, exercise Penny, her beautiful horse, but she was sure about one thing, she wouldn't let this drop without an explanation.

Sipping his water Roger pondered on the attacks on himself and the night clubs. Also the call centre, not much harm done there. Mina and Jana were shaken up, but no permanent damage. He had questioned them separately then together, then separately again. Repeating previous questions, noting previous answers. They were clean. Innocent victims. All Roger had achieved from his questioning was that the guys were foreign. Mina thought maybe Serbian; she recognised some of the words that the two thugs had spoken to each other from her mother language. He thought about the damage the two of them had caused. The computers could be replaced, reprogrammed, all the data they contained had been carefully stored in back up files, in a separate system in the office above the call centre. The loss of telephones was little more than a minor irritation. The clowns who caused the damage hadn't had the brains to check the rest of the building. Which made him think; whoever set up the raid had knowledge of the downstairs of the premises but not what was above it. Roger would go through every person, every name who had been in that building in the last couple of years. It would not be too difficult, the operation had been quite secretive.

The nightclubs would be repaired, the windows bricked up. He would give serious consideration as to what he would do with *Sam's*. Bad enough that a policeman had been shot and killed in there three years earlier, but now three young girls and a young man were dead, consumed by the flames that had engulfed the dance floor. Also another six young people were still in a serious condition in the burns unit of Chelsea and Westminster Hospital. Another fifteen had been discharged after receiving treatment for smoke inhalation.

He had time to think about it, there would be a full investigation by the police. The Health and Safety executive was also involved. *Sam's* would not be reopening anytime soon.

He blamed himself. He had lapsed into too comfortable a lifestyle, gone soft. *Respectable business man!* He allowed a slight smile. What had he been thinking? Roger Scott was not cut out or meant to be anything other than what he was, a south London criminal. It was what he was good at.

He had arrived at the gym at 5.00 am the last two mornings, like he used to, three years ago, before Sam, before he went soft and comfortable. *Leisurely breakfasts with fruit, smoked salmon and the odd glass of Champagne.* Not bothering to think about his business ventures until the day was half way through. He drank some more water; then headed for the shower. He kept a wardrobe at the gym. After showering and changing into a suit he drove to the call centre. The traffic was not too bad this time of the morning, he would be there by 8.30.

At the same time in Kent, at a country mansion near Cliffe, Sam had opened her eyes as the first rays of sunshine entered her bedroom. She lay for a while thinking again about the previous three days. How in such a small space of time the dramatic events had unfolded. Deciding she couldn't do much about it Sam had eventually got out of bed. She had eaten a light breakfast that Mrs. Cowens had prepared, and then taken a shower.

Sam had spent the previous afternoon on the marshes, there had been nobody around for miles, *or so it appeared,* just her and her beloved horse Penny. She had felt relaxed, happy despite the recent events in London. As Sam had gently encouraged Penny to the edge of one of the many manmade lakes that covered the area, she paused to look at the array of birds fluttering in and out of the bushes, then skimming across the surface of the mill-pond like water, catching some of the many flies that hovered above the lake. The pink flamingos perched one-legged on the manmade island not two hundred metres from her. It was a different world, peaceful and tranquil, a million miles from the recent events in London. Sam had tried to put the nightclub attacks and the four guys who were outside the Chinese restaurant behind her. For now, but it wasn't going to go away. She wanted answers, answers from her husband.

Pulling on her riding jodhpurs and boots, she selected a tweed jacket to go over her silk blouse. Sam checked she had her front door keys and shouted goodbye to Mrs. Cowens before closing the door behind her. She then headed across the cobbled yard to the stable block. She felt a little better; the sun was up and starting to warm the dewy morning. Sam looked up at the blue sky as she slid the bolt across the stable door, she then pulled the top part of the split door open. She stepped back in readiness, smiling. Sam knew Penny would bound towards the opening in a boisterous welcome. She waited. There was nothing, no sign of Penny. Sam took a tentative step forward calling out the name of her beautiful pet, her best friend, her loyal companion of the last two years. Opening the bottom part of the door and allowing the sunlight to illuminate the stable she stepped inside calling out for Penny. Sam saw her lying in the corner. Her mind raced, was Penny ill? She was fine last night when Sam had bedded her down. Sam took a step further. Then bending down she looked at Penny.

Then screamed.

Assistant Chief Constable Ted Walton groaned his discomfort; he pressed the back of his hand gently but firmly into his stomach, as he sat behind a desk in an office he had commandeered in Camberwell Police Station. The desk was covered in notes and files that he had ordered to be retrieved from the archives. Most of what he looked at was around three years old. Most of them made grim reading. Failed police raids on brothels, failed police raids on nightclubs. The increase in drug distribution at around the same time. An unarmed undercover detective gunned down in a nightclub. He read that particular file again, tried to stem a tear for his son, *his secret son*. Sitting back, Ted Walton realised that all that was spread out in front of him had the same connection, the same common denominator. The same name mentioned on each file; *Roger Scott*. He studied further.

He picked up a file that had been closed three years earlier due to lack of evidence. The suspicion at the time was that Roger Scott was controlling prostitutes that operated from private flats, according to the report in front of him the appointments were made via a call centre in Peckham. The problem was that when it was investigated there was nothing to find. The flats contained innocent women, and the phone numbers to the call centre were disconnected. There was talk at the time of a mole in Camberwell Police Station, although nothing or nobody was ever found. Ted sat back and thought about the situation. Yes the case against Roger had gone cold, but why? Maybe three years ago there was a bent copper here. Maybe high enough in authority to cover up the evidence. Ted had ordered a constable from Camberwell to retrieve the files. He picked up the phone on the desk. He groaned to himself again, attempting to relieve the pain he was suffering as he pressed an internal number.

In an office at the other end of the building a police constable also groaned as he glanced at the phone as it rang in front of him. P.C. John Jenkins knew who was on the other end of it. Why did the Assistant Chief have to pick on him to be at his beck and call? Yes he was involved with the case against Roger Scott three years ago, but now it was dead. There was no case to answer. He wearily picked up the phone, listened to what was said then stood up and left the office. As he headed to the other end of the building he thought about how much he hated this job. He had never been really interested in police work from day one, but it paid the rent and kept his bitch of a wife reasonably happy. He thought some more, he was nothing more than some kind of trophy to her, something to show off to friends and family. "My husband, a policeman." *Fucking frigid bitch.*

Putting his thoughts behind him he knocked on the office door and walked in. The superior officer looked up at him and nodded towards an empty chair. As Jenkins sat down Ted Walton passed a sheet of paper over the desk. P.C. Jenkins looked at it and listened.

"What you are going to do is off the record, for now. The investigation I have started is at an early stage and I want it keeping quiet until I say different. So if you want to have any kind of future as a policeman you will listen and listen good," He looked at the constable, waiting for some kind of reaction; nothing. He continued;

"That is the address of an office in Peckham. I am thinking that maybe you have been there before, around three years ago. Which is why, if you value your career you will follow my orders. I want you round there now. You will take two other constables with you. Gain entry and find out what you can. There will be people on phones making appointments with prostitutes. There will be computers and no doubt paperwork. You don't have a search warrant so bluff your way in. Make it look like a friendly visit. If you feel there is enough evidence in there to incriminate them we shall arrange an official full scale raid."

P.C. Jenkins looked at the address. He showed no sign to the Assistant Chief Constable that he had indeed been there before. Many times. Since the night he had gone too far in being unable to control his lust in one of Roger Scott's massage parlours. Whilst naked and in a state of sexual excitement, he had almost attacked the girl who had been massaging him. It had been captured on CCTV. He had been in Roger's pocket and at his beck and call ever since, forewarning him of any police investigation before it got too close. He hated Roger Scott as much as he hated his wife, but for now he had no other choice but to do as he was told. Jenkins stood and answered *"Yes Sir"* then walked out. Ted Walton watched the P.C. close the door behind him before once again attempting to stem the pain he was suffering.

Roger sat at his desk in the upstairs office of the call centre. He had told Mina and Jana to take a few days off, take a break, they needed it. He had given more thought to his predicament as he travelled from the gym. Clearly the events of the last few days had been more than mere coincidence. Somebody wanted to hurt him. Not only him personally and physically but also his business interests. Both his nightclubs had been hit, his call centre attacked. Not to mention the Silk Road Restaurant and the attempt to cause him serious damage. Now he sat opposite Jeff. Tom was sitting downstairs, in his usual place, at the table at the back of the building, watching the small television. Roger checked his watch. Sam would be safely in Kent, in his country house in its own grounds, enjoying her time with her beloved Penny. It was a secure haven for her. Not even Jeff or Tom or any of his past employees had been there.

He thought about the guy with the walking stick at the corner table in the Silk Road Chinese. He recognised him, but where from? He would keep him in mind. He had gone through the CCTV from *Sam's* on the night of the arson attack again. It could have been his imagination but a guy near the bar wearing a white jacket had been talking to a pretty girl, who had disappeared into the ladies toilet maybe a minute before the attack. The guy had looked a little concerned; his concentration appeared to be focussed between the window and the dance floor. Also he kept glancing at his watch. Roger watched the video again, twice. He would give it a closer look.

Jeff and Tom had interrogated the guy in the warehouse for many hours, Jeff verbally, Tom forcefully. By then there was not much left of him to bury deep in the 6,000 acres that was Epping Forest. After questioning Jeff at length it dawned on Roger that maybe the guy was foreign, maybe he didn't speak or understand English. A slight smile, if someone starts a war there will be casualties.

It was time for a change. Time to become the Roger Scott of three years earlier. He looked at Jeff. As usual Jeff didn't speak, he just sat waiting for Roger's next order. Roger sat back in his chair. He would get his guys back; once more become a threat to all who knew him. He would find those responsible for what had been happening. They would pay, pay big.

He was shaken from his thoughts by a loud banging at the back door downstairs. Roger pressed a key on the laptop in front of him, making the screen change to a view of the yard at the rear of the call centre. He shook his head at the picture in front of him; three uniformed policemen. He smiled to himself as he noticed police constable John Jenkins looking up at the camera. Roger turned to Jeff and told him to go and let them in. He sat back in his chair; apart from the night in the Silk Road Chinese Restaurant he hadn't seen the useless copper for a couple of years. Roger remembered him well. Three years ago Jenkins had been undercover in one of Roger's massage parlours, under orders to catch one of the girls offering more than just a massage. His sexual excitement had got the better of him. He stood in front of, and then threatened one of Roger's girls whilst wearing nothing but a hard on. Then the panic as he was confronted, then to be slapped around a little and then be very firmly in Roger's grasp. As he had been ever since.

It was twenty minutes later, after finding nothing but an empty room downstairs, and nothing at all upstairs other than Roger's desk and two chairs, that Jenkins sent the other two officers back to wait in the car, while he had a final word with Roger Scott. He now sat in front of Roger unable to keep the smile of his face. He spoke;

"How did you know Roger?" Roger glared at him. Another example of how soft he had become, even this plod was showing no respect. He leaned forward into the policeman's face;

"It's Mr. Scott to you, you fuckin' prick!" He nodded to Jeff who took a step forward and grabbed Jenkins by the throat. Roger moved from behind his desk. He stood towering over the shaking policeman. He spoke again;

"I still fuckin' own you. I can drop you in deep shit or make you disappear any time I feel like it. You got that?" Jenkins tried to nod his head, Jeff squeezed harder. Roger continued;

"It is pure coincidence that this place is empty. So tell me, and make it good; why didn't I know you were going to pay me a visit today?" He glanced at Jeff who released

45

his grip slightly. The P.C. trembled as he spoke;

"I…I haven't heard from you for a couple of years. I never thought you would be here. Even if we had found something I would have covered it honest."

Roger sat back. He knew this was his own doing. More proof if he needed it of how he had let things go. This idiotic copper needed a lesson, a reminder. He thought quickly then answered;

"So, you have had an easy time recently, but it all changes now. Get rid of the tin soldiers out there and be back here tonight in your uniform. Six o'clock. Now fuck off!"

Jenkins nodded his head then scurried out as Roger's phone rang. He answered. It was a tearful Mrs Cowens.

***

July 2012.

The man in the wheelchair stopped, and then slowly reaching up he pulled his baseball cap down further to conceal more of his face. He had been watching a gang of maybe six or seven guys, all in their late teens or early twenties. *All wearing similar hooded jackets.* They were standing on the corner of Peckham Road and Bellenden Road, near the Burger King, near the array of scruffy looking shops, near the *Vegas Slots* gaming salon. It was the fifth day in a row he had been there. The gang was laughing out loud, making fun of everybody who walked past them. Nobody answered back, not around here. The street gangs had taken over the area over the last couple of years. The police didn't appear to want to get involved.

Five days ago when the man in the wheelchair approached the same gang in passing he spoke to one of them. Nothing much, just an *"Alright mate"* as he steered around them. The smallest one of group had stuck his chest out, arrogant, loud, asked what he was looking at, and then threatened to let his tyres down before laughing loudly. The rest joined in with the ridicule. The second day the man in the wheelchair had travelled along the road, next to the kerb. He stopped where the guys were standing, then attempted to get the front wheels of his chair onto the path. He looked up at the gang, a pleading look on his face. The smaller one laughed again, pointing at him. The rest watched smiling as the crippled man struggled. Then one of them stepped forward, a big guy, maybe the leader. Moving behind the chair he grabbed the two handles and helped to lever the wheelchair onto the path. The seated man smiled and raised his arm, as if he wanted to shake hands with the helpful guy. The rest of the gang stood in silence, watching the proceedings as their colleague stood over the wheelchair, hands on hips, looking threatening. Then a slight shock as they noticed the twenty pound note in the hand of the wheelchair occupant. The guy snatched the money from him then turned in triumph waving it at his friends, grinning from ear to ear. The man in the wheelchair pressed the four-way switch on the right hand armrest and moved off along Peckham Road. The procedure continued for the next two days, the man in the wheelchair looking to struggle in one way or another as he neared the gang. The youths falling over themselves to help him. The twenty pound notes doled out again.

Now as he approached them for the fifth time they all turned to look, some smiling, some expectant. They clearly recognised him as the guy who paid well for a bit of help. Only today he clearly didn't need any help. This time as he moved towards them he was looking at the big guy, maybe

47

the leader, the one who he had given the money to the first day. He made a beeline for him.

Roger put his foot to the boards as the BMW engine screamed in response. His mind was in turmoil. Mrs. Cowens had babbled uncontrollably down the phone. Somebody had broken into his premises in Kent. Roger tried in vain to calm her down, to try and get some sense out of her. To find out what had happened. He told her to go and bring Sam to the phone. Mrs. Cowens continued with her hysterical cries. She said that Sam was curled up in the corner crying. When she tried to approach her Sam had screamed at her saying it was all Roger's fault. That she hated him. Eventually Mrs. Cowens had managed to reveal the cause of the upset.

Roger pressed his foot onto accelerator even harder in an effort to gain more speed. He was thinking hard. How did whoever was trying to damage him know where his country residence was? How did they know Sam would be there without him? They could have attacked the property at anytime but it seemed like they were waiting for her to arrive. Clearly they didn't want to harm Sam physically. Just devastate her feelings. As he crossed over the M25 Roger thought about Penny. He was not an animal lover, but she was a lovely trusting horse and his wife's pride and joy. He thought back to when he first bought her. It had been around two years earlier, a first wedding anniversary present. He and Sam had looked at several horses before she spotted Penny. It was exactly what she wanted. Perfect temperament, she had been broken and trained to accept the most novice rider. For Sam it was love at first sight. She had squealed with delight as the driver of the horsebox reversed into the courtyard, then opened the rear door before leading Penny out. Roger had never seen his young wife so happy. Now as the BMW sped along the A2 his mind returned to the present.

Penny did not deserve a crossbow bolt through her eye.

***

Marion Hill had been brought up in a small Lancashire seaside town. Her Father Jake had sold his soft drink delivery business many years earlier, after the large hypermarkets had seemed to appear in almost every town in the land. Amongst many other items they were selling cheap plastic bottles of the same drink as Marion's father, but at a fraction of the cost. With fuel and other delivery overheads he had no choice but to sell up and move on.

The family headed for south London where he found work in a small engineering company. They were happy with their new surroundings and Marion had settled in well at her new school. She left the Peckham Academy after three years and moved around several jobs, mainly shop work. The evenings would be spent hanging around Peckham Road or sitting in the Burger King with her friends from her schooldays. Listening in awe as they regaled her with stories of violence and of the gangs that ruled the area. Even though she knew that maybe a lot of the stories had been elaborated on over the years she loved every minute of it. They made it sound like something out of the movies. Marion noted that the name Roger Scott was mentioned on almost every occasion. Sometimes as a local hero, a Robin Hood character, but most of the time as a man who should not be crossed or messed with.

One day around three years earlier she had noticed a new gaming salon being opened on the site of previously disused shops. She applied for, and after being interviewed by a lady called Mina, she accepted the position of manageress of the *Vegas Slots*. Marion enjoyed her work, it was a warm clean environment and for most of the time she was her own boss. She would open up in the morning and lock up at night. She didn't let it get to her when she saw housewives losing hundreds of pounds in less than an hour, then leaving in tears only to return a few days later to repeat the process. It didn't worry her when men would enter the premises on a Friday evening and lose their entire week's wages in a matter of minutes. It was a job, a good job, well paid and she felt secure.

Marion's only contact with the management was when every second day two large men, obviously twins, would arrive to collect some of the takings. She liked the one called Jeff, he came across as a gentle giant, his brother seemed a little strange she thought, never spoke, just looked, a bit menacing, but he never troubled her. All in all she was happy, and after a few months of employment Marion found out that she also had bragging rights, although she had never met him she was now working for the infamous *Roger Scott*.

Marion glanced at her watch, almost time to lock up for the night, she was pleased, it had been a busy day. As she walked towards the door, keys in hand, Marion had her mind on events planned for later the same evening, a bottle of wine to wash down a take-away from the local Indian restaurant. She smiled to herself; she was looking forward to a quiet night. As she approached the door she stopped as she heard a male voice, a loud shout;

"Hoodies up."

Marion stepped back away from the door wondering what was happening. Outside the biggest of a gang of six or seven guys, all in their late teens or early twenties, *all wearing similar hooded jackets,* kicked the door open. They barged through as one, knocking her out of the way as they went. One of them then kicked the door shut then leaned against it, blocking it from the inside. The rest knew what to do; they had been told by the man in the wheelchair. He had given them clear instructions as to what he wanted. They went around each machine in turn, paint spray cans in each hand. Every slot that would normally receive coins or banknotes was filled with paint. Half a can or more in each machine. Marion stood watching, shaking her head, a slight smile on her pretty face. She spoke;

"Do you boys know who owns this place?"

They carried on spraying the paint, ignoring her. She continued;

"If you did you wouldn't be doing this."

They still ignored her. In less than five minutes every gaming machine had been irreparably damaged, the paint leaving the machine entrance and running down into the inner workings. Marion watched then spoke again, louder;

"Roger Scott, *that's who.*"

One of the smaller guys walked towards her. Loud, arrogant; "So who the fuck is Roger Scott." The biggest one grabbed him by the arm. He shouted at Marion;

"What did you say?"

Marion smiled, more confident;

"Roger Scott. You boys are in big trouble."

The big guy pushed the smaller mouthy one towards the door;

"Out, everybody, and keep them hoodies up."

He walked to the door himself and followed the rest out into the street. Nobody spoke until they crossed the road and headed towards Sumner Road Park. The big guy spoke;

51

"Hope you all had your faces covered, that crippled prick back there didn't tell us Roger Scott owned the fuckin' place."

They carried on walking, the big guy, maybe the leader, talking quietly. Explaining who Roger was. Relaying some of the tales of violence and murder that he had heard about over the last few years. They listened in silence until he had finished. The smallest one of the group, the loudest, stuck his chest out. He spoke;

"So, he doesn't frighten me, we rule this area. If he wants to start something it's his problem."

The big guy slowly shook his head as they carried on walking.

In a dark shop doorway the man in the wheelchair watched them go, he allowed a slight smile. It had been easy, maybe too easy. They were arrogant, thought they were invincible. They had taken the two hundred pounds he had offered them to wreak havoc on the gaming salon. He had told them that if they did what he wanted there would be more similar raids in the pipeline. He pressed the four way switch on the right hand armrest and moved slowly away in the opposite direction. He wouldn't be back in the area, and he wouldn't see them again. Inside the door of the *Vegas Slots* Marion pressed a speed dial button on her phone, it rang out once then she heard Mina answer.

***

Roger stood in the stable looking down at the stricken horse. The velocity of the crossbow bolt at that range meant that Penny would have been killed instantly. The cowards who did this must have known that Penny was a friendly trusting animal; she would willingly approach anybody who entered the stable. He walked around, looking at the floor. Boot prints in the sawdust, big, maybe size ten, one set. He walked to the door. Two more prints, different. He crouched down looking for signs of damage... nothing. Somebody knew what they were looking for, what they wanted. Somebody who must have been here before to check the place out, maybe more than once. Either somebody who knew Roger or somebody who had been sent by somebody who knew Roger.

He walked along the side of the stable, then around the back. Roger stood and looked at the twenty year old tractor, a slight smile as he stared at the large shovel shaped attachment that hung on the back. The ancient machine only had one use; it had never ploughed a field or spread any kind of fertiliser. Its role was solely to dig holes, holes maybe around six feet deep, holes maybe around eight feet long, holes big enough to conceal the numerous bodies of people who were once Roger's enemies. As he returned to the front of the building he thought some more, he was ticking off names in his head. Roger should know who they were.

In the lounge of the country house Mrs Cowens whispered gently to Sam, trying to soothe her as she wept uncontrollably. Sam looked out of the window, she saw Roger examining the stable door. She looked back at Mrs Cowens, eyes red and sore from the tears. Mrs Cowens smiled, trying not to be patronising. She gently pulled Sam's head to her breast. She spoke;

"There there Sam, don't cry dear." Sam pushed herself away from Mrs. Cowens. She stood, hands on hips watching again as Roger examined the undamaged door. Watching as he stepped back, stared at the stable before walking around the courtyard. Sam was upset and fuming at the same time. Roger had entered the house a little while

53

earlier, he had given her little more than a quick cuddle before telling her to stay inside. He then headed outside to the stable. No explanation as to why he had ordered Mrs. Cowens *and told* Sam not to involve the police. Sam wasn't having any more of it. She glanced at Mrs. Cowens before striding through the door and slamming it shut behind her.

"Roger!" Sam shouted as she stormed across the courtyard. Roger turned to face her. Sam stopped, hands on hips, glaring. She shouted;

"What is going on Roger? You have been attacked in the street, my nightclub is ruined, and now my Penny is dead, and still no police. What is going on?"

Roger looked at her, he shook his head and walked back towards the stable. Sam followed him, repeating her questions. He turned abruptly, so abruptly the Sam almost walked into him. He spoke. Aggressive;

"You can see what is going on! I am being attacked from all sides."

"So call the police, let them investigate."

Roger gave a quick shake of his head as he looked at her, a look that Sam had seen a few days earlier, a look she didn't like, a look that frightened her, He spoke again, quietly, a little menacing;

"Listen, and listen good. The police are worse than useless, they don't help the likes of me, I sort my own shit out," Then patronising;

"So be a good little girl and go back inside. Leave this to me."

Sam burst into tears, not for the first time today. She turned and ran back to the house. Ignoring Mrs. Cowens she ran straight to the stairs, up and into her bedroom. Sam threw herself on the bed and buried her face into the pillow.

Roger had seen enough. He entered the house and approached Mrs. Cowens. He told her he had to go. There would be somebody here soon to take the remains of Penny away. A man called Jeff would also be here shortly to look after her and Sam. Sam knew Jeff, she would recognise him. Sam was to stay here until she heard different. He glanced around and headed for his car, opening the door his phone rang. It was Mina. She sounded distressed.

Assistant Chief Constable Ted Walton hid his discomfort as he glanced at the black clouds gathering over the well kept lawn and garden. He was sitting in the lounge of his good friends James and Cassandra Austin. He thought the clouds were an appropriate colour. They suited the mood and situation. He was aware that he was maybe glancing out of the window a little too much. Endeavouring to concentrate on the reason he was there, he turned to look at his two dear friends. He had known them both for a long time. He had first met them at the local golf club and then socialised with them for many years. Both he and his wife Olive had attended their wedding and been god-parents to both of their daughters.

Ted Walton was troubled; he struggled to speak, to find the right words. The three of them had cried and hugged each other before sitting down. Assistant Chief Constable Ted Walton was slightly embarrassed and upset at the same time. He had been well aware of the fire at the nightclub in Camberwell. He had known there had been casualties, that young people had been killed and injured. He hadn't bothered to check who they were. Why would he, it was just another tragedy, a not unusual occurrence in the UK's biggest city.

Cassandra and James Austen had gone through the full

circle of emotions. Shock then upset then hysterics then anger then calm. Now blame. Cassandra hadn't wanted her little girl, her baby, Emily to go to that horrible nightclub in the first place. She glared at her husband accusingly. He should have known it was owned by a gangster, he should have remembered that a policeman was killed there three years ago. Why didn't he back her up when she said that she wanted the birthday party at their house? If he had, Emily would still be alive, not killed in the most horrible of circumstances. She cried again, uncontrollably, she pushed James away when he tried to comfort her. Ted Walton looked at his friends as he took in the proceedings. He already had it in his mind that the nightclub owner was responsible for the death of his son, *his secret son*. Now this, his beautiful god daughter dead, his good friends devastated, and it was all down to Roger Scott. The Assistant Chief Constables decision had already been made. No going back. Now even more determined.

Despite the pain he was in, he would not rest until he had finished Roger Scott. *One way or another.*

Sam lay on her bed; she had heard Roger slam the door as he left the house two hours earlier. She had heard a wagon arrive, the sound of a small crane, the thud as the dead weight of Penny was unceremoniously dropped to the flat bed of the horse transporter. She had heard Jeff explaining to Mrs. Cowens who he was. She had shouted to Mrs. Cowens that she was to let him into the house. She had heard quiet talking downstairs. She had never left her room.

Now as she lay there staring out of the window through glazed eyes Sam was in deep thought about Roger. About his refusal to answer her questions. About his refusal to involve the police. About the various attacks on them both, but more so the way he had changed, changed towards her. Nasty, aggressive. It was as if she didn't know him anymore. What had happened to her loving caring husband of the last three years? Sam thought back again to before they had become an item. She knew little about him or his business in all the time she had worked for him. Was he really a gangster? Was he really involved with drugs and prostitutes? Then the events of the last few days. Something was not right about Roger Scott.

She lay still, quietly sobbing. Looking through the window at the cumulus clouds changing shape, each one bearing a resemblance to Penny. Some showing a long nose, then changing again as if her eyes were appearing. Sam knew that it was her imagination but she carried on looking, tearfully watching as her beloved Penny continued to change shape before her eyes. Until the darkness started to block her vision of the clouds in the night sky.

Sam closed her eyes, thinking of Penny she fell into a restless sleep. As she dozed lightly they were back on the marshes, nobody around, just her and Penny in a mad fast gallop. They moved together as one in perfect harmony. Fences and trees disappeared as they approached. Nothing could stop them. Sam and Penny, together again. She slept on. Then she drifted into a different dream with Penny. Sam heard the sound of soft music, accompanied by angelic voices; *then a soft whinny as Penny gazed down at her;*

> *The good Lord wanted a mount he could ride,*
> *He wanted the best, your joy, your pride,*
> *He looked at Penny, beautiful and able,*
> *Then took her away to heavens stable,*
> *Now she is watching from high above,*
> *She wants you to know of her undying love,*

Then another soft whinny. Penny still gazing down.

You were together as one for a time too short,
Penny loved you with all of her heart,
She will never forget you, your love your care,
So think of the good times, don't despair,
She is happy again looking down at you,
Now she roams free on pastures new,
So please don't be sad, do not feel pain,
One day you will be together again.

Sam opened her eyes. The morning sun was starting to rise, the first rays appearing through the bedroom window. She sat up and glanced at her swollen dark rimmed eyes in the bedside mirror. Enough was enough. There were no tears left. She quickly showered and dressed, then after throwing some clothes into an overnight bag she went downstairs. Mrs. Cowens had laid the table and prepared breakfast. Jeff was sitting in an armchair nursing a cup. Mrs. Cowens looked at Sam and smiled as she entered the room;

"Morning dear, you sit down and I will bring you some coffee."

Sam carried on walking. Ignoring Mrs. Cowens and Jeff she continued towards the front door. Without turning she spoke;

"No thank you, I'm going."

Jeff stood quickly; he strode towards Sam, trying to get between her and the door. Sam turned, defiant, staring at Jeff as she opened the door. Then in a raised voice;

"Don't try to stop me Jeff, I'm leaving, I have had enough."

Jeff stopped in his tracks, wondering what to do, if it had been one of Roger's male employees he wouldn't have had a problem exerting his authority, using force if necessary, but this was different. Sam was a small girl, his boss's wife. He hesitated, maybe a little too long. Sam was gone, the door slamming behind her, then into her car without a backward glance. She started the engine and drove across the courtyard and into the country lane away from the house, eyes focused on the road ahead. As she wiped a tear from her eye she didn't notice a small motorbike pull out of a farm entrance behind her. She headed through Cliffe towards the A2 and away from the sadness of the last two days. Back at the house Jeff watched through the window as Sam disappeared. He then picked up the phone to make the call he was dreading.

July 2011 One year earlier.

The man in the wheelchair hated being strapped into this motorised contraption. He had suffered two years of agonising operations and now he had to make regular visits to the Royal National Orthopaedic Hospital which housed The London Spinal Cord Injury Centre. He sat in his chair in the waiting room with various other outpatients who were in a similar predicament. Young and old, male and female, black, white and Asian. There was clearly no discrimination as to who received their terrible injuries. On the positive side, if there was one, he was meeting people on a regular basis, people in wheelchairs or on crutches and getting to know them. People from far and wide. People whose injuries were so severe that they too had to attend this hospital, even if it meant travelling many miles.

Since his life had changed in such violent circumstances he had become a loner, not wanting to mix or talk to anyone. Now, sitting in the waiting room he recognised some of the others, maybe just a nod of the head to some of them, maybe just a *good morning* to others. One

59

guy in particular would be more friendly towards him than the others. He was from south London, he didn't need a wheelchair. After many months of ongoing treatment he was now able to manage with just the aid of crutches. Now after further medical attention he could get around slowly and painfully using just a walking stick. The man in the wheelchair tolerated him but he didn't like his foreign accent. He had endeavoured to give him a wide berth.

Then three weeks ago things changed. The man with the walking stick had cornered him as he drank coffee in the small canteen that was set aside to use after treatment. Maybe the man in the wheelchair was feeling particularly lonely that day, but he decided to listen to the guy. Like everybody else in the room he spoke about his injuries and how he had received them. It had been two years earlier, just before he himself had suffered his own appalling injuries.

They had talked at length and had then decided to wait for each other after their individual physio sessions. They drank coffee and talked, finding out that they had more in common than most of the other unfortunates who attended the hospital. Apart from the fact they were both from south London, they had one thing very much in common. One man. *Because of one man*, the same man, they were now suffering their respective disabilities.

July 2012, present day.

Roger stood inside the *Vegas Slots* gaming salon. Jeff stood next to him. He had told Jeff to return to London after he had made the call to Roger to tell him that Sam had left the house in Kent. Marion Hill sat at the counter where she would normally serve tea or coffee. Against all previous instruction Marion had rung the police after she had spoken to Mina. They were still there when Roger arrived. Roger surveyed the damage as the WPC Joan Shaw questioned Marion; "*Yes she thought she recognised them, even with their hoodies up.*" How could she be sure? "*Because she had seen what looked like the same gang standing on the corner of Bellenden and Peckham Road quite often when she finished work.*" Would she be able to pick them out in an identity parade? "*No! They were wearing hoodies for fucks sake.*" Roger stepped forward. He looked glaringly at the WPC. He spoke;

"It's nothing but a few kids messing about, bit of vandalism, I am not pressing any charges, you can go when you are ready." He nodded his head towards Marion, then;

"She is a bit upset, she wasn't hurt" Then leaning closer to the policewomen;

"She has told you all she knows, so why don't you go look for some real criminals?"

WPC Joan Shaw was about to protest when her sergeant stepped forward telling her that they had enough evidence to take matters further. They were leaving but they would be back. Roger nodded at Jeff who opened the door for them to leave. He knew they wouldn't be back. Just another day in lawless London to them.

Roger watched them go then turned to Marion; about to shout, to tell the stupid tart she was sacked, tell her she went against all his rules about involving the filth. Tell her to get the fuck out of his premises. He looked at her tear-stained face. He walked towards her. She stared at him, wide-eyed, frightened. He had second thoughts. He spoke, quietly, a little menace in his voice;

"Are you sure it was the guys who you have seen standing down the street, on the corner?"

Marion looked at the floor then back at Roger, it was

the first time she had met him, she could see that behind that handsome face and cold dark eyes that there was something evil lurking. She answered;

"Yes. Mr. Scott I'm sure. They were there again when I walked past earlier, one of them was smirking at me. When I looked again I noticed he still had some paint on his hands."

Roger told Marion they would take her home. Then he would get the insurance company to visit and then an engineer to see if any of the gaming machines were salvageable. With Jeff driving and Roger in the back of the BMW with Marion, they drove slowly along Peckham Road. Jeff slowed the car even more as they approached the corner of Bellenden Road. Marion looked out of the window;

"That's them Mr. Scott, I'm sure of it." Roger and Jeff followed her gaze taking in as much detail as they could. Six maybe seven guys, all in their late teens or early twenties. *All wearing similar hooded jackets.* They dropped Marion near her house and headed for the Pot Black snooker hall. Roger had ordered Jeff to contact all of the massage parlours that he once owned. To speak to each one of his old gang personally, to tell them to be at the *Pot Black Snooker Hall* on New Cross Road. There used to be seven people in total, all could be trusted. All of them had been loyal. Roger wished he had never let them go in the first place, the clowns who were now working in his nightclubs as security couldn't lace their boots.

Again he thought, his own fault, being lax, letting not just himself go but also his business interests. Roger had given a lot of thought to the events of the last few days. He was short of numbers, vulnerable. He was once one of the most feared men in south London, commanded respect; nobody would have dared to try the tactics that had recently occurred. Three years ago Jeff would not have let Sam past him. Three years ago none of his employees would have contacted the police under any circumstances. Roger needed help, he needed manpower. He needed to get his crew back together.

***

Assistant Chief Constable Ted Walton took a last look in the full length mirror. He was in full dress uniform. Immaculate in every way from the peaked cap bearing the Metropolitan Police insignia down to his highly polished shoes. It was a day he had not being looking forward to. The grey cloudy sky seemed appropriate for what lay ahead. He had attended many funerals over the years, both private and on official police business.

Today was different, today was both, today was the day he and many others would say their final goodbyes to Emily Austin. *His goddaughter, his best friend's daughter. The sweet innocent girl who had been cruelly taken in the worst way possible. Taken in Roger Scott's nightclub.* He glanced at his reflection in the mirror one last time before leaving the bedroom and heading downstairs where his wife Olive was waiting. She asked him how he was feeling; he smiled sadly, telling her that he was bearing up under the circumstances, that funerals were never easy. He knew she was enquiring about the pain he had been in lately, not his emotional feelings. Despite his best efforts to hide it from her Olive had known her husband long enough to recognise there was something more than indigestion wrong with him. He now forced a false smile, said he was fine. They then left their house together without speaking further, both too upset to talk.

Roger Scott had been following the funeral cortege at a discreet distance. Over the past few days he had checked the deaths in the local newspapers on a daily basis. Then he read the announcement that the family of Emily Austen were sad to report the loss of their dearly beloved daughter, followed by the details of the funeral arrangements. He wanted to attend, not the church service, not the final farewell at the crematorium. Just the last part, the part where all the friends and relatives gather outside. To look at the wreaths, read the condolence cards. To hug each other, to try and find the right words to say. Words that have been repeated millions of times but still don't sound appropriate. Roger wanted to watch for anything unusual, anybody looking out of place, maybe gloating. A slightest clue as to who was behind the attack on *Sam's Nightclub*.

He sat in the driving seat of the BMW as the church service took place. He followed the convoy of cars to the crematorium. He waited, then some thirty minutes later he alighted from the car and moved to stand at the edge of the crowd of mourners, as if he was maybe a relative or maybe a family friend. To watch, to be discreet.

Roger had been standing for maybe ten minutes when he noticed a face he recognised. She was standing tearful with what could only be her parents. A pretty girl, she looked different without the pleasant smile that she had been wearing the last time he had seen her. Standing at the bar, with a guy in a white jacket, a guy who was watching a window at the precise time a petrol bomb crashed through it. A window in *Sam's Nightclub*.

At the same time Assistant Chief Constable Ted Walton was watching Roger Scott. He was curious. What was he doing there? Ted wanted to approach him, ask him what the hell was going on. He stopped himself, not the right time. He would wait, maybe have him arrested for something, maybe pay him a visit, but not now, not today.

Roger was having similar thoughts; he wanted to go over to the pretty girl who was clearly the sister of the unfortunate Emily Austen, question her about the guy in the white jacket, find out who he was, did she know his name? Not the right time. He would wait; maybe go to her house as the sad and upset nightclub owner. Offer condolences. Then ask the question. Roger had also noticed the guy who was very clearly some kind of high ranking policeman looking at him. He vaguely recognised him. He would find out who he was. He turned and headed back to his car, slipped inside and left.

Sam had spent the last two nights staying in the London penthouse that she and Roger had shared for the last three years. She wanted to be alone to gather her thoughts. She stared out of the window as she sipped a glass of wine; going over and over in her head where it had all gone wrong. What had caused the dramatic change in their otherwise idyllic life? What had got into Roger? Why had he changed so much towards her? Penny was her pride and joy, Roger knew that yet he couldn't even show her the slightest bit of sympathy or comfort. Sam sat down in the plush armchair, putting her feet up on a small stool she closed her eyes, thinking hard, trying to make some sense out of what was happening. She cast her mind back to the beginning.

She remembered the day around three years ago that a Detective Constable Nixon had summoned her to Camberwell Police Station. The Detective had got her there under the pretence of finding out who had kidnapped and hospitalised her cousin. Only to then press her for information about her boss; Roger Scott. He then proceeded to tell her his thoughts on Roger, how he was a drug supplier, a gangster, a man who ran brothels. At the time Sam hadn't believed a word of it, but now? She then thought back to the kidnap of her cousin and how a guy called Shane had told her Roger was behind it. Whatever happened to Shane? Sam had not seen or heard anything of him for three years. He had disappeared around the same time as her ex-boyfriend, a guy called Mike Smith. What had happened to Mike? Had Roger been behind his disappearance as well?

Her mind returned to the present. The guys waiting outside the restaurant. The man that Roger threw into his car boot. What for? What happened to him? Her poor beautiful horse Penny. The attack on *Sam's Nightclub*. The attack on *Club Mina*. Her mind was in turmoil. Sam thought some more; *Club Mina,* Why was it called *Club Mina*? Maybe Mina herself could answer some of her questions. She had worked for Roger prior to Sam being employed. She also appeared to be closer to her husband than any of the others. Maybe Sam could ask her questions that her husband refused to acknowledge. She drank some more wine. Maybe that was the answer. Roger wouldn't talk to her, no use approaching Jeff, yes, maybe talk to Mina.

The Pot Black Snooker Hall contained twenty four snooker tables and four pool tables. A long bar ran down one side of the room. This was where the clients would pay for their tables and maybe a drink or two. Up until three years ago they were also able to purchase small bags of white powder amongst other illegal substances. That had all stopped. Roger didn't do drugs anymore. There were still two ladies available upstairs for the more wanton clients, the clients who maybe told their wives they were merely going for a game of snooker. Behind the bar was a single door that led to another room that contained only one snooker table. Nobody but Roger and invited guests were allowed in there, which was where Roger Scott was now. Jeff in his usual position, standing behind Roger.

Roger looked around the three guys and one woman sitting in front of him. They were once his most trusted of allies. Johnny, six foot four inches tall, a good brain and a vicious temper. He had gained his credibility the hard way in the back streets of London. Roger looked at Harry, similar in size to Johnny; it was thought he had earned his cred by doing a kill in his younger days. Nobody asked him about it and he never spoke about it. Not the brightest of guys but he had common sense, maybe that's why he had never been caught. Next to him sat Mary. Evil temper and could hold her own against most men despite her five foot six height. She was a similar size in width. The last guy was Alan. Three years ago he was a new recruit, but had proved himself on more than one occasion. He was ex army with many kills to his name, proficient with his fists and with the Ruger LCR five shot revolver he quite often kept in his shoulder holster.

Roger spoke;

"Thanks for coming." He glanced at Jeff then looked at Johnny;

"What happened to the rest?" Johnny glanced at the others, and then clearing his throat he answered;

"George disappeared off to Spain. Somewhere near Marbella we think. The massage thing wasn't him. Apparently he's doing alright freelancing as a bodyguard." Roger nodded. Johnny continued;

"Ron's dead, two brothers tried to take over his massage

parlour. He followed them outside. They stuck him with a knife. All we know is they were Serbian. There has been quite a few of them moving into the manor in the last year, throwing their weight about. They are now running Jack's, Ron's and George's parlours."

Roger looked back at Johnny, little surprised, it was worse than he thought; one of his guys killed without retribution or revenge and Jack's business had been taken over. Johnny watched Roger's face; he read his thoughts, then;

"Jack's doing a three year stretch, GBH. He was being stalked by his ex-wife; she was causing him all sorts of shit. One night she went too far, he caught her outside his new flat. She shouldn't have even known where he lived. He had taken enough, he just snapped. Thing is he never laid a finger on her, you know Jack, he would never hit a woman. He just got hold of her, shouted and shook her about a bit. It wasn't that bad but apparently she'd been shagging a copper. Looks like he pulled some strings to get Jack arrested. He's still in jail." Roger looked on, Johnny continued;

"We had to have a word with him, the copper. He ain't a copper no more, been invalided out, dodgy knees apparently" Roger nodded his approval then shook his head;

"When did this happen?"

"Just over two years ago."

Roger pondered. Then;

"So he should be due out then. Good behaviour and all that" Johnny slowly shook his head;

"No. Don't think so. It seems they stuck him in a cell with a bit of *Stoke-on-Trent*. One night he tries it on and Jack spreads him all over the fuckin' place. So it looks like he'll be doing the full stretch."

Roger was fuming;

"Why didn't I know all this?"

It wasn't a question, more of a statement. Johnny spoke;

"You have been out of the game Roger. Three years ago you would have known, three years ago you wouldn't have allowed the shit you are in now to get anywhere near you."

Roger looked shocked, what the fuck was going on? None of his boys spoke to him like that. It was *Boss* or *Mr. Scott*. He stood, pushed his shoulders back. For the first time in many years he was stuck for words. He eyed them all for a full minute. He could sense that they were different towards him, a look of defiance, not with the respect he once commanded. Three years ago Johnny or the rest of the guys wouldn't have answered him back. They would have waited for him to finish, wait till he gave them a sign to answer. Johnny continued;

"The word on the pavement is that you are finished Roger, and if that's true then its wide open for other gangs to move in."

Roger clenched his fist behind his back; it was all he could do to stop himself from launching at Johnny. He sat back down thinking quickly. He told them to be here to get the gang, *his gang,* back together. They were here, but more like strangers. Not the people he would have trusted with his life three years ago. He was losing the meeting and he knew it. He needed to win them back, and quick. Roger thought some more; they had turned up, they didn't have to, that meant something. He wondered how much or little they knew. He changed his tact;

"Okay Johnny, thanks for that, I am very aware of what you are getting at which is why I asked you all here. You are right, I'm being attacked on all sides and it's my own doing. It's true I have let things go a little, been distracted by marriage. Maybe I should have got Sam pregnant, gave her a hobby."

He saw Ron smirk and Mary shake her head; he was on the front foot. He continued;

"Of the four guys who were waiting for me outside the Silk Road Restaurant three are in hospital, the fourth one is dead." He looked at Jeff, they followed his gaze. Jeff unsmiling nodded grimly. Roger carried on;

"They were Serbian. Maybe part of the same family that fire bombed the nightclubs." Roger wasn't sure about what he had just said, but he remembered the guy who the twins had tortured probably couldn't speak English. He watched as their faces softened. Then;

Tonight Jeff, Tom and I will be having a word with the fuckers who damaged my gaming salon. As for any other crap you might have heard that's what it is *crap*. Roger looked at them all, maybe thirty seconds, not speaking, thinking that if they had heard about the attack on his house in Kent he was in deep shit. Then;

"Now it's up to you four. I want you all back on the team. You will be well paid and respected." He didn't wait for an answer he spoke again, quickly;

"These twats are going to pay, and pay fuckin' heavy." He stood and walked round the table, he raised his voice;

"If you are in here tomorrow, midday we can get it back together, and at the moment it's not just me that's vulnerable. You are all on your own, and remember something, they won't stop at me. They have already taken three of the massage parlours. We are all at risk."

Roger walked to the door, Jeff opened it for him. He turned, nodded his head. He glanced at Jeff and they both

walked out. At the snooker table nobody spoke or moved;
Until they heard screech of brakes followed by a loud bang.

It was starting to get dark when the white transit van with a tinted windscreen and blacked out side windows moved slowly along Peckham Road. Past the Burger King, past the array of scruffy looking shops. Past the now closed *Vegas Slots* gaming salon. It slowed and stopped a little further down the road, on the corner of Bellenden Road, where six or maybe seven guys stood, all in their late teens or early twenties, *all wearing similar hooded jackets.*

The pretty girl in the passenger seat was wearing a skimpy vest and no bra. She was twenty one years old and very petite, her name was Sasa. The driver of the van sitting next to her was the same age but looked much older. She was also very pretty and very scantily clad. She was called Nina. Sasa pressed the switch on the door and the window slowly wound down. The guys on the corner stopped their banter and looked at the two girls, a little curious. Sasa leaned out of the window; she smiled sexily then spoke, slightly broken English;

"Hi. We lost; can you tell me where is Burgess Park?" One of the guys approached the van while the rest shouted obscenities; *"Get yer tits out, I'll show you something you can park on."* They all laughed raucously. Sasa smiled sweetly, then in a little girl voice;

"We really lost; maybe you could show us way there, back doors are unlocked." Then more seductively; "We would be very grateful."

The youngest, loudest of the group walked quickly to the back of the van and opened the doors, he looked inside to see a double mattress and a crate of beer. He laughed out loud shouting to the rest to come and look. They all gathered at the back of the van, peering in. The biggest guy, maybe the leader walked back to the passenger door, he opened it and shoved Sasa across the double seat before getting in himself. "We'll show you how to get there" The rest piled in the back slamming the doors behind them.

Roger and Jeff had walked out of the Pot Black Snooker Hall leaving their four former colleagues behind. Roger was in deep thought. He had a strong feeling that the guys he had just left would be returning tomorrow, but maybe they needed a slight push, something to convince them a little further that they couldn't do without Roger Scott. He pulled out his phone. He looked through his contacts as Jeff pressed the remote control to unlock the BMW. Roger was now scrolling down his phone as he walked round the front of the car.

The sound of a high revving engine made Jeff glance up and notice a blue Ford that was hurtling along the road around fifty miles per hour. It was getting closer to the BMW without showing any signs of slowing. Roger looked up as Jeff shouted a warning; he saw the Ford as it was almost upon him. As he jumped on to his car bonnet to try to avoid the blue car it smashed into the front wing of the BMW then continued along the full length of the car. It went from the front to the back doors causing sparks to fly and glass to shatter. Roger had now rolled over the front of the BMW and landed on the pavement at the other side. He looked up to see the blue Ford speeding away. A car going in the opposite direction braked hard to try and avoid a van in front that had stopped to take a look. The car's tyres screeched in protest as it skidded and crashed into the back of the van. Roger and Jeff watched as the blue Ford disappeared out of sight.

Burgess Park in the Southwark area of south London consists of one hundred and forty acres of land that was formerly housing and industry. Although various Mayors of London had promised money to have work on the park completed, it had never been finished and was still riddled with roads from a bygone era. Which was where the white transit van was now, slowly moving towards the wooded area off Albany Road. In the front the two girls and the big guy could hear the sound of laughter coming from the rear of the van and shouts of who was going to go first, followed by more laughing. Nina steered the van through the park and into a copse that was shielded on both sides. She stopped and applied the handbrake. Then looked across at Sasa and smiled. The big guy who was sitting by the door looked at them both whilst rubbing an erection through his jeans. He couldn't wait. Sasa and Nina had told him they were meeting another two girlfriends at the park. To enjoy some beers, or maybe something stronger. Sasa rubbed the guy's penis whilst smiling seductively. She spoke;

"Maybe we could start before our friends get here."

The big guy couldn't believe his luck, two white girls and two more on their way, all gagging for it. He released the door catch and swung his legs out, then nonchalantly strolled along the side of the van to open the back doors for his friends.

He walked round to the back and into a baseball bat. It hit him squarely in the face catching both his nose and mouth. He staggered back and collapsed on the floor, moaning through his broken teeth and nose. He looked up to see Jeff standing over him, the baseball bat held above his head. He was wearing his usual evil smile. Sasa and Nina had moved to the back of the van and had a hand on each door handle. They looked at Roger, who had appeared out of the trees. He nodded. They swung the doors open and stepped back. The first member of the gang jumped out, a big smile on his face until Tom's bat hit him across both knees while he was still in mid-air. He screamed loudly as he somersaulted then fell awkwardly to the ground. The rest of them, all five stood in shock, their smiles gone. They starred at their two friends and then at Roger, and Jeff and Tom.

Five minutes later after being tied and beaten, they were back in the van, sitting in two rows along each side. Jeff and Tom towered over them, baseball bats hovering threateningly. Roger stood outside in full view of them all. He spoke;

"You boys have been naughty." He waited a few seconds then continued. "You really think you can fuck with Roger Scott and get away with it?" One of the guys near the door opened his mouth to speak, maybe to apologise, maybe to beg. Tom's bat crashed into his shoulder blade. He screamed then remained quiet. Roger shook his head. He carried on;

"I talk, you listen. That's how it works." He looked at them all then continued; "So here's what I am thinking might happen. Just so the rest know we mean business, maybe we are going to have to kill one of you." Gasps all round the van. Roger spoke again;

"So then the rest of you will know that now from now on I fucking own you." He paused watching their faces, one of them would bite, which one? Then;

"So from now on you all work for me until I tell you different. You got that?"

The smallest one, the loudest one bit, he shouted;

"You think we are fuckin' frightened of you, you old git. You won't kill anybody, and when we get out of here

74

you are…" The biggest guy, maybe the leader shouted at him to shut the fuck up as Roger nodded to Jeff. The base ball bat came crashing down on the smaller one's head, four, five then six times. The rest of the gang looked on as their friend's skull split open, white bone quickly replaced by blood and grey matter. Roger shouted;

"Out of the van the lot of you." He watched as Nina sliced through the ropes that were holding their arms behind their back. Then;

"Unless you want the same as him be at the *Vegas Slots* in one hour. You know where it is. Now fuck off."

They filed away, across the park. One of them limping badly, another one holding his sleeve against his nose and mouth. They were maybe one hundred metres away when they heard a *whoosh* followed by a loud bang. They turned to see the white transit van in a ball of flame. Doors closed, their friend still inside. No sign of Roger or the twins or the girls.

***

At the dining room table in a terraced house in Peckham Rye, Bojan Duric was talking slowly and methodically. It had been three years since two of his three sons had been hospitalised for many months. The scars were still evident. Their once handsome faces changed forever. The elder of the two, Aco still limping, still needing the aid of a walking stick to get around. All *because of one man.* The same man they were discussing, a man called Roger Scott. Bojan had questioned his two sons over and over. He had gone through every detail of what had happened on that fateful night in that scruffy nightclub in Peckham. He hated the owner, the man responsible for his sons appalling injuries, the man called Roger Scott.

The Serbian accepted the maybe his sons had gone about things the wrong way. Maybe a less aggressive approach to start with would have been better. Maybe get to know a bit more about Roger Scott and his operation before attempting to muscle in. He looked across the table at his damaged boys. There was no need for the amount of punishment they had received. They could have been given a warning and maybe slapped around a little, without the injuries being inflicted in such a serious manner. He then looked towards the door as it opened and his wife showed three guys into the room. Bojan nodded towards three empty seats. They nodded to him as they sat. Bojan stood. He walked round the table. He stopped then glared at his three visitors. He spoke;

"Where the fuck you been? Should have been here hour ago." One of them answered;

"Mosque, afternoon prayers."

Bojan nodded, he respected the fact that they were Muslim, but he was still angry. He spoke again;

"Four of you against one. What fuck happened?" He then listened carefully as they explained how it going to plan until a big guy turned up and surprised them. Bojan was fuming;

"So two of them and four of you. Scott should have been down before other guy come." He looked at them waiting for an answer. Nobody spoke. Bojan hit his fist off the table;

"What happen to Vlado?"

"Don't know, we wake up and he gone, maybe Scott take him."

Bojan shook his head. He could not believe what he was hearing. These four guys had been feared and respected in Serbia. Although Bojan had been in London for many years he had kept in touch with old contacts, old friends.

The four guys, who were now three, had been made to fight, to learn how to kill. How to survive. They had no choice; it was kill or be killed. Because although they were Serbian they were also Muslim.

He had gone to a lot of trouble and expense to get the four of them to London. Now they were three. He sat down in deep thought. He wanted revenge. He wanted Roger Scott to suffer. He glanced up at the three men standing in front of him. Nobody knew them. They were still of use. He needed them for now. Bojan changed his tack. He forced a smile;

"OK. Maybe not all bad. Vlado cannot speak any English, so if Scott have him it is no problem. Also you did good job with horse and with wrecking office. Scott will be worried."

He paused, then; "If only for a little while." He stood and walked around the table;

"The night before you come Dorde set fire to Scott nightclub. Much damage. Now closed." Bojan sat down again. He forced another smile, looked at Anto, Boro and Danko in turn. Then;

"This is what we do next."

Half an hour later after pats on the back and shaking of hands the three Muslim Serbs left the house. Bojan watched them go. He smiled again, this time it was not forced; Roger Scott was starting to pay for ever getting involved with Bojan and his family. Now it was time for the next stage. The next piece of his plan. The next payment was due.

Roger stood looking at the damage in the *Vegas Slots* gaming salon. Sasa and Nina had gone back to their flat, the flat that Roger owned, the flat with a red light in the window, back to work. He shook his head then turned his attention to the six guys in their late teens or early twenties, *all wearing similar hooded jackets* that were sitting on the floor, still in shock. One of them still holding his sleeve to his mouth and nose, another one occasionally massaging his knees. The rest looking back at him, their faces etched with fear. Jeff was standing over them, mobile phone in his hand. He had just taken close up pictures of all their faces.

The young gang members had talked about what had happened in the park as they strolled towards the salon. They didn't want to be there. One of them had suggested they disappear for a while. He had argued that it was a trap, if they turned up as Scott had instructed they would be sitting ducks. The biggest guy, maybe the leader shut him up by telling him they couldn't just disappear. You could not hide from Roger Scott. They had seen first-hand what he was capable of, and if he wanted them dead it would have happened back at the park. They would have all been in the van when it exploded. He knew they had been set up. The piece of shit in the wheelchair must have known Roger Scott owned the *Vegas Slots*. No, they had little choice; they would turn up and see what he wanted.

Roger walked towards them. He stood looking down at them for a full minute. He had seven pieces of paper in his hand. He shook his head again then spoke;

"Listen, and listen good you shower of shit." He paused, looking at each on in turn, then continued;

"You are going to do as I tell you, when I tell you and then you might, *just might,* live a while longer." He dropped the pieces of paper in front of the big guy, the obvious leader. He continued;

"Seven addresses, all massage parlours. Here's what is going to happen."

78

The new black BMW had been delivered that morning, a replacement for the one that had been wrecked outside the snooker hall. Now Roger was sitting inside with the air conditioning on as he looked at the detached house in a quiet leafy avenue in Dulwich Village. He had been there for over half an hour. He was a troubled man, metaphorically kicking the shit out of himself for letting his business and his reputation slide into some kind of oblivion. His lazy life of the last three years was now moving at what seemed like a hundred miles an hour. He knew he was in deep trouble and also knew that he had to act quickly. The longer he left the problems that had suddenly and viciously reared their ugly heads the worse they would become. So now sitting in this tranquil setting he cast his mind back to the start of his current situation. Start at the beginning; the raids on his nightclubs. Roger had gone through the CCTV footage of the incident at *Sam's* nightclub. Something or rather someone was troubling him. The more he looked at the guy in the white jacket talking to the pretty girl who he now knew was Emily Austen's sister, the more suspicious it looked. The guy was definitely watching the window as he listened to the girl talking. Roger had zoomed the camera in on his face. The more he studied the footage the more he seemed to recognise the guy, or maybe someone like him. Roger sat back in his car in deep thought. Something crossed his mind. While the nightclub was being attacked he was with Sam in the Silk Road Chinese Restaurant. He thought about the CCCT footage taken from the restaurant. He had studied it closely. The guy in the corner, the guy who had been watching Roger. The guy who had appeared to press a digit on his mobile phone as he and Sam had got up to leave. The guy with the walking stick who now looked suspiciously like the guy wearing the white jacket in the nightclub. Maybe related, maybe brothers. Maybe not, but if they were it was too much of a coincidence to be left without further investigation.

Which was why Roger Scott was sitting in his car, outside the detached house in a quiet leafy avenue in Dulwich Village.

Johnny, Harry, Mary and Alan sat at the table in the back room of the Pot Black Snooker Hall. It was the day after they had last been there. Roger had shaken hands with them all as they had entered. He was now seated at the head of the table. He smiled then spoke;

"Thanks for coming." He looked at them all in turn. Something was wrong, they were not happy. He stood, spoke again, unsmiling;

"You all ok?" Johnny answered;

"No we fuckin' ain't. Seems like you were right boss." Roger was listening, watching their faces. Johnny continued;

"After seeing you nearly get killed yesterday we had all agreed to that we were coming back to work for you. Then last night each of our massage parlours was hit; the word out there is that the other three, the ones the Serbs are running got hit as well." Roger looked at Johnny, silent, then;

"What do you mean hit, what happened?" Johnny replied;

"Nothing too serious, a gang of young lads came in, pushed the girls and punters around. They didn't cause any damage to the place. Just stole what cash there was then ran off. Did the same thing to all of them."

Roger looked back at them all, as if in deep thought.

He spoke;

"Anybody recognise them? Was it anybody we know?

"No. Same mob at all of them though. Young lads, maybe late teens, early twenties. They were all wearing hooded jackets, faces covered." Roger thought for a while, then;

"If they are young kids they must have been told what to do, somebody must be controlling them, I'll see what I can find out." He smiled inwardly, they had come back. He thought they might after what he had set up the previous night. Also Johnny had called him boss. *A good sign.*

Roger forced a smile as he pressed the doorbell on the well preserved front door of the detached house in the quiet leafy avenue in Dulwich Village. He felt lost, alone. He was out of his comfort zone. Roger Scott was used to taking what he wanted when he wanted. This was different. Not his usual situation of sending some of his boys round to extract the information he needed, one way or the other. *No.* After seeing that copper that was maybe from Scotland Yard, at the funeral of the girl who was so tragically killed in his night club, he decided he had to make his visit sympathetic. Look sad for their loss. Show respect. *The grieving nightclub owner.*

Cassandra Austen heard the doorbell. Her husband had left home half an hour earlier. After an attempt to kiss his wife on the cheek, James Austen had got into his car and left the paved drive an unhappy man. Not only had he lost a daughter he loved dearly, he now felt he was losing his wife and life as he knew it. It was if she had blamed him and him only for the death of their daughter, and now she had built an impenetrable barrier between them.

Cassandra heard the bell and walked to the door

81

suspecting her husband had forgotten something, maybe his keys or maybe his wallet. It wouldn't be the first time. Roger heard footsteps approaching on what was maybe an oak floor. He stood, ready, still struggling to smile. The door opened and a middle aged lady with sad red eyes stood looking at him. She too tried to smile a welcome but struggled. She looked. A *can I help you look*. Roger relaxed his features. Then;

"Hello, I'm Roger Scott. I own the nightclub where your tragic loss took place. May I come in?"

Cassandra Austen was taken aback. So this was the gangster who was partly responsible for her daughter's death. Not what she expected to see at all, she assumed that gangsters were scar faced rough looking people. What Cassandra saw on her doorstep was an immaculately dressed good looking man. She stared unable to speak for what seemed like an age. She continued looking at him with hatred in her still tearful eyes. She wanted to tell him to go away, to never come to her house again, go now or she would call the police. Cassandra didn't do any of what she wanted. She stepped to one side and allowed Roger to walk past her and into the lounge.

Roger stood awkwardly. He tried and failed to raise an assuring smile, he had never felt so nervous. The old Roger Scott would have been shouting and threatening. Demanding answers to his questions. He couldn't bring himself to behave in that manner. Maybe it was the sadness he had witnessed with Sam and Penny. Maybe he remembered the sadness and upset at Emily Austen's funeral. Maybe back to the root of his problems, the fact that he had gone soft over the last three years. Or maybe it was the look of the lady standing on front of him, a beaten look. All tears cried, that made him break the silence;

"Mrs Austen, I can't begin to tell you how sorry I am for what happened in my nightclub." Cassandra opened her mouth to scream at him. Tell him it was his fault. He was thug of the worst kind, he should be in jail. Instead she looked at him. He appeared to be genuinely sorry. She composed herself. Then;

"Thank you. Please sit down."

In the upstairs office of the call centre Roger stood facing Mina; Jana was downstairs manning the phones. *The new phones.* Tom was in his usual place, in the downstairs room at the back, sat at the table, watching the small television. Roger had decided that Tom would be on guard there for the foreseeable. If for no other reason than to make the three ladies who worked there feel more secure.

Roger eyed Mina closely, she looked quite calm. It was her first time back at work since the attack on the call centre. Roger had been watching her closely as she worked, answering the phones, then asking the caller which girl he was interested in, then contacting the selection, then making the appointment then ringing the client back with confirmation. She seemed happy enough. Roger knew that due to her background, first as a kidnapped and forced sex slave in a dirty Serbian brothel as a teenager, and then being sent to London and forced to work in an equally dirty environment, that she was a hard and resilient lady. He had also altered the way the CCTV covered the back of the building. Now that at any time Mina or Jana could simply press a key on their laptops and the screen would show the outside of the back door.

Roger had explained briefly about the nightclub attacks and the guys who were waiting for him outside of the Silk Road Chinese Restaurant. He hadn't mentioned Penny.

He warned Mina to be extra vigilant when accepting and making the appointments, not to accept any callers who withheld their phone numbers. If they weren't traceable she had to ignore them. The last thing he needed was the girls in the flats being attacked. He asked her if she was happy to continue working for him. Mina answered that there was no problem, both herself and Jana had experienced a lot worse in their lives. Roger was satisfied that she was telling the truth, both of the girls would be able to carry on working as normal.

Roger and Mina went back a lot of years; she had been a loyal employee as he was an equally good boss. Although married to Sam he still had a lot of affection for Mina. So when he told her the meeting was over and asked if she needed anything from him Mina smiled. Not for the first time. A smile that Roger had seen many times over the years. He smiled back and gave a slight nod of his head. Mina knew what to do. She stood, turned round and quickly slipped off her pants before raising her skirt and bending over the desk. Roger unbuckled his belt and moved behind her.

Sam pulled up in her car at the back of the call centre. She had been there before. Since Roger had closed his main office this was the only place he worked. Sam didn't like the place at all; she thought it was dark, dingy, almost sinister looking. Nothing like the plush marble floored office she once worked in prior to their wedding. Roger had told her that since their marriage his business interests had changed. He had closed down some of his enterprises so therefore the large expensive office was no longer needed. He could manage all his dealings from here.

Sam applied the hand brake, stepped out and locked the car. She was now standing outside the large back door. It opened and she was greeted by a smiling Tom. Sam smiled back and mouthed *Mina* to Tom. He pointed to the stairs and then stepped aside to let her enter.

Camberwell Police Station.

Police Constable John Jenkins stood to attention in front of Assistant Chief Constable Ted Walton. He was still in shock from his latest episode with Roger Scott. He thought that he had seen the last of him a couple of years or more ago. He hadn't expected to be on the receiving end of the man once again. *The man who he hated nearly as much as he hated his wife.* Now he was shuffling his feet and stammering as he did his best to lie to his superior. The constable had explained how he and two police colleagues had turned up unannounced at the premises that were thought to be Roger Scott's call centre. How they had gained entry only to find that apart from three desks the room was empty. Roger Scott was there and he answered all their questions. He had no knowledge of a call centre ever existing in this building. He used it as an administration office for the running of his nightclubs and gaming salons. In fact the whole place was about to be refurbished as he was giving serious consideration to selling the building. Scott had invited the policemen to have a look around if they wanted to. They did and found nothing.

Jenkins then told his superior that Roger Scott had questioned him about the investigation into the attack on one of his nightclubs, and the tragic deaths of the young innocent people in attendance on that fateful night. Were they any closer to finding the culprit responsible? Scott had emphasised how helpful he had tried to be. Also how surprised he was that nobody had been brought to justice yet.

The Assistant Chief Constable was furious. He had broken many rules in the way he had instructed Jenkins to mount the raid on the premises. For what? He knew this waste of space standing in front of him was lying. He glared at the constable for a full minute, struggling to disguise the pain he was in. Then;

"All the evidence points to that building being a front for a call centre. Which was being used to arrange appointments with prostitutes that Roger Scott is controlling?" He continued, angrily;

"So you tell me Police Constable Jenkins. How the hell did he know you were about to make your visit?"

Jenkins stammered an answer about not knowing. That maybe it was a genuine admin office. Ted Walton attempted to stand up quickly; a severe pain across his stomach stopped him. His voiced raised he told the hapless P.C. to get out.

Sam eyed Roger and Mina suspiciously. She was sitting in the corner of the office as Mina sat opposite Roger who was seated behind his desk. Sam was not happy. She had already tripped as she ascended the third stair causing herself to slip noisily back down to the bottom. She knew that Mina must have heard the commotion, but she hadn't even bothered to open the office door to see if Sam was alright. Not until she had dusted herself down, climbed the stairs for the second time and reached the top step had the door opened, and to her surprise Roger was standing there, asking if she needed any help.

Now as she sat listening to Roger giving Mina instructions on the new security arrangements she got the feeling that it was a forced conversation. Mina was being a little too attentive, maybe nodding her head a little too much. After a couple of minutes of what Sam thought was pointless waffle Mina stood up, then with a quick nod of her head in Sam's direction she opened the door and returned downstairs. Roger stood and moved across the office, he risked a quick glance down to check that he had arranged himself properly, flies up, shirt tucked in. He looked out of the window as if in deep thought before turning to look at his wife. He smiled, it was difficult. He sat back down and asked her how she was. At first she didn't answer. She was inwardly fuming.

Then she lost it. Maybe it was the events of the last few days that had got to her, maybe the grieving for Penny, maybe the fact that Roger had not been in contact with her at all, maybe it was all three things that made Sam explode. Roger watched as Sam stormed around the office shouting about what had happened, about her beloved Penny. Getting more and more angry due to him not answering her. Eventually appearing to calm a little. Only to start again when he refused to acknowledge her questions. Roger watched as the full circle of emotions went through Sam. Then;

"Sam. I can see you are upset and I understand why, but you have to let me handle this my way. It is me they are after; all the attacks, even the attack on your horse was to get to me."

Sam screamed. She'd had enough;

"Horse! Fuckin' horse, she had a name!" She glared at Roger. Then spoke quietly, calmly;

"Her name was Penny, and she meant more to me than you ever will again." Sam stood, then looking at Roger with a mix of tear and hate filled eyes she stormed out slamming the door behind her.

Roger watched out of the window as Sam got into her

car and sped off. He shook his head. That was a close call. He couldn't blame Tom; he would have been more pissed off with him if he had refused Sam's entry. He would need to be more careful in future.

Sam was still fuming. She had never been so angry. She had gone there to get answers to some questions off Mina. She hadn't expected Roger to be there, now she was no further forward. Sam thought about the atmosphere in the office. Something wasn't right, both her husband and Mina were hiding something. She cast her mind back to when she first fell for Roger. To the many times that he would lock his office door while they made love on the sofa that sat in the corner of the room. Then returning to her desk, grinning like the cat that had got the cream - knowing that anyone who looked at her in the next half hour would clearly know what they had been up to. How she would look down then up, glance out of the window, maybe at her computer screen, anything to avoid looking at the face of whoever it was in front of her. Similar looks and mannerisms to what she had just witnessed Mina doing.

Sam was not happy when she had first entered the call centre. Now she felt ten times worse. She drove aimlessly; she didn't want to go back to the house in Kent ever again. She didn't want to go back to the London penthouse. Sam drove a little further then indicated to turn left. She would go and visit her cousin Adie, chat to her. Play with little Meg, Adie's beautiful daughter. Maybe a complete change of scenery would help her mood. Maybe not, but she did not want to see her husband again anytime soon. Feeling a little better, she continued out of the London suburbs towards the quiet area where Adie and Meg lived. Still thinking deeply, still confused as to what was happening to change her life so dramatically. Sam failed to notice a small motorbike following her car.

Roger sat back down at his desk. He had left the Austen household after about one hour. He was pleased he had made the visit. After a few minutes of being there Jane Austen had descended the stairs looking tired and drawn. Her mother had introduced Roger and explained who he was. After the initial shock had passed Jane relaxed and listened as Roger told them both about the CCTV footage. He told lies quite easily as he explained to them that he was talking to as many people as possible who had been in attendance on the night of the tragedy.

Roger was now more than aware that there was some kind of relationship between the high ranking copper who was at the funeral, and the Austen family. He chose his words very carefully, saying that the police were doing a very good job under difficult circumstances. However it seemed that witnesses, maybe through fear, were not coming forward to make statements. Therefore he himself was trying to help in any way he could.

Mother and daughter listened as Roger lied about the different people he already spoken to, how he was building up a picture of what happened in order to help the already overworked police. Cassandra and Jane Austen felt a little better, a little more relaxed after Roger had left their house after an hour. Roger felt better too. He had a name, a name of a man in a white jacket who had been talking to Jane in *Sam's* nightclub. A man of Serbian decent. A man named Rodovan.

Roger Scott pondered over the last few days. Cleary he had been followed, the people who killed Penny knew where he lived. Also the attempt on his life outside the snooker hall, somebody must have followed him there, and then waited until he came out. Maybe for the foreseeable he would use taxis and make them drive through the bus lanes. Roger looked at the evidence he had. A guy called Rodovan, maybe Rod, who could well be the brother of the man who had been watching him and Sam in the Silk Road restaurant. Maybe that guy had also followed him. Four photographs of the clowns who had waited for him outside that same night. Somebody on a motorbike who had attempted to attack *Club Mina*. He had questioned the yobs who had sprayed the paint on his gaming machines. Through their fear they had told him in detail about the guy in the wheelchair paying them to do the damage. They also told him that the same guy had suggested there would more work for them.

Roger thought about it. A man in a wheelchair and a man with a walking stick. Clearly it was all linked together, but how? If he was to write down all the names of the people who had had their legs broken, due to owing him money and other reasons, he would have a list as long as his arm. He also knew they would not want to cross him again.

Roger turned his attention back to the gang of paint sprayers. He had reminded them that they not only worked for him, but that he also owned them, and they would tell him as soon as they were approached by anyone wanting to do him damage. He had watched their faces. They seemed to accept what he was saying, but Roger also knew that at some point they would rebel if he kept up with the threats. He would need to bring them closer to him. Make them feel more of a part of what he was doing. Maybe pay them some money; *or maybe kill another one.*

October 2012.

Adie stared at the padded walls, the cushioned door, and a bleak single bed. A table and one chair screwed to the floor. No window, just four walls to look at.

Her head hurt, she didn't know how long she had been in this awful place. She looked down at the loose fitting gown that covered her otherwise naked body. She could smell the disinfectant emanating from both herself and the one item that covered her modesty.

Adie lay back on the bed. She thought of Meg, her beautiful daughter, she closed her tear filled eyes. Weeping quietly as she tried in vain to cast her mind back as to how she finished up in this place. Her thoughts went back to her first memory after coming out of an induced coma three years previous.

It had been a bright sunny day when her cousin Sam had collected her from the hospital. Adie had held her baby Meg tightly but gently in her arms as the car, with her cousin Sam driving pulled away from the smiling waving nurses. Sam had told Adie that she was taking her and Meg to a nice new home. Adie couldn't believe her eyes as they entered small but well- proportioned bungalow. It was beautifully decorated with one of the two bedrooms laid out as a nursery. Sam stayed with Adie for the first few nights to help her settle in.

A physiotherapist and speech therapist visited her twice a week, also an occupational therapist and social worker called to check on the progress of both herself and Meg. As the weeks went by Adie's health and confidence improved rapidly, to the point where she was confident and able to cook, clean and look after the bungalow with the minimal help. Now she was also happy to converse with neighbours, and invite some of her cousins who had visited her in hospital to her house. Sam was also a regular visitor, calling every few days, playing with Meg. Sitting in the garden with Adie, encouraging her to talk, trying to steer the conversation away from the past whenever Adie brought it up. Adie had even thought about looking for part time work at some point in the future, when Meg was old enough to be installed in a nursery school.

She had been happy, content in her own little world, looking forward to the future, the new life ahead of her.

Then in one short night all her plans were shattered.

July 2012 Present day.

The man on the small motorbike sat at the end of a quiet street. He had followed the Porsche 911 as he had been told to. He had now listened to his next instruction, which was quite simple; to stay there, where he was, and to keep an eye on the other house where the girl in the Porsche lived. Not the one in Kent. The London one. Then to only ring back if the car moved.

Inside the house at the other end of the street Sam sat on a settee with Meg leaning against her knees smiling up at her. Adie was in the chair opposite. She had been overjoyed when she received the call from Sam asking if it was ok to pop over to see her and Meg. Speaking slowly and smiling happily Adie told Sam about how well Meg was doing. She loved running around and playing in the garden, and she had made friends with some of the other children who lived nearby. Meg asked Sam what was the red stuff on her lips and why was it there and did Sam have any babies? Then, where did she live and where was her Mummy? Sam smiled for what seemed like the first time in many days as Adie watched her daughter chattering about anything and everything that entered her little head.

Looking out of the window at the small garden that backed onto open fields Sam's mind drifted to both Adie and Meg three years earlier. How she had visited them both in hospital until the day of their discharge. How happy she had been watching Adie's face as she viewed her new home for the first time. Sam then thought about the night many months prior, when she saw the battered bruised face of Adie on the television news. How the same night she had confronted Adie's then boyfriend, a horrible man called Shane. Sam thought again about what went through her mind previous to that. About Shane telling her that Roger Scott was behind what had happened to her cousin Adie. How he had arranged the kidnap because Shane owed him money.

It was some thirty minutes later that the man on the small motorbike saw, then recognised the blue Ford with blacked out rear windows slowly approach the house where the Sam had left her car. A slight acknowledgement from one of the three occupants as they got out of the car. He started the bike then pulled away in the opposite direction.

Sam was startled back to the present now as little Meg pulled at her skirt asking her if she wanted to play football in the garden. She smiled at the beautiful little girl in front of her and said of course she would. She loved playing football and could she go in goal? It was then, as she stood up and glanced again out of the window that she saw them. Two men at the back of the house. At the same time she heard a crash as the back door was kicked open. Gathering up Meg into her arms Sam stood frozen as three guys wearing stocking masks ran into the small lounge. Adie was still sitting in the armchair, with shock and fear as one of the men shouted;

"Which one of you bitches Sam?"

Sam looked back at him horrified; she trembled as she tried to answer, her mouth opened but no words came out.

The guy stared at her then turned to look at Adie. He spoke again, quieter, more menacing;

"I ask again, and this time I want fuckin' answer. Which one Sam?" Adie stood only to be stopped by a fist to her chin. She dropped back down into the chair. Even though she was hurt and frightened she wanted to protect Sam. *Sam, the girl who had been there for her for the last three years.* Adie spoke slowly but clearly;

"Me, I am Sam, now leave my friend and her baby alone." The guy smiled, this is exactly what he wanted. He turned and nodded to one of the other guys who produced a sack which he roughly pulled over Adie's head. Sam screamed, telling him that she was *Sam,* to leave Adie alone. One of them silenced her with a back hand to her face. The third guy stepped forward, looked at the first one. Then;

"If get this wrong Bojan kill us. Take both." The guy then pulled a second sack from his pocket. He snatched Meg out Sam's arms and threw her to the settee. For the first time Meg started to scream. The two girls were then dragged out of the back door and towards the side of the house, where the blue ford had been parked. They were then pushed roughly onto the back seat, one of the guys got in with them, the other two jumped into the front. Doors closed the car reversed off the drive. Adie was crying hysterically, moaning into the sackcloth; *"Where is Meg? What have you done to my baby?"* Sam sat in silence, listening for any clues as to who they were, or where they were being taken. She already had a name; *"Bojan."*

Now she had her hands clasped together, not tied in any way. With both her and Adie having sacks over their heads surely somebody would notice them, maybe ring the police. She wasn't to know the rear windows were blacked out to the extent that nobody from the outside could see in. As she and Sam had been pushed into the rear of the car Sam had finished up next to the opposite door, with Adie in the middle and one of the guys next to her. Sam was thinking hard, if she could get one hand near the door handle maybe she could open it and jump out, start screaming, attract attention. She hoped that the door's child lock had not been activated.

She moved her right hand down towards the bottom of the sack. The material concealed her movements. Sam moved her hand very slowly until she could feel the door handle through the sack. The three men were taking no notice of her. The two guys in the front seats were arguing with the one in the back. He was supposed to know what Sam looked like, he was the one who had followed the Porsche all the way to Kent and most of the way back. He was trying to defend himself, saying that he had to keep his distance, and they both had long blonde hair, that they were similar looking when you were wearing a crash helmet.

They were still not taking much notice of Sam. She felt the car slowing a little, she thought some more, maybe they were approaching traffic lights, or maybe a roundabout where they would have to stop to give way to other traffic. Sam waited for her chance. The guy in the back was still protesting that it wasn't a problem, they had two girls, one of which they knew was Sam. Once they met up with Bojan he would know which one she was. The one in the front passenger seat replied telling him that was true but it still made them look fuckin' amateurs. That they had already fucked up once that night in Camberwell. Sam's ears pricked up at that comment. Three men, speaking in broken English. There were four on the night outside the restaurant. She thought briefly about the fourth guy. The one who had finished up in the car boot. Sam shuddered as she felt the car slow down further, She got herself ready. As soon as it stopped she would fling herself out, start shouting and screaming. Do anything to attract attention.

John Davis had been in his back garden pulling up a few weeds out of the hard ground, doing a bit of tidying when he heard a crash. It appeared to come from the house three doors away from his own. The one where that girl lived. The one who came across as a bit slow. The one who lived there with just her daughter. He thought there was something odd about her, never any sign of a man around. Maybe the crash was the little girl dropping something, maybe a cup on the tiled kitchen floor, or maybe a box of Lego or some other toy. He was close to the fence that separated his garden from his next door neighbour. John looked over towards the source of the noise; he couldn't hear or see anything. He turned back to the job in hand. *Bloody weeds!* Why do they have to grow so quick without the aid of expensive feed or fertilizer. Why can't the flowers do the same bloody thing? Shaking his head he bent back down to pull out another of the offending little wastes of garden space. *Then a shout. A loud shout. Somebody in distress.* Standing back up he looked with horror as he saw three men dragging what looked like two struggling hooded figures around the side of the house. He shouted. One of the men paused, a quick glance in his direction then carried on as if John was invisible. John ran into his house, grabbed the phone and dialled *999*.

Sam sat in rear of the car patiently awaiting her chance. She was thinking about Roger talking about the four guys who were waiting for him outside the Silk Road Chinese Restaurant. How he had called them "amateurs." Now there were three men talking openly in front of her and Adie in broken English. It had to be the same people. As the car continued moving slowly Sam heard the unmistakable sound of continuous bleeps indicating they were approaching some kind of pedestrian crossing. She heard the driver swear as the car came to halt. Sam waited, she wanted to jump out but not until the car was starting to move again. She didn't want anybody to come after her.

After what seemed like an age Sam finally heard the engine note change. As the car inched forward she screamed loudly. At the same time pulling on the small lever to release the door catch. A sigh of relief as the door sprang open as she put her weight against it. *No child lock.* Shouting as loud as she could Sam tumbled out of the car and onto the road. Inside the car the two guys in the front seats turned in shock to see what had happened. The guy in the back put his arm around Adie's neck to stop her following Sam. He then shouted;

"Go, go, fuckin' move. Now! Move." The car sped off leaving Sam screaming and crying on the ground. Passers-by looked in horror at the tangled wriggling figure that was rolling around the road.

***

Marion Hill was standing inside the *Vegas Slots* gaming salon. She was tired. She hadn't been sleeping well since the paint spray attack. Marion was also frightened. She had lain awake in her bed rehearsing how she was going to resign from her post as manageress of the salon. Maybe it would have been easier before the attack, maybe easier before she had met Roger Scott personally. Marion had never been so frightened as when Roger had walked through the door with the twin brothers.

Marion looked at the double doors at the back of the premises; she had opened both earlier for a large van to reverse up to them. She watched as two men in overalls moved each of the damaged machines out of the doors and into the van. Roger had been in touch with her and told her to come back to work. Although she was still very upset she thought it might be the best thing to do. Roger had been there one hour earlier. He had explained that all the affected machines were to be taken to a warehouse, to be stored until he worked out what to do with them. New machines would be arriving over the next two days. He wanted Marion there to supervise the changeover, then to get the business back up and running. Maybe through fear she had agreed. Any thoughts of resignation had quickly been forgotten when she heard Roger's voice.

Now as Marion watched the machines being moved she was more worried. The local newspapers had been full of pictures of a burnt out van that had been found in Burgess Park. The remains of a male body had been found inside the back of it. There was another picture of a young guy who had gone missing at the same time. The police were asking for witnesses. Anybody who thought they might have seen the van in the vicinity of the park, should contact them immediately. What was troubling Marion more was that a few minutes earlier there had been a knock at the locked front door. Thinking it might have been to do with the expected delivery she had opened it. Marion was shocked to see five guys standing there. Maybe in their late teens to early twenties, *all wearing similar hooded jackets.* She thought they looked a bit nervous. Only one of them spoke. The biggest one of them, maybe the appointed leader;

"We have to come to say sorry for the other night. It was us that came in with the paint."

Marion looked at them all in turn. She had remembered each one. Only there was one missing, the smallest one. The loud mouthed one. The one whose picture she had seen in the newspaper. The one who was dead. She slowly nodded her head as the guy continued;

"We are going to keep an eye on this place. You won't have any more trouble." They turned and walked away.

Sam sat in the back of the police car. She was bruised and had some small grazes but she felt a little better knowing that she had escaped the kidnappers. Sam was more concerned as to what would happen to Adie. It was due to her that her poor cousin had been taken, as if she hadn't been through enough. The two officers in the front had been responding to a call from a worried neighbour called John Davis reporting what looked like the kidnap of two people. They were on their way to the address when they received a second call from the station telling them to detour to Forest Hill Road. Several members of the public had phoned the police after seeing a body or a person being thrown from a car. Sam wiped away a tear as she spoke to the two policemen;

"Why are we just sitting here? My cousin has been kidnapped and you are doing nothing about it!"

"Please keep calm madam. We have alerted every squad car in the area. We have to wait with you until the ambulance arrives." Sam was fuming;

"I don't want an ambulance. I want you to find Adie. Her little girl is all… Oh my god! Meg is alone in the house. We have to get round there now."

One of the officers turned to look at Sam;

"What little girl? Who are you talking about?"

Sam was close to hysterics;

"Little Meg. Adie's daughter, when they took us they left her there alone in the house. She was crying and upset. We have to go there now. *Please.*"

Bojan screamed at the top of his voice;

Idiots, you fuckin' idiots. That not her, who she?"

The three Serbs shrugged their shoulders, looked at each other, wondering who to blame. Anto answered;

"She girl in Porsche, we saw car."

They had driven into an underground car park beneath the flats where the three kidnappers shared an apartment. Then half carrying, half pushing Adie into the lift, they went up three floors and through a door to where Bojan was waiting for them. It was then after roughly pulling the sack off Adie's head that the realisation that this was not Roger Scott's wife hit the Serbian. Adie opened her eyes, she was terrified. Not knowing where she was, she looked at the surroundings as four foreign sounding men argued in front of her. The door was still open and Adie could see the lift to the left. It was still as they had left it with the doors apart. She glanced at the four men who were still blaming each other.

Looking back at the open door she decided to take her chance; glancing again at the arguing men Adie turned and ran. If she could get to the lift and close the doors she might have a chance to escape. Adie got as far as the inside of the lift. She was frantically pressing buttons; she had to get down and out of where ever it was she was being held. She felt overwhelming relief as she heard the door start to close. At the same time one of the Serbs had glanced back in her direction. He shouted and started running towards her. Adie looked in horror as the guy got nearer to her. The doors were closing but too slowly. Then relief as she saw the guy stumble, it slowed him enough for the doors to shut tight. The lift began to move; Adie breathed a sigh of relief.

She leaned back then started to shake in disbelief as the lift started to go up not down. Adie watched as the floor numbers on the small digital screen counted upwards. She could hear voices. Angry voices. The unmistakable sound of footsteps echoing around the concrete stairs that served the upper floors of the tower block. Adie pressed herself to the back of the small compartment that was taking her away from the kidnappers and what she was certain was some kind of captivity.

The lift continued its ascent. Adie watched the door as the lift slowly ground to a halt. The door opened, she took a tentative step forward. She peeped out nervously looking from side to side. Nobody there. Stepping out, Adie glanced at the stairs to her left. Should she risk running down them or go back into the lift and press the button for the ground floor? She hesitated. The lift doors closed. Decision made for her. Adie turned and took the six steps down then turned a corner that would lead her to the next few stairs. She risked a glance over her shoulder, nobody there, another sigh of relief.

She then turned and ran into the chest of a large Serbian man who was smiling as he stood in the stairwell.

Around a mile away Sam sat in Adie's lounge whispering gentle reassurance to Meg who snuggled into her. She was still crying; "Where's my mummy, why did nasty men take her away?" The young policewoman smiled sympathetically. They were waiting for a social worker to arrive. With no sign as yet as to where Adie was and also that Meg was on the social services watch list they had a dilemma as to what would happen to the infant. Who would look after her until they were sure Adie had been found and was able to care for her child herself. Sam had been quite adamant that she would stay at Adie's house and care for Meg for as long as it was necessary. The policewoman told her that it was not possible. They had to use dedicated foster parents who had been vetted and police checked. They had at any one time, emergency carers they could call on. Also forensics were on their way to look at the scene of the crime, and a detective who wanted to question her. Sam sighed in frustration. What else could go wrong? Her life had been turned around in dramatic fashion over the last couple of weeks. She couldn't help thinking that it was Roger's fault. The guys in the car had mentioned the restaurant in Camberwell. They had also asked which one was Sam. Clearly it was her that they were attempting to kidnap, and now poor Adie, who had suffered more than enough over the last three years was out there somewhere, through no fault of her own and in grave danger.

Adie screamed as the big man pushed her down the stairs. From three flights down Bojan heard the commotion and came running upwards. Meeting Adie and the big guy halfway he grabbed them both by their throats and spoke quietly;

"Shut fuck up, both of you." Adie stood silent in total fear as Bojan continued;

102

"You, idiot, get rid of her, wrong woman. Get rid now, quietly. People listening."

Bojan was right, people were listening, but from behind closed doors. In this area of town, in this building, it was a regular occurrence to hear the shouts and screams of desperate women who suffered at the hands of their brutal husbands or partners. They listened but kept their doors firmly closed. It would never cross their mind to contact the police.

The Serb turned Adie around and started shepherding her down the stairs. He would get her back in the car. Blindfold her then dump her somewhere quiet. Adie had no idea where she was as her head had been covered until they had reached the apartment. She was terrified, not knowing where she was now going or what was going to happen next. They reached the bottom of the stairs, passed a door that would lead outside, then towards another door that would take them down to the underground car park. The Serb still had hold of Adie's collar as he opened the door. Adie saw the darkness and started to panic at the unknown in front of her. As she tried to turn to get back out through the door, the Serb's hand slipped from her. Adie lost her balance and screamed as she fell down the concrete stairs behind her, hitting her head on almost every step as she went tumbling to the bottom. The Serb watched as Adie landed in a heap. Unconscious and bleeding from various wounds around her head, he turned and ran back up the stairs. Bojan was waiting for him at the top, hands on his hips, glaring.

Twenty minutes later the apartment was empty of all clothes and belongings. Bojan, Anto, Boro and Danko were driving away from the block of flats without looking back.

Roger Scott looked at the sheet of paper that lay on the desk in front of him. He was in the upstairs office of the call centre. He went slowly down the list. Kenny Ray was the first name on the sheet. Kenny ran his empire north of the river. Drugs, prostitution, and debt collection, along with a casino he owned. Roger had clashed with Kenny three years earlier after some of his guys had been badly beaten while trying to take over one of Roger's clubs. They had since kept to their own side of the river. Next was the name of all the guys who had not only worked for Roger over the years but had also visited the call centre at some point. He looked further down at the names of two policemen. Jenkins and Blunt. Although they had been on his payroll at some point, he could never be sure he fully trusted them. Blunt was now retired; he had been well paid by Roger to keep him informed of anything the police were planning that might affect him. As for Jenkins, in Roger's opinion he didn't have the brains to be dangerous. He thought again, are brains needed to be dangerous? Maybe not. He crossed Blunt's name off.

Until a couple of years ago, Roger hadn't trusted anybody. Another sign, if he needed it, that he had gone soft, let things go. Mina had thought the two guys who had damaged the call centre were Serbian. She might be right. In which case, who on the list in front of him had briefed them? Roger sat back in his chair in deep thought. The name of the guy in *Sam's* nightclub he had taken from the Austen girl was Rodovan, was that a Serbian name? The guys who jumped him outside the Silk Road were also foreign. Maybe also Serbs. He looked at the list again. Decided to assume they were the same people or related in some way. Picking up a pen he began to cross names off. Names of the people he knew would not need or use outside help to get to him. He smiled as he looked at the four names he had left.

***

Two miles away Linda Harton was not in a good mood. She had been arguing with her husband's mother. Although he was thirty seven years old, her spouse Nev still happily accepted and appeared to enjoy being treated like a child by his *"Mummy."* Linda thought it was pathetic to watch, a grown man being asked if he had washed his hands before she would serve tea. She had left him and their eldest son at the nearby football pitch while she took their two younger children home. Her head was throbbing due to the constant bickering between her two youngest;

Linda had heard enough of the two children arguing.

"Be quiet you two! We are nearly home." It was always the same when they had been to their Nan's house. She was too soft with them in Linda's opinion. Spoiling them with sweets. Buying them clothes and giving them money to go home with, even though she couldn't afford to. Linda, although unhappy with the situation tolerated it. After all Nan's worked for nothing, so she was handy to have around at times of school holidays or illness. If she complained, Linda would simply stop her from seeing her grandchildren for a few weeks. That seemed to work. Her wimp of a husband let her get on with it even though it was his own mother who was being used.

Linda pressed the remote control and waited impatiently for the garage door to open. Turning on her headlights and selecting first gear she slowly pulled into the underground car park. She then negotiated around the other parked cars before stopping at her allocated bay. She sighed as the back doors swung open and her two children jumped out still arguing. Linda got out and pressed the key fob to lock the car then heard her daughter scream; *"Mummy."*

Linda shouted;

"Ralphy, leave your sister alone." The little girl carried on screaming as Linda walked quickly towards her. *"Just wait until I get you two indoors."* She then stopped dead in her tracks as she saw the reason for her daughter's anguish.

The ambulance had arrived within ten minutes of Linda making the frantic phone call. She had found a lady, maybe in her late twenties sprawled out on the garage floor. Her head was covered in blood as were her arms and legs. The two paramedics quickly got the girl onto a stretcher and took her to hospital. Now, an hour later Linda sat, still shaking as she described to the two police officers how she had made the discovery. They listened patiently before showing her a photo of Adie.

In a quiet cul-de-sac Sam eyed the two people in front of her with suspicion. Spike and Yvette sat on Adie's settee wearing what Sam was convinced was a false smile. They didn't look right, a little scruffy, disinterested. They all listened as Lisa, the social worker explained that the police had found Adie and she was in hospital. It looked like she wouldn't be out anytime soon. Little Meg was in need of temporary care until her mum was well enough to return home. Sam protested that as she was a blood cousin, she should be allowed to look after Meg. The social worker was quite adamant that it wasn't allowed. Spike and Yvette had been vetted and checked. They were the approved foster family in this area. Sam looked at them both suspiciously;

"So how long have you two being doing this line of

work then?" There was venom in her voice. Before they had chance to answer Sam continued; "and how much money are you getting for this?"

Lisa jumped up and stood in front of Sam;

"Sam! There is no need for this. I know you are upset, we all are, but this is not achieving anything, the decision has been made. Maybe you should say goodbye to Meg and leave."

Sam's eyes filled with tears, she glared at Spike and Yvette; "I want your address, I want to visit Meg and make sure she is alright." Lisa stood;

"That is against all rules Sam, now please leave."

"OK. I'm going." She turned and faced the social worker; she pointed her finger into her face. Then quietly with menace in her voice;

"You Lisa, would do well to remember the case of Baby P." *"When you clueless fuckin' people sent that little boy to his death."*

Lisa opened her mouth to protest. Spike and Yvette smiled. A strange smile, self-satisfied, almost cynical.

Sam turned and stormed out. She headed for the hospital.

Sam had parked her car outside the Kings College Hospital and was now sitting in the waiting room. Looking around the dull walls, her mind filled with bad memories. Memories from three years ago. The last time Adie had been rushed in there. The last time she had been kidnapped and discovered in a WW2 bunker near Southwark. Tears streamed down Sam's face as she recalled the pain and torment that poor Adie had gone through. The many months in intensive care. The painful recuperation. Then finally being allowed home, only for history to now repeat itself. Sam couldn't help thinking that Roger was involved in some way, as maybe he was three years ago. She was snapped out of her thoughts by a man she recognised from her previous visit to this place. A man who had a habit of delivering bad news; Dr. Ahmed spoke;

"Sam. How nice to see you again. I wish it could have been under happier circumstances. How are you?" Sam looked and tried to smile at Dr. Ahmed. She remembered him very well from her visits to Adie three years ago. It was his expertise that had released Adie from the coma that had been induced, due to the horrific head injuries she had suffered.

"I am fine thank you. I have been checked out at the accident and emergency. A little bruised and a little shaken but ok. How is Adie?"

The surgeon shook his head slowly. A grave look on his face. He spoke;

"She will live." He stopped and glanced towards the door that concealed the high dependency unit which housed Adie. He continued;

"She has several head injuries. She was found at the bottom of some concrete stairs, it looks like the damage was done as she fell down them. She is heavenly sedated. The X-rays show nothing fractured or broken. I worry more about the psychological damage the fall may have incurred. We won't know for a little while. Not until she comes round and we get the opportunity to talk to her."

As Sam opened her mouth to answer Dr. Ahmed, the door that led to the corridor that led to other parts of the hospital opened, and what was very clearly a detective entered. He gave a friendly glance in Sam's direction, and then addressed Dr. Ahmed;

"How is she doctor? Well enough to be interviewed?

"Afraid not, she is still sedated, it could be some time."
Then turning towards Sam he spoke;

"This is Detective Constable Farrell. He is investigating Adie's kidnap." Then looking back at the detective;

"This is Sam Scott, she is Adie's cousin."

In Camberwell police station, Assistant Chief Constable Ted Walton sat at the back of a room. He would have preferred to stand, to show a presence, to be commanding. He had tried but the pain in his stomach didn't allow him to for more than a minute. So he sat and watched as the five detectives had filed into the room and taken their seats. He had tolerated the useless P.C. Jenkins long enough. He had realised that he should not have attempted to do things off the record. He had arranged a previous meeting with Detective Inspector Terry Thompson and made it very clear what his intentions were. Now he looked on as the D.I. stood in front of a magnetic whiteboard facing the five detectives who were now seated. They listened as they made notes. Held to the board were three photographs. The first one showed a white transit van. It had been severely fire damaged. The picture next to it was of a youth, maybe late teens. The third, a handsome looking man, maybe around mid thirties. The D.I. pointed to the photo of the young man then spoke;

"Denzil York. Age nineteen. He was found in the back of this van, which was found in Burgess Park. It looks like he had been locked in the back before it was torched. It's early days but it also looks like his head had been caved in. There appears to be several skull fractures. From what we know so far young Denzil here was part of a gang of youths, who had a habit of being a nuisance to the public around the Bellenden Road area. We also know that a few days ago a nearby establishment known as the *Vegas Slots* was vandalised. The manageress, a lady we know as Marion Hill, gave us a description of the perpetrators. Although they were all wearing hooded jackets and had their faces covered Marion suspects that they were the same gang that Denzil belonged to."

He glanced at the photos again then turned back to face the front:

"I want the other gang members found and interviewed. Look at any CCTV footage of the area surrounding the gaming salon, look for movement of the white van prior to it entering Burgess Park. Find and speak to any witnesses who were in the area at the time. It is a busy main road, somebody must have seen something. Talk to other gangs who hang around the area, they must know about what has happened. I want posters of the van and of Denzil putting up in the nearby shops, also speak to the shop owners; they may have seen something to give us a lead."

He paused and looked round the room. Then looking at Ted Walton he continued;

"You will have all noticed Assistant Chief Constable Walton is present today. He would like to say a few words, but before he does, think about what I have said. I want this solved, I want results!" D.I. Thompson glanced at the pictures on the board then sat down.

Ted Walton knew he had made a big mistake in ordering P.C. Jenkins to make an unauthorised raid on Roger Scott's premises. A mistake that would not happen again. From now on everything he did in order to nail Roger Scott would be official and above board. He stepped forward, slowly, gingerly. He turned to face his audience. He pointed to the third picture.

"This gentleman is called Roger Scott. Some of you

may have heard of him. He owns the previously mentioned *Vegas Slots*. He also owns the nightclub in Peckham known as *Sam's*. The same nightclub where five young people died recently, as a direct result of a fire. A fire which we now know was arson. On top of which you may or may not remember that three years ago one of our colleagues was shot and killed in the same premises."

Ted stopped talking to take a deep breath. Then;

"Last night we received a call concerning a kidnap in the Brockwell Park area. Two young ladies were snatched from a house in broad daylight. One is in a bad way in hospital the other is next door waiting to be interviewed. The lady in question is Roger Scott's wife. I will be speaking to her personally after we finish here." He paused and looked at each member of the audience in front of him. He turned towards a nearby desk and chair, he sat down then;

"I am of the firm belief that there is more to Roger Scott than we see here in front of us. There is evidence of his involvement in prostitution and drug supply. The night that one of our colleagues was killed in his nightclub a person we wanted to talk to in connection with the sad events disappeared. He was found the following day. Not only dead but it looked like he had been brutally tortured prior his demise. Nobody was ever found or charged with that murder." He continued;

"D.I. Thompson will be in charge of this investigation. He will tell you what is required next. He will also report directly to me."

He put both hands on the desk in front of him. Leaning forward, looking down at the detectives like some kind of imposing bank manager trying to intimidate a bankrupt applying for a loan. He spoke whilst attempting to hide his obvious discomfort.

"There will be no mistakes this time. No cock ups. Roger Scott is guilty of more than one crime. It is too much of a coincidence for this young man to be found brutally murdered soon after Roger Scott's gaming salon was vandalised. Your job is to solve this case. Leave no stone unturned in this investigation." He raised his voice;

"I want results!"

***

Two miles away Roger stood over Sam, imposing.

"What did you tell them? The police! *What the fuck did you tell them?*"

Sam sat back on the settee in the plush lounge of the London penthouse that she and Roger had shared for the last three years. She was shaking as Roger walked around the room, every muscle in his body straining with anger. Sam had arrived back from the police station annoyed and upset. She had gone to the hospital to find out about Adie, then found herself being accompanied to the police station by detective Farrell.

She had started to shout at Roger, calling him uncaring, selfish. She had been kidnapped and had fallen from a moving car. Had the stress of seeing two undesirables take charge of little Meg. Then not only having to go hospital for herself and by herself but now the worry of her cousin Adie suffering severe head injuries. Roger had not even asked how she was feeling. All he was interested in was what had happened at the police station.

Roger watched her for a minute then cut her off. Speaking quietly;

"I want word for word, every question and every answer." Then shouting; *Fuckin' now!*"

Through her tears Sam did her best to explain the

112

events of the day leading up to her being in hospital then being asked to accompany the detective sergeant to Camberwell police station. She told Roger that she was questioned first by a senior looking guy. Clearly someone in authority. He wanted to know about a gaming salon called the *Vegas Slots*. Did she know if Roger owned a white transit van, where was he three days ago? What time did he arrive home? Did Roger have money problems, because it was very clear that the attack on the nightclub had been arson. Sam told Roger that she said she had been in Kent three days ago. That her husband was staying at their London apartment. No, he did not have any money problems, both his nightclubs were thriving. The senior officer had then left and a detective arrived. He had hit her with more questions. Sam said that she had answered the questions truthfully, that almost all of them were to do with the kidnap. She stopped and looked up at him scowling;

"Don't worry, I didn't tell him it was the same people who were waiting for you outside the restaurant the other night." Roger looked at her, surprised. Sam spoke again;

"Yes, that's right, the same people. I heard them talking in the car. Nor did I tell them that somebody called Bojan had sent them to kidnap me and Adie."

Sam continued, telling Roger that the only mention of him from the second detective was to do with his office in Peckham. Did Sam know what it was used for? She told Roger that she had made it clear that she did not know anything about his business. She had then attempted to turn the tables on the detective by asking why she was there. What were they doing to find the kidnappers? He was far too experienced to fall for it. He told her in no uncertain terms that she was there to answer his questions.

He made it clear that she was not under caution and she could leave anytime she wanted.

Roger was relieved; he studied his wife's face. He knew that the last few days had been different from anything she had experienced since she had met him. It was his own fault; he had let her get too close to the business, *his business*. While at the same time losing concentration himself. He relaxed his voice. Spoke gently in a softer, quieter manner. He sat down next to her. Sam stiffened, she didn't want this, she was still angry, still frustrated, still upset. Roger went to put his arm around her. Sam stood and screamed at him to *fuck off*. She went into the guest bedroom and slammed the door shut behind her. Roger watched her go. He didn't move, didn't go after her. He was slightly shocked. It dawned on him that in the years he had known Sam he had never heard her swear, until the past few days.

He sat thinking. It was starting to fit into place. Clearly they had followed Sam to Adie's house; they must have been waiting near the call centre. The same people. The same clueless people that had waited for him outside the Silk Road Chinese. No doubt in his mind that they were also responsible for the attack on his call centre. None of them very bright. He stood and walked across the room, still thinking. The guy Rodovan in the nightclub had told the Austen girl that he was Serbian. He needed to find this guy. Then what about the guy in the wheelchair who had paid the gang of kids to attack the *Vegas Slots*. Was he involved with the Serbs? Maybe, maybe not, if not then who was he? Who was he working for? The young gang had said he was English, no foreign accent. Roger went back to his thoughts of a few days earlier. A guy in a wheelchair *and* a guy with a walking stick. Coincidence or connection? Now a name; so who was Bojan?

114

Roger gazed out of the window as he thought some more. They had now had two goes at Sam and several at himself; he needed to do something about her. He picked up his phone. He dialled a number, a number of a mobile in Spain.

***

Police Constable John Jenkins was nervous, he was more than nervous, he was metaphorically *shitting himself*. It was five minutes to six. He was standing outside the rear door of the call centre. Roger Scott's call centre, as he had been ordered earlier. He wasn't happy. He thought he had seen the last of Roger Scott three years ago. He had played Roger's game, giving him information. Giving him prior warning of any impending raids or investigations.

Jenkins was more than aware that his problems were of his own doing. He also knew that three years ago he had been set up. That tart in the massage parlour had led him on. Making him believe that there was more on the menu than a simple massage. Not for the first time he had been unable to resist the temptation. Not for the first time it appeared that his brains had been in his balls. Or were they? Maybe if that bitch of a wife hadn't been so fuckin frigid, maybe it wouldn't have happened, but it had, and it had all been captured on CCTV. Which had led to P.C. Jenkins being in Scott's pocket, doing as he was told when he was told.

Then nearly three years ago it had gone quiet. As if he was no longer needed by the bastard named Scott. Now it had all changed back to how it was. He was back in the firm grasp of Roger Scott. Now he had blatantly lied to the Assistant Chief Constable who he knew was not stupid. Ted Walton had seen through him. Jenkins knew that, and now he was standing outside of Roger Scott's call centre, nervous, more than nervous, he was metaphorically *shitting himself.*

The next day.

Roger stood in the Pot Black Snooker Hall. He was in the back room, the room that contained only one snooker table. The room where club members were not allowed to enter. In front of him sat Johnny, Mary, Harry and Alan. Jeff stood next to Roger. Tom at his usual post; standing by the door. Also at the table was a new guy. His name was Steve. Like the rest of the males present he was a big guy, solidly built. Johnny had told Roger earlier that he had started this guy working for him around last six months earlier. A bit of extra security. He said that he was from up North, a small place near Durham.

Roger was not happy with Steve being there. He liked to bring his own guys into the fold, after they had been checked out, watched and tested. Then put on trial. He looked at Steve. The look was not returned; Steve just sat, impassive, staring across the table. Roger spoke;

"So what's your background?" Steve looked up at Roger, then in a strange accent he answered;

"Left the Para's five years ago. Been running private security up North. Protection of anybody who needed it and was happy to pay." Roger nodded, Steve continued;

"It went well for a few years then about a year ago an Arab, who had come over to buy Newcastle United paid me to watch his back. It was going well until the fat bastard who owned the club gave him a load of bullshit and lies. Apparently he is good at that. The shit hit and one of the owner's minders caught a stray bullet. The Arab quickly disappeared, some sort of political asylum deal, and so did I. Been down here ever since."

Roger looked at him. He was thinking hard, he remembered hearing about the story. It had reached the national news. Apparently most of Newcastle had wished it had been the football club's owner who got the stray bullet not one of his boys. There appeared to be little or no concern from the police. Roger nodded slowly. Still not happy, but forewarned is forearmed. Steve would need to pass a test and he would be watched and checked out. He spoke;

"You are all aware of what has been happening the last few weeks. I am now convinced it is down to a gang of Serbians who we know have taken over three of what were our massage parlours." Roger then produced two photographs, a little grainy, clearly taken from CCTV footage. He slid them across the table;

"Take a look at these two." They all glanced at the pictures before passing them round. Johnny was the last to receive them. He looked closely then was about to pass them back to Roger. He stopped, picked them both up, looked again. He put them down then made an acknowledgment to Roger.

"What is it Johnny?"

"Seen one of them before boss, one of two brothers, foreign. Sure it's one of them." Roger looked at Johnny waiting for him to continue. Johnny looked again at the photos, then;

"Couple of years back, maybe more, they come into the nightclub throwing their weight about, saying they were going to take the place over. You flattened the fuckers then we took them out the back and finished them off. Never forget a face I've stamped on."

Roger nodded, thinking. Johnny was right; he remembered them now, total amateurs, full of shit. He had watched as his boys had dragged them out the back, but then didn't give them much more thought.

"These two pricks need to be found. The one in the white jacket was in the night club when it got firebombed. He's called Rodovan. I thought there was a likeness between him and the guy in the second picture. He was in the restaurant the night those four clowns were waiting for me. He uses a walking stick. We now have another name, the guys who kidnapped Sam were sent by somebody called Bojan. We need to bring them out in the open. Before I tell you how we will do it there is something else to get out of the way."

He nodded at Jeff. Jeff acknowledged it with a glance then walked to the corner of the room. He slid the bolt back on a large door and opened it to reveal some sort of store cupboard. Jeff stepped inside and pulled out a uniformed policeman. He roughly led him across the room and pushed the shaking man down on to one of the empty chairs. Roger stepped forward and stood over him. He spoke;

"This piece of shit has been paid handsomely by me over the last few years; he has also kept his job and his marriage because of me. Now he has decided to take the fuckin' piss."

Police Constable Jenkins looked around the sea of faces in front of him. He recognised most of them from his past dealings with Roger. He was frightened. He didn't know why he was there. Jenkins had turned up at the call centre at 6 pm the previous night, as instructed by Roger Scott. In full uniform, again as instructed. He had been shouted at, pushed around and then put in the back of a van and taken to the snooker hall, where he had been warned and locked in a cupboard overnight. Now he was sitting in this chair wondering what was going on.

Roger stood behind the stricken Constable. Then;

"Two days ago he decided to take the piss by leading an unauthorised raid on my office in Peckham. Clearly they found nothing as I run a legitimate business. The problem is, as you gentlemen know, and this clown is about to find out, nobody takes the piss out of Roger Scott."

Reaching inside his jacket he pulled out a handgun. It was fitted with a sound suppressor. He waved it in front of Jenkins's face. Roger looked around the room then pressed the barrel into the back of the P.C.s head. He looked at Steve as the policeman whimpered. Then;

"You, round here now!"

Steve stood without flinching and walked round the table to stand behind the shaking copper. Roger handed him the gun. He stared menacingly at the new guy. He spoke, quietly;

"Do it."

Steve took the gun without hesitation and stepped forward. He checked the safety catch, then pressing the gun into the back of Jenkins' head, he squeezed the trigger. Jenkins screamed as the firing pin quietly clicked into an empty chamber. Steve looked at Roger who smiled, and then held out his hand to receive the gun. He handed it over then nodded at Roger before heading back to his seat. Steve had quickly weighed up what was happening. He hadn't really expected to walk into Roger Scott's inner circle without some kind of trial. He also knew by the weight of the gun that it was empty. Roger watched him walk round the table; he expected to see a slight swagger, maybe a smirk, maybe a touch of arrogance. All he did see

119

was nonchalance, as if what Steve had just done was the most natural thing in the world. He may have passed the test but Roger Scott still wasn't sure about him.

Turning back to the job in hand he grabbed P.C. Jenkins by the collar and pulled him to his feet, then shook his head as he looked down at the urine stained trousers on his captive;

"Will ring you sometime, be ready. Anymore fuck ups and the next time the gun will be loaded" He nodded to Jeff who dragged Jenkins out of the back door. Roger watched them go, then;

"Right this is what is going to happen."

Marion Hill sat in the Copper Tap pub on Peckham Road. She was in deep thought. She was also worried, *more than worried*. It was supposed to be a few drinks with two of her oldest friends. A few laughs, a good time, but Marion had a lot on her mind. The events of the last few days had caused her to lose sleep with the stress and worry about what might happen next. When she had first started to work at the *Vegas Slots* it was a thrill telling her friends that she worked for the infamous Roger Scott. It gave her bragging rights. She was admired and looked up to. Although she had never met Roger until last week, she had him down as some kind of modern day Robin Hood. Now Marion was worried, it was alright talking about her boss's reputation, maybe elaborating a little, but this was different. Maybe she hadn't believed a lot of what she had heard; maybe she was just happy to be carried along with the tales of violence and murder; but now she was worried, *more than worried*.

She had read the local newspapers, seen the picture of a youth. A youth whom she recognised. A youth who it had been reported had been locked in a van that had then been torched. The police had been back to see her for a second time, shown her a picture of the now deceased youth. They had put more pressure on her, asked her to go over again what had happened that night. That night when the *Vegas Slots* had been attacked by a gang of youths, maybe in their late teens or early twenties. *All wearing similar hooded jackets.* The youths who had sprayed paint into the slot machines. The slot machines owned by Roger Scott. The police had left after telling her that the next time they spoke to her it would be in Camberwell police station.

"Marion!" She jumped in her seat, startled back into the reality of the quiet drink with her friends. She looked over her glass at her friend of many years, Nan; Nan was not her real name but due to looking many years older than her true age, it was a name that had stuck with her. She didn't appear to mind.

"Sorry love I was miles away." Marion looked down at her glass then back at her friend. Nan had been chatting merrily to Totty, their other friend. Like Nan, Totty was not her real name, just something that had stuck with her since her misspent youth. Nan and Totty had not been taking much notice of Marion. It was when they paused their conversation and saw that Marion was in deep thought that they stopped talking and turned their attention towards her;

"What is it, what's wrong?"

Marion looked directly at Nan, her tear-filled eyes glistening;

"It, it's nothing, just a few problems at work, a few things getting to me."

"So resign, pack it in, no job is worth stressing over. Is it Totty?" Totty looked back at Nan, disinterested; "No love, she should pack it in."

121

Marion looked into her glass again. She would like nothing better. *If only it was that easy.*

Two of the gang of guys who were in their late teens to early twenties, *wearing similar hooded jackets* stood with two large men. One with a strange accent. They were outside of a massage parlour near Nunhead. They had met with Roger and his giant pet gorilla who they now knew as Jeff, a couple of hours earlier. They had been told in no uncertain terms that they should never mention to anybody that they had visited the parlour before. Their instructions were simple. They were to follow the two guys into the premises after about one minute. Then to go round the whole place, every room, and wreck them beyond repair. Any males, clients or employees or otherwise were to be beaten senseless. Remembering what had happened in Burgess Park, they had reluctantly agreed.

It turned out to be easier than they thought. As the two of them had burst through the door they were greeted by the sight of two prone and bloodied bodies of what was clearly the establishment's security. The two of Roger's guys who had gone in a minute earlier had been confronted by the now unconscious figures, and quickly set about them with fists then boots. The two young guys followed their instructions quickly and efficiently. Every room, every piece of furniture, every massage bed, every mirrored wall, was completely destroyed. Surprised clients, some in a state of undress, most in a state of sexual embarrassment, were dragged to the floor then kicked and beaten. The girls, most of them naked, were herded into the reception area. Within a matter of minutes the two young guys and Johnny and Steve were quickly walking away from the massage parlour, or what was left of it. In the back alley behind the building stood seven naked girls. Shaking and frightened. Locked out of the now ruined premises.

At two other similar establishments less than two miles away Alan, Mary, and Harry had inflicted similar damage to the one known as *The Soft Touch*. Jeff, Tom and the rest of the gang of youths had left the other one, *Fingertips*, after delivering the same punishment to the premises, the employees and the clientele. More frightened naked girls standing shivering in the street behind the massage parlours. Following his instructions they had made it clear to everyone in the parlours that Roger Scott was responsible. To tell their bosses that if they wanted a war they had got one.

***

Two miles away Sam stood, hands on her hips.

"I am not going to Spain and you can't make me."

In the London penthouse that Roger and his wife had shared for the last three years Sam was shouting through her tears. Roger had explained that things were about to get messy. That he had arranged for George, one of his former employees who now lived in Spain to meet her at Malaga Airport. How it would be better for her to be out of the way for a few weeks. Sam argued that being in Spain wouldn't help anything. That she needed to be here to help the police find Adie's kidnappers, and to be available for Meg if she was needed. Roger shouted back at her. He reminded Sam of what had happened to Penny, and about the second attempt on his life. Sam had seen the damage to the BMW and knew he was telling the truth. Roger went on to tell her that it had been three weeks since the attack on the nightclub, *her nightclub*, and the police were still nowhere near finding who was responsible. He stood over her, large and imposing. He dropped an envelope on to her lap. He spoke;

"Ticket for the five o'clock flight. Tom will be here in half an hour. He will get you to Gatwick. George will be waiting for you in Spain. He knows you and you should recognise him. I will be in touch when it is safe for you to come back." He bent his knees and crouched in front of her, forcing a smile he took her hand in his. Then;

"Sam, it's for the best. These are dangerous people we are dealing with. There are now six dead from the nightclub fire and the police are not interested."

Sam pulled her hand away from his and glared up at him;

"You bastard!" Roger looked down at her. He was shocked; Sam had never spoken to him like that before, never. He stared at her, Sam stood, she walked a couple of steps then turned to face him;

"Fine, I will go to Spain, but don't ever think I don't know the real reason you are sending me there." Roger looked back, quizzical. Sam continued;

"Don't think I am so stupid not to realise that there is something going on between you and that whore Mina, and I know that you had something to do with my cousin Adie's kidnap three years ago." Roger was shocked, he stood, silent. Sam was on a roll;

"Yes, that's right, around the same time that Mike Smith and Shane Reardon disappeared, the same time that a policeman was shot in your nightclub that happened to be full of gangsters at the time. I will go to Spain but when I come back." She paused, lowered her voice, quiet, angry;

"Not when, *if,* and only *if* come back, *I want answers.*"

She walked out slamming the door behind her. Roger watched her go. Then under his breath;

"Speak soon."

In the back room of the snooker hall on New Cross Road, Roger stood at the top end of the table. In front of him sat Johnny. It was 2.30pm. The rest of the crew, *his crew*, were due at 3 pm. The other guys, the ones in their late teens or early twenties, *the ones who wore similar hooded jackets* had been ordered to attend at 4 pm. Roger had decided that Johnny was to be trusted, as he was three years ago before the demise of his empire as he knew it. Johnny was the one who Roger had allowed to get close to him. His number two, second in command, although he never allowed Johnny to know that officially;

"All go to plan?"

"Yes boss, smashed the place to fuckin' bits. Left all the tarts bollock naked out the back. The two bouncers, if that's what they were are probably in hospital."

Roger nodded; "You made sure they knew who was behind it?"

"Yes boss, mentioned your name a few times, told them they would regret fuckin' with Roger Scott."

"What about the new guy? Steve?"

"No worries boss, seemed to enjoy himself."

Roger nodded his approval;

"Well done, I have some idea who is behind all this shit but we need to bring them out into the open. They caught me unawares." He paused clearly not happy to admit his mistake. Then continued;

"We'll be ready next time." Roger walked round the table, as if pondering something else. He looked at Johnny, not speaking, waiting maybe a full minute. Then;

"Cast your mind back two or three years. To the warehouse in Felixstowe. The time I got you and Alan to sort out those two knobs who were trying to set up against us." Johnny nodded, he remembered;

"Yeah boss, I remember, one of them is still at the bottom of the sea. The other one was Mike Smith. When we left him in Felixstowe he didn't look well at all. Doubt there was many bones left unbroken."

"But still alive?"

"Yeah just, but that's what you wanted boss, one dead, the other one hurt."

Roger put his hands in the air, a sort of mock acceptance that he appreciated they were following his orders.

"No problem Johnny, just need to be sure. I get the feeling that this is a revenge mission, they don't appear to be after my business and nobody has attempted to demand any money. This is personal, it is me they want. Somebody involved knows too much about my set up. If it is the Serbs somebody must be feeding them information. We know Mike Smith, if he is behind it, he cannot be working alone.

Johnny pondered, then; "Never known anybody come back for more after a beating like that, think he would have learned his lesson. So what happens next?" Roger looked at him, he paused again. Then;

"We keep going, we find out what else they have. The rest are due here just now, they have had the pictures of the two guys who I'm pretty sure are involved, let's see what they've got."

Two hours later the rest of his crew and the youths had been and gone. The young guys very happy that Roger had smiled at them each in turn. Told them that they had done good. Told them that he was pleased with the result. Then not happy when Roger told them in no uncertain terms that they were still in his debt, he still owned them, that there would be more work to do. Then leaving on a high after Roger had handed them two hundred pounds each and told them to wait for his next call.

Roger sat alone in the back room of the snooker hall. Progress he thought, Mary, Alan and Harry had done well in the massage parlours. Followed his orders to the word. No sign of the guy with the walking stick or white jacket man but the bait had been laid. Just a matter of time before they showed themselves. He thought more about Mike Smith. Johnny was right; nobody had ever come back for revenge. The beatings administered were enough of a deterrent. Maybe this was different.

Roger knew that Mike had more reasons than most to want to go against him, the main one being Sam. The girl Mike had hoped to marry, to spend the rest of his life with. His first love. Mike and Sam had been an item for around six months, regularly sharing the same bed. Mike was planning to ask her to move in permanently, to be his bride. He had already bought the engagement ring. Then while he was away working for Roger in Greece, Scott stepped in and took her. Mike found out when he had returned. He was about to propose marriage. He had been devastated. His feelings had got the better of him. Mike had attempted to set up a rival gang, to take over Roger's empire. Roger had found out. Mike had gone against Roger in the worst way possible, *and had suffered in the worst possible way.*

Roger thought some more. Jealousy was something he had never experienced. Women were there to be used; there were plenty of them available without the need to be possessive. Maybe Mike did have something to do with what had been happening. He took a piece of paper from his briefcase. He looked at the four names he had written on it. He put a line under Mike Smith's name.

230 miles away the man in a wheelchair sat in the dining room of a Victorian house. His two brothers watched as he moved the chair slowly to the table. He activated the arm control turning himself round to face them. He forced a smile; his brothers looked at him, expectant. They had also suffered the last three years. It had hurt them more than they showed to see their elder brother in this terrible state. He had been their mentor, the guy who had watched out for them as they grew up in a racist era. He had taught them to look after themselves against all the odds. They had worked together to build a successful drug business. Now they were struggling, their drug supply had gone along with their credibility on the streets of this hard northern city. He turned his head to look at his brothers, cursing inwardly at his inability to turn his body. He spoke;

"Three years now in this fuckin' thing. *Because of one man*". His brothers looked on, trying not to appear patronising while trying to show sympathy. He continued;

"Time the London man suffered. Time he felt my pain" He looked back at his two brothers. He continued;

"One of the guys who worked for him three years ago rang me, said he wants to talk. Said the Scott man had put him in one of these fuckin' things." He hit his fist of the armrest. Then;

"We go to London tomorrow to see him, maybe we stay awhile, maybe kill the Scott dude when we there."

His brothers looked at each other then back at their elder sibling. Not sure what to say. The biggest one; Kang, cleared his throat, shuffled his feet, glanced at the third brother then spoke;

"Who is the guy? Why he contact us? Don't trust no one from down there no more. Look what happened last time."

He briefly thought back to how Roger Scott had lured them to his snooker hall, only to beat up the eldest brother and threaten them to stay out of London for good. He continued as his two brothers looked on;

"We was set up, could have been killed. I say we don't go."

The man in the wheelchair glared at him;

"It aint you that's in this fuckin' thing. I want to go. Sort the London man for good."

His brothers looked at each other. They knew that there was no way they could get him to change his mind.

Bojan sat at the dining room table in the terraced house in Peckham Rye. He was watching his two sons as they counted the money on the table in front of them. All hard cash, happily handed over by the unfortunates who had no other choice than to succumb to their suggestions, or maybe the threats of retribution. He smiled as he thought about how well they were doing. Despite the terrible injuries inflicted upon them by Scott they had still managed to keep their business of debt collecting and protection of various local premises intact. Bojan knew in the back of his mind that it was his reputation that had gone before them, the foundations he had laid over the years and the training he had given them had put them in a position of respect in the local community. He also knew that they needed more of their own street credibility. He would not be around forever.

He thought about his third son; Rodovan. He was a good boy, maybe too good. Always smartly dressed, always taking pride in his appearance. Spending hours making sure he was immaculate in every way. He had never shown any interest in the family business. Yes he would do the odd job with them, maybe act as a lookout, maybe help with setting up the odd target, but that was where his involvement ended. He was not and had never been a violent person, never got himself into a situation like his brothers where Bojan had to rescue him and gain some revenge.

He happily attended night school four evenings a week. During the day he worked as a junior accountant at an office in the City. He planned for a future without crime. To be successful in his own way.

Rodovan would not ever be part of what his father and two brothers were doing. Never be part of the family business. Bojan looked again at his two elder sons, reflected on their injuries; maybe it was good that Rodovan was different to them.

Bojan thought back to a more pressing problem. He was looked up to by all in his local manor, in particular the many other Serbian immigrants who had settled in this area of south London. Many of them had only been in England for around two years but in that time some had managed to establish themselves. Setting up small businesses, corner shops selling speciality Serbian food. Some buying into existing operations.

Four Serbians, two sets of brothers decided to do it the easy way. Taking what they wanted. Using their experience gained from the corrupt regime they had left behind, they had looked at various businesses in the area. In Belgrade after leaving the army, they had been involved with the movement of young girls into the cruel and illegal brothels, that appeared to operate in every back street, every lorry park and every nightclub. It was easy money. No matter how poor people were they always managed to find enough for sex. There was no shortage of girls to work in these unsavoury establishments. Odd young ladies came voluntarily; but most were the young and vulnerable, often homeless and drug dependent, often kidnapped. They would be taken under the wing of a corrupt pimp, who plied them with more drugs and kindness until they were hooked. Then to be held by violence and fear.

The two sets of brothers had been in the country for around a year when they had approached Bojan.

Bojan was aware of their involvement in various crimes. He was not concerned, yet. He knew that they had already taken control of three massage parlours. Two were easy. By coincidence the former owners had disappeared. The third proved a little more difficult. They had approached and threatened the owner, a large guy called Ron. Unexpectedly he had been tougher than they expected. He had put his hand inside his jacket. Then told them to get out. Maybe he had a gun, they weren't sure. They walked to the door, maybe to come back later, maybe to form another plan. The big guy, the owner, followed them into the quiet street, maybe too quiet. Turning quickly one of the brothers pulled a long bladed knife. Spinning round quickly he surprised Ron who took a step back. The knife slashed across his shirt and into the flesh across his chest. The shock caused Ron to look down at his injury. The knifeman continued his attack by bringing the knife back and then forward into Ron's chest. The two sets of brothers then ran off leaving him dying in the street. No witnesses, or if there were, none came forward with a statement as to what they had seen.

Three days passed and nobody seemed interested in what had happened. The massage business carried on regardless. It was then that one of the two sets of brothers entered the parlour to announce it was under new ownership. Within a month they had seized control of the two other similar brothels.

Now full of confidence, they had learned that in that particular part of London another Serbian guy called Bojan ran things. From money lending to debt collecting to protection. They had watched his movements, watched how he operated from back street pubs. Noticed how he commanded respect through fear. The two sets of brothers decided it would quite easy to take his business, but first they needed to get closer to him.

Bojan and his two eldest sons, Aco and Dorde were sitting in the back room of the Gowlett Arms in Peckham Rye. They had been collecting dues owed to them by local business owners, and now they were planning their next visits.

One of their "clients" was owed four thousand pounds in back rent from one of his shops he'd let. The Polish guy who ran the business was taking the piss. Telling the owner that turnover was down, that he would pay what he owed when things picked up. The owner knew that business was good but the Polish guy was big, and aggressive. The owner was a businessman not a fighter. So with that in mind he had approached Bojan. The Serb had taken over the debt by giving the guy two thousand pounds. Now they were going to pay the Pole a visit. Collect the four grand plus another two interest, and maybe a break an arm to remind him who he was dealing with.

Dorde approached the bar to order more drinks when four men walked into the front room of the pub. He watched through the gap in the wall that separated the two rooms, as they swaggered to the bar. The temporary bar manager, who didn't want to be there, he had been sent to cover the premises until a permanent licensee could be found, glanced at Dorde then back at the four new faces. One of them leaned towards him, menacingly. He spoke;

"Which is Bojan?" The manager pointed to the back room. The four strangers walked through the adjoining door to where Dorde had rejoined his father and brother. He whispered that four guys were looking for him. Bojan glanced up as they entered the room; he knew who they were, clearly the two sets of brothers who were trying to make a name for themselves. He ignored them as they walked towards him.

"You Bojan Duric?"

Bojan continued talking to his sons as if the four guys weren't there. Then the guy spoke again, louder;

"Which is Bojan Duric?"

Bojan stood quickly, his face half an inch away from the spokesman. The guy felt Bojans breath on his face;

"Who the fuck asking?"

The guy stepped back quickly, shocked, then very slowly brought his right hand forward to offer a handshake while forcing a smile.

"My name is Zivco. This my brother and my two friends. We very happy to meet you."

Bojan looked suspiciously at the four men standing in front of him. He knew who they were; their activities had not gone unnoticed. He had planned to meet them at some point, but now they had found him. Thinking quickly he decided against an aggressive retort. Without smiling he introduced his two sons before pointing to four empty seats for the guys to sit down;

"So, what do you want?"

He listened as Zivco, who appeared to be their leader explained that they had heard about Bojan, that they were keen to meet him, maybe to join forces with him. They knew how he was highly respected in the community. They didn't want to cross him. After all they were all Serbians and in London for the same reason. Bojan nodded his head in the right places, at the right time. He didn't believe a fuckin' word. They were up to something, after something. He interrupted the guy;

"So if you four so good why did your massage parlours get attacked?"

Zivco paused, how did Bojan know about the parlours and the attack? He tried to hide the look of shock that threatened to show on his face. He answered quickly;

"We were taken by surprise, it was unexpected, we know who responsible, somebody called Roger Scott, we find him and we kill him."

This made Bojan more interested. He briefly wondered why Scott had picked on them, then thought that maybe he could use these four, use their grudge against Scott to cause him more damage. He already had three of the four guys who he brought over from Serbia in his pocket. Did he need more men? Maybe. Maybe not. Bojan sat back thinking as Zivco continued. He had a lot on his plate with Scott; he didn't need a war with these four. But maybe now that they had something in common he could use them. He decided to let them get closer; it would make them easier to manage, easier to keep an eye on. Easier to move them if and when the time came. He let the new guy talk for more than an hour before offering his hand and telling them that he looked forward to working with them. They would start straight away.

He had a job for them. *A test*.

It was a warm pleasant evening in south London as Maureen Turnbridge and her friend Pauline walked their dogs near the park, close to Lucas Gardens. It was a nightly routine while their husbands were at the local club enjoying a beer or two. The two ladies had known each other for many years. In their twenties they had worked together at the local bank. Then eventually they both took early retirement. As they strolled along the tree lined avenue they chatted happily about their forthcoming visit to Spain. Both the ladies and their husbands had bought a house there some years earlier. Both were looking forward to their third trip of the year. The many beach parties, the numerous barbecues with various friends. They were regular visitors to an area which was not far from Gibraltar.

Still chatting, Maureen stopped at the side of the road to allow her dog, Boss, to use a lamppost. It always amused and baffled her at the same time how Boss managed to find exactly the same spot each evening to empty his bladder. They were about to start walking again when both ladies heard what appeared to be more than one female voice, sounding distressed, clearly very upset. Then more voices, some crying, one or two close to hysterics. Looking at each other they followed the stricken sounds that led them into the mouth of an alleyway. Pauline gasped as they were confronted by several naked young girls, huddled together trying to gain some sort of comfort from each other. Not wanting to go any closer they found their mobile phones and rang the police.

D.I Terry Thompson stuck three addresses to the white board. P.C. Jenkins sat in silence; he wondered why he was there. As this was an investigation that was being handled by the CID, why had he been told to attend? He listened as his superior explained that the previous evening three massage parlours had been attacked at more or less the same time. All had received the same treatment. The whole of the premises wrecked. Clients and male employees beaten up, the working girls thrown naked onto the street. The problem was that there had been no complaints made by the owners or the employees or the clients. It had been brought to the attention of the police by two worried ladies who happened to be walking their dogs in the area; also there had been calls from the local hospital reporting that several people had been admitted at the same time.

The naked girls had been taken back to their homes. None of them would tell the police anything other than their address. The male clients, the majority being married were maybe worried about their wives finding out about their nocturnal activities, they also refused to talk. Two constables had called back to all three sets of premises earlier in the day to find all of them closed. The doors had extra padlocks on them and all the windows were boarded up. Nobody around to interview or talk to. Neighbouring shops and small businesses were approached. The owners had not seen or heard anything. Not normally a problem, they couldn't investigate a complaint if one hadn't been made.

Except, as D.I. Thompson went on to explain, the three massage parlours in question were formerly owned by a Roger Scott. Too much of a coincidence? He spoke;

"I want to know what happened. We have the addresses of the working girls. Visit them, put pressure on them. Threaten them with jail or anything else, but get one or more them to talk, to tell us what happened." He looked around the room, his eyes stopped on P.C. Jenkins;

"Jenkins, I believe that you have had experience with Scott. The reason you are here is to tell us what happened three years ago, when you were part of an investigation led by the now deceased D.S. Nixon. Our colleague who was killed in one of Roger Scott's nightclubs. You were also involved in raids on the three massage parlours in question. Can you enlighten us in any way?"

Jenkins felt like he wanted to shrink into his chair. So this was why he was here. Yes, he was involved in the raids on the massage parlours three years ago. That was when his problems had started, it was since then he had suffered at the hands of Roger Scott. He had to say something. D.I. Thompson had clearly gone through the records. He would also have been briefed by the Assistant Chief Constable. Jenkins was also aware that if he implicated Roger Scott in any way he would be dead. He stood up, stuttered, then cleared his voice;

"Yes Sir. Three years ago D.S. Nixon was quite sure that he had a case against Roger Scott. We raided the massage parlours, the three in question and also several more. There was nothing untoward going on in any of them. We tried to raid his nightclubs only to find they were boarded up and closed. We looked into every aspect of his business but found nothing to charge him with, or arrest him."

"After D.S. Nixon was killed the case went cold. Nothing has happened since. No complaints against Scott, nothing about him or his business interests have been reported. The recent arson attack on his nightclub, and the subsequent investigation is the first time since that his name has been mentioned."

He sat back down. D.I Thompson stared at him for maybe a full minute. He knew that Jenkins was lying, or maybe not divulging all that he knew. There was something not right about this guy. The Chief Constable had told him that in his opinion Jenkins was a useless waste of public money. Maybe he was right. Thompson had enough on his plate without being hindered by this idiot. He would watch him closely.

Joe the Pole, as he was known locally, was in a happy mood. He had only been in England for two years. Now he already had his own business, a thriving business. He watched from behind his counter at the almost full cafe. He had a good profitable turnover. From the early morning workman in overalls who enjoyed a hearty breakfast, through to the shoppers coming in from the local precinct for morning coffee and cakes. Lunchtimes were his most fruitful. He had built up a regular clientele of locals who were keen to sample the delights of traditional Polish food.

He looked around as he prepared Pierogi filled with Sauerkraut and Mushrooms. *"Yes"* he thought, a good business made even better by the fact that the premises were rent free. The skinny owner seemed to have accepted the fact that the business was as bad as Joe told him. Either that or the aggressive manner in which the Pole got his point across. Either way Joe wasn't bothered. The cafe, *his cafe* was thriving with little or no overheads.

Joe was shaken out of his thoughts as the door swung open and four strangers walked in. He looked at them and offered a welcome smile. The four guys maybe two sets of brothers thought Joe, ignored him. They looked around the cafe before moving to a vacant table near the window. The Pole wiped his hands on the grubby apron that was tied around his waist, before walking from behind the counter with his pen and notepad. He smiled;

"Morning gentlemen, what can I get you?" the biggest of the four stood quickly, his face close to Joe's;

"Seven thousand quid." Joe stood his ground;

"Only do food and drinks here, and there aint that much money in the world, is there?" He tried to smile.

The four guys' stood as one. The main man had his hand inside his jacket, spoke;

"You have been taking money from owner, we are here to collect." Joe stood frozen, trying to think, he wanted to answer. He couldn't. The guy leaned closer. Then;

"Through the back, talk, or maybe we kill you here."

Joe looked around the cafe; the rest of his customers could sense something was not right. One by one each table slowly emptied. Worried customers leaving money on their tables, maybe more than they needed to, then scurrying towards the door, heads down. Joe watched them go, knew he was in trouble; he had been happily taking the piss out of the owner for too long, and riding his luck. He was on his own. He forced a smile, a slight nod of his head before turning and walking through the beaded curtain that led to the room behind the cafe. One of the guys closed the door before bolting it. The four of them then followed Joe into the back room. As he got through the curtain Joe turned quickly, fist clenched, about to lash out at the nearest one of the four guys. He then stopped in his tracks as he found himself staring at the wrong end of a gun.

***

Malaga Airport is the fourth busiest in Spain, handling over 19 million passengers a year and around 141,000 flights. It is also one of the most complicated for passengers arriving for the first time. Sam wandered for what seemed like miles, passing departing travellers; she followed the signs for baggage reclaim, only to find herself walking through the duty free as if she too was departing. Sam was not a happy lady before she alighted from the plane. She had endured a screaming child who kicked the back of her seat for the entire flight. A man with bad breath who insisted on wanting to know every detail about her. She had tried to sleep without success due to the flight attendants trying to sell her some overpriced rubbish every two minutes. Then there were the numerous thoughts revolving around her head. Bad enough that she had been sent to Spain against her will, but on *fuckin' Easyjet!!!*

Sam fought her way through the crowds who appeared to be as baffled as she was as to which way to go. Eventually after reaching what looked like the exit, she had to fight her way through countless white shirted, sweat dripping people. Most of them holding signs bearing names above their heads, while blocking the doorway. Sam pushed her way through muttering obscenities to anyone who was within earshot. Eventually reaching the outside only to be stopped again by overweight holiday makers, wearing their matching Matalan clothes, standing less than a yard from the door. Most of them with a fixed grin and commenting on how nice the weather was. Sam cleared the crowd and looked to the right where other travellers were heading towards the taxi rank. Then;

"Sam!" She turned to see a large man, around six foot six, she vaguely recognised him. He walked towards her, hand extended, smiling brightly:

"Sam, George. Good flight?"

"OK thanks. Yes, no. Awful. Can you get me out of here please?"

George leaned towards her, his large hand relieving her of her suitcase. Sam followed him across a road, through various doors, many stairs to eventually find the car park.

George had been surprised to receive a phone call from his old boss Roger Scott. As far as he was concerned Roger was part of a previous life that had long gone. George had lived in southern Spain for almost two years. In that time he had established himself as a trusted and renowned bodyguard for the many Russian and Eastern European gangsters, who ran their drug and vice empires that were based in the Marbella area. He had established a reputation within the criminal world of being reliable, but also ruthless when needed.

Sam looked on as George pressed the remote that unlocked the door of a newish looking Mercedes. Placing her suitcase in the boot of the car, he opened the door for her to get inside. Ten minutes later, travelling along the AP7, the coolness of the air conditioning, and the views of the Andalucía landscape made Sam a little more relaxed, she spoke;

"Sorry George. I know that this is none of your doing but Roger sent me here against my will. I don't want to be here. I didn't want to come here."

George carried on driving, silently. Roger had contacted him a couple of days earlier. He had chatted for a little while about the old days, about how things had changed. About how things were different now. Roger said he was having a few problems. He didn't go into any details other than he wanted Sam out of the way while he sorted it out. He wanted George to look after her. Find some decent accommodation. Keep an eye on her until Roger told him it was safe for her to return.

George had accepted it, albeit reluctantly. He had enough going on without being a fuckin' childminder. But Roger was his old boss, a guy who he once looked up to and respected. He told Roger he would make sure she was safe and looked after. He drove on as Sam carried on with now nervous chatter, George nodded his head in the right places but he wasn't really listening. Eventually leaving the Peaje he steered the Mercedes past Estepona, before explaining to Sam that he didn't want her staying in Marbella. Mixing business with pleasure was not a good idea. He had booked a hotel for her in a quieter area, not far in driving distance from Marbella, but far enough away so she would not be involved with his work.

Sam dreamily gazed out of the window as George turned off the A7 and headed towards Puerto de la Duquesa.

***

The man in the wheelchair was in deep thought as he manoeuvred the hated contraption along the edge of Peckham Rye Park. Glancing at the vast array of greenness that covered the Victorian landscape, he stopped to gaze momentarily at the children playing, the people exercising their dogs, the elderly couples seated on one of the many park benches. His sadness returned as he watched the pleasant peaceful scene before him. It reminded him of how his life had changed. Changed forever. *Because of one man.* The thought of him brought the man in the wheelchair back to reality, the reason he was in this area of south London.

He knew how Roger Scott operated. By now he would have found the guys who had vandalised his gaming salon. He would have hurt them, maybe permanently damaged one or more of them. They would have told him who had paid them to do the damage. Depending on their attitude they would have disappeared or maybe be on his payroll. By now he would have put two and two together. Worked out who had put them up to it. Would Scott remember who it might have been? Thinking back three years there were a lot of people badly hurt after crossing him, maybe a lot more since. Would Scott know who was behind it?

Roger Scott was methodical, thorough, seemed to know everything that was going on around him. As the man in the wheelchair steered himself along the cracked footpath in Peckham Rye he thought some more. He had been injured in the most horrendous way three years ago, left for dead by the two guys who were clearly following Roger Scott's orders. He cast his mind back. He smiled, no, he was one of many, there was no way Scott would remember him. Pressing the four way switch on the right hand armrest the chair turned and then stopped outside a terraced house with a small garden in Peckham Rye.

***

"Shut that fuckin' brat up you lazy bitch, or I fuckin' will."

One mile away in a two up, two down terraced house on the edge of Brixton, Spike lay back on his settee; he opened another can of cider then pressed the remote control to increase the volume on the television, to drown out the pathetic cries of Meg.

"Can't hear the fuckin' racing for the noisy little mare."

Yvette stormed over to the low chair where Meg sat crying hysterically. She leaned close to the infant, cigarette dangling from her mouth. Her face less than an inch from the frightened child;

"Shut the fuck up or I will lock you in that dark cupboard, you don't want that again do you? Now shut it!"

Meg tried to push her little body into the back of the chair as the smoke from Yvette's mouth made her cough. Spike threw the remote control across the room before standing up and striding towards the petrified child. He put his face next to Yvette's;

"You are a stupid waste of fuckin' space. How the hell

did you get past that fuckin' test they gave you?" He glared at Meg. Yvette answered;

"You didn't say that when you heard about how much money we would be getting did you? No! You didn't mind then, when you thought about how much you would have for the booze and that fuckin' weed you smoke did you? It wasn't me who wanted to get involved with all this looking after kids shit? First kid we get and look at you. We have only had her a week and you have started already. It was you who saw it as an easy number. Money for fuck all was what you said. Well that sums you up. Fuck all, that's what you are and that's what you do." She glared menacingly, then;

"It's you that's the waste of fuckin' space."

Spike glared at her, wanting to lash out, wanting to give her an answer, but he had tried that before. Only to be beaten by Yvette. He was frightened of her and she knew it. He sat back down.

Yvette roughly pulled the crying Meg out of the low chair and stormed out of the room.

A mile away the sun shone brightly as Bojan and his two elder sons sat at the dining room table in a terraced house in Peckham Rye. He was thinking again about the problem. If Zivco and the other three were any, good how come their three massage parlours had been wreaked, and they had approached him? Yes they had returned to him with four thousand pounds within a few hours of him giving them the order. Joe the Pole had given them all he had on the premises. He had been beaten up and told that they would be back for the rest in two days. If he didn't want his legs broken he would have the money. He would receive a broken arm regardless.

The four Serbs had passed the test he set them, but was it too quick? Too easy? He thought again. Yes, his reputation went before him, but reputations didn't count for much in Serbia. They were there to be taken, to be seen as a way of gaining credibility. The four of them had come to him cap in hand, not guns blazing. Why? Because they were new to the area? No, they had already managed to acquire the massage parlours. No, they wanted more than friendship, they wanted an *in* to his business, or maybe all of his business. Yes it was a problem, but he would be one step ahead.

Bojan's thoughts were brought back to the present by the door being opened, and his wife stepping to one side after announcing they had a visitor. The three men watched as a wheelchair entered the room. Aco smiled warmly as he recognised his friend from the London Spinal Cord Injury Centre. He raised himself unsteadily. Then leaning on his walking stick he extended his arm to shake hands with Mike Smith.

October 2012.

Adie looked up from her pillow as she heard the key enter the lock of the cushioned door. She didn't bother trying to sit up. No point, it would be the same routine. Two nurses, a bowl of water, soap and sponges. Then being made to stand naked, undignified, as they roughly rubbed soap on her before rinsing and drying her. She kept her eyes shut as the footsteps drew nearer. She hated this place and her head still hurt. She thought again. "Why me, why is it always me?" The footsteps stopped, Adie waited. Then;

"Good morning Adie, are you awake? Do you remember me?"

145

A voice she thought she recognised, not the nurses, a man's voice. She lay still trying to think. She gradually opened her eyes. A smiling face leaning over her. A white gown. He spoke;

"Do you recognise me Adie? My name is Dr. Ahmed."

Adie looked at him, something familiar, a man who had helped her get better maybe. She thought hard, her head hurt again. She forced a half smile. She remembered.

"Yes, you made me well again." More tears, a slight sob, then;

"Please help me. Why me? Why is it always me? Why am I here, I want to go home. I want to see Meg." Adie closed her eyes sobbing quietly.

Dr. Ahmed sat in the chair and looked at Adie. He remembered the day she was admitted to the Kings College Hospital, the first time, three years go. Adie was very thin, very weak, undernourished and had appalling head injuries. She had been found in a disused WW2 bunker, she and her new baby both starving. He had put her into an induced coma due to a skull fracture putting pressure on her brain. Adie had been in intensive care for many weeks before being moved to a side ward. Her recovery had been nothing short of miraculous. Eventually and after many months of treatment, both she and her baby were discharged.

Dr Ahmed continued looking at her, sadness in his weary eyes. He had no idea what the circumstances were behind Adie being admitted to this out-dated psychiatric hospital. In his opinion their methods were crude and old fashioned. He had discharged her from his care three years ago, only to find her being readmitted just over two months ago. He had kept her in intensive care treating her head and body injuries until she was well enough to be moved to a side ward. After monitoring her for two weeks and being happy that she was fine physically, he then suggested that she may need psychiatric help. Dr. Ahmed never intended that Adie should finish up in this Victorian hell hole.

He stood, and after a parting glance at Adie he went to door, closing and locking it behind him, he then headed for the office of the hospital director.

July 2012 Present day.

Roger was waiting; he was thinking that he had done enough for now to get the Serb's to react. The problem was they hadn't. It struck him that maybe more than one gang was involved. Was that likely? So far his house in Kent had been attacked. Both of his night clubs and his call centre. Then there was the personal attack on himself at the Chinese restaurant. Along with the attempted hit and run outside the snooker hall. Then his gaming salon being hit. Too much for one man or one gang to organise? Maybe, but all the attacks tied in together.

Then the attempted kidnap of Sam; it had to be the same people responsible. From what Sam had told him about the kidnap attempt, it had to be the same hapless gang who had waited for him outside the Silk Road. He thought some more. Where did Mike Smith come into it? Was he involved at all? The description the young guys had given Roger made him think he was. Maybe Mike Smith was nothing more than an informant. Possible and probable if he had got to the right people. Roger stood and walked to the window, gazing out, still thinking hard.

Apart from the collateral damage what were they trying to achieve? By now there should have been a visit from one of them. Maybe some kind of demand. Maybe a warning to get out of town. Maybe the threat of more trouble unless he paid them a lot of money. There had been nothing. No contact, no demands, no warnings. Which meant Roger was right in what he thought earlier, it could only mean one thing; *revenge*. He thought some more, revenge for what? Was it to do with the two young pricks who tried to take his nightclub a couple of years ago? But then they weren't capable, who then, he had the name Bojan, was that the connection? Maybe, if somebody was feeding then information, maybe somebody like Mike Smith.

So what now? Wait for their next move? Surely wrecking the massage parlours should have provoked some kind of reaction. He sat back down thinking; what would he have done? How would he react if the tables were turned? Closing his eyes he cast his mind back three years. *The Roger Scott of old.* Would he have waited for a reaction from whoever it was trying to harm him? No was the answer. No, he would have been more proactive, a step in front. Nobody ever got that close to the Roger Scott of old. The answer hit him. He smiled, it was right there in front of him. Roger picked up his mobile phone and hit a speed dial number.

***

Joe the Pole screamed as Jeff went to work on him with a Stanley knife. It was Jeff's favourite toy, his close interrogation weapon of choice. It hadn't taken Jeff too long to work out that if he put two blades into the knife together then wedged a matchstick between them, it would inflict more damage on the unfortunate victim. Damage that could not be fully repaired. Damage that even the best surgeon would find impossible to stitch satisfactorily due to the two cuts being close, but not too close together. The Pole jabbered in his own language as Tom leaned over him, an evil cruel smile. Tom and Jeff, the closest of twins, were never happier than when Roger Scott ordered then to extract information from an unfortunate victim who had something he needed.

Mary and Alan had been visiting some of the pubs and bars in the Peckham Rye area. It was common knowledge that a lot of the recent influx of Serbian immigrants had settled around there. The group of guys, all around late teens to early twenties, *wearing similar hooded jackets,* were walking the streets around the same area. Stopping on the odd corner, being mouthy, slightly aggressive to any passerby who looked at them the wrong way. Roger had instructed them to stay down there as long as it took to find out what they could about who was running the streets. Mary and Alan were taking a more sedate approach, the couple out for a drink, blending in with the locals, listening into bar conversations. They didn't attract too much attention; they were rough, hard looking, like most of the clientele in the establishments that populated the area.

It had been in the third pub they had visited, *The Gowlett Arms,* that they watched as four guys were standing at the bar, maybe two sets of brothers, not twins, but very alike. They were talking quietly, but loud enough for the odd snippet of conversation to be heard.

One spoke slightly louder than the rest. He appeared to be on a high, talking about how easy it had been. About how the Polish guy in the cafe was close to shitting himself before he handed the money over. About how they should be doing it more, but for themselves. Not to hand the cash over to that prick and his two backward sons. Another of the guys was glaring at him, leaning close telling him to keep his voice down. They had stopped talking and quietly sipped their drinks for a few minutes.

Mary and Alan talked quietly about nothing important. Stopping the conversation frequently to listen to the four guys at the bar. As Alan stood to order more drinks one of the four spoke;

"Zivco, it is good what we did but we have our own problems, what we do about our massage parlours?" Zivco looked back at him, he was glad that his friend had changed the subject. He answered;

"We leave them another week Toma, then we reopen with more security. When we see Bojan later we will mention Roger Scott again. When I said his name in that back room." He nodded towards the gap in the bar; "I saw Bojan's face change. I think he knows who this Scott man is. Bojan has been here many years, maybe he will tell us where he is. Then we will find him and kill him" The guy nodded slowly, smiling in acceptance.

At the nearby table Mary and Alan glanced at each other and then at the owners of the three massage parlours. Now they knew who was responsible for Ron's murder. They also had three names.

Around two miles away Joe the Pole sat bleeding and frightened. He was tied to a chair in what he thought looked like a small warehouse. When five young guys. Maybe late teens to early twenties had walked into the cafe, he didn't think anything other than that they were just like a lot of his customers. Maybe on their way to somewhere, maybe just finished work. He mused and wondered why they always wore similar hooded jackets. As if it was some sort of uniform. It was when they began to get rowdy; smashing plates and cups that Joe stormed from behind the counter to confront them. He grabbed the biggest one and forced him out of the door. The rest followed, laughing and mocking Joe. Dancing around him with their fists up shouting, taunting.

The street was fairly quiet as it was near closing time for the small cafe. Joe stood solid with his hands on his hips. He was a big strong man, fully matured, not like these kids who still had a lot to learn. As he stared defiantly he failed to notice the black BMW slowly pulling up behind him. He failed to notice a large man walking towards him from around the nearby corner. He also failed to notice the metal cosh that came crashing into the back of his head. As Joe's knees gave way, the boot of the BMW opened. The young guys moved as one, catching Joe and bundling the now lifeless body into the car, then quickly closing it before it sped away.

Joe had woken up some time later, tied to a chair, completely naked. Two big, mean looking men standing over him. He thought quickly though his head was throbbing. What did they want? He didn't have to wait long to find out. One of the big guys' leaned over him;

"We heard you had some bother with four foreign knobs. Who were they? Who sent them?"

Joe shook his head. He didn't know who the two hoodlums standing over him were, or what they wanted. What he did know was that the day before he had never been so frightened in all his life as he handed over four thousand pounds to four guys who had beaten him all over his body, whilst threatening him at gun point. They were to return two days later for another three grand. Joe would have the money ready, he feared for his life. He looked up at his captors. He didn't know how far they would go with their interrogation, but he was convinced that his punishment would be much worse if he revealed any information to the two that stood over him.

He shook his head as he spoke:

"It was no trouble, a few guys pushed me around, made some demands, but like I said, it was no trouble."

Jeff shook his head as he glared at his captive. His right hand moved at lightning speed. Joe saw the glint of metal reflecting from the single overhead light bulb. He felt the blood gushing across his chest a split second before he felt the searing pain. Eyes tightly closed, Joe screamed before slumping down into the chair, his whole body devoid of the strength needed to support himself. The chair now in a pool of bodily fluids as both his bladder and bowels released their contents. Jeff smiled as he leaned towards Joe, then stepped back as the smell hit his nostrils. He waived the knife in front of the stricken prisoner as he spoke;

"Want to try again?"

At a dining room table in a terraced house in Peckham Rye a Serbian called Bojan watched in silence as his eldest son Aco chatted to Mike Smith. It was as if they had known each other all their lives. After the initial pointless but courteous questions, the *"How are you, how's the injuries?"* They got down to the reason they were there, which was to talk about their main protagonist, the reason for their disabilities; the reason they were in the same predicament; *because of one man.* Roger Scott.

Mike had explained how it was he who was responsible for the damage that put the *Vegas Slots* out of business. He asked if the information he had supplied about Scott's house in Kent and the description of Sam, Roger Scott's wife had been of use. The address of the call centre in Peckham, and the bastard's favourite Chinese restaurant, which he frequented on a regular basis. Aco nodded enthusiastically as he told Mike that the information had been good, that Roger Scott was, and is still, suffering.

Getting carried away with the euphoria of the recent apparent success Aco patted Mike on the arm and started to tell him about the nightclub attack. How the fire had devastated the place. Totally wrecked it. Bojan stood. Aco was about to continue to divulge the details of the attempted hit and run on Roger. How they had laughed as the car sped away while Scott was laid on the pavement. Bojan leaned over, he had heard enough. He raised his voice;

"Nothing achieved yet. We lost one man. Three of our friends massage parlours closed, and Scott is still in control. So this no time for laughter or celebration."

Aco opened his mouth to protest, in his opinion they were doing good, starting to achieve what they set out to do. He looked at his father then decided against it. Mike turned his head;

"Sir, can I tell you what else I have been working on?"

Bojan took his eyes off his son and looked closely at Mike Smith. He was curious, what could a cripple achieve that he hadn't? Fine, he had paid some yobs to smash up a gaming salon, he had given some information that had proved to be useful, but what else? Intrigued he nodded for Mike to continue. The man in the wheelchair cleared his voice then spoke.

Joe the Pole looked up as the cafe door opened and two guys entered. He recognised them as two of the four Serbs who had paid a visit two days earlier. These two he noticed did not look like brothers. Maybe one from each family he mused, before forcing a smile and gesturing with his head to the opening at the back, that led to the kitchen area. The slight movement he gave caused him severe pain. The beating he had received from the four Serbians earlier in the week was still painful but nothing like he was feeling from his strapped up and heavily bandaged body, that had been tortured by Jeff and his twin brother Tom.

The two guys' glanced around the empty cafe then one of them turned and locked then bolted the door. Zivco had decided that Joe was a beaten man. There was no need for four of them to visit the cafe on this occasion. Two people would be enough. He had sent his brother along with one of the other brothers. Bojan had received the first instalment of the money that Joe had originally owed the landlord. The next bit would be easy. The dumb Pole would have the rest of the money ready and be more than happy to hand it over. Although he would still receive more punishment as a reminder of who was in control.

Joe walked through the beaded curtain letting it drop behind him; he then continued walking through an open door that led to an alleyway at the back of the cafe. One of the guys shouted at him, demanding to know where he was going. Joe carried on walking as the two strode after him. So intent on watching Joe they didn't see the two figures step behind them from the door that led to the stairs. The first Serb dropped to the floor like a stone, as the powerful blow from the cosh that Mary swung caught him behind his ear. The second one turned quickly but not quickly enough to avoid Alan's swinging baseball bat. The blow hit him square across the face, pushing his nose back into his head. He hit the floor unconscious.

Not a word was spoken as the pair were then dragged out of the back door of the cafe, and thrown through the open rear doors of a waiting van. Alan stood over the shaking Joe as Mary told him he had done good, but maybe he should close the cafe for a while, maybe take a long holiday. Poland is nice, maybe he should try there. Joe didn't argue, just gave a slight nod. He would go to Poland, but not for a holiday, he had taken enough, he would go for good, never come back. Joe then watched the van drive away before closing and locking the door.

***

In a small but luxurious hotel near Manilva in Southern Spain, Sam lay naked on the bed; she watched as Roger undressed. His muscular lean body hadn't changed in the three years that she had known him. He looked back at her, smiling that smile, the smile that made her melt. The smile that she had fallen in love with three years earlier. She returned the loving look. Removing the last of his clothes Roger moved towards the bed. Sam gazed at him as he lay down beside her, she could feel the wetness between her legs as she parted them in anticipation. She couldn't help purring softly as Roger began to caress her. Sam slid her hand across his warm body. Roger was panting with pleasure as she slowly licked his face then chest before moving her hand down to grasp his erect penis. Sam's dampness increased along with her breathing.

Then her smile disappeared as she touched a mop of hair, not pubic hair, but a head of hair, the head was bobbing up and down on Roger's hardness. Through the half light of the moon that illuminated the bedroom, Sam looked in the direction of the hair. She shrieked as the head stopped its movement and Mina looked up to smile at her. Then licking her lips Mina turned back to Roger's penis to continue the fellation. Sam wanted to jump out of the bed, to push Mina away. It felt like she was frozen, paralysed. She turned her head to Roger who smiled before speaking;

155

"Thought you would like a threesome. Bit of fun. Something to liven up our boring sex life." Sam lashed out with her right hand; fist clenched aiming for her husband's head. She then screamed as it hit the small bedside cabinet.

Waking up abruptly she lay panting, bathed in sweat. She shook her head violently, her eyes filled with tears as she recalled the latest nightmare. It was the second time in a week that Sam had woken up in shock. The second time in a week that she had dreamt that Mina had been in bed with herself and her husband. Sam leaned across to the cabinet and switched on the bedside light. Glancing at her watch she cringed, 3 am. There was no way she would be going back to sleep now. She sat on the bed, putting her head in her hands she began to quietly weep. How could her life have changed so dramatically? How in the space of a couple of weeks had she been reduced from the confident, self-assured girl she was, into this quivering wreck? Moving to the small table at the other side of the room she pressed the switch on the kettle and placed a tea bag in the waiting cup.

Sitting back on the bed she glanced at her mobile, she thought about ringing Roger, telling him how she felt. How upset she was. How could he send her to Spain against her will? Something inside stopped her, she couldn't quite put her finger on it, but she had a feeling in the back of her mind that she was afraid of what she might hear on the other end of the phone. Sam tried to force a smile; it was only a bad dream, just her imagination. At least it was better than the previous one. *The one where Mina had galloped away on Penny after sticking a knife through Sam's heart.*

***

Calpol, according to the manufacturer's guidelines is

an *Infant Suspension*. Meant to be used in moderation for teething pain or fever or a sore throat. Maybe earache or a cold. It has also been used as a lazy way of overdosing an infant in order to make it sleep, sometimes for several hours.

At 1pm Lisa the social worker sat in her car outside the two up two down terraced house on the edge of Brixton. She had knocked on the door three times, there had been no answer. She was getting frustrated and annoyed at the same time. She had telephoned Yvette an hour earlier to inform her that she would visit shortly. As part of the agreement in place she had the right to visit Meg or any other child who was with temporary foster parents at anytime, day or night.

Leaving her car for the second time, she approached the front door then knocked again, louder. Lisa stepped back as footsteps could be heard from inside the door. The door swung open and she was greeted by a smiling Yvette, a hand on her hip and a questionable look on her face. Lisa forced a smile as she spoke;

"May I come in?" Yvette's face showed concern as she briefly glanced over her shoulder before answering:

"Is there a problem, because this is very short notice?"

"It is not short notice Yvette, I rang you over an hour ago, and there is no problem unless you tell me there is one, now may I come in please?"

Yvette took a step back to allow Lisa to enter the small dingy hallway. Lisa followed Yvette along a short corridor that opened into the living room. Yvette turned to her and made a hushing sound as she put her index finger to her lips. She pointed to a small cot in the corner of the room. Lisa followed her gaze to see Meg asleep in the corner of the cot. She looked further around the room to see clothes and dirty washing strewn across the sparse furniture. Yvette was watching Lisa's face as she made her critical assessment. She spoke, slight nerves in her voice;

"Sorry about the mess, I haven't had time to clean up yet, what with getting Spike up early to get him to work and then sorting little Meg out and taking her for a lovely walk, then…" Lisa stopped her with a wave of her hand;

"No need for explanations Yvette. My concern is for Meg not the state of your house."

Lisa walked towards the cot and leaned over Meg, she was sleeping soundly. Lisa stared. Meg had only been in this house for just over a week but she appeared to look a little drawn. A little thinner than the last time Lisa had seen her. She turned back to Yvette;

"How long has she been sleeping?" Yvette stuttered;

"Err, erm, just got her off, she had being having a great time running in the park with some other children, poor little mare has worn herself out." She forced an unsuccessful smile. Lisa looked around the scruffy room, seeing a single empty chair she walked over to it and sat down before opening her bag to retrieve a pen and notepad. She looked at Yvette then;

"So does Spike always go to work so early? Because at the interviews you both attended you indicated that he only worked part time."

"Er, yes, he has found a new job, full time." She paused looking at the cot then back at Lisa. Lisa answered;

"You do know that we must be informed of any change in circumstances. I want to know the name and address of his new employer."

Yvette smiled again and sputtered an apology, telling Lisa that she intended to but she had been busy caring for Meg, which was her main priority, and as it was a new job she wasn't sure where it was or what the company was called. She said that as soon as Spike came in from work she would ask him and then inform Lisa. Lisa looked on, suspicious. Yvette spoke again, her voice betraying a slight tremor;

"I would offer you a cup of tea but as you can see I have a lot to do. Is there anything else before you go?"

Lisa stood and walked towards the front door without replying. She was not happy; she made a mental note to return sooner rather than later. Opening the door she turned to speak to Yvette. Then heard a thud from upstairs. Lisa glanced up, following the direction of the noise, then back at Yvette. A questionable look on her face. Yvette stepped forward putting her hand on the door handle and opening it fully before leaning towards Lisa in an effort to get her through the door. Then with a sly smile;

"Walls are as thin as paper in these places. Neighbours kids running riot again. I'll have a word now that you are going, don't want them waking poor Meg up now do we." She closed the door almost before Lisa was through it.

Lisa sat in her car. She was in deep thought. The noise she heard was not from the house next door. It was very clearly from the room above, as if somebody was falling out of bed. This troubled Lisa, but not as much as the empty bottle that she had noticed through the half open door that led to the kitchen. The bottle with a label that read "Calpol"

In a small warehouse in Southwark two naked men sat back to back tied to two wooden chairs. Their faces and bodies were a mass of blood and bruises. They had woken up in this position some time earlier. They had little recollection of how they had got there. The last thoughts they had as they walked confidently into the kitchen area of the Polish guy's cafe, was how easy it had all been. They had collected part of the debt a few days earlier, and they were about to collect the next instalment. Now they were in a small warehouse, naked and tied to two wooden chairs. The smaller one of the two was crying, promising to answer any question the two giant lookalike guys who circled them asked. His colleague screaming at him to shut the fuck up. Calling him a coward. When his brother found out about this the two English would be dead.

The smaller one's problem was that the two English giants hadn't asked any questions. They had silently spent the last hour smiling as they inflicted the terrible damage on the two captives. It was a well-used system they had perfected over the years. They knew that if enough pain and fear was delivered their victims would say anything for them to stop, but anything was not what they wanted or needed. They required the truth, therefore the torture came first, and when the questions were eventually asked, with further threats of violence, the truth would be forthcoming. The one who was crying looked in horror as one of the big guys approached, not for the first time, brandishing a large knife. Then a slight sigh of relief as he did nothing more than slice through the rope that was securing his comrade.

Without speaking, the two lookalikes worked as one, dragging the struggling form across the bare concrete floor. The crying man watched in horror as his friend had a rope tied around both ankles before the other end was thrown over one of the girders that supported the roof. The two captors then pulled the rope until the guy was hanging upside down, still naked, still bleeding. The two Serbs then watched fearfully as the quiet one of the two big guys dragged a large toolbox to the middle of the floor. He then opened it and arranged a cordless electric drill on the floor, followed by a blowlamp and then a large pair of pliers.

As the two prisoners gasped at the sight and thought of the forthcoming torture, the door opened and Mary entered with Alan.

***

Marion Hill was frightened, very frightened. It was the first time that she had been inside of a police station. Not just inside but in an interview room, with two detectives standing over her. When they had approached her in the *Vegas Slots* gaming salon they had been smiling, friendly. They had explained that she was not in any trouble, that all they wanted was for her to answer a few questions. Then the surprise that the questions they wanted answering would be asked at the police station.

Now she sat on a hard wooden chair. One of the detectives had sat down opposite her, smiling, the other stood to the side of him, glaring, menacing. They had told her that she was not under arrest or any kind of caution, but due to the seriousness of the investigation they were going to record the conversation. Marion was too nervous to disagree. The seated Mr. Nice smiled at her, thanked her for attending, told her to just relax and answer their questions. She was not in any kind of trouble, they merely needed her help. He then slid a photograph across the table and asked her if she recognised the young man pictured. Marion looked at it. She remembered him as one of the gang who were wearing hooded jackets who had wrecked the gaming salon a couple of weeks earlier. The youngest one. The loudest one. Marion looked at the picture, maybe a little too long, she hesitated, looked up at the guy seated in front of her. He smiled, he read her face. He spoke;

"Miss Hill do you know or have you seen this man before?"

"Err, yes, no, not sure, Maybe, they was wearing hooded jackets, their faces covered."

The Detective who was standing leaned towards Marion, unsmiling;

"Who was Miss Hill? All we asked was had you seen this person before. Clearly you have. Now when was the last time you saw him?"

Marion looked up at him, more frightened, tears filled her eyes. Mr. Nasty continued;

"Miss Hill, the young man in this picture was brutally murdered before being locked in a van that was then set on fire. He died in the most horrendous way. He had parents and younger brothers and sisters who are clearly very upset, just think about if it had been a member of your own family."

He paused. Mr. Nice continued;

So Marion, hope you don't mind me calling you Marion, you need to tell us where and when was the last time you saw, or think you saw the person."

Marion looked again at the photograph. She began to cry.

Assistant Chief Constable Ted Walton had finally given in to his wife's demands and made an appointment to see his doctor. Olive could see the pain that her husband was in. She had nagged, shouted and eventually pleaded with him to get his condition checked out. Ted had reluctantly agreed. In his younger days Ted was a renowned amateur boxer, hard, could take and give a punch. When he first joined the police he was immediately selected for the force rugby team. A no nonsense player who showed little fear of any opponent. He had fought with hardened criminals over the years as they attempted to evade arrest. Ted Walton was a fearless combatant in every discipline.

But Ted Walton also had more than an intense fear of doctors and dentists. Ted Walton was petrified of them.

The pain in his stomach was getting worse. Some days it was quite unbearable. Recently he had spent more time, almost a daily routine, locking himself in either his bathroom or study, in an attempt to hide the discomfort from his wife. It hadn't taken his doctor long. After asking him a few questions, he listened through his stethoscope before applying pressure to the affected area. He watched as Ted flinched then attempted to hide his pain. The medic then told his patient that he was referring him to hospital for X-rays. In his opinion he needed checking out sooner rather than later. It would not be a written referral; it was a phone call there and then. He wanted Ted admitted immediately.

By the time the Assistant Chief Constable had reached the hospital a Dr. Gantar was waiting for him. He was rushed through to the X-ray department without any delay. As Ted lay on the hard bed waiting for the X-rays to begin he gripped the sides until his knuckles were white. He tried to take his mind off the fear that was coursing through him. Tried to think about something else, eyes closed, he was immediately somewhere else.

His thoughts went back to where they usually did. Where they had been for almost every waking hour since the fire at *Sam's* nightclub. The horrendous way in which his beautiful god daughter had been killed. Then before. The death of his son, *his secret son,* in the same nightclub.

163

Now as he lay on the hard bed waiting for the X-ray machine to do its work he tried to convince himself that the pain in his stomach was nothing more than an ulcer, or maybe two. Maybe brought on because of the stress he was suffering, due to the same cause. *Yes* that's all it was, stress, all *because of one man*. Roger Scott. For whatever reason he and his colleagues were no nearer making an arrest. Scott appeared to be either clean or a step in front despite their best efforts. Ted winced again as the pain shot through his stomach. He inwardly tried to smile. He felt better inside. *Yes* an ulcer, maybe two, easily removed. Then back to work. Back to the promise he had made to himself. To take down Roger Scott. One way or the other.

Mary smiled warmly at the two bloodied captives; she walked over to the guy who was hanging upside down. She crouched so that her head was level with his. Mary smiled again before turning and walking over to the man who was still tied to the chair. She nodded her head towards Alan as she spoke;

"My friend here is not a very nice man. He gets very annoyed and upset if he doesn't get the answers he wants." She looked at Alan. The two captives followed her gaze to see him bending down over the toolbox as if he was selecting which item to use. Mary continued;

"You will talk; eventually you will tell us what we need to know. In fact, you will beg us to listen. It is up to you as to how much pain you can stand before you do."

She nodded to Jeff who stepped forward and turned the chair round, so that the guy who was tied to it had his back to the other Serb. He looked up at Jeff in horror as he heard the cordless drill start to revolve and then his friend begin to scream.

It was a little more than an hour later that Mary sat on the now vacated chair, looking at the five names and three question marks on the sheet of paper in front of her. She glanced up to see Jeff and Tom sealing the two forty-five gallon metal drums that contained not only the two dead Serbians but also a considerable amount of sulphuric acid.

Bojan Duric listened as Mike Smith told him about the events three years earlier. About how he and his friend Shane had been set up. How Shane was dead and Mike was left for dead. *Because of one man;* because of Roger Scott he was destined to be this wheelchair for life. Bojan yawned, so what. It wasn't his problem. He had enough on his mind without this prick whinging at him. Mike continued; he said he had been working hard to find out everything about the build up to the shooting of a detective in Scott's nightclub, and about the disappearance of a guy named Mal, who was found dead the following day. He still had contacts from three years ago, people who had fallen foul of Roger Scott.

"What this to do with me?"

Bojan had tried to keep his voice calm, he didn't quite manage it. Mike noticed, he continued quickly;

"Three brother's sir. They ran their empire up north, Liverpool. Scott not only finished them but also put the head guy in a wheelchair. I have been in touch with them, spoken to them. They want to help in bringing Scott down. They are coming to London tomorrow, I am meeting them, maybe you might want to..."

"No! We don't need help!" Bojan shouted. "My sons are crippled, you in wheelchair, now another cripple to look after. No! Don't need help. I will take down Scott myself!"

Mike held up his hand as an apology. "Sorry Sir, no problem. Maybe it's time I was leaving." He touched the four way switch on the chair arm and smiled an apology at Ajo. As Bojan went to open the door to allow Mike through there was a loud banging from the other side. Standing solid he opened the door quickly to see Zivco standing, ashen faced;

"Bojan, I need talk to you." He walked into the room, past Mike and towards the dining room table. He dropped a padded envelope onto it and turned to face the rest of the occupants. Bojan looked back at him; he noticed the glassiness in his eyes. He nodded.

"My brother and one of the other guys went to Polish cafe to collect the rest of money. They didn't return. I go there to see why. The owner was there, little man, he said he had received phone call to go to cafe. He said it was empty when he get there. He found this on counter with my name on it."

He picked up the padded envelope, it had already been opened, he held the bottom and tipped contents onto the table. Ajo leaned further to get a closer look, then reeled back quickly as he saw a severed ear; it still had an earring attached. A small sheet of bloodied paper had also come out of the package. Zivco spoke;

"That is my brothers ear, recognise earring. Letter says that is all that is left of him and his friend." He looked at the ear sadly then back at Bojan. He spoke;

"Letter then said something else." Bojan looked at him, waiting for him to continue. He did;

"At end it say; "Regards Roger." Will be in touch."

Roger studied the five names followed by three question marks on the sheet of paper. Mary and Alan were sitting opposite him in the back room of the Pot Black snooker hall. Jeff, as usual stood behind Roger, his brother Tom at the door. Roger looked up at Mary;

"Either they didn't know as much as we thought or you killed them too quickly, there are two names missing."

Mary didn't answer; she risked a quick glance at Alan who looked on impassively. Roger stood, he smiled;

"Nothing much to worry about, well done both of you, it's clear that this Bojan bloke is the father of Ajo and Dorde. The two you have just left are also brothers of these two." He pointed at the two names at the bottom, Zivco and Toma obviously the last names to be divulged.

"So it's fair to assume that the three question marks are the mob that waited for me outside of the Silk Road restaurant." He looked at Mary again;

"No names?"

"No boss, they didn't know them, just knew of them. They said that they had never met. All they knew was that there were three other guys involved with the Bojan Serb. If they had known them they would have told us after what Alan was doing to them."

Roger smiled. Mary continued to tell him everything the two unfortunates in the warehouse had said. That they had joined Bojan with their two brothers to take over his business. With only him and his two crippled sons they saw him as an easy target. They had found out about the other three a few days later. They said over and over that they had never met them and they didn't know their names. Mary said that she was convinced they were telling the truth. Roger spoke;

"No mention of a Rodovan or a Mike Smith." Mary and Alan looked a little baffled as she shook her head. Roger continued;

"Yes, Mike Smith is still alive, maybe in a wheelchair but still alive. I'm pretty sure it was him who paid those guys to wreck the gaming salon." Mary spoke;

"So this Rodovan, he was one of the guys in the picture you showed us last week, the one wearing the white jacket, maybe another of Bojan's sons."

"Maybe, they look alike, and he was in Sam's nightclub the night the firebomb came through the window, he was looking suspicious, as if he was waiting for it to happen. So where does this Bojan live?"

Mary shook her head as she spoke;

"Said they didn't know, they would meet in the back room of a pub, *The Gowlett Arms*. It's the same pub that me and Alan first saw the four of them."

Roger nodded as he sat back down. He told them he had another job for them. A few minutes later he then reached under the snooker table and retrieved two packages and slid them across the table to Mary and Alan.

***

Lisa screamed at her boss. He had made her wait in the corridor outside his office like some naughty schoolgirl for over half an hour. She had spent the next half hour explaining her concerns about one of her latest cases. She was very worried about young Meg who had been left in the charge of a certain Yvette and Spike. Her boss appeared to be listening but in Lisa's opinion he was disinterested. He had then told her to go away and find some proof before submitting her thoughts in writing. He was quite clear that just because she had noticed a bottle of *Calpol,* and that the man of the house had found a new job, it did not warrant any further action at this stage. Lisa was exasperated;

"Sir, there was something not right in that house; the woman was lying through her teeth, in my opinion that baby looked ill and under nourished. I demand that action is taken before something serious happens."

Her boss was fuming, he was not happy to be spoken to in that manner; nobody made any sort of demands of him. He answered;

"Listen young lady. We have a vast shortage of suitable foster parents in that area. That couple have been through a very stringent and thorough check. I was personally involved with that particular selection, which I might add they passed with flying colours. Now let me remind you that you are at the moment employed as a social worker, you are not here to tell me how to do my job. So I repeat, unless you can find some proof of your allegations and show me them in writing, I have nothing to act on. So might I suggest you get back on with your work. Close the door on the way out."

Lisa stormed out slamming the door behind her. Her boss watched her go before picking up the phone on his desk and dialling an internal number.

P.C. John Jenkins sat in front of Roger, Jeff sat behind him. He tried but failed to smile, he had even less success at trying to keep his hands from shaking. Jenkins through fear had made contact with Roger after the previous day's meeting at the police station. The meeting where Detective Inspector Terry Thompson made it very clear to all present that Roger Scott was very much responsible for and guilty of various crimes that had not been solved in recent years. Thompson had instructed his team as to what he wanted next. As they were no further forward in their investigations maybe it was time to bring Scott in.

Due to the information gleaned from Marion Hill there was evidence, albeit circumstantial that Roger Scott was behind the murder of the young man named Denzil York.

The youth who had been found dead in the back of a burnt out van in Burgess Park. They had enough evidence to question Scott and possibly make an arrest. They needed him to be put under pressure, maybe he would give something away. Something that maybe revealed a weakness, something they could home in on.

Unbeknown to the constable, as the detective inspector gave his orders he was watching P.C. Jenkins face for some kind of reaction. He did not trust this guy. How many policemen would have served as long as he had without any aspirations or ambitions of furthering their career? Nobody joined the police force for money; the pay was not any kind of incentive. In Terry Thompson's opinion, the people who decided to wear the uniform did it to serve the public and make the streets a safer place. Which was why after the meeting had closed, he put a watch on John Jenkins. He knew that a certain WPC Joan Shaw did not have a very high opinion of the constable. She would be more than happy to do as she was instructed; to follow his movements, look for anything that was untoward or detrimental to the investigation. Joan Shaw relished the challenge.

Roger looked at the hapless copper thinking that he was nothing more than a rip off to the tax payer. Jenkins spoke;

"You need to be ready Mr. Scott. You are about to be arrested."

Roger looked at Jenkins, looking for a clue in his face or mannerisms. Any slight giveaway that he could be lying. Maybe a trap. Maybe trying to set Roger up for a fall. Jenkins showed no emotion. Roger answered;

"Go on, and make it good."

"In the next few hours or maybe few days, I'm not sure when, two detectives will arrive. They will talk to you about the arson attack on your nightclub, about the attempted kidnap of your wife. They will drag up the night that a detective was killed in Sam's nightclub three years ago, and what do you know about a guy named Mal, who was found murdered the following day. Then about the damage to your gaming salon that happened shortly before a youth was murdered in Burgess Park. They have the CCTV footage of the victim, along with several others entering the back of a white van, which stopped quite close to the gaming salon. The same van that the victim was found in, dead and burned beyond recognition. We have been ordered to find these youths and question them."

Roger nodded, P.C. Jenkins continued;

"Three massage parlours that you once owned were wrecked the other night. There have not been any complaints made but we have been told to find out who was behind the attack."

Roger put his hand in the air to silence the constable. He looked at him closely. Roger was thinking like he used to, three years ago, before he had gone soft. Before he had let himself and his businesses go. He spoke;

"So how do you intend to do that?"

"We have been ordered to find anybody or everybody who was inside the massage parlours that night, prostitutes or punters. We have to pay them a visit, put them under pressure, get them to tell us exactly what happened. See if there are any clues that you were behind it." Roger nodded, then;

"Why is your mob taking such a big interest in me? It is me who is the victim."

"Not sure Mr. Scott, but it appears to be coming from higher up the pay scale. Ted Walton, the Assistant Chief Constable is taking a big interest in you. It looks personal."

Roger continued looking at the policeman, he could see

the fear. He thought some more, about the arson attack on *Sam's* nightclub. About the funeral of Emily Austin he attended afterwards. About the fact that the same Assistant Chief Constable was in attendance. Standing very close to the victim's family. Jenkins could not hold Roger's stare, he looked down, then up, then towards the window. Then jumped as Roger shouted at him;

"Out with it! Now."

The Roger Scott of old was well experienced in the body language of whoever it was in front of him. When they were lying, when they were merely nervous. When, as in this case they were hiding something. The constable shook. Then;

"Two detectives pulled in a Miss Hill. The manager of your gaming salon. It seems like she told them that she had seen the guy who was killed in Burgess Park in there the night it was attacked with paint."

"Go on!"

"I'm not sure what or how much she told them but the conversation was taped. I saw her come out of the interview room, she was crying, very upset."

"Was she arrested?"

"No, I don't think so; she just walked out of the station in a hurry."

Roger sat back in his chair. So Marion Hill had opened her mouth to the police, what had she told them? The yobs who attacked the gaming salon had been wearing hooded jackets, faces covered. She had pointed the gang out to Roger when they had been standing on the corner of the street. Had she told them that? Would she have noticed that there was one less when they had returned to apologise? Maybe, but he could have been anywhere, maybe decided not to go with the rest. No, all they had was the speculation of what might have happened. Roger stared at the P.C. for a full minute; he was convinced that he had pushed him as far as he could for now. He spoke;

"Ok. We will see what happens when your boys get here. You can go."

Jenkins stood, he turned and after a brief glance at Jeff he left the call centre via the back door. Across the yard and out through the gate. He turned left and headed along the alley that would take on to Peckham High Street. Hands in his pockets and his head bowed he walked quickly out into the street of boarded up shops, betting shops, charity shops. His mind was in its usual whirl after leaving Roger. A mix of fear and relief, but most of all hatred. He hated Roger Scott.

Which was why he failed to notice a W.P.C. Joan Shaw watching him.

Big Steve, as he was known in the small town near Durham where he had lived before moving to London, sat in the corner of the grubby bedsit he rented. One table, one chair and a single bed. He studied the photographs that he had spread out on the bed in front of him. The first few were happy memories of his time in Catterick Garrison before joining the 2nd Battalion of the Parachute Regiment. He looked at the faces on the group picture, going through each name in his head. The odd smile as he remembered some of the good times. The picture of him lifting the silver football trophy after winning the inter garrison final. Then the show of sadness at the comrades who hadn't made it through the wars in Afghanistan, Bosnia and various other places.

He turned to some more recent pictures. Pictures that had been taken a few months before he had left the forces.

He gazed at one in particular; it showed himself and his best friend. The guy who he had been closest to. The guy who had saved his life many years earlier after they had been ambushed near Kabul. The guy called Mal, who had contacted him three years ago with an offer of work. The kind of work he was good at. The kind of work he had been trained to do.

Steve had been ready to leave, to come and join Mal. Then he not heard anything, his best friend had just disappeared. Despite his best efforts there appeared to be no way of contacting him. Steve thought that maybe there had been a change of plan; maybe Mal would be in touch when the time was right. So he continued his life. He knew Mal would contact him when he was ready.

It was two years later after attending a reunion that he heard and realised why he had suddenly lost touch with his best friend.

He pushed the photos to one side and sat back in the chair. Looking out of the window at drab bedsits, burnt out cars and graffiti covered walls, he closed his eyes and went through the past few days. He had now met the infamous Roger Scott. He had managed to infiltrate his inner circle. Passed the feeble and obvious test that Scott had given him. It was easy enough, maybe too easy. There was an element of truth in the story he gave Johnny and Roger about his security business up north. Yes there had been a shooting but it was nothing to do with him, he had contracted that particular job to another firm across the City. Steve had been too busy. Busy working on finding out what had happened to his best friend. The guy who had saved his life many years earlier.

Now, after many hours of trawling the internet for old news and back issues of local newspapers, he had built up a picture of what had happened around three years ago in a nightclub in Peckham. In particular what had happened to his best friend. He would not rest until he had found the man responsible and taken his revenge.

***

In a nearby cafe the owner was frightened, very frightened.

"I am nothing more than a small business man. What do you want from me?" Alan stood over the shaking man as Mary, who was never the prettiest of women, snarled at him;

"The Polish prick that was ripping off your cafe has gone, gone for good. You should be grateful to us for arranging that. We know you paid someone to frighten him into paying off his debt. The people your man sent there are dead, just like you are going to fuckin' be, unless you tell me who you paid to set this up."

The small man shook, he was out of his depth. He thought it would be easy, Bojan Duric ran this area, he had done for the last couple of years. Any debts that needed collecting were offered to him, and you then got paid straight away, albeit a lesser amount. Whatever happened after that was down to Bojan.

Mary was losing patience. She didn't have time for playing games with this little prick. The back of her hand flew violently into the small man's face, it caught him unawares. He was sent spinning from the chair, screaming as he crashed to the floor. Alan leaned down and used one large hand to lift the guy off his feet and slam him back down into the chair. Mary leaned close to him. The small man had taken enough. He sobbed;

"Duric, Bojan Duric. He is the man who bought my debt."

175

"Address!"

"I don't know." Then another scream as he flew off the chair for a second time.

Twenty minutes later Mary smiled at Alan as the car pulled away from the hospital car park. She had the name and address she wanted. The shop owner had been dumped in the corner of the car park. Away from the tell-tale CCTV cameras. Somebody would come across his badly beaten body sooner or later. He would live, but with the knowledge that if he wanted to live a bit longer he would keep his mouth shut.

***

Puerto de la Duquesa. Southern Spain

Sam swirled her drink round her glass, watching dazedly as the ice melted. It was 2pm. The sun was blazing to the point of making her sit in the shade. After her latest nightmare, her latest restless night, her latest disturbed sleep dreaming about the adventures of her husband and that fuckin' skank Mina, Sam had showered and decided to go for a walk. Maybe discovering the local area would take her mind off the situation back in London. Take her mind off how three years of married bliss had suddenly turned into another bad dream.

She wandered aimlessly around the pretty Puerto de la Duquesa, pausing to look at the numerous and varied boats that bobbed gently on the still water. The many restaurants offering various dishes from various parts of the world. She thought it strange that there were no or very few traditional Spanish options.

Sam ordered a coffee and a *"famous"* quiche in a cafe bar called *The Coyote Runner,* which was served by a large smiling man. He looked like he was about to stop and chat to her, but then wandered away after hearing a lady's voice, telling him that the boat was ready to leave, and so was he! Sam glanced at the lady who stood with one hand on her hip. The big guy walked out.

After finishing her coffee and gazing at the beautiful blue sky Sam had left the port, deciding explore further. She walked out through an archway, then followed the road to the left and eventually climbed a hill that led her to a small square that housed more bars and eating establishments. Which was where she was now, swirling her drink around her glass, watching the ice melt. She glanced at some children as they careered around the square on various wheeled toys, intent on wrecking the well tended flower beds. Then;

"Get yer another love?"

Sam was snapped out of her thoughts by a pretty blonde lady, clearly the owner of the *"Bar Trish"* where she had been seated for the last half hour. Sam forced a smile as she asked for another Gin & Tonic. She knew that it was a little early in the day for alcohol but she didn't care, maybe it was down to the mood she was in. The drink appeared a minute later, delivered by the same lady who now introduced herself as *"Kelly."* She seated herself next to Sam. Then;

"Not seen yer here before love, on holiday are yer?"

Sam relaxed a little, the lady seemed really nice, friendly, it was maybe what she needed. It dawned on her that although George was there if she wanted anything, she still had nobody to talk to. She answered;

"Yes, not sure how long for, just needed to get away for a little while."

"Oh well, hope yer enjoy yourself love, there will be a few locals in soon, happy hour starts at three."

Sam thanked her thinking if only she had someone there with her to enjoy a meal or maybe a drink, or maybe nothing more than some company.

With that Kelly returned to the bar. Sam watched her walk away; she sipped her drink and thought how happy Kelly looked.

Sam glanced at the other eating and drinking establishments around the square. *"Teds bar"*, proclaiming to be the best sports bar around. *"The Grounded Rat"*, a blackboard showing various tapas. In the corner of the square she noticed *"Bronte's"*. Sam could detect the smell of barbecued meat emanating from that direction. The whole area looked so lovely and tranquil compared to the mad crowded rush of London. It dawned on her that for the first time in weeks, that although lonely, she actually felt relaxed. Maybe she would return to this square, it appeared to attract more locals than holiday makers, maybe she could meet some new people. She smiled at the thought; apart from Adie she had lost contact with almost all of her past friends. Another legacy of the way she now felt.

Sam tried not to reflect on the happenings of the previous few weeks. The tragic death of her beloved horse, Penny. The fact that her idyllic life would probably never be the same again. Her mind whirled and turned, the many questions, mostly unanswered that still troubled her, the change in Roger, yes Roger; all of this was his doing, and his skank Mina, Sam hated that woman. Then there was poor Adie, back in hospital with horrible injuries for the second time in three years, and what about Meg? As if she hadn't had a bad enough start in life without now being palmed off to two very unscrupulous looking foster carers.

Sam was getting more and more angry. So what now? Stay here like the good little wife and do as her *master* tells her? Wait for the call to go running back like some loyal cocker spaniel? Try to get back into the life prior to the last few weeks? Sam felt her eyes start to glisten at the mess of it all. Suddenly her relaxation turned to anger. Who the hell did he think he was? He had treated her like some insubordinate child since the trouble began, not the loving loyal wife that she was, and had been for the last three years. She took another drink of the G and T still thinking. Why had he really sent her here?

She could have stayed in a hotel in London if he was worried about her safety. They could have told the police their concerns and asked for some kind of protection. He could have done a whole host of things other than send her to Spain. No, there must be another reason he wanted her there. Becoming even more angry she gulped down the Gin and Tonic, her thoughts then went back to Mina. Why? Why Mina? She thought. Mina was well past her sell by date in both looks and figure. Sam was doubtful that she was ever pretty even in her younger days. Another hour went by; another two Gin and Tonics went down, except it turned out to be four G and Ts. Sam not realising that happy hour meant that every time you buy a drink you receive two. *"Bastard man."* she thought. *"Well if that's the way he wants to play it."* Now feeling both tipsy and resentful Sam picked up her mobile phone. She rang George.

***

Bojan looked at the severed ear, looked again at the distraught Zivco. He sat down in deep thought. It was not going as planned; one of the four guys' who had come over from Serbia was missing, no doubt dead. Zivco's

179

brother and one of the other two brothers were also dead. The word on the street after the three massage parlours were wrecked was that Roger Scott was behind it all. His name had been mentioned more than once, and now it had spread to almost every drinking house in the area. There was no doubt in Zivco's mind that Scott was also behind what had happened at the Polish guy's cafe. The letter that arrived with the severed ear clearly stated "Roger" at the bottom of it.

Bojan was in agreement with the street talk, he was losing credibility and he knew it. This was supposed to be easy, frighten Scott by beating him half to death, by nearly killing him with a car, by wreaking havoc on his business, on his marriage, on his personal life. Take him down slowly; ruin him, change his life forever. Just like Roger Scott had done to Ajo and Dorde, his two precious sons. Bojan looked again at the stricken Zivco, then again at his brother's ear, then at the letter, then at Mike Smith. He spoke;

"Rules have changed. I still want his property and business damaged. I still want him ruined." He paused, looked again at all in front of him. Then; "But now I don't want Scott hurt. *I want him dead.*"

***

In Camberwell police station Detective Inspector Terry Thompson stood in front of the five detectives, the same five that he had addressed a few days earlier. He was not happy. The detectives, backed up by uniformed officers had visited every person they could find who had been in the massage parlours on the night of the attacks. The girls who had been taken home, the clients, some of whom were still in hospital. All but one said they didn't know anything;

they were going about their business when several men came in and wrecked the place.

The detectives tried heavy handed tactics, threats of arrest, to be named and shamed, their pictures in the newspapers. More harshly spoken words, off the record. Again, no response. Many of the male clients were married, in fear of their wives finding out where they had been. Some of the girls did not speak English. Only one of the older, more experienced prostitutes said she had heard the name "Roger Scott" mentioned, but had refused to make a complaint or give an official statement. She told them they could jail her if they wanted, it wouldn't be the first time, and it would be safer than facing Scott. After assuring all who they spoke to that they would have protection if they would make a statement, their words still fell on deaf ears, the detectives left.

Terry Thompson addressed his audience;

"It would appear that we are hitting a brick wall with every part of this investigation, maybe now we know why. As most of you are aware our Police Constable Jenkins has been suspended pending a disciplinary meeting. It would appear that he was seen leaving the premises of our friend Roger Scott. He had not informed anybody he was going there, and he could not offer any defence or answers as to why he was there when he was confronted. So maybe we now know why Roger Scott has been one step ahead of us in certain parts of our investigation. The disciplinary meeting will take place here but it will be conducted by another force. On that basis we will not discuss it any further."

He watched their faces, no emotion, no surprise, he moved on;

"Detective Farrell. What's the latest on the CCTV

footage of the white van?"

Farrell stood, shoulders back;

"Not good sir. We have footage of the van stopping near Bellenden Road and several youths entering the back of it. The windows at the front were blacked out. So we could not identify the driver. Through the cameras we traced it towards Burgess Park, but as we all know the CCTV cameras in that area are only for show. None of them are connected or monitored. We lost sight of it. Nothing after that until a concerned local saw the smoke and flames and made the call."

Thompson shook his head;

"So what happened to the rest of the gang? Several were seen entering the van but only one found inside after it had been torched." Farrell replied;

"We don't know Sir. We have footage, albeit low quality, of a gang of youths leaving the area at the time, but it also shows a few other gangs roaming in the vicinity. That's how it is over there. We have made regular visits to the area they were often seen around and there is no sign of them, it's as if they have disappeared. We have spoken to Denzil York's family. They knew he hung around with a gang of youths but they either didn't know their names or they don't want to tell us."

"So we are no further forward?"

"Not as far as the van is concerned. It had been stolen two weeks prior to the incident. We have appealed for witnesses, apart from the usual timewasters wanting their fifteen minutes of fame nobody has come forward. It would appear that maybe the locals know that Roger Scott is involved which is why there is no cooperation."

Terry Thompson looked at the blank faces in front of him, then with a voice slightly raised;

"Assistant Chief Constable Ted Walton has some kind of bee in his bonnet over this Scott character. Although I tend to think there are more important issues that need attending to out there, it has been indicated in no uncertain terms that this man is to be taken down. This has come from the top. He is not going let it go. So, do any of you have anything that we can use to incriminate Roger Scott?"

The five Detectives looked at the notes in front of them, one or two shuffled in their seats. Uncomfortable, they knew as well as their superior that they had little or nothing to go on. Thompson looked on. Then from the back, Angie, the only female, a lady who although an experienced investigator was fairly new to Camberwell. She raised her hand. Thompson looked at her briefly. He was aware that she had recently been transferred by her own request from Gibraltar. Whilst there she had solved many cases, and had received a medal of bravery for helping to evacuate cruise ship passengers, when the threat of an explosive device had been reported. Due to her actions nobody had been hurt in the forthcoming explosion, but because of the close proximity of Angie it had permanently affected her hearing.

D.I. Thompson also knew that she had been living with a Spanish guy. It was some sort of relationship break up that had made her want to return to the UK. Terry Thompson was unhappy about her being there. He was aware that Gibraltar was relatively small in both size and crime wave compared to south London. It had not been his choice to have her transferred to Camberwell but at this stage he was ready to listen. He acknowledged her;

"Detective Paco?"

Angie cleared her throat, then;

"Sir. We are all aware that there was a plan in place to

visit Roger Scott and maybe arrest him. We also know that it was put on hold due to a certain P.C. Jenkins. But now that he is no longer working maybe we should get Scott in here, behind closed doors, on his own. I'm sure he will have answers but there may be some kind of slip, maybe a mistake if we put him under enough pressure."

The lead detective looked at her. It was something that had been on his mind, something that was going to happen, only for that clown Jenkins to put paid to the plan. He nodded his head then looked at the rest of the room. He answered;

"So how do we do that?" Angie continued;

"We get serious Sir. We put twenty four hour surveillance on him. We bug, tap and listen to his phone calls. We put a tracker on his car. Follow him and hound him until he drops his guard, which he will, then we bring him in to help with our enquiries.

D.I. Thompson resisted the urge to shake his head. He tried to hide what he was thinking; *"Is this woman for real? This is the real world, not some shit that she has seen on fuckin' T.V!"* Regaining his composure he nodded "thanks" in Angie's direction. Then;

"Anybody else?" Blank looks, it was as if they weren't interested. He couldn't blame them. He had known the Roger Scott types before. They were wasting their time; Scott would have enough alibis in place to cover himself. D.I. Thompson had an in tray full of unsolved crimes, some of them suspected murders. Many of them much more important than this case. But when the Assistant Chief Constable is personally involved he had to act accordingly.

***

Marion Hill looked up as the front door of the *"Vegas Slots"* opened. Then she took a sharp intake of breath as she saw her boss enter. Roger Scott was not smiling, far from it. He looked angry as he walked towards her. Behind him was a lady, bit rough looking, maybe pretty once but not anymore, she had a weather beaten look about her. Roger spoke;

"Want a word Marion. Mina will keep an eye on things out here, back room now!" Marion shook as she turned to walk away, doing as she was instructed. Roger followed her through the door then closed it behind him.

"I hear you have had a day out at Camberwell Police Station. Want to tell me about it?"

Marion opened her mouth to answer but nothing came out. How did he know? She had not told anybody, not even her best friends. She looked up at him, shaking. Roger forced a smile, tried to look relaxed, less frightening. He sat down on the only available chair, now Marion was looking down on him. He spoke again, softer;

"Marion, you are not in any trouble, I just need to know what they wanted, what did they ask you? What did you tell them?"

Marion was still shaking; she hadn't got over the questions and the grilling from the two detectives yet, now she was having to face another interrogation. She attempted to calm herself, be composed, telling herself that she had done nothing wrong. She finally answered;

"They told me they just wanted me to help them, they said that I wasn't under arrest or anything. One of them was really nice, friendly. Then they showed me a picture of a young guy. They said he had been brutally murdered. Found dead in the back of a van. They asked me if I had seen him before, did I recognise him as one of the gang who came in here with the paint cans. I told them that they were all wearing hoods. Then the other policeman became really nasty, shouting, He twisted everything I said, saying he knew that I recognised the young guy. That I must tell them when I had last seen him. He frightened me so much so I told him the truth."

Roger stared at her. At first disbelieving what he was hearing. Then thinking; again his own fault, another example, if one was needed, that he had gone soft, employing law abiding people. Three years ago everybody on his payroll, apart from Sam, was there because Roger had some kind of hold over them, maybe a debt, maybe fear, maybe because they all knew Roger's reputation. None of them would have told the police a single thing. He spoke quietly, menacing;

"Which was what Marion! What was the fuckin' truth?"

Marion began to shake again. Maybe the fact that he had sworn at her, on the two occasions she had met Roger she had found him to be quite pleasant. Eyes filling with tears, she answered;

"The newspaper." Roger continued looking at her, somewhat bewildered.

"There was a photo in the newspaper last week; it said that the person in the picture had been found dead in the back of a van, it was saying if anybody had seen him they should come forward. It was the same picture as they showed me. So that was the truth, that was the last time I saw him. In the newspaper. They weren't happy; the nasty one said I was taking the piss. He said I knew more than I was telling them. I had heard enough, I told them again that was all I knew. I started to cry. They told me I could go but they would want to see me again."

Roger smiled, relaxed a little. Softened, he asked

186

Marion if she would like the rest of the day off, she said no, she was fine. Roger stood, reached into his wallet and pulled out £500 which he handed to her. Marion attempted a smile as she took the money then watched Roger walk out.

Big Steve, as he was known in the small town near Durham before moving to London watched as Roger Scott left the *"Vegas Slots"* gaming salon. He was sitting in the nearby Burger King, unhappy to be surrounded by excited noisy children. He had spent the last few days alone; there had been no phone call from Johnny lately, and no offer of further work. In fact it was as if he had appeared to have disappeared. It suited Steve, it had given him time to achieve what he had come to London to do, which was to avenge the murder of his closest friend, the man who had saved his life. The ex- Para who had disappeared three years ago.

He knew about the Pot Black Snooker Hall, and now the gaming salon. He had visited some of the brothels that Roger had once owned and requested the more experienced girls for his services, after a couple of tries he had found three girls who had been involved with the brothels for many years. After further visits with the same girls they had opened up a little to his questions. Steve had told them he had also known Roger for many years and that he used to work for him, before he had given up ownership of brothels. Steve said that he himself had been offered one of them to run but had decided to head back north.

It was on the fourth visit to the *"New Secrets"* parlour that Steve had managed to get a lady called Lotte to open up a little more; with a bit of goading and reverse psychology he had fed her certain questions that eventually she had answered whilst thinking it was her own idea. She talked about how Roger Scott's empire as such had come to an abrupt end. Lotte herself had been more than friendly and accommodating with a guy called Jeff who was one of Roger's minders. She had remembered that it all happened after a detective had been shot and killed in one of his nightclubs, the one called *"Sam's."* Steve said he remembered it well, she believed him and carried on talking. Steve let her chat as she continued the massage. Eventually he spoke;

"Yes, I remember two or three of the guys disappearing after that night, I'm sure one of them was found dead, err, it was, err, what did you call him again?" Lotte jumped in;

"Well the one the police found dead was somebody called Mal, apparently he was in a hell of a mess, bits of him missing we heard. The other two they looked for and didn't find was err, Shaun or maybe Shane somebody, he was quite new, hadn't been working for Roger very long. The other one, well, there was talk of him being involved with Roger's wife, err, Mike I think, yes, Mike Jones, or maybe Smith, Some kind of common name."

Steve smiled, he had what he wanted, for now. He slowly lifted the towel that was covering his nakedness;

"All very interesting sweetheart but those days are history. There is a fifty in my jacket pocket, you know what to do."

Lotte smiled as she unclipped her bikini top.

***

Sam sat opposite George in *"Ted's Bar"* She had rung him earlier to enquire if he was busy, as she needed to see him. George said he could spare her some time due to most of his work occurring after dark. He had the odd daytime

188

job but not often. As he drove the fifteen miles towards Duquesa he was wondering what was so important. Sam had been very vague over the phone. Not quite insisting or demanding that he should meet her but maybe being a little persuasive. Clearly she had been drinking; the slight slurring of her words as she spoke made that very clear. He had wanted to ask more questions, ask what was so important that she needed him there now. But remembering he had told Roger Scott that he would look after Sam while she was in Spain he had left himself with little choice other than to meet her. Even after three years he still did not want to cross Roger. Now as he sat opposite Sam outside of *"Ted's Bar"* George looked at her across the table while at the same time forcing a smile;

"So Sam, what can I do for you?"

Sam took another drink; she smiled crookedly across the top of her glass;

"Just needed some company, you don't mind do you?"

George looked back at her, thinking. She looked different; the pretty smile had been replaced by a scowl as she spoke, which sounded slightly aggressive. He knew from when he had collected her from the airport in Malaga that she had been unhappy. Roger had told him very little on the phone other than that he was to look after her. He forced another smile as he answered;

"Don't mind at all Sam, it will be a pleasure. How have you been?" Sam placed the glass back on the table then attempted to answer without sounding a little drunk. She didn't manage it;

"Fine, I'm fine, bloody fine, never been fuckin' finer." She looked across the square, then at the ground, then back at George who remained silent;

"Just needed some company. The people here are

189

friendly, that bald guy with the glasses across there," she nodded towards *"Bar Trish"* then continued, "was a little too friendly, which is why I changed bars, but I don't know anybody, so I thought you might not mind giving me a little of your time."

George glanced across the square to see the bald guy smiling and waving at Sam, then blowing a kiss. Then pointing to his own eyes and mouthing; *"I'm watching you."* George stood and went to walk towards him. Sam took in what was happening. Then placing her hand on his arm;

"Leave it George; please don't do anything, not here."

He looked down at her face, then at her hand, then back across the square. Sam's face looked a little pitiful, her hand remained on his arm. Baldy with the glasses had disappeared. He sat back down. Not for the first time since he arrived he attempted to look relaxed. He had better things to do than babysit Roger's drunken wife. He may have been mistaken, but the scowl Sam was wearing earlier appeared to have been replaced by a pleasant smile. Her face had softened. A flutter of the eyelashes maybe? He took another sip of his drink as he watched her closely. He may be imagining things but it looked like Sam was flirting with him. What was she up to?

Roger had explained, albeit briefly that he was having a few problems back in London. Things were getting a little out of hand, somebody would maybe finish up being hurt. Which was why he wanted Sam out of the way for a little while. George thought about his time working for Roger, if past experiences were anything to go by the current problems shouldn't take too long to sort out. Then he could get back to normal. He answered her;

"Like I said, I don't mind at all Sam, it's a pleasure being with you." He looked around his surroundings as he sipped his drink. One or two of the locals taking more than a passing interest in him. Then glancing around looking at the different bars as they began to fill. Mainly men in their work clothes in search of a well earned beer after what looked like a day of painting. Smartly dressed ladies chattering happily after making their way back from their work in Gibraltar.

Sam picked up her glass, she leaned closer to George. He didn't move as she kissed him on the cheek before slurring a *"Thanks."* Then the echo of cheers and comments of *"Sack the juggler"* as the glass slipped from her fingers and smashed across the floor. A pretty barmaid appeared behind them with a brush and began to clear the broken glass. A small lady, maybe a Scottish accent, smiled warmly at Sam;

"Dinnea fash yer sel hen, these things happen." A big guy, cigarette hanging from his mouth, a glass of dark beer in his hand, maybe the landlord, slurred an insult. Sam thanked the barmaid and the Scottish lady before producing a twenty euro note. She looked at George as she unsteadily got to her feet;

"Can we leave please? Maybe go somewhere else?"

George smiled; "Maybe a good idea."

George steered the car away from the square as Sam struggled to fasten her seatbelt. He glanced in his rear view mirror to see two or three locals sitting on a wall, smoking as they watched the car pull away. He spoke, smiling;

"So, where to Madam?" Sam thought before answering;

"I'm feeling a little hot and sweaty; can we call into my hotel so I can change into something fresh?" He didn't answer as he indicated left to head towards Manilva and the direction of Sam's temporary home. Five minutes later George glanced sideways at Sam has he pulled into the underground car park. He noticed a strange look about her, a sort of drunken but satisfied smile.

Sam had been thinking hard as she had spent the afternoon drinking alone. She was convinced that her husband had sent her to Spain because he wanted more time with that ugly slag Mina. Maybe he had been attacked; maybe the nightclub fire had been malicious, maybe not. Sam's drunken mind played games with her emotions. Failing to make any kind of sense of what was going on. The car had now stopped. Sam pulled on the lever to open the door, then as if to put her left hand down for support she rested it on George's knee, briefly smiling before leaving the car. George followed her out, then after locking the door with the remote key he followed Sam towards the lift.

***

Zivco and Toma, the other Serbian man, were mourning the loss of their respective brothers. The two of them and their respective brothers had been friends for many years. They had served together in the Serbian army under Slobodan Milosevic during the war that had commenced due to the breakup of Yugoslavia. After the conflict was over they had somehow managed to avoid the extensive criminal trials for war crimes that had been carried out. They and many of their now illegal army colleagues had rampaged across various Muslim villages committing murder and rape as they went. Somehow despite being also guilty of ethnic cleansing and other crimes against humanity they had never been brought to any kind of justice. After the war they had survived on a life of crime. The lawless streets were a haven for the two sets of brothers. They very quickly found the vulnerable, the weak, the people who couldn't fight back. Teenage daughters kidnapped and forced to work in filthy brothels. Money and goods taken from various families. A corrupt police force that didn't care as long as the bribes kept coming in.

Then a couple of years ago the net started to tighten on Zivco and Tomo and their brothers. The government and police were finally starting to clampdown. More and more war criminals were being found and tried. It was time for the two sets of brothers to move out. Their reputation had grown, now they were well known. Not only were the police and government forces after them but also other criminal gangs. Belgrade had been territorially divided. It was an unwritten law that encroachment onto another gang's area would result in the worst possible kind of revenge.

More so the Muslim population, who had been so horrendously persecuted while the world watched, were now starting to seek revenge. The two sets of brothers had decided like many others to move to England. Stories of free housing and endless state handouts were common knowledge throughout most of Europe and beyond. Sure enough, even to their surprise, they had been looked after, given rent free accommodation and more money to live on than the true British who had been born there.

All was well until they decided to want more. Old habits of taking what they wanted when they wanted, fuelled by the desire for an even better life than they had, took over their better nature. By now they had already acquired three brothels that were fronted by the guise of being massage parlours. Then they wanted more, more but without the work or effort. They had approached Bojan Duric thinking it would be easy. Simply get close to him, gain his trust, before stepping in and taking over his small empire. That done, they would then grow their business, be renowned and feared throughout London and beyond.

Now it had all changed. Zivco and Tomo, the other Serbian man, were mourning the loss of their respective brothers. Made more difficult because there was no funeral to arrange. No relatives to inform. No flowers to order. No bodies to identify. *The only grieving to be done was over a lone ear.*

Which was why they were in the back room of the *Gowlett Arms*. Looking suspiciously at three guys, brothers with strange accents, one of them in a wheelchair. Another guy in a wheelchair they already knew. They had met Mike Smith at Bojans house. Zivco and Tomo the two remaining brothers, although mourning the loss of their respective brothers were waiting for Bojan Duric and his sons.

***

Lisa could not believe what she was hearing. She was sitting opposite her supervisor, who was doing her best in her soft voice to explain that due to internal changes, one of the cases she was looking after was being allocated to another social worker. Lisa watched the lady sitting in front of her lying as she said that there was nothing wrong with the way she did her work, it was because of the other person being better qualified for the particular case in question. Lisa shook her head in despair as she spoke;

"Let me guess who we are talking about." The lady on the other side of the desk looked back at her.

"Meg, who is with a certain Yvette and Spike." Then voice raised; "Am I right?" Her supervisor put a hand in the air, a *don't shoot the messenger* gesture. She squirmed around her seat as she attempted to explain that it was normal procedure to move cases around from time to time, and that Lisa herself would be given a different case to look after. Lisa was fuming. It was clear that this was a result of her making a complaint to her boss a couple of days earlier. Lisa had felt at the time that something was not right. The guy did not want to hear what she was saying. Now this, not only was she more than worried about Meg, but there appeared to be something underhand occurring within this department.

"I want to see him now, the boss; I want to speak to him." The supervisor answered;

"I'm sorry Lisa that is not possible; he is in a meeting and will be for the rest of the day. The best thing you can do is get back to work and accept the decision." Lisa stood, tears in her eyes, she shouted;

"No! No! I won't do that! I want nothing more to do with this department or this job. There is something not right about the two who are looking after Meg and I don't want to be a part of it. Lisa stood and walked to the door before turning to face the supervisor. Voice low, controlled but angry;

"This doesn't end here. I will find out how the hell those two got on the preferred list of foster carers. Do not expect me to disappear quietly."

***

At the same time around two thousand miles away in a hotel near Manilva;

"Gay! What do you mean you are fuckin' gay?"

Sam had never felt so foolish in all her life. Half an hour earlier, after entering the hotel room she had looked seductively at George, smiling as she poured him a drink, telling him to make himself comfortable, that she wouldn't be long, she just needed to freshen up. As she soaped herself in the shower she felt like a naughty schoolgirl, it was the first time she could remember that she had played *the tart*. It had given her a warm feeling as she let the water cascade over her now shaking body. It gave her a feeling of satisfaction that she was about to get her own back on Roger for shagging that ugly bitch called Mina.

After drying herself, Sam had wrapped a fluffy towel around her naked body and walked back into the bedroom. She asked George if he was alright, explaining that her clean clothes were in the wardrobe, that she had forgotten to take then into the bathroom with her. Was it the mix of alcohol coupled with wanting to get one back on her husband that made Sam decide her next move? Maybe just a little devilment? Maybe the recent nightmares had a bearing on it. She didn't know which as she turned to George, smiling as she let the towel fall to the floor. She slowly walked towards her guest, still smiling. Wallowing in her nakedness. Moist between her legs with anticipation.

It was then that George had stood and announced his news.

"Really?" Sam had replied with a nervous smile, maybe waiting for a punch line, maybe waiting for him to undress and take her there and then. None of that happened;

"Really!" Slight anger in her voice this time. George stood impassive, looking at her face, ignoring her nakedness. Sam's smile had quickly disappeared as she grabbed the towel off the floor and ran passed George and into the bathroom. Sitting on the closed lid of the toilet she burst into tears.

George got up to leave, walking out of the door and closing it behind him; he was smiling and shaking his head at the same time;

"Did Roger really think he would fall for that one? It was clearly a test. Typical Roger Scott tactics." Driving back to Marbella George continued his thoughts;

"Shame really, Sam was fit, wouldn't have minded giving her one. Never mind there was always later." He was looking forward to escorting a nineteen year old Russian girl around Puerto Banus that evening. He smiled again; Helga was always keen to show her thanks after a night out, and he was always keen to accept them.

Back in the hotel room, Sam curled up on the bed hiding her face as she cried drunken tears into her pillow.

***

Assistant Chief Constable Ted Walton sat with his wife Olive in an office in the Kings College Hospital. He was worried, very worried. The previous day he had received a call from Dr. Gantar, who said that he had the results of his recent examination. He said that he would like to see him in person. He said that it might be a good idea if his wife also attended. Ted Walton was more than worried. The door had opened and Dr. Gantar had entered, but he was not alone, he was accompanied by the hospital administrator, a lady called Mrs. Graham. Now Ted was very worried. In true police tradition if there was bad news to be broken, there were always two people, often a lady to break it. Dr. Gantar spoke;

"Thank you for coming in Mr. Walton, and to you also Mrs. Walton. How are you feeling today?" Ted answered, irritated;

"We are not here to walk on eggshells Doctor. It is clearly bad news. Can we get on with it please?"

The Doctor looked at the policeman, then down at the sheets of paper on the desk in front of him. He took a quick sideways glance at Mrs. Graham, he cleared his throat. Then;

"I'm afraid it is bad news Mr. Walton. The X-rays show a lot of dark shadows around the entire inside of your stomach. I would like to conduct further tests but the initial results are showing advanced stages of cancer."

Ted slowly nodded his head; in the back of his mind he had known what he had was more than indigestion, more than an ulcer or two. He looked back at Dr. Gantar as his wife Olive reached across to squeeze his arm. He wanted to shout, he wanted to cry, he wanted to be angry with somebody, he wanted to wake up from a bad dream. He looked at the lady next to the doctor, then his wife, then at Dr. Gantar;

"How, how long have I got?"

"Without further tests it is difficult to tell, I would like to do an exploratory operation. It would mean going inside you to examine the full extent of the disease. But looking at the X-rays, I am quite sure that it has gone too far. I also fear that your body, bearing in mind the extent of the illness, would have difficulty handling an operation of that kind."

The Assistant Chief Constable slowly nodded his head;

"So best and worst case scenario, how long do you think I might have."

The doctor tried to look more sympathetic as he answered;

"I would suggest that without looking at the full extent of your illness, we cannot answer that question accurately; as I said earlier, I would like to explore every possibility. We can look at chemotherapy and other options, but to answer your question, best case six months, worst case a matter of weeks."

Ted Walton stood. His wife stood with him, he thanked the doctor, told him he would be in touch the following day. With a glance around the room he walked out.

Bojan said goodbye to his wife as he and his two eldest sons left the terraced house in Peckham Rye. They were on their way to a meeting in a pub called *The Gowlett Arms*. A meeting that he had called as a matter of urgency. There would be his three friends from Serbia there along with Zivco and the other Serb who were still mourning the loss of their brothers. They hadn't met yet but Bojan knew that as they were all Serbian there wouldn't be any problems. After all he was the boss. When he talked, they listened. Bojan expected Mike Smith and the three brothers from Liverpool to also be in attendance. It was time to get serious with Roger Scott, time to finish him for good. There would be no mistakes this time, he had enough people. People who all had reasons to want to do serious harm to Roger Scott. Bojan and his two eldest sons were on a mission as they strolled away from the terraced house in Peckham Rye without looking back.

If they had turned to look back maybe they would have noticed a van being driven slowly along the street, before stopping a short distance from the terraced house they had just left. Maybe they would also have seen a large man leaving the van and walking towards their house, pausing for more than a passing glance, more than a casual look, more than just taking in his surroundings before returning to the van. But they didn't, being on a mission they were focussed on the forthcoming meeting. The meeting where they hoped to seal the fate of Roger Scott.

A few miles away in a two up two down terraced house

199

on the edge of Brixton an argument was occurring. Meg pushed her little body back into the low chair, screaming in fear as Yvette and Spike shouted at each other;

"Send the little shit back, I can't stand the noise in here any longer. I can't hear the telly or the radio and I can't fuckin' sleep because of the row that git makes."

Yvette stood up, her face less than an inch from Spike;

"And what about the money? So she cries, so fuckin' what? You don't seem to notice or care when the cash lands do you? How are you going to buy your cider and weed, eh? Remember it was you that made me shag that foul breathed boss of social services so we could get on the list. It was you that said it was easy money; wipe her arse and nose now and again and that would be it. Any idea what it feels like being humped by a fat sweaty pervert like him? Do you know the things he makes me to do, things he wouldn't dare ask his wife to do? No you don't do you? Well it was your idea and I didn't put up with all that shit for nothing, we are keeping her until we are told, or I tell you different."

Spike threw the empty cider can he was holding across the room making little Meg scream louder. He stood, and with a glare in the frightened child's direction he stormed out of the room.

The fight had started without warning. Bojan and his sons had approached *The Gowlett Arms* when they noticed the three Muslim Serbians, Anto, Boro and Danko waiting for them outside. After brief greetings and shaking of hands they all went inside. Bojan first, he led them across to the bar. He ordered three bottles of lager and three bottles of water. He handed a bottle to each person and then headed to the door that connected the bar to the back room. Opening the door he glanced ahead and acknowledged Mike Smith, Zivco and Toma the other sad looking Serb. His gaze then went to the three strangers, one in a wheelchair, obviously the brothers from Liverpool. He stepped further into the room followed by Aco and Dorde. The six occupants of the room watched them enter followed by the three Serbians.

Then a stunned silence followed by a shout. That was when the bottle flew across the room smashing into the wall at the back after narrowly missing the two mourning Serbs. Bojan and his sons were knocked aside as Anto, Boro and Danko ran towards their former countrymen. Fists and bottles flying they mounted their attack as the rest of the men in the room looked on in shock. Zivco and Toma were quickly beaten to the floor, fists and feet raining down upon them. Bojan was the first to react grabbing Anto round the neck while shouting at the other two to stop.

By now occupants of the front bar had gathered at the door after hearing the commotion. The temporary manager was also shouting, telling anybody who would listen that the police had been called and they were on their way. Bojan shouted to Aco and Dorde to open the fire door at the back of the room, Aco reacted first by hitting the bar on the door and pushing it open. Bojan released his hold on Anto's neck and shoved him towards the door with a kick to his back. He then turned his attention to the next nearest attacker. He threw a fist to the back of the neck, which Boro did not see coming. It sent him sprawling though the still open door. By now the two recipients of the attack had got over the initial shock and were attempting to fight back. Bojan shouted at two of the Liverpool brothers to get in the middle of the fight. The

201

two of them jumped forward solidly and stood between the remaining three.

Bojan looked around the room; a broken table and shattered glass covered the floor. The fighting had stopped; now there was nothing more than hard stares between the attackers and the attacked. He looked at the crowd of people at the door, still looking into the back room. He ran towards them, kicking the door shut as they backed off. Then turning back to face the scene of the altercation he ushered everybody out and into the back alley, then away from the pub.

End of October 2012.

Adie was now sitting up in the chair that was screwed to the floor in the padded cell. She looked around at the four bare walls. She felt a little stronger, a little better. Her head still hurt from time to time, but now she felt the inclination to leave the bed and walk around room that she classed as her prison cell. The two strict looking nurses had been and gone after leaving her washed and humiliated. They had left some tattered magazines for her to read. She ignored them. Adie's thoughts were clearer now; although she couldn't remember everything that had led to her being in this awful place, she did remember being in her house with her daughter Meg and her cousin Sam, when some men had smashed their way in and taken both her and Sam away.

In the last few days a policewoman had visited three times. The first time appeared to be more of a social call. Being friendly, talking to Adie about nothing in particular, maybe how a neighbour or a relation would pass the time of day. On the second visit she had been a little less familiar, maybe a little more official. She had asked Adie what she could remember about how she finished up in hospital. Could she describe what had happened that day? Adie had told her bits that she could remember, before her head had started to hurt again. On the third visit Adie had opened up a little more. She told the policewoman that she had been taken to what looked like a block of flats, there were three, maybe four men, how she had tried to escape, then falling into something dark. Then nothing.

Adie looked up as she heard a key turning in the door. She remained seated, not moving as the door opened and a man she recognised put his head round smiling. Adie tried but found it difficult to return the smile as Dr. Ahmed entered the room.

"Adie, how are you feeling today?"

"Sad, lonely, depressed, when can I leave this horrible place? Why does nobody come to see me? Where is my baby Meg?"

The doctor sat down on the single bed facing Adie. He answered;

"You still need to be kept under observation Adie, you are still poorly, but I have been speaking with Head Nurse and she tells me that she is pleased with you. We will monitor your progress over the next few days and if it continues to improve we will have you moved to a general ward. From there we will get a better idea of when you will be ready to go home. Then it will mean daily visits from nurses who are qualified in this particular field to make sure there is no danger of relapse."

"And what about my baby?"

Dr. Ahmed hated lying, he hated even avoiding the truth, but he didn't know the answer. He forced a smile;

"Little Meg is safe and being looked after, soon as you are a little better I will arrange for you to see her."

For the first time in what seemed like months Adie managed to relax.

August 2012 Present day.

In a terraced house in Peckham Rye eight men stood around a dining room table. Three Muslim Serbs glared angrily at the grieving Zivco and Toma, who faced them across the table, their faces battered and bruised. In between them stood Bojan and his two sons. Mike Smith and the three brothers from Liverpool had been told to wait in the lounge at the front of the house. After leaving *"The Gowlett Arms"* and the sound of police sirens nearing Bojan had ushered them along a series of back lanes and alleys until they had eventually reached the back of the house in Peckham Rye. He now looked slowly at each of his former countrymen as he spoke;

"What fuck was that about?" No response. Bojan stormed around the table until he was face to face with Anto, Boro and Danko who had started the fight;

"I ask again, what the fuck that about." Anto pointed across the table then answered;

"Those two bastards and their brothers burned our houses while we still inside, some of us got out, but my elderly mother didn't. They then hounded us and the remaining members of our families until we were forced to leave. It was lucky for us that you asked us to come to England Bojan. We were happy in Serbia but them and those like them murdered many of our friends because we have different religious belief." He looked briefly at Bojan and then his two comrades. Finally back at the two across the table. Then;

"I never forget faces, the way they laughed as they threw

the petrol bombs through our windows."

Bojan looked at each person in turn, finally stopping at the two accused;

"This true?" Nothing. He shouted. *"This true?"*

Zivco shuffled his feet, then answered quietly;

"It was a war Bojan, we had no choice. We were under the orders of Milosevic himself."

Anto shouted;

"War was over, you did it for enjoyment, you did it because we are Muslim. No other reason."

"We were following orders. we were told what we had to do."

"Shut it all of you." Bojan turned to the Muslims;

"You three stay here." Then to Zivco and Toma; "Come with me."

***

Roger Scott smiled, shaking his head. The two detectives who had turned up unannounced with what Roger knew were flimsy excuses for some kind of trumped up charge were wasting their time. He had refused to talk to them. Refused to answer any questions. Other than telling them that he didn't need his solicitor he said very little, apart from telling Jeff to sit down and keep quiet. It wasn't the right time to rip their fuckin' heads off. To keep calm, his turn would come.

Now he was sitting in an interview room in Camberwell Police Station. Although they hadn't charged him with any crime they said that he had been asked to accompany them to help with their enquiries, as he was a suspect in a recent murder case.

Detective Inspector Terry Thompson eyed him closely, so this is the infamous Roger Scott. This was the guy who the

Assistant Chief Constable had ordered them to bring in. He then turned to D.C. Farrell. A nod of his head. Farrell pressed the start button on the recording equipment. He spoke:

"For the benefit of the recording D.I. Thompson, D.C. Farrell and Roger Scott are present. Mr. Scott was asked if he required a solicitor, an offer that he refused."

He turned his attention to Roger;

"We are investigating the kidnap and murder of a Denzil York. We think he may have been in the *Vegas Slots* gaming salon on the same night he was killed. The same gaming salon which is owned by yourself."

Roger nodded. Then;

"Keep thinking; you're doing alright so far."

"Do you remember the deceased being in the gaming salon?"

Roger thought for a moment, then;

"Don't remember seeing any dead bodies in there."

Farrell continued;

"Mr. Scott, can you tell me where you were on the evening of July 10th between the hours of 6pm and midnight?"

Roger answered; "Which year?"

D.I. Thompson interjected;

"2012. You are not doing yourself any favours by attempting to be smart."

"As it happens I was in my gaming salon, assessing the damage that had been caused by some young vandals."

"How do you know they were young?"

"There were no wheelchair or Zimmer frame marks on the floor." The two detectives glanced at each other.

"Can anybody verify the fact that you were there?"

"Yeah, two of my employees, Tom and Jeff." *Good luck with that one thought Roger.*

"Why do you think they targeted your premises?"

"You tell me, you're the detective."

Detective Inspector Thompson leaned over the table, his eyes locked on Roger's;

"You are going to make this very difficult for yourself Mr. Scott. It will be better for you if you gave us your full assistance." Roger smiled. He leaned closer, eyes still unflinching. He spoke;

"Ok then, for the benefit of the recording Roger Scott is about to give his full assistance and come clean with D.I. Thompson and D.C. Farrell." The two detectives glanced at each other then looked back at Roger. He continued;

"I have no idea who kidnapped and murdered Denzil York, I have no idea who wrecked my gaming salon. I have no idea who firebombed my nightclub. I have no idea who attempted to kidnap my wife. As it is very clear that you two and the rest of your outfit don't have any idea either, it looks like we are all in the same shit. So unless there is anything else, I will leave you gentlemen to it."

Thompson answered;

"Mr. Scott I would respectfully request that you stay seated and answer our questions."

Roger smiled again, he shook his head again. The detectives persisted with their questions.

The game of cat and mouse, or in this case mouse and cat continued for another hour, every question that Roger was asked, was answered either with a question back or a sarcastic comment. He continued to antagonise them by sometimes keeping quiet, and doing nothing other than smiling, with a slight shake of his head. Roger knew they were speculating, hoping for him to say something that would back him into a corner, no way out, guilty as charged. It was never going to happen. He had heard enough.

Roger stood up; he looked down at the two detectives. They had got the message; they knew that they were not going to get anywhere, not on this occasion. D.I. Thompson leaned across the table and switched off the recording equipment. He glanced at Farrell. Then;

"We will be in touch, but don't think this is the end of it, and now that we are off the record, I will tell you that I think you are a murdering bastard, and mark my words we will get you."

Roger Scott looked back at them both in turn, another smile, another shake of his head. Then;

"And now that we are off the record, I will tell you that I think you two are a pair of clueless fuckers, who are dancing on the end of somebody's string. Good luck." He walked out.

***

Sam had checked out of her hotel and was now sitting in a taxi as it took her to Malaga airport. She was in a daze as the Andalucía Hills rolled past the speeding car. Sam hadn't slept at all the previous night, once the effects of the alcohol had worn off she felt more foolish and embarrassed than she had done previously. She was giving herself a mental beating. How the hell could she have done what she did? Why did she do what she did? Even if George had taken full advantage of the situation and had taken her to bed, how would she have felt this morning? She was a married woman! It was a situation that she had never experienced before.

As Sam had lain awake through the night she had tried to make sense of her actions. It was true that she didn't want to be in Spain, but that was not a good reason to throw herself at George and behave like the local whore.

What must he be thinking? Would he tell Roger what had happened? Sam put her head in her hands as the reality of the previous evening sank in even more.

Now sitting in the airport lounge she wondered if because of her recent behaviour it was all her own fault? Roger had sent her to Spain against her will. Sam had put two and two together and come up with Mina. Maybe the jealousy had clouded her judgement. Sam cast her mind back to where it had started to go wrong, when her life had changed so dramatically. The four guys waiting for them outside the Silk Road Chinese Restaurant. The arson attack on her nightclub that happened almost at the same time. Was that Roger's fault? He didn't appear to know much about it. Certainly Sam had blamed him for the murder of her beloved Penny. Maybe none of it was Roger's fault, maybe she just wanted to lash out, take her problems out on somebody. Sam then thought about the kidnap of herself and Adie, again Roger's fault? Did he know? Surely not, he would have done something about it. Stopped it before it had happened.

Sam was now thinking about her life prior to the recent events; for three years her life had been idyllic. A big house in the country and an apartment in south London. Money never a problem. Penny, her beautiful horse, holidays, wining and dining at the finest restaurants, but most of all a loving and caring husband.

Now the same husband had packed her off to Spain for her own safety, made sure she was looked after while she was there. Maybe he knew that George was gay, maybe he had arranged it that way so she would avoid any unwanted attention. Yes, that's what it was; Roger was only concerned for her wellbeing. Sam wiped away a tear as she glanced up at the electronic information board that told her to proceed to gate 33.

As the plane cruised at 35,000 feet over the Bay of Biscay Sam felt a little better. It had dawned on her that she hadn't told Roger about her impending return to London. She had left the Manilva hotel in such a hurry and embarrassed state of mind, that it had never entered her head to inform anybody. She knew now that it was all her own fault, her lovely caring husband only had her safety in mind when he sent her to Spain. She had witnessed the violence at first hand, it was a serious situation and Roger was right when he said the police were not doing anything about it. Sam relaxed back in her seat and sipped a Gin and Tonic; she smiled for what seemed like the first time in weeks. She now realised that she had the best husband in the world and now she was on her way back to tell him exactly that. She would surprise him, and then make it up to him.

At the same time in a terraced house in Peckham Rye, Bojan Duric sat at the dining room table facing Anto, Boro and Danko, his three Muslim friends. He was explaining that he would tell the other two Serbians to leave. That they were no longer needed. He apologised to the three men. He said if he had known the circumstances he would never have got involved with the brothers. The three Muslin Serbs accepted that Bojan was telling them the truth. They said that they were happy to carry on working for him. It was back to business, back to get their revenge on Roger Scott. Bojan had told them it was time to get serious about killing Scott, but first they had to bring him into the open. He was proving illusive since the night at the Silk Road Chinese Restaurant and the incident outside of the snooker hall.

They had listened as he laid out his plan; they were to return to Roger Scott's mansion in Kent. Bojan didn't care if anybody was in the house or not. He wanted it burned to the ground. House and stables, nothing left. Guaranteed to bring them the response they wanted. After an hour Bojan watched them leave. He then opened the door to the lounge at the front of the house before entering to greet Mike Smith, the three brothers from Liverpool and Zivco and Toma, the two grieving Serbians.

Bojan studied the six men in front of him. Anto, Boro and Danko, his three Muslim friends had now left the terraced house in Peckham Rye. They were bound for a mansion in Kent to carry out the mission Bojan had set them. Despite meeting two of the many who had persecuted them and their families back in Serbia, Bojan thought that they appeared to be happy to continue their work for him.

Now as he stood in the front room of the small house in Peckham Rye looking at the seated men, he shook his head. Two of them in wheelchairs, two of them who fought like girls back at the pub, and the last two with strange accents who had done very little. He spoke;

"You can all go; I don't need any of you."

Zivco and Toma looked at each other, this was unexpected, they had thought that Bojan would have told the Muslims to go. After all, it was their opinion that everything bad and evil in the world emanated from them and their Koran.

They had talked earlier, their original plan was to get close to Bojan, to be trusted, to watch how his empire operated, then remove him and take it over for their own. It hadn't gone to plan; both of them had lost a brother they loved, in the most brutal way that they could only imagine. Only one ear left for both of them to grieve over. They decided to stay close to Bojan, to stick with the original plan. They felt that they owed their dead brothers that much. Toma thought quickly;

"Why Bojan? We are close to what we set out to achieve, why stop now?"

"Who said anything about stopping? This will never stop until Scott is dead. Now on I do it myself. Look at you all. Two cripples, two idiots who can't look after their own massage parlours. By now whoever did damage to them should be dead. In this business we rely on credibility and respect. You two have none; even both of your stupid brothers could not perform a simple task without getting killed."

Zivco jumped up, opened his mouth to protest, to get angry. Bojan turned to him, shoulders back, square, solid. He stopped Zivco with a wave of his hand then continued;

"Nothing left but an ear. Yes, very sad, but how much do you think they told them before they were killed? You are nothing but a liability. So maybe you all fuck off now."

Bojan opened the lounge door. At the same time Aco, his eldest son opened the front door then watched as they all left. Zivco was the last to go. He turned to Bojan as he passed him, he pointed a finger;

"Maybe you think it ends here; *but now you have more than one enemy.*"

Bojan didn't answer. His eyes followed the two wheelchairs and the rest of them as they left the garden and went through the gate. With a shake of his head he closed the front door.

***

Big Steve, as he was known in the small town near Durham before moving to London, sat in a small scruffy internet cafe. He had paid his two pounds for half an hour use of the battered laptop that was housed in a small cubicle. After days of studying every copy of every three year old local newspaper he could find on line, he had built up a picture in his mind of what happened in the nightclub known as *"Sam's"* three years ago. Some of the papers had acquired stills from the CCTV footage, that had covered every minute of the night a detective had been shot dead, and Steve's friend had disappeared. One paper had given a pictorial blow by blow account from the shooting to the aftermath. Steve zoomed in on every grainy photograph until he could picture the full series of events. His friend appeared to be crawling then crouching, then making his way to the back of the room and towards the emergency door. That was the last picture of him. Steve then moved onto the days after the event. The main stories were covering the sad loss of a promising detective; apparently shot twice by one of his own armed police response units.

Steve continued, searching every page of every paper which covered the story over the coming days. Eventually a small piece gave a mention to a body being found mutilated on some waste ground near the Thames that was popular with dog walkers. It was thought to be a man known as Mal who the police had wanted to speak to concerning the shooting in *"Sam's"* nightclub a few days earlier.

Steve sat back in his chair. That was it, nothing more. The only mention of his friend, the man who had saved his life, was stuck in a small paragraph at the bottom of page eight in a local rag. He switched off the laptop and headed back to the rented bedsit.

Anto, Boro and Danko, the three remaining Serbian Muslim friends, never gave much thought to Vlado, their

213

missing comrade. They had been unconscious or in too much pain as they lay on the pavement outside of the Silk Road Chinese Restaurant to notice what had happened to him, but as he was the only one of them who could not speak English they knew that despite any amount of torture administered, he could not divulge who they were.

Now, after several weeks had passed they assumed he was dead. A casualty of the war that they were waging against Roger Scott. A war that he had started and they were about to finish. They had accepted the apology from Bojan and understood that he would have had no idea that the Serbian brothers had killed their families. They were happy to carry on working for him and finish what they had started.

The three had been up early, washed and said their morning prayers. Asked Allah for guidance and to watch over them today and all days. Now as they sat in a blue Ford with blacked out windows, not half a mile away from Roger Scott's Kent mansion they went over their plan again.

It would be quite easy. Over the previous two days they had been doing a reconnoitre of the surrounding area. Every bridle path, every country lane explored. All exit routes out of the village of Cliffe covered to become more than familiar with. Two of them had visited before, in the dead of night. They hadn't stayed long, just time enough to open a stable door and release a crossbow bolt. Now all three were there waiting for darkness to fall.

The plan was quite straight forward. They had not seen anybody other than an old lady leave or enter the house in the time they had been there. It appeared she went to bed around 10 pm. They would wait, and then take three 20 litre containers of petrol to the front door. Two would be emptied through the letterbox; the third would then be poured in a line from the door to the stable block. There had been little or no rain for the past ten days. The ancient stables, like many of the older buildings in the area were made of wood. Very dry wood. The remaining petrol would be tipped around and on the stable door. The fuel would be ignited mid way between the two buildings, allowing a sheet of flame to reach the house and the stable at the same time. The petrol soaked rag that would be hung out of the letter box, on the door of the main building, would quickly drop its deadly cargo onto the inside of the house, and onto the 40 plus litres of petrol that would be pooled on the floor. They went over the plan again, and again. They were happy, it would be straightforward. They waited.

The suspended P.C. Jenkins looked lazily across the lounge at the source of the noise that had disturbed his afternoon nap. The vibrating phone sat on the coffee table near the window. He let it ring; he wasn't in the mood to talk to anybody. He had been sitting in the lounge for three days now. Sad, upset, maybe regretful, he wasn't sure which. Three days ago he had told his wife about the disciplinary meeting with his superiors, about him being in serious trouble, about how he knew he had no future in the police force. They would sack him for sure.

Despite her protests he had refused to answer her questions as to why he was in such a predicament. In the ensuing row he had found out his wife's true feelings towards him, how she should have listened to her mother. How she had the choice of suitors, she had only chosen him because he was a policeman, and now he wasn't. Three days ago his wife had left him, not saying where she was going. He had watched her go without protest.

Now, after three days of being sad, upset, and maybe regretful, he sat in the lounge contemplating his next move. He thought about his wife. Deep down he wasn't bothered that she had left, in fact he was more than happy to see the back of the moaning bitch. There were no children to worry about. Their sex life had been virtually nonexistent over the last few years. It was not very exciting before that.

An hour had gone by before he glanced at the phone again, then slowly lifted himself out of the armchair and moved towards the coffee table and the offending mobile. Retrieving the missed call he recognised Roger Scott's number as it flashed across the screen. P.C. Jenkins gazed at it. He began to sweat, he wasn't sure why. Fear perhaps? Anger maybe? After all, it was because of Scott, *because of one man* that he was in this mess. *He hated Roger Scott.* He looked at the number, his finger moved towards the return call icon. He hesitated, then taking another mouthful of whisky he pressed it to ring the cause of his problems.

Mrs. Cowens had known Roger Scott for many years. When Roger had first bought the mansion in Kent he had advertised for a live in housekeeper. Mrs. Cowens who had been widowed since the 1960's, and lived in nearby Cliffe Woods, applied for the position immediately. Roger thought she was perfect and offered her the job there and then.

The mansion had been built around one hundred and fifty years earlier. It had been renovated many times; the most recent being after Roger had bought it. It had been built on an elevated position to take advantage of the surrounding fields of flat landscape. On a clear day it was possible to see for many miles from the upstairs. Now after what had happened to Sam's beautiful horse Penny, a couple of weeks ago, Mrs. Cowens spent a lot of her time gazing out of the upstairs windows. Southend on Sea was visible from the back of the house, the Q.E.2 Bridge at Dartford from side window. From the front where she spent most of her time it was possible to see across to the A2 road that ran from the M25 to Canterbury. Although Penny being killed had been a frightening experience Mrs. Cowens did not scare easily. She was happy to remain in Roger's employ and continue to keep the house in good order.

Unbeknown to Roger, during the 1950's prior to his death, Frank Cowens had been one of the most feared gangsters in north London. Mrs. Cowens had seen a lot over the years, from gang warfare to kidnappings and worse. She had moved to the Kent countryside after being widowed, to start a new life where she would be relatively unknown.

She often thought about the old days; some were violent, but most of them were happy. Which was why there was maybe something inbuilt or inbred that made her telephone Roger, to report that a blue car had been driving near the entrance to the house very slowly, on more than one occasion, in the space of the last two days. The occupants appeared to be taking a great interest in the property. Roger had immediately despatched Johnny and Harry to the house and also Mary to tour the local area. On their arrival they hid their car behind the stable, next to the ancient tractor.

Now they stood next to Mrs. Cowens behind a lace curtain in an upstairs bedroom at the front of the house. Very soon they too saw the blue car, a Ford. They told Mrs. Cowens to pack an overnight case. Johnny then contacted her daughter and said that as a reward for her hard work and loyalty her mother was to be treated to a Spa Hotel for the night, and a meal at the Don Vincenzo restaurant in the Dickensian High Street of Rochester. It was a favourite of Roger Scott's housekeeper.

Roger's country house was covered and monitored by strategically placed CCTV cameras. Johnny and Harry watched the television screen as Boro and Danko, two of the Muslim Serbians alighted from the blue Ford. They noticed that another guy remained in the car. The screen was in the lounge at the front of the country mansion near the village of Cliffe. They had been watching all day. Two hours ago they had received a phone call from Mary, who had been sitting in the car park of the local pub known as *The Six Bells*. She had reported seeing a blue Ford with three guys inside, passing more than once, as if they were checking the area, getting to know the layout of the roads and lanes around the vicinity. She recognised them from the pictures Roger had taken of the four unconscious men outside of the Silk Road Chinese Restaurant some weeks earlier. She was convinced it was them, no doubt in her mind.

Back at the mansion Johnny and Harry continued their surveillance as the car slowly pulled away. Switching the screen to show a different camera angle they saw the blue Ford park around fifty metres away, along the adjacent lane and out of sight of the house. The two guys who had left the car earlier were now carrying what looked like three plastic containers, as they walked quickly towards the front door of the country mansion near Cliffe.

Johnny stood, and with a prearranged gesture to Harry he moved back through the lounge, through the dining area, through the kitchen and quietly out of the back door. Walking quickly he circumnavigated the house, to find

218

himself at the side of the stable block. Now he looked at the two men as they approached the front door. He watched as they poured the contents of two of the plastic containers through the letter box before stuffing a wet looking rag into the same orifice. He continued watching as they then began to spread their deadly liquid in a line, from the front door towards the stable block.

Inside the house Harry had quietly placed a fire extinguisher that he had been holding onto the floor. He then moved a large aluminium open container slowly away from the front door, being careful not to spill any of what was now clearly petrol, onto the wooden floor. It had been left close to the door, below the letterbox. Due to its size and shape it had caught almost all of the petrol as it had spilled through and into the hall. Moving slowly he transported it through the lounge, passed the dining area, and into the kitchen. Then out of the open door before placing it on the cobbles in the back yard. Harry quickly ran back to the front door, he picked up the fire extinguisher and waited.

The two Serbians were within five metres of the stable block. They had left a very clear trial of petrol, which was pooling in the cobbles in a line from the house. Such was their concentration on the job in hand that they failed to see a large figure moving in the darkness from the side of the stable. Boro turned as he noticed a shadow on the ground at the side of him, then dropped to his knees as something hard and cold hit his temple. Danko turned to his friend, only to walk into a backhand blow from the same weapon. The front door opened and Harry ran towards the commotion carrying the fire extinguisher. Noticing the two prone figures on the floor and Johnny standing over them he slowed, and then retraced his steps, whilst releasing the contents of his burden onto the pools of petrol, rendering them harmless. The two injured men groaned on the ground as Johnny and Harry made sure the area was safe from any danger from the petrol.

Sitting in a blue Ford, parked around fifty metres away, along the adjacent lane and out of sight of the house, Anto, the third Serbian friend of Bojan checked his watch. He looked over his shoulder to see if his comrades were returning, to see if there were any signs of flames. He saw nothing. He would not worry just yet. His friends were competent. The operation had been well planned. The mansion was empty apart from a little old lady housekeeper. It was straightforward enough to burn the whole place, including the stable to the ground, no witnesses, only one casualty, an old woman. Who cares.

Six miles away in the Don Vincenzo restaurant, in the Dickensian High Street of Rochester, Mrs. Cowens and her daughter Sharon smiled contentedly as they touched glasses to toast Mr. Scott.

The petrol ignited with a whoosh as the flames shot skywards lighting up the darkness all around. The screams of the two burning men were quickly stifled by the heat and smoke then shock. Johnny and Harry stood back and watched. They had questioned the two men; who had confirmed that it was someone called Bojan who had sent them. The information was extracted quite easily as the remaining petrol was poured over them. They begged for mercy before being reminded that the old lady in house would have been shown none. They then shouted at Johnny and Harry, calling them infidels, and how they would rot in hell. Harry had smiled as he told them they had nothing to worry about; after all, they were now going to enjoy loads of virgins and wine. It didn't appear to appease them.

Anto sat in the car fifty metres away and waited. He had seen the flames, allowed a smile, job done. His friends would be back very soon. He had started to be concerned a few minutes later when there was little sign of the house and stable block being on fire, in fact, instead of the flames increasing in size they appeared to be diminishing. He started the car in readiness and waited. Two minutes turned into five, he was getting increasingly concerned. Then after looking again into his rear view mirror, he noticed two figures moving towards the car. He felt relieved that his two friends had returned, then dismay as the car door was wrenched open and he was dragged from his seat to the ground outside. Fists and boots rained upon him until he was a bloodied mess. He felt himself being dragged to his feet and thrust back inside the car, into the driving seat. A large head leaned towards him;

"Tell Bojan, Roger Scott knows every move he makes before he makes it. Your two mates are toast. Now fuck off."

Johnny and Harry walked back towards the house as Anto struggled to select first gear. They turned to see the car splutter slowly away.

***

Assistant Chief Constable Ted Walton and his wife Olive had spent every available moment together over the weekend, they had tried not to talk about the hospital consultation. They had looked at the family photo albums, then reminisced about the day they had first met. Ted was captain of an exclusive golf club. On that hot July day he had led his team to victory in the County Championship. Olive was lady captain of one of the opposing teams. After

221

the presentation of trophies and the usual photographs, Ted had found himself sitting next to Olive at the captain's table, they had chatted, found out that they were both single. They had been together ever since.

Sitting on the settee holding hands, they talked about, amongst other things their favourite holiday destinations, favourite restaurants, TV programmes. They tried not to, but inevitably their conversation somehow steered itself back to Ted's illness. Without wanting to argue, Olive had suggested that her husband should speak with the consultant first thing Monday morning, have further tests. Radio and Chemotherapy even the exploratory operation that had been suggested. Ted said nothing. He knew Olive was aware that he disliked going to see doctors or dentists. What his wife didn't know was that it was more than a dislike; it was pure fear, not a phobia, he was petrified. He nodded his head in her direction, tried to smile as if he was taking in what she was saying. Ted wasn't taking anything in; he had already made his mind up. He had reached a decision.

As he lay in bed later that night Ted Walton was alone with his thoughts. He had already decided, he had done some research. Google may be a wonderful way of gaining information and knowledge, a way to find out almost anything on any subject in the world thought Ted, but now he was wishing he hadn't bothered to type in his symptoms. He had thought about only searching for the facts on how he had felt a few months ago. Maybe before his illness became too serious, before it had taken hold. He knew he would have been fooling himself. He knew he had to find out the true extent of the terrible disease, that had taken over his body uninvited. He could only find out by looking at the experiences and expertise of others.

Ted Walton now accepted that he was dying, pure and simple, *fait accompli*. Ted had also decided that in the remaining time he had left, while he still had a little quality of life, he would finish what he had started; the Assistant Chief Constable knew he was going to die, to once again meet his son, *his secret son*. Now he also knew that he was going to see that Roger Scott was dead before him.

***

The following morning on New Cross Road the traffic was unusually quiet. Roger had arrived at his snooker hall earlier than expected. He had arranged for Johnny and Harry to meet him there, to brief him as to what had happened the previous evening. Now he sat in the back room of the Pot Black, with Jeff standing behind him and Tom by the door. They all listened as Johnny explained the details of the previous night at Roger's mansion near the village of Cliffe, in Kent. He had been right to have the two of them stationed there. Roger knew he had inflicted enough damage on Bojan Duric to create some kind of response. It hadn't taken as long as he thought it might have. Job well done, it would be highly unlikely that they would make another attempt on his house. Did he think that Bojan would go this far, to attempt to burn his home to the ground? Maybe, maybe not, but it had told Roger that the Serbian was now getting serious.

After the car with the third Muslim Serb had driven away, Johnny and Harry had dragged what was left of the burned corpses to the back of the stable block and buried them in a deep grave. The old tractor with the large shovel shaped attachment on the back was still reliable. Roger told Johnny and Harry to take a few days off, disappear for a little while. They were happy. They had a package of cash each, as they left the room. Roger turned to Jeff;

"You two sure you got the right house in Peckham Rye?"

"Yes boss, we saw the Bojan guy leaving and entering a few times with his two sons, no mistake, and one was limping, using a walking stick."

"Okay, so the prick wants to play with fire, here's what we are going to do."

At the aging dining room table in a terraced house in Peckham Rye, Anto, the one remaining Muslim was shaking with shock; dried blood covered his face and hands. He was doing his best not to cry. Bojan stood over him, Aco and Dorde sat opposite. Anto explained what had happened at the mansion in Kent, the one near the village of Cliffe, on the Hoo peninsula. He thought it had gone to plan. They had watched the house and planned their route of escape. The other two, Boro and Danko had left the car and carried the petrol towards the house. Anto had waited as agreed. He then watched through the car window and saw the flames shoot skywards. He started the engine only to be ambushed by two big guys who beat him up, then told him his friends were dead and Roger Scott was responsible.

Bojan wanted to shout at him, tell him he was an idiot, tell him they should have planned it better. He didn't get the chance. Anto stood shakily; he gripped the chair back for support. He spoke, slowly, carefully;

"I am leaving Bojan, I have had enough. All of my friends are dead. You have tried to get me to work with the very people who tortured our families back in Serbia. What they did can never be forgiven or forgotten." He looked away then back;

224

"The Scott man is too clever. You should leave it alone before you all die." He walked towards the door and opened it before turning back to Bojan and his sons. Bojan spoke;

"Ok. That's what you want. You go back to Serbia and a life of persecution."

"No. I am Muslim; there is nothing for me there. No friends, and my family are all dead. I am going to Finsbury Park Mosque. I hear there are people there who help me. I will get my revenge on all infidels very soon." He walked out closing the door behind him.

Bojan let him go, maybe it was for the best, Anto looked broken, of little use. It was not a problem; maybe it was better without him. Roger Scott had pushed things too far. Now there was somebody Bojan needed to meet. He turned to his two sons;

"Come with me, we have things to do." He shouted a goodbye to his wife as they all left.

***

With a relative density of 0.63 when compared with air, natural gas, unlike propane tends to rise in the event of a leak, until it meets a solid mass, then the area would start to fill with the deadly noxious fumes. When the same area, if contained, was full, it would not take much of a spark or flame to ignite the gas with devastating consequences.

Only in this case it wasn't a leak as such. At a terraced house in Peckham Rye an oven door had been left open, and the gas control was on its highest setting; all four gas rings on the hob were also turned on to their maximum, as was the eye level grill. None of them were lit. Due to the age of the oven there was no thermocouple fitted, thus allowing the gas to escape at its full capacity. Very quickly it was filling the room from the ceiling downwards. With the curtains being closed and both doors being shut, and with towels against the bottom of them, the room was almost completely sealed.

Bojan's wife, Mila, sat on one of the dining room chairs, oblivious to the obnoxious smell. She was also not aware of the long smouldering cigar that was in an ashtray, on the floor at the opposite side of the room to the kitchen area, at the furthest point from the oven.

When the doorbell had rung half an hour earlier, Mila had happily answered it, assuming that it was her husband or one of her sons, returning to the house for something they had maybe forgotten. They had only left ten minutes earlier saying that they wouldn't be long, just a little bit of business to attend to. Instead she saw two large men, one of whom pushed her violently back into the hall of her house as the door was still half open.

A few minutes earlier after watching Bojan and his two sons leave the house, Jeff and Tom had casually strolled from the van to the front door, checking that nobody was watching them before pressing the doorbell. Then as Mila, Bojan's wife answered it one of them had kicked the door forcefully. She had staggered back as they quickly followed her into the house before closing the door behind them. Tom had held the stricken woman to a chair as Jeff pressed a chloroformed cloth over her nose and mouth until she had passed out.

Now Mila sat on the same chair in the dining room come kitchen of a terraced house in Peckham Rye, still unconscious. One of the big guys had lit the cigar and then placed it in an ashtray. Due to its length the cigar would stay smouldering for around half an hour. More than enough time for the room to fill with the escaping gas. To add fuel to the impending fire, Jeff had removed the two, one pint glass bottles from his pocket and spread their contents around the room. They had then moved quickly as the smell of petrol mixed with the fumes of the escaping gas.

The explosion, when it happened sometime later was heard as far away as the River Thames and beyond.

Rodovan, Bojan's youngest son had finished work for the day. He had left the office and after two Tube journeys and then a short walk through Peckham Rye, he had made his way up the garden path and inserted his key into the front door. He didn't get the chance to turn it before the door had flown outwards and into him, knocking him backwards, and taking a large piece of his head several yards across the front garden. The house windows were also blown out of their frames, showering him with masonry and shattered shards of glass. The houses next door and opposite also lost their windows. Inside the dining room come kitchen the ceiling came crashing down as the contained blast found the weakest point of release.

The fire that raged throughout the house would leave little or no evidence as to what had happened, other than that some sort of tragic gas leak had occurred. Within minutes the acrid black smoke could be seen from as far away as the parked cars queuing on the QE2 Bridge, to the sightseers at the top of the Shard in central London. From the end of the street Jeff and Tom stood back from a bus stop they had been standing in, and watched as the flames raged fiercely through the gaps in the house where the door and windows had once been. They then got into the van and slowly pulled away.

***

Sam dozed on the plane that was about to enter British airspace. She was happy in her thoughts about Roger, she had realised that it was she who had been wrong, she had been selfish, not thinking of anybody else's problems, just her own. Now she was looking forward to seeing the look on her lovely husbands face when she surprised him. Sam felt better, she relaxed a little.

Around 150 miles away Roger Scott sat in his London penthouse. He was in deep thought. He had just left the bedroom after an hour's exertion with Mina. It was the first time he had indulged in sex with her in his own apartment. He was normally happy to bend her over his desk at the call centre when the need took him, Mina was always happy to accommodate. Now with the attention from the police and the attempted attack on his Kent mansion he had decided to stay away from the call centre and the snooker hall for a day or two. He had told Mina to get a taxi to the penthouse in order to give him an update on how busy the flats had been; which girls were not paying their way, which girls would require a visit from Jeff to deliver a reminder. With all that had been going on around him he had somewhat ignored his usual business activities.

Mina went through each girl in turn; almost all of them were showing a good return. That done, Mina had smiled, a little embarrassed, as she asked if she could have a tour of his penthouse. She had never seen such luxury before. Roger was happy to oblige, why not? It wasn't as if anybody would find out. Mina knew better than to divulge any sort of information that concerned Roger Scott.

He showed her the kitchen area first. Mina stared at the modern appliances, thinking that she had no idea what some of them were or what they did. Then smiling as she noticed that the kitchen contained a separate glass fronted fridge that housed only Champagne. They then moved through the door and into the lounge. Mina stood in awe as she gazed out of the large picture window, taking in the views across the City of London. It was a sight that she would be happy to look at all day. Then moving through to the bedroom, she looked at the bed; she had never seen one so big. The room itself was larger than the whole of her flat. Then a questionable look as she noticed the Jacuzzi, through the open curtains that led into an adjoining room. To her it looked like a giant bath, but why were there little holes everywhere?

Roger glanced at his watch then decided to show Mina how it all worked. He poured her a glass of bubbly as they waited for the bath to fill. Smiling warmly at her Roger suggested she undress and try sitting in it. Mina loved it; she lay naked with various bubbles caressing various parts of her body. Roger had then joined her with more Champagne before they finished up in the giant bed.

Now as Mina dozed it crossed Roger's mind that he was still married, that he was still Sam's husband. He had given little or no thought to his wife since she had reluctantly agreed to go to Spain. He stood, leaving Mina sleeping in the bed; he then wandered across to the window. Gazing out at the London landmarks it dawned on him that he hadn't really missed Sam. He had thought a few weeks ago about the fact that he was bored with his life. Maybe Sam was the reason; she was a different person to him. She loved the foreign holidays, going to the theatre, the nights out. Roger thought at first that he was also enjoying the change in lifestyle. Then the boredom set in.

At first he ignored it, maybe swept away with the excitement of being married to a pretty young wife. It had never happened to him before; women were there to be used, to work in his brothels, to accommodate him with the odd freebie when it was required. Roger had never been in love before, never known love, didn't know what it felt like. Sitting back down he poured himself another drink. Still thinking; was he or had he really been in love? Now with Sam being away from him he wasn't sure. Had he enjoyed the last three years? Yes, maybe, well most of it, maybe some of it. So what was the problem? Roger analysed what had happened recently, not just since Sam had gone to Spain, but the preceding weeks that led up to him deciding to send her there.

It dawned on him. He smiled. It was staring him in the face. *He was Roger Scott.* The man who was never meant to fall in love, the man who was never meant to be happily married, the man who was never meant to settle down. Yes being married to Sam had been good. But not in the same way as the last few weeks, and not as good as his life had been before. Roger Scott was the man who had started with nothing. He had stolen, conned and killed to get what he wanted, it was what he was good at. Not for being the Lord of the manor. He missed the thrill of the chase. Being actively involved in the everyday running of his business. Being one step ahead of the police, the taxman, his rivals and his enemies.

Mina slept on as Roger sat in his penthouse waiting for P.C. Jenkins to return his call. He knew the useless, clueless waste of space would do sooner rather than later.

When it happened a little while later, Roger got a surprise. The voice on the other end was not the usual grovelling wimp of a constable, far from it. What Roger heard was an angry man, shouting that his life was in ruins, that his wife had left him, that he had been suspended from his police duties and would surely be dismissed. He had been humiliated and ridiculed, beaten up and threatened. He raised his voice higher;

"All because of one man. You, you bastard." Jenkins said he had taken enough. He told Roger to do his worst; show the fuckin' video to who he wanted to. From now on he didn't give a shit. Then to Roger's surprise the ex-policeman told him to watch his back, because one day he would get his revenge. With that the phone call was ended. Roger smiled at the phone before placing it back down.

Interesting he thought. *"That waste of oxygen with less than half a brain cell was going to exact his revenge?"* He then wondered why people always questioned his parentage? Smiling to himself, he pictured the hapless ex copper; on his own, maybe full of drink, depressed, maybe watching some crap on television where the underdog always wins and the bad guy always gets his comeuppance; and now threatening Roger with violence! He made a mental note to have one of his boys pay Jenkins a visit.

About an hour earlier Sam had been jolted out of her nap as the plane touched down at Gatwick Airport. She stretched and smiled at the same time. She had unintentionally travelled light; leaving Spain in such a hurry she had left most of her possessions behind. Sam wasn't worried; with no hold luggage she would get through the customs and into a taxi much quicker. She would be on her way home to make up with her lovely husband even earlier.

Around a mile away Big Steve, as he was known in the small town near Durham, sat on the bed in the scruffy rented room. He had closed the frayed curtains and locked the door. Now he carefully lifted a small holdall from the bottom of the wardrobe that stood in the corner of the dump. Lifting out a rolled up piece of cloth, he slowly started to unwrap it, the smell of fresh oil getting stronger as he removed the cloth completely, to reveal a 9mm handgun. Although big Steve had left his digs in Newcastle in a hurry, he had managed to pack a case with some small, personal items. Quickly and expertly he stripped the gun down. Carefully cleaning each piece before reassembling it. Reaching back into the holdall he retrieved another rag covered package. This one contained a cardboard box that held thirty rounds of ammunition that matched his gun. He was ready. It was clearly obvious to him now that Roger Scott was the man, who his friend Mal had wanted help in removing three years ago. It was also clearly obvious that Roger Scott was the man who either killed Mal or had ordered the killing. Big Steve had done his research; he knew where Roger Scott lived, the call centre where he worked, the snooker hall where he held his meetings. He looked at the gun again. It was new, never been used, untraceable. It would be disposed of after he had avenged the death of his friend, after Roger Scott was dead. Carefully packing the gun and its ammunition back into the holdall he laid back on the bed. For what was maybe the first time in weeks he smiled.

Bojan and his two sons, Aco and Dorde, could hear the sirens as the fire engines raced passed the *Gowlett Arms*. They paused their conversation until the noise had passed. They were back where they had started several weeks earlier. Just the three of them. Bojan had decided that as it was his fight it would be he who would finish the job. He had been foolish to think that he could enlist the help of others when they clearly had their minds elsewhere. He went over the information he had gained from Mike Smith. Bojan now knew the location of the snooker hall where Scott held his meetings. He also knew where his office was, the one where the ladies made phone calls. Mike had also given him a rough idea of where the London penthouse was. It would be easy enough to find the exact apartment. He would then finish the *Scott bastard* himself.

Checking his watch he waited another five minutes, then right on time the door opened and a large man entered. Over six foot tall and wearing what looked like a multi coloured tea cosy on his head. Under his arm was a package, about the size of a shoebox. He walked towards Bojan without speaking; placing the box on the table he walked back to the door, closed it and leaned against it stopping anybody else from entering. He watched as Bojan peeled back the brown paper that had been wrapped around the package and then slowly lifted the lid. Aco and Dorde leaned over to get a closer look at the contents. They then nodded their approval at the aged but workable 9mm handgun. Replacing the lid Bojan stood, he walked towards the man by the door while at the same time retrieving an envelope from his inside pocket. The big guy accepted it; he opened it and quickly flicked through the bundle of fifty pound notes. Then still without speaking he stuffed the money into his pocket, opened the door and left.

Bojan closed the door behind him then turned towards his two sons, he was about to speak when it was flung open again. A young boy maybe twelve years old ran into the room. He was out of breath as he spoke;

"Mr. Durik, you must come quick Sir. Your house, it is on fire."

***

Outside of the two up two down terraced house on the edge of Brixton, Lisa sat in her car and watched as the Head of Temporary Foster Care parked his Range

Rover. Since walking out on her role as a social worker she had spent a lot of time there. She was making notes, how many times did Yvette and Meg leave the house. Was Spike really leaving for work on the odd occasion that he left home; it was becoming very apparent that Meg never left the house. There were occasions that Lisa would see Spike and Yvette leaving together with no sign of Meg. Lisa had followed them to the nearby pub, she was very tempted to walk through the door and ask them who the hell was babysitting.

Now as she took photos with her mobile phone, she could clearly see her ex- boss trying to hide his smile as he got out of the car. He locked it with the remote control and made his way to the front door. He rang the doorbell then stepped back while pushing his hair over from the side in a futile attempt to hide the top of his bald head. Lisa continued taking snaps as the door opened and a smiling Yvette invited him in. Lisa put her phone down and made more notes.

The Head of Temporary Foster Care now sat in the small lounge asking pointless but official questions; how was Meg progressing? How were she and Spike coping? Were they still enjoying their work? Where was the little mite now? Yvette answered each question, telling him what he wanted to hear. That everything was fine, Meg was doing really well. Spike had taken to her as if she was his own daughter. In fact right now they were at the park, she loved feeding the ducks.

He then explained that she would not be seeing Lisa again. It had been deemed that she wasn't suitable for this particular case, in the next day or two a new social worker would be making contact with her to arrange an appointment.

Yvette knew this was all rubbish, she knew the real reason for him ringing to say he was going to pay a visit, which was why Spike had been given ten pounds and sent out to the pub for a couple of hours, and why little Meg was fast asleep upstairs, after once again being force fed with *Calpol*. Yvette felt sick as she watched him waffle, it looked like he was about to start drooling at the mouth. She waited. Then;

"So when do you expect Spike and Meg to return?"

Yvette knew it would be no good putting him off. After the first time he had slobbered over her with his bad breath and his foul smelling penis, she had been told what was expected of her if she wanted to remain on the preferred list of foster carers. She stood, tried and failed to smile. She answered:

"Maybe about an hour. So can we get this over with, and please be quiet, the walls are paper thin, I don't want the neighbours to hear."

With that Yvette slowly walked up the stairs, she was wearing a short skirt and no pants. She could hear him slobbering behind her. She wondered if her plan would work; to get him so excited before they entered the bedroom that it would maybe be all over quickly. *It didn't.* Yvette stripped naked and lay on the bed watching as he undressed, as before his trousers came off to reveal stockings held by suspenders, and a pair of flimsy open crotch knickers. He then produced a small riding crop and a feather duster from his briefcase, throwing them to Yvette before bending over the end of the bed. He squirmed and whimpered for the next ten minutes. Then it was Yvette's turn.

It was an hour later that Lisa saw the Head of Temporary Care leave the house. It was two hours later that Lisa

235

filmed Spike on her mobile phone staggering along the street, clearly very drunk. Lisa started her car as Spike went through the door. Closing it behind him he found Yvette fully dressed with her head in the toilet as she vomited.

***

Bojan ran as fast as he could, leaving his two sons and the package containing the gun behind. He reached the end of the street of terraced houses in Peckham Rye, to be met by the sight of tens of people staring at the still burning house. *His house, his home for the last twelve years, his family home.* He pushed through the watching crowd only to be stopped by three burly policemen. He protested that it was his house that was on fire. That his wife was in there and maybe his son. They held him as he looked despairingly at the three fire appliances and two ambulances that stood in the distance. Bojan looked again at what was left of the house. The flames albeit smaller due to the dousing the fire fighters were administering, were still visible from where the windows and the front door had once been.

He could see a stretcher being carried to one of the ambulances. He relaxed his body, the policemen relaxed theirs. He let his legs buckle as if in shock or denial or maybe going to faint. One of the uniforms let go of him. Bojan sprang up and head butted the man before pushing the other two aside and sprinting along the street. He headed for the stretcher and the ambulance. He was shouting for his wife as he ran. The two men that were carrying the stretcher stopped as they saw a big man running at them. Bojan also stopped then looked at the prone figure on the stretcher. He saw a badly burned body, where the skin wasn't black and charred it was cut to ribbons, pieces of glass sticking out of various parts of the body. Bojan looked away; he was finding it difficult to grasp what was happening.

Then the shock as he looked back again at the head on the body, on the stretcher. Or what was left of the head, it appeared that half of it was missing, or maybe just mangled, or maybe just some sort of deformation. Bojan's legs gave way for the second time in the space of two minutes. Only this time it wasn't a ploy to escape the strong arms of the law. This time his body succumbed to the reality of what he was witnessing. Out of nowhere another medic appeared, out of nowhere somebody had found a chair and placed Bojan on it. He was panting, sweating, trying to make some sort of sense of what was happening.

It took over two hours before the flames had been held enough for the fire fighters to don their breathing apparatus and enter the ruined burned remains of what was once a cosy family home. Even the most hardened and experienced of them were shocked when they discovered the kitchen and the source of the inferno. Even more shocked to see the remains of what was clearly a human form now reduced to little more than ashen bones. As a precaution the gas had been turned off at the meter at the back of the house. Now as the four men and two women from the Peckham fire station looked around the blackened room for more victims, there was little to see. What may have been tables and chairs, what may have been kitchen worktops. What was maybe a sink or a fridge or a washing machine was nothing more than a ghostly apparition, something more akin to what might have been seen in a horror film.

It was around three hours later when the grave looking doctor approached the three sad looking men who were sitting outside of the operating theatre at the Kings College

Hospital. The three stood as one. The doctor had removed his surgical mask as he walked towards them. He spoke;

"Mr. Duric?" All three nodded their heads.

"It is bad news I'm afraid. Your son is still alive, but he has massive head injuries. We have operated on him but a large proportion of his skull and brain was hit by what looks like a blunt instrument, the force has also embedded glass into the same area."

Bojan sat back down, his two sons stood in shock. The doctor continued;

"He has multiple breaks and fractures to his neck and back, and it appears that his legs and arms are also severely damaged." Aco spoke;

"Will he live?"

"We don't know, he may survive but his quality of life will never be the same. The next twenty four hours will be crucial."

Bojan began to cry, he knew it was all his own doing. His youngest son, the brains of the family, the one who was going to make something of himself without resorting to crime would be either dead or have a life as some sort of cabbage. He had seen head injuries during the Bosnian war. He had seen soldiers with half their heads blown away only to survive and spend the rest of their lives not knowing anything that was going on around them. He got up and walked away, out of the door, Rodovan was finished, Bojan knew that. As he headed away from the hospital his mind went back to Mila, his wife for over twenty five years. He had seen close up what was left of the devastated house. Now he was clinging to the forlorn hope that maybe his wife had left their home before the explosion, maybe to go shopping or visit a friend or just for a walk. He knew he was grasping at straws.

Mike Smith and the three brothers from Liverpool sat in a cafe opposite the Pot Black snooker hall on New Cross Road. Mike had apologised for what had happened in Bojan's house. He told them that the plan had been to join forces in their vendetta against Scott. The plan was to kill him, and with so many of them involved it would be harder for the police to find the culprit. Mike had said that he didn't know about the history between the two sets of Serbs. He told them he also hadn't expected Bojan to tell them all to leave. He thought there would be a rethink, maybe another plan, maybe separate the two sets of Serbians, maybe a two pronged attack on Roger Scott. The three brothers from Liverpool nodded their heads in unison as they listened. Mike could see that although they were looking at him and making the right movements, they were not really taking much notice of what he was saying. Then one of the three brothers, maybe the youngest one, spoke;

"Look man, look at that. That looks like the Serb dude's place."

He pointed to the corner of the cafe and towards the small television that was silently showing the local news. There was footage of a burnt out shell of a house. Fire appliances could be seen in the background. They all continued to watch. Mike knew the house, he had been there before. They all had. They all recognised the house where Bojan and his family lived. They watched in horror as the camera panned around showing the full extent of the damage. The youngest one continued;

"I say that we go back North man. We know what the Scott dude is capable of, we was set up last time. He did that fire, he must have. I say we go while we can."

The eldest one, still watching the television replied, loudly;

"We fuckin' stay until he is dead. So maybe he did the fire. The Bojan dude should have seen it coming. He should have been ready. We stay until we finish what we came here for."

They all sat in silence as he looked around the small cafe, there was nobody in there but them. He opened his jacket to reveal a 9mm handgun. He spoke again;

"My life is fucked man, stuck in this wheelchair forever, I would be better off dead. So before that happens I am going to kill the man. The Scott man."

***

Roger looked at Mina as she quietly napped in the giant bed. He smiled; he would let her sleep a little while longer. Mina was a good employee; she had been loyal to Roger for many years. He had no love or affection for her but remembering the hard life she had gone through, maybe a small treat now and again wouldn't go amiss. Looking at his watch he decided to take a shower. Then maybe get Mina a taxi back to the call centre. Tom and Jeff would arrive in an hour. They were going to take Roger to the mansion in Kent. Roger wanted to have a look for any clues from the latest attempted attack that might incriminate him at some point. He also wanted the twins to stay down there. Not only as security, but it might also be a good idea to have them disappear for a few days. Somebody could have seen them before the fire in Peckham Rye.

He was in deep thought as the water cascaded over his body. By now the Serbian who had ordered his Kent mansion to be fire bombed would have received the message, that if you play with fire you may get your fingers burned. Would that be the end of it? The end of all that had gone on in the last few weeks? He thought some more; probably not. After what Jeff had told him about the damage they had inflicted on Bojan's home, would he come back for more retribution? Possibly but Roger doubted it. Then there were the two remaining Serbians whose brothers had met their maker. Maybe they would have another go at him. By now they would know that he was behind their demise.

He thought some more; these guys were serious killers, they would try again. He would get in touch with Mary and Alan. They managed to find them last time, only this time they would not be there to observe and report back. Roger wanted the two Serbians dead.

Only one of the four that had waited for him outside of the Silk Road Chinese was still alive; would he come back? Roger doubted it, he would still be running. Maybe all the way back to Serbia. He smiled to himself at the thought.

Then mentally going down his list he thought further, what, if any damage could Mike Smith do? None, but maybe he was still worth finding, maybe have another quiet word. Then there was the copper, the one that was near the top of the pay scale, the one who had taken a big interest in one of the night club victims. No, he had nothing. They had feebly tried to make the arrest and Roger had made them look like the amateurs that they were.

He then went through each member of his own gang; could any of them be a danger? No, he would have spotted anything untoward, anything out of their normal behaviour. They were all as loyal now as when he ended his business affairs with them three years ago. The new guy Steve? Again no. Johnny was a good judge and he had known Steve for months, also Roger hadn't seen or heard from him lately. Still thinking; the only recent threat had come from the useless P.C. Jenkins. Roger smiled to himself; not much to worry about there. He briefly cast his mind back to the gang of youths, *the ones that wore similar hooded jackets*. He would leave them be for now, maybe forever, let them get on with their lives. After what he had done to them they would be in fear of him for the foreseeable. He thought some more; maybe it wouldn't do any harm to have one of his boys give them the odd frightener now and again.

Switching off the shower, Roger grabbed the towel off the rail. The extractor fan was still running noisily; the door was still firmly closed. He was rubbing the water from his ears when he thought he heard a shout, maybe louder than a shout, maybe a scream. He stood silent for a moment, listening for any sound of intruders. Maybe somebody had got past the security guard downstairs. Maybe one of the guys he had been thinking about moments earlier. Then another scream, then shouting, then another scream, maybe a different voice. He looked around the bathroom. He picked up a bottle of aftershave, the only container in there that was made of glass. He stood, ready, and then slowly opening the door he quickly stepped through and into the bedroom. The screaming was now much louder.

To his surprise Roger looked to see Mina sitting up in the bed, with nothing but a single sheet covering her nakedness. Sam was standing over her shouting almost every obscenity that she could muster. Roger stood by the door watching. Sam then stopped her shouting; she looked at Roger then back at Mina. Mina was whimpering softly, trying to mumble some sort of apology. Roger didn't say anything. Sam turned her wrath and attention to him;

'Bastard, bastard. How can you do this? Bring this fuckin whore into our bed, our fuckin' marital bed? Then turning to Mina;

"Out, out now! Get the fuck out of my flat."

242

Mina looked at Roger who nodded his head. As Mina got up to find her clothes, Sam looked at the aging well used body that her husband had preferred to hers. She burst into tears. She shouted *"bastard"* one more time then turned and stormed out of the door.

***

Zivco and Toma, the two grieving Serbians sat together on a park bench. They were discussing their next move. They were angry, very angry. Bojan had humiliated them by expecting them to work with Muslims; in their opinion that was unforgivable. Then he took the piss out of their dead brothers. Also to then tell them that not only were they no longer needed, but to say it in front of those two cripples. Who did he think he was? Their original plan was to take over his business. To ruin him, maybe run him out of town. Now their anger had changed the plan. They both agreed that they would make him suffer, kill him like a rat. After all that is what he is. A sewer rat.

First they were due to visit the massage parlours that had been wrecked a couple of weeks ago. They had reopened the day before. For added security they were all linked via speed dial on a direct dedicated line. At the first sign of trouble at any of the brothels the receptionist would press a hidden button to alert the other premises. That would in turn give them chance to alert their own security and be ready for whoever it was that was about to pay a visit. They did not want a repeat of the previous damage.

Talking further they mused about the fact that they had also become embroiled with a gangster called Roger Scott, the man responsible for the deaths of their two brothers. They wanted their revenge on Scott; it was something that they had agreed they would have to do themselves. Bojan had been trying long enough with no results, and he was still no further forward. It was time to get serious; they had connections, people they knew who could supply weapons. Their next move was to contact them, acquire the guns they needed and take out both Bojan and Roger Scott.

Mike Smith had left the brothers from Liverpool in the cafe opposite the Pot Black Snooker Hall; he had told them that to try and kill Roger Scott would now be near impossible. They had lost the element of surprise. Scott would be onto them. They had seen what had happened to the two Serbs, only an ear left between them. Now they had all witnessed the television footage of Bojan's house. Roger Scott had to be behind it. Mike went on to tell them about the time he worked for Scott. He regaled them with some of the stories of torture and worse that had been inflicted on Roger's victims. He described in detail what had happened to himself. How he had been a streetwise, street fighting amateur boxer. How he was lucky to be alive. How he thought the two of Scott's gang who administered his beating were going to kill him. Instead they gave him a life sentence in a wheelchair.

Mike went on to tell them how Roger appeared to have eyes everywhere and an equally ruthless gang to back him up. Mike told them to go back to Liverpool while they still could. It was over. Roger Scott was not winning, he had won, and there was nothing they or anybody else could do about it.

The elder of the three brothers listened in silence before reiterating that it would not be over until Scott was dead. Mike said *"good luck"* then shook his head before leaving them in the cafe. Now with his right hand on the four way lever that controlled the wheelchair, he powered forward and away from the snooker hall. Back along New Cross Road, he thought he would travel the three or so miles towards Tower Bridge then find a train out of London. He wasn't sure where yet, he would just disappear; he was now more than aware that even he had underestimated Roger's power. Mike thought it would have been a lot easier. Cause a bit of damage to various parts of his business; draw him out into the open then leave the rest to Bojan and his family. Now he wasn't even sure if they were still alive. If they had been inside the house as it had burned down they surely wouldn't be.

Mike knew that Roger would not stop there. He would track down every last person who was involved in the plot against him. Yes, he had made the right decision, he would disappear.

***

Sam slammed the door of the London penthouse that had been one of her homes for the last three years. She ran down the stairs crying and screaming at the same time. Glaring at the security guy as she passed, she walked out onto the street with her head down; she was finding it difficult to stem the tears, even though the path was crowded and she was aware of people staring at her. *How could he? How could he take that skank of a woman into bed, their bed?*

Sam walked for miles in deep thought, what was happening? It was bad enough that she had thrown herself at George only to find out that he was gay. Then thinking that all the problems were her own doing. How stupid had she been to try to surprise Roger, only to find out that her husband preferred an ugly old woman to her, and not just in the office but in her bed, *her fuckin' bed!*

Still walking, still thinking, she now found herself heading in the direction of Peckham High Street. She wondered why, She had no idea or intention of being anywhere near the call centre, the call centre where that bitch Mina worked, *the slag who had been shagging her husband.* Sam never wanted to see her again, so why was she now standing opposite the sinister looking blacked out shop front? She still had her head down in an attempt to avoid eye contact with other passersby. She turned away, her mind in turmoil. Not sure where to go or what to do. Maybe she would find a hotel for now, get her thoughts together. Maybe find out how Adie and Meg were. Maybe contact one or more of her cousins. Somebody to talk to, somebody to listen to her tale of woe. Now with her head down she walked on, still not taking much notice of which direction she wanted to travel.

Then a noise behind her, a bell, maybe like a bicycle bell. She carried on walking, straight ahead; not moving left or right, not deviating from her chosen path. The bike behind her shouldn't even be on the footpath. The bell sounded again, nearer, persistent. Sam had taken enough for one day, her temper was frayed to start with, now some idiot on a bike thought he had right of way, expecting her to move. She span round, ready, this prick was going to get the brunt of her wrath. She shouted;

"Who the fuck do you think…" Sam stopped in both mid sentence and in her tracks. The offending bell was not on a bicycle, to her horror it was on a wheelchair. Head down again; spluttering an apology she stepped aside to allow the wheelchair and its passenger to pass. More tears ran down her face. As if her day could not get any worse. The wheelchair drew level with her then slowed to the same speed as she was walking. She didn't look, she was too embarrassed to face the poor person who was sitting in it. Then she heard her name, not loud, more of a question, as if the owner of the voice wasn't sure he had the right person. Sam vaguely recognised the voice of the man who was asking. She lifted her head, through the mist of her glassy eyes she found herself looking at Mike Smith.

In a terraced street in Peckham Rye, Bojan and his two remaining sons, Aco and Dorde, stood in front of what was left of their family home. The fire fighters, albeit not as many as earlier were still in attendance. The fire was now fully extinguished but there was still evidence of the odd bit of smouldering, maybe a piece of floorboard from an inside cupboard or maybe one of the roof trusses that the water from the hoses hadn't quite reached. It could have been the fact that the heat had been so intense that it would take a little while for the house to finally be at rest.

A policeman, clearly of a senior rank approached them. He introduced himself then slowly and gently told them there had been no survivors of the fire. He then asked them how many people may have been inside the house when the fire had started. Bojan said that he hoped that there would have been nobody inside; he said that he hoped his wife had not been there. Then looking gravely at the ground in front of him he said but maybe she had been. The policeman said that although it was early days in their investigation it did look like they had found the remains of at least one person. Bojan looked at the devastation in front of him, the house was a shell, surely it would have to be demolished. The adjoining houses, four either side had been evacuated. Maybe they would have to come down also. He looked back at the policeman. Then;

"What caused this to happen?"

"The investigations are continuing Sir. They will for some time, but at the moment it is looking likely that it was caused by some sort of gas leak. Do you have anybody you can stay with?"

Bojan answered that they had. The policeman said he would need an address and all three of would be interviewed as part of the investigation into the cause of the fire. Bojan put an arm round each of his sons and led them away from what was left of their home.

It was an hour later that Bojan received news from the hospital that he was half expecting; that his youngest son, Rodovan, his pride and joy had passed away. Although it was not a surprise it still saddened him to the point of tears falling again. He knew it was for the best. Rodovan would never have been the same again. He was better off dead.

Now they were sitting in the back room of the *Gowlett Arms*. Where they had been when they received the message earlier, that their house was on fire and Bojan had ran out of the pub. Dorde had picked up the box containing the gun and handed it to the bar manager, telling him to hide it and also guard it with his life. The guy didn't argue, he took the package and locked it in the safe.

Now with it safely back in Bojan's hands they sat in silence, it was maybe half an hour later that Bojan spoke;

"It was Scott who did it." Aco answered;

"Maybe father but also Zivco and Toma also made threats as they left the house."

"They did, but they would not have used fire, that was revenge for what happened at his Kent house, fire for fire, I now know how Scott thinks. It was a message to me. He knew where we lived. Those two idiots who got themselves caught by him must have talked before he killed them, told him everything. I am glad they are dead."

Both his sons slowly nodded their heads. Then;

"What do we do next father?" Bojan looked at his two remaining sons. He thought before answering. They were cripples, without him they had nothing. What was left of his life? Rodovan gone, his wife gone. Now feeling bitter he answered;

"You two do as I tell you. This is all your doing. If you had thought about what you were doing three years ago, before going into Scott's nightclub none of this would have happened. Now your brother is dead, and your mother is dead. There is nothing left for me here." He glanced at the box on the table in front of him. He continued;

"I am going to kill Scott myself; if anybody gets in my way I will kill them also. Your crippled friend told me where he lives and the snooker place where he meets his gang. I will watch both places, I will wait until he is alone. Then I will kill him." His two sons nodded in agreement. Bojan continued;

"Before that I will take care of those two idiots, Zivco and Toma, how dare they threaten me in my own home? Who do they think they are dealing with?

On the fourth floor of the aging building that acted as Camberwell Police Station, Assistant Chief Constable Ted Walton sat in his office; it was the Monday afternoon after his hospital consultation. He had the file that covered the Roger Scott investigation spread out in front of him. There was nothing in there that had any chance of incriminating him. The two detectives who had brought Scott in were amateurish. Ted had listened to the recording of the interview. Scott must have laughed all the way home. Ted gripped the desk tightly making his knuckles white, as the pain shot across his agonised stomach. Gritting his teeth he sat back in deep thought. Then there was a knock at the door, he shouted for whoever it was to come in.

Detective Inspector Terry Thompson entered. Ted nodded towards the empty chair for him to sit down. Then;

"What is it Terry?" The D.I. answered.

"We have a break Sir. There was a gas explosion at a house of a known criminal in Peckham Rye two days ago. The lady of the house was killed. We have spent most of yesterday going through CCTV footage taken from a London bus. Also by chance a motorist was stopped in the next street for using one of those new Russian dash cams. They are still illegal here so it was confiscated. First of all the bus has a camera pointing to the door so that the driver can see people getting on and off. We checked it several times and it clearly shows two men who are known to us, loitering not far from the house. Due to that we went through the dash cam. As the car was being driven along the road near to the house the same two men can clearly be seen entering the front garden."

Ted Walton hid the pain that was shooting through his body. Then;

"Is there a point to this Detective?"

"Yes Sir, the two men in question work for Roger Scott. They are twin brothers, as I said earlier they are known to us."

"So you think they are involved with the fire?"

"Well we know that Scott had his nightclub fire bombed, we know that his gaming salon was wrecked and we know that there was an attempted kidnap on his wife. What we also know is that Roger Scott has never made any attempt to help us find the culprits. It's as if he didn't want them caught. So maybe this fire is some kind of retribution."

The Assistant Chief Constable nodded slowly, taking in

what Thompson had said. Then;

"Do we know if the fire was started deliberately?"

"Investigations are still ongoing Sir, but it just seems too much of a coincidence for his two guys to be there shortly before the fire was reported."

"What did the house owner say about it?"

"Nothing as yet Sir, he is still in shock. Not only was his wife killed, but his youngest son has since died from injuries incurred in the aftermath. It appears he was caught up in the explosion that started the fire."

Ted Walton thought some more then;

"OK. Let's bring them in, sooner rather than later. We'll see what they have to say."

Mike Smith had looked up at Sam; at first he wasn't sure if it was her. He was in a hurry to get away from the area; and this woman was in his way, and what were the chances of this person being her, south London is a big place. He had assumed that she was still with Roger Scott; the nightclub had still been called *"Sam's"* There had been times when he had thought fleetingly that maybe Roger had tired of her. Force fed her drugs, turned her into a dependent addict, and then made her work in one of his brothels or flats, which Scott was more than capable of.

There had been many times, when Mike had worked for Scott that he had witnessed young girls getting themselves into debt, due to the extortionate interest rates that were charged for his illegal loans. When they couldn't pay they were taken away, to be injected with heroin, under their arms or behind their knees, so that the merchandise wasn't damaged. In a short space of time they were too helpless to realise that they were being offered to the paying public.

A few weeks earlier when Mike was outside of what was

once his flat, he had watched the red light in the window being turned on then off; the thought that it may have been Sam behind the closed curtains had sickened him. He had never stopped loving her even though she had left him for her boss.

Now as Sam stopped and turned to look at him, an angry look that then softened, he could see there was no mistake. The tear stained face belonged to his ex girlfriend. They looked at each other, recognised each other, no words spoken, just a look of surprise from them both. The world seemed to have stopped. Sam spoke first;

"What's happened Mike? Why are you in that wheelchair?"

Mike looked back at her, he wanted to answer her, tell her everything in one sentence. He was in the wheelchair *because of one man,* her husband. No words seemed appropriate, or nothing would come out. Instead he managed to force a smile.

Twenty minutes later they were sitting together in the *Copper Tap* in Camberwell. There was no excited talk, no smiles, no reminiscing from when they were an item. It was as if they couldn't face each other or maybe they were both too embarrassed by the situation they had found themselves in. Eventually after a second drink Sam had asked about his disability, how did it happen? She then sat back in shock as Mike told her that Roger had ordered two of his guys; Johnny and Alan to break almost every bone in his body. They had done just that before leaving him a bloodied tangled mess in a hospital car park. Amongst many of his injuries the damage to his spinal cord was irreparable, he was crippled for life. He told her about the events leading up to the attack, then without hesitation Mike said that at the same time her husband had ordered the execution of a guy called Shane.

252

Sam sat back in horror, she remembered Shane, three years earlier he had been living with her cousin Adie before she had been kidnapped and left for dead. It got worse for Sam as Mike went on to tell her that it was Roger who had ordered Adie's kidnap. He planned to ply her with heroin and put her to work in one of his massage parlours, which were a front for his brothels. Scott wasn't aware that Adie was almost due to have her baby. When he found out that she would not be any use as a prostitute he arranged for her to be left in a disused WW2 bunker. Adie was alone and frightened until he himself had discovered her, almost dead.

Mike then stopped talking; it was as if he had got three years of pain off his chest. He took a sip of his drink and looked at the girl he was once in love with, the girl he was about to propose marriage to, when his boss stepped in and took her. She looked pitiful, broken; he had never seen her like this. Sam looked back at Mike; she wiped away a tear then spoke;

"Mike I am so sorry, I thought you had forgotten about me when he sent you away on that job. I thought you didn't care, Then one thing led to another then…" Sam stopped talking and burst into tears; "I was so stupid, I should have listened to what everybody was telling me about him."

Mike waited for her to compose herself. He watched as she dabbed her eyes with her handkerchief. She took a drink herself then started to talk. Mike listened as Sam told him about the nightclub attack, the fight outside the Chinese Restaurant. About her beautiful horse Penny being killed and about the attempted kidnap of herself and Adie. She stopped talking as another tear trickled down her cheek. She then went on to describe the injuries that her poor cousin Adie had suffered for the second time in three years. Mike watched her as she spoke. Yes, everything she was saying was sad and upsetting, but he could see that there was more, something else was getting to her. After a pause Sam continued;

"Do you remember a woman called Mina?" Mike answered;

"Yeah, she worked in the call centre, making appointments for the perverts to visit the flats that the poor girls were forced to work in." Sam gave a little gasp then;

"A couple of hours ago I found her naked in my bed, Roger was in the shower, it was very clear what they had been up to." Mike waited, Sam continued;

"I'm quite sure it wasn't the first time, I think he's been screwing her in his office, I nearly caught them at it. Then two weeks ago he sent me to Spain, by myself. Now I know why." Sam picked up her drink, she felt a little better; it was as if talking about her discovery made it easier. She put her glass to her mouth then stopped; stared at Mike, then;

"What do you mean making appointments for perverts?" Mike slowly shook his head then answered;

"You don't know a thing about what he does, do you? The call centre, it is there to handle the business for the ten or so flats he owns. Mina and the others make the appointments, the drugged up girls do as they are told. Tom and Jeff collect the money."

Sam sat back, the shock of this news showing on her face. Mike smiled; he didn't know why but he was starting to enjoy this. Maybe because of the pain he had suffered. Yes Roger had ordered the two thugs to half kill him, but it was Sam who had jumped into bed with that bastard Scott as soon as his back was turned. Yes he had loved her, yes he had never forgotten about her, but it was clear that she had very quickly forgotten about him. He stopped feeling sympathy for his ex-girlfriend. He looked at her, the shock was still showing on her face. He couldn't resist. Go for it he thought. He continued;

"So how come you have been married to him for three years but never knew about the flats or the massage parlours, or his drugs business or the amount of people he killed, or arranged to disappear?

"Arranged to disappear?"

"Yeah, most of the girls in the massage parlours are there because they got behind with the payments from his money lending game. So they were drugged up and made to work until they were past their sell by date. Until nobody fancied them anymore. It was then more drugs to overdose them or a one way trip to the Thames. Like I said earlier, that was Scott's plan for Adie, your cousin, until he found out she was pregnant."

Sam didn't answer Mike; she put her head down as she listened to the latest revelations about her husband. How could she have been so stupid? He owned a penthouse in one of the better areas of south London. A mansion on the Hoo Peninsula in Kent. The holidays, the cruises, the west end nights out. How was it all paid for? A couple of less than salubrious night clubs? A snooker hall and some gaming salons? The reality hit her. Mike was telling the truth. The life style she had enjoyed over the last three years could only have been afforded through crime, and the suffering of others.

She thought some more; *killed people! How many, what for?* Sam looked up at Mike. He now felt sorry for her. He had enjoyed making her suffer for the last few minutes, but now his emotions had changed again. She had both heard and had enough, Mike smiled. Reaching across from the wheelchair he offered his hand. Sam took it as she cried out loud.

***

Mary and Alan sat in a car one hundred metres from *The Soft Touch* massage parlour; they had watched the two Serbians, Zivco and Toma, enter the premises a few minutes earlier. They had followed the two of them from one of the other newly reopened parlours. Roger had ordered them to track the two Serbs down. It had been easier than they thought. Mary and Alan had found the gang of youths, the ones that liked to wear *similar hooded jackets*. Mary had asked them nicely to station themselves outside the three massage parlours that they had wrecked two weeks earlier. Then to let them know when the two owners showed up. They readily agreed before Alan had let go of the two biggest, that he had pinned against the wall behind them.

Mary had known that the brothels had reopened and thought it would only be a matter of time before the two Serbs showed up at one of them. Sure enough one of the hooded youths, maybe the biggest one, maybe the leader, had rung her an hour earlier. Picking up the new throw away mobile phone Mary rung Roger to report the findings. He told her that there was a good chance they would go to their third massage parlour next. Roger told Mary to head to *Fingertips* now, make sure the car was far enough away not to cause any attention, then both her and Alan to go inside and wait for the two Serbs. He said that they knew what to do next. Mary ended the call; she took the back off the phone and removed the sim card. They drove half a mile, about halfway to Nunhead before stopping the car. Alan got out and dropped the card down the nearest drain before placing the phone on the road in front of the car. He got back in, Mary selected first gear and pulled away, driving over what was left of it.

***

"How long do we wait here man?" The youngest of the three brothers from Liverpool was sitting in the driver's seat of the blue Lexus. They were about two hundred metres from the Pot Black Snooker Hall. "We stay here much longer we will be noticed, there are cameras everywhere." The oldest brother sat alone in the back seat, his folded up wheelchair was in the boot.

"Long as it takes. Start the car, turn round and then we drive the other way, watch from somewhere different."

"Then what, you have the shooter, you want to do the dude, how the fuck are you going to kill him?"

The crippled man was getting angry, firstly at his two younger brothers but more so at himself. He knew his plan was bad. They were in a car that was registered to him, and he was going to do a drive by shooting as soon as he saw Roger Scott. He didn't care about getting caught, that wouldn't happen. If the law got anywhere near he would use the remaining bullets to take as many of them down as he could. He would save the last one for himself.

As each day had passed since he had been sentenced to life in the wheelchair, he had hated Roger Scott more and more. He wanted Scott dead. He didn't care what would happen after that. He didn't want to spend another day in that fuckin' four wheeled contraption. His two brothers could say they had nothing to do with it, that they didn't know that he was carrying, or what his intention was. He would stick to the plan, keep driving past the snooker hall, wait a while then turn and repeat the process. Until he thought of something different, something better.

Mary and Alan had been inside the *Fingertips* massage parlour for over half an hour. They had paid the receptionist £100 for one hour and chosen a plain girl called Vicky. They had explained that although they were happily married they enjoyed the occasional threesome. They asked for the theme room nearest the reception area.

Now as Vicky sat on the massage table with a sock in her mouth, held there with gaffer tape, they waited. Mary was standing by the door, listening for the first sound of Serbian voices. When it happened the gag in Vicky's mouth would be removed and Alan would make her scream. Mary would then open the door and walk out quickly. She was sure that after the place being wrecked two weeks ago, the two Serbs would enter the room to find out what the commotion was. Mary would then follow them back in and do what was needed.

The problem was, they had been inside the Fingertips massage parlour for over half an hour and there was still no sign of the owners.

Roger had ended the conversation with Mary. Now he sat back on the settee in his London penthouse. Tom and Jeff would be there in around ten minutes to drive him to the mansion in Kent. It had been almost two hours since Sam had left and then the taxi arriving for Mina. He smiled to himself; the two remaining Serbs would be dead by now. Coshed unconscious, tied and then powerful weed killer poured into their throats, they may have woken up briefly, but it would not have been for long; the weed killer was of industrial strength, not available over the counter. Almost immediately it would begin to wipe out almost every vital organ in their body. Maybe it would be better for the two victims not to regain consciousness, the pain they would endure as the poison swept through their liver, then their kidneys, not before attacking the walls of their stomach on its way would have been unbearable. Two more of the clowns who decided to pick a fight with him out of the way.

Roger looked at the list in front of him, it had changed somewhat in the last couple of weeks, since he had began to compile it, but the nucleus was the same; the high ranking copper who had it in for him. Bojan plus a couple more. He could forget three of them, they might have a grudge against him but there wasn't much they could do about it. It was Bojan that needed the attention. Roger knew that he had broken his spirit, it had been widely reported in the local papers that in the aftermath of the fire in Peckham Rye there had been two casualties, and who it was thought they were. Would Bojan be angry or upset or both? He remembered that it was Bojan's two sons who had probably instigated what had occurred in the last few weeks, by trying to muscle in on his nightclub a couple of years ago. Roger wondered why they had taken it this far, over the years various rival gangs had tried and failed, as had the odd pair of pricks like those two, but the grudge had never lasted this long. The punishment he and his boys inflicted was normally enough to deter a repeat performance.

He thought some more; Bojan was still the immediate threat, but what was left of his gang? As far as Roger could work out his back up had diminished quite considerably. He still had his two sons but what real use were they? Both crippled, hardly anything to worry about. Roger reached a decision, like he would have done three years ago, before he had taken his mind off what was happening around him, before he had gone soft and comfortable. *Before Sam.* He thought briefly about his wife then; *Bojan had to go the same way as his Serbian friends.*

Big Steve, as he had been known in the small town near Durham, before he left for London studied the table, looking thoughtful as he rubbed the blue chalk onto the end of the snooker cue. Leaning over he took his shot and potted a red ball. Standing back straight he smiled at his opponent. Steve had not been in the Pot Black Snooker Hall since the meeting in the back room when Johnny had introduced him to Roger, and he had frightened the skinny copper half to death. He had wandered in an hour ago, spoke to the guy behind the bar, told him he wasn't a member but he was a friend of Roger Scott's. The manager hadn't argued; anybody who knew Roger would not try a bluff of any kind. Steve didn't have to wait too long before another lone male walked in looking for a few frames. He had introduced himself before racking up the snooker balls into the triangle.

Now as he played and chatted to his opponent he was looking around the room, taking in the full layout. The entrance and the emergency exits, the toilet doors. There was one set of stairs that led to what the guy behind the bar had said was "alternative recreation." Apparently there were two teenage girls from Bosnia available today. Steve wasn't interested. He looked beyond the bar to another door; it led to the back room where Johnny had taken him earlier. Three doors, the one at the other end that he and the rest had used a couple of weeks ago. A door at the back that opened into the yard at the rear and this one that led from the bar. This was going to be easier than he thought. At some point Roger would be in the back room by himself, or maybe with one of his pet gorillas. Maybe they would both be with him, it wouldn't matter. Steve doubted very much that any of them would be carrying. He would establish himself as a paying customer, when he knew Roger was in the back room, he would ask the barman to let him know that a friend of his was playing snooker. Like anybody Scott would be curious, maybe acknowledge him, maybe invite him through to the back. If not Steve would ask Roger if he had a minute, could he have a quiet word, bit of business. Once in the back he would pull the gun and shoot the murdering bastard. If Jeff or Tom got in the way they would receive the same punishment. Steve would then leave through the back door, along the alley to where he would have left his car. The car that he had stolen earlier. Then head back up north, as far as Peterborough, then leave the car in some rough council estate, keys in, doors unlocked. Steve would then get a train the rest of the way to Newcastle. Maybe buy a bottle of bubbly on the way to toast Mal.

A job well done. His best friend's death finally avenged.

About a mile away in Nunhead, Mary heard the phone on the desk in the reception ring, and then being answered. She then heard a panicked voice, then the sound of a chair being hurriedly scraped back along the floor, then a loud banging on all the doors leading off the reception. Including the one they were standing behind. She turned and nodded to Alan who roughly pulled the gaffer tape off Vicky's mouth. Before she had chance to scream Alan replaced it with his hand while putting a finger to his lips to tell her to keep quiet. Mary stepped out quickly closing the door behind her. The receptionist was shouting for everyone to leave, that everybody must get out quickly. Mary

261

watched as doors flew open and naked girls ran out in a state of panic. Behind them men in a semi-state of undress followed, desperately attempting to pull their clothes on as they went. Mary roughly grabbed the receptionist by the arm, twisting it painfully behind her as she marched the stricken woman back into the room. Spinning her round towards Alan she spoke;

"What the fuck is going on?"

"There is trouble at one of the other premises, *The Soft Touch,* lots of trouble, people are being hurt. The same thing happened two weeks ago, it happened here also. We must get out before they come here."

Mary released her, looked at Alan, then they walked back out of the room, and out onto the street, trying not to smile at what she had just witnessed. She turned to Alan;

"What do you think happened?" He answered; "Don't know, but maybe we should take a drive up there and find out."

An hour earlier and a mile away from the *Fingertips* massage parlour, Bojan had been inside *The Soft Touch.* He knew that it had reopened the day before. He knew that the owners would be diligent in protecting what was theirs, after the damage that had been inflicted two weeks earlier. He had watched them enter their first parlour half an hour ago. He had then ordered his youngest son, Dorde to drive him and Aco to *The Soft Touch* to lie in wait. Then leaving the two of them in the car he had entered the premises alone.

He told the girl on the reception that he was a friend of the owners, and would they be in later? She answered by saying that she didn't know, she had only met one of them briefly yesterday when she had started work. She had heard from a friend that there was a vacancy for a receptionist.

After paying her £60 for half an hour with a skinny spotty girl, Bojan then entered the room nearest to the outside door. He didn't have to wait long. His phone flashed a message from his sons. They were parked a little way from the parlour but close enough to see Zivco and Toma arrogantly enter the premises.

Bojan had heard them raising their voices at the girl on reception, calling her a lazy cow, and if she didn't want to be working in the massage rooms, she had better get on with the job she was paid to do. The girl looked back in horror, she had only started to work for these guys the day before, they hadn't even told her their names, now she was being threatened by them. She decided that this would be her last day.

Bojan listened until they had finished their diatribe, then he himself had shouted loudly at the girl inside the room, an aggressive annoyed shout. Zivco and Toma looked at each other. It was one thing for them to shout at and bully the unfortunate girls who worked for them, but there was no way it would be tolerated from any of the punters.

Thinking the door would be locked from the inside Toma ran towards it shoulder first. Bojan heard the footsteps and opened the door as Toma hit it. With nothing to stop his momentum the Serb careered through the opening and into the room before crashing into the massage bed. Bojan had stepped to the side as he sped past. As Zivco followed his friend through the door he ran into the machete that Bojan was now holding out in front of him. Zivco screamed in both shock and pain as the sharpened blade sliced through his shirt and into his stomach. He looked down in horror as his blood spurted from the wound, before collapsing to the floor. Bojan withdrew the machete from the dying man and turned to face Toma. At the same time Toma had bounced off the massage bed and stepped quickly towards Bojan. He received the same fate as his friend.

Bojan then calmly walked out of the room. He paused to look at the receptionist; she was peering past him, through the open door, a look of horror on her face as she could see a prone figure laid in the doorway and an ever increasing pool of blood. She couldn't see that his friend who lay behind the door was in a similar state. Bojan looked at the girl then pointed to the body in the doorway. He spoke;

"Dead man, your boss, is Bojan Duric and my name is Roger Scott. Don't you forget that. I will be back"

He walked passed her and out of the door that led to the street. Turning left he gave a slight acknowledgment to his sons who were sitting in the car watching him. He carried on walking as they drove off in the opposite direction. Inside the receptionist hurriedly picked up the phone.

The two grieving Serbians who were still trying to get over the loss of their respective brothers lay together on the floor next to the massage bed. Their blood pooling as one. Eyes open, they still had a look of shock on their faces. The receptionist was not medically qualified but even she could see that the guy who was visible to her, the guy in the doorway was very much dead.

Mary stopped the car outside of *The Soft Touch* massage parlour. Alan got out of the passenger door and walked around the car towards the entrance. He stopped as a crying, screaming lady rushed towards him. Mary lowered the car window and listened as the woman spoke in broken English. She said that there had been much trouble, two men were dead, they had been attacked and there was blood everywhere. Alan listened then:

"Attacked by who, how many of them?"

"Just one man, a big man he said his name was Roger Scott and that he had killed my boss Bojan Duric"

Alan glanced back at Mary as they heard the sound of police sirens approaching, he jumped back into the car and they sped away.

***

The pain was getting worse, as he expected it would. No amount of indigestion pills or liquid or powerful painkillers were helping. Assistant Chief Constable Ted Walton let out a small gasp of discomfort as he examined the papers on the desk in front of him. There were details of various crimes that had been committed in the area over the past three days. Two armed robbers had been caught red handed as they attempted to hold up a jeweller in Blackheath. Clearly amateurs or maybe their first attempt, they had blatantly walked into the jewellery shop, no masks, no disguise, and no clear plan other than to demand that the valuables were handed over. The hidden alarm button had been pressed and a passing police car informed.

The next sheet had details of an attempted mugging outside of one of the few remaining banks that was still in operation. An off duty policeman had been passing and had disarmed a would be robber from behind, relieving him of the 9mm pistol he was attempting to use.

The last one appeared to be some sort of revenge attack. A man had forced his way into a house where his ex wife lived with her new lover. She had managed to talk and placate him while her daughter had contacted the police using her mobile as she hid in the toilet. They had arrived within minutes and overpowered the man before disarming him.

Ted had found what he was looking for. All three incidents had involved a handgun; all three incidents had ended without any weapons being fired or anybody being hurt. All the suspects were in custody awaiting trial. All the evidence and firearms were safely locked up in the basement of the building. Four hand guns, with ammunition.

Sitting back in the chair he gently massaged his stomach. It didn't seem to help other than giving him a little bit of comfort. He thought some more; his task would be simple. He would use his authority to access the evidence holding area; he would tell whoever was on duty that he needed to examine all four of the items seized from the recent attempted robberies. Ted would then approach Roger Scott on official looking business. He would use one of the confiscated weapons to kill him in cold blood. Ted Walton would then go to his impending grave at peace, not only for himself but also for his beautiful goddaughter, Emily Austen, and his son. *His secret son.*"

November 2012.

The ambulance slowly came to a halt outside Kings College Hospital. The nurse sitting next to Adie smiled as she stood to unbuckle her seatbelt. Adie tried to smile back; she was the first lovely, friendly nurse she had seen recently. Adie shuddered as she thought about the last few weeks, the humiliation of being made to stand naked while two disinterested woman who had somehow been appointed as nurses, roughly washed her with foul smelling soap. Adie allowed the nurse to lead her out of the ambulance and into a waiting wheelchair. As she was pushed toward the door Adie noticed Dr. Ahmed smiling as he waited for her. One hour later Adie was sitting up in a newly made bed, she relished the smell of clean sheets as she looked around the ward and acknowledged the other lady patients, who were smiling in friendly acceptance of her presence. Dr. Ahmed stood by the bed as he gently but clearly explained that her injuries had all but healed. He went on to explain that he would like her to stay in the ward for a few weeks, until he was sure that she would be able to fully look after herself upon her release. Dr. Ahmed answered Adie's questions about Meg as best he could without elaborating as to what she had been through. He went on to explain that Meg was in good hands and being looked after. He was quite sure that they would be reunited sooner rather than later.

A few miles away Louise smiled lovingly at Meg. It had taken a few weeks of reassurance, then gentle encouragement, then more reassurance before Meg allowed Louise to get anywhere near to her. Now when Louise entered the room Meg attempted what looked like the beginnings of a smile. It was progress, recognition of somebody who Meg was learning to trust. Louise knew it would take time but Meg was moving in the right direction. Maybe another week or maybe two she would try to introduce the infant to the other tiny residents of the nursery.

August 2012 Present day.

Detective Inspector Terry Thompson stood in front of the five detectives. It had been two days since Assistant Chief Constable Ted Walton had ordered him to arrest the twins known as Tom and Jeff. The detectives, along with the uniforms allocated to them had searched the local area; they had been to the last known address where the twins shared a flat. They had watched Roger Scott's call centre and his snooker hall. They had found nothing. Two pictures were stuck to the board behind Thompson; Tom and Jeff, identical twins. Roger Scott's minders and maybe the people responsible for the fire at a terraced house in Peckham Rye, where two innocent people lost their lives. D.I. Thompson addressed his audience;

"They can't have just disappeared. Roger Scott is rarely seen without at least one of them. So where are they?" He looked at each detective in turn. D.C. Farrell answered;

"We have had two officers stationed outside their flat in Peckham; also we are watching the snooker hall where Scott appears to spend a lot of his time. I have another two at the shop on the high street that he fronts as a call centre. Thus far there has been no sign of the two suspects or of Roger Scott for that matter. Clearly they are hiding from something, and I'm pretty sure we know what that is."

D.I. Thompson sighed heavily. This was not what he wanted. It was bad enough that the Assistant Chief Constable wanted Roger Scott arrested. Not only had he failed to do that but now he couldn't even produce the two suspected murderers who worked for him.

At that point a knock on the door was followed by it opening and a uniformed officer entering. He nodded an apology in the general direction of all before approaching the D.I.;

"Sorry Sir, but this is something you need to see." He handed over a sheet of paper. Thompson looked at it;

"When did this come in?"

"A few minutes ago, the receptionist of a massage parlour dialled three nines to report that a man had been murdered. A car was dispatched and they found two males dead. It looked like they had been attacked with a large knife or an axe. The girl that made the phone call was screaming that the killer had told her his name."

The Detective Inspector was reading the sheet of paper as he listened. Now he looked up;

"Roger Scott. The witness has said that the perpetrator was Roger Scott." He paused while looking at the sheet of paper. Then;

"This changes things, we now have four people dead and what seems like the same suspect or suspects." He looked at them all; it was time for action, time to stop pussy footing with Scott. He spoke;

"Back here in one hour, fully armed and ready, we will have search warrants and back up. I want each of his premises hitting simultaneously. We will force entry and search everybody present and every inch of every room. No stone unturned. I want him and his two thugs found. Now get to it."

Sitting in the back of his BMW Roger watched the Kent countryside flash by. Tom was driving, Jeff sitting next to him. He was thinking about the police interview. He knew that he had made them look like the amateurs that they were. He also knew that they wouldn't stop in their efforts to pin something on him. Maybe more so now after the fire in Peckham Rye, and by now they would know about the Serbians who owned the massage parlours being killed. According to Mary the girl had said that Roger Scott was responsible. Clearly he was being set up. He needed time to think, to work out who was capable of a double murder and who also had a grudge against him.

With this in mind he had decided to stay at his country residence near the village of Cliffe, in Kent. Before leaving London, Roger had been in touch with Johnny, instructing him to get some of his guys and keep a watch on the snooker hall and his penthouse. Also have one of them near the gaming salon. Then to report back to him at the first sign of anything untoward or suspicious occurring. Although he knew the police had little to go on he was still concerned, it was the first time he had let them get this close. Three years ago he had a high ranking detective in his pocket, he would meet Roger if or when necessary, to inform him of any investigation that was been carried out against him. Since then the guy had retired. Roger now regretted not replacing him. One more example of how he had let things go.

Roger glanced out of the window at the flamingos standing one legged on a small island in the middle of the manmade lake next to the cement works. He smiled sardonically. He had ordered Mary and Alan to terminate the two Serbians; now somebody had got there before them and completed the task. It could only have been Bojan Duric. Who else would know the two dead Serbs? Who else would have a reason? Who else would say that one of the dead guys was called Bojan, and that he was called Roger Scott? He had clearly worked out how Roger got his address. The two dead Serbs would have told him about the brothers severed ear. Bojan would have known that they would have talked before they begged for their lives. But more important; who else would try to pin the blame on Roger Scott? The guy was more dangerous than Roger had first anticipated. He needed moving sooner rather than later.

He thought quickly. Get every available member of his gang to find Bojan and eliminate him. Forget watching the various premises he owned, they would have to look after themselves. Picking up his mobile he went to ring Johnny.

He paused a moment; what if it was Bojan who had been killed in the massage parlour? He could have been there to see the two other Serbs, maybe something happened? Maybe Bojan is already dead. Roger thought a little more then went to press the speed dial that would contact Johnny. The phone rang as he touched it.

Marion Hill sat at the counter sipping a cup of tea. She mused on how quiet the day had been. A few lunchtime punters from the nearby office block squandering their hard earned. A few young fat arsed tracksuit bottomed girls, one or two of them heavily pregnant, smelling of stale tobacco and alcohol, as they departed with their family allowance and other state handouts. Marion was past caring. The last few weeks had changed her attitude to working in the *"Vegas Slots"* She had been caught up in a suspected murder case. Frightened by the police and intimidated by the infamous Roger Scott. So now she would do her job and pick up her wages, nothing more. If another gang of young men wanted to launch another attack with paint spray cans, they could get on with it. She would gladly open the door for them. Now she was tough, experienced, not easy to frighten or upset. She smiled to herself; *try me, bring it on!*

As the door crashed open and five heavily armed police stormed in Marion screamed before collapsing behind the counter. The lead policeman screamed louder;

"Everybody down! Now, on the floor, hands where we can see them!" Two of the office workers hit the floor, hands behind their heads, one of the fat young mothers started laughing. The rest ignored the armed police, one carried on feeding notes into a roulette machine, oblivious to all that was going on around her.

At the same time the Pot Black Snooker Hall was receiving the same treatment. The barman stood impassive, he was well trained. They could shout and scream as much as they wanted. Nothing untoward was going on; even the girls upstairs had been briefed as to how to handle the situation. He leaned against the bar watching as most of the punters did as they were told, then a slight smile as he noticed the big guy who was apparently a friend of Roger, was on his back with two armed police standing over him.

Roger's call centre was a different story. Mina and Jana were at their desks receiving calls from expectant punters. They had none of their usual protection from Tom, and it was still only two weeks since they had been attacked whilst at work. They hit the floor as one, did as they were told as they stared into the barrels of various weapons.

The small semi retired security guy that manned the entrance to the block of luxury apartments and penthouses, happily pressed the button on his desk, in order to release the catch that secured the two glass doors in front of him. The lead armed policeman thought about telling him to get on the floor, but a second look made him change his mind. He merely stood in front of the old guy as his comrades rushed past him and up the stairs.

***

Big Steve from the small town near Durham had a problem; there had been no sign of Roger Scott in the three days he had been attending the Pot Black Snooker Hall. He had turned up at various times of the day. He had left and returned the same day. He had chatted confidently to the guy behind the bar on each visit. Mentioned again that he and Roger were good friends, and that he was looking forward to seeing him again. The guy gave little away other than Roger would be in when he was in, not before. Steve was getting impatient, he wanted Scott dead sooner rather than later. He could be here for days. Who knows how long it would take for his target to arrive.

Sitting at the side of the room watching the other punters play their game he sipped a beer. Steve was thinking hard. He was starting to look suspicious, it wasn't as if he was any good at snooker, the day before he thought he noticed his opponent looking at the inside of his jacket as he leaned over the table to take his shot. Today he had left the hand gun back at the bedsit. Maybe he would try to get nearer to Roger before carrying it again.

It dawned on him that apart from the snooker hall, the gaming salon in Camberwell, and the building where Scott's penthouse was situated, he knew very little about Roger's movements. No idea where he spent his time or where else apart from the two nightclubs he would visit. He thought back to his first meeting with Scott, in the back room of the snooker hall, after the skinny copper had left. How they had planned to wreck the massage parlours, how they had used a gang of youngsters, to help smash the places to bits. The ones who always appeared to be wearing *similar hooded tops*. It struck him that he needed numbers, more feet on the ground. Somebody or some people to help with tracking down Roger Scott. Steve quickly finished his drink before moving towards the door. He didn't make it. He was about one metre away when they were violently smashed open. Now Steve lay on the floor looking up at the barrel of a gun that was being pointed at him.

Outside the snooker hall a blue Lexus containing three brothers from Liverpool was passing for the third time in an hour. The occupants had been to a bed and breakfast overnight. The elder brother had finally taken notice of his siblings. The previous day one of them had noticed what looked like a plain clothes policeman entering and leaving the cafe opposite, on more than one occasion. He reasoned that if they constantly patrolled the area they would certainly be noticed. With that in mind and also the need for food drink and toilets he decided that they should leave and return the following day.

They saw the blue flashing lights of the blacked out van before they heard the sirens. The youngest brother who was driving tried not to panic as the police vehicle screamed to a halt in front of them, Kang, the brother next to him shouted for him to turn the car round and get out of there. Spinning the steering wheel and flooring the accelerator he spun the car across the road to go in the opposite direction. He watched his rear view mirror as the back doors of the van flew open, and several armed police rushed out and ran towards the snooker hall. As he watched he failed to see a second black van coming towards him from the opposite direction. Foot still hard down he saw the van too late, stamping on the brakes he could not stop the Lexus from hitting it. Both airbags released themselves into the faces of the two front seat occupants, the elder brother in the back seat shouted in pain as the seatbelt cut into his body. The three brothers sat dazed, expecting guns to come through the windows at any moment. Then still watching as the rear doors of the van opened and armed police alighted and ran towards the snooker hall.

Remarkably their car engine was still running. The driver watched as an unarmed policeman, maybe the van driver opened his door and asked if anybody was hurt. The brother took his chance; he slammed the car into reverse and pressed his foot down. The police guy was knocked backwards by the still open door as the Lexus shot backwards, before the driver found first gear and rounded the van. Getting back up the uniformed policeman grabbed at his radio as the car escaped along New Cross Road.

As the BMW pulled into the driveway of the mansion on the Hoo Peninsula, near the village of Cliffe, Roger answered his phone. He didn't speak, just listened as Johnny explained that he had posted one of the guys near to every one of Roger's businesses including the two nightclubs. Roger thought that there wasn't much point as they were both closed. Johnny explained that each guy was close enough to see what was going on without been seen themselves. He then went on to say that at almost exactly the same time, apart from the nightclubs, armed police had raided each of the premises. They were still inside the buildings. Roger felt a vibration as his other mobile; his private one received a call. He quickly told Johnny to instruct the guys to stay put and that he would ring him back in half an hour. Answering the other phone Roger listened as the security guy who manned the door at his penthouse, reported that armed police were inside his property. He thanked the man and closed the call.

Now sitting in the lounge of his country residence he was in deep thought, going over in his head the recent events that had led to situation he was in. Clearly the reason for all the police raids was to find him. Two Serbians were dead, murdered and the guy who did it had named himself as Roger Scott. Problem? Maybe, but once the girl who had witnessed it all had seen Roger she would know that it wasn't him who was responsible. Roger mused that if the useless coppers had taken the trouble to look at the

275

CCTV from the massage parlours, they would also see that it wasn't him. *Fuckin' clowns.*

Maybe it was as he had thought earlier, a complete setup due to the way he had took the piss out of the two amateur detectives. Maybe. Then there was the high up copper, the one Jenkins had told him about, the same one who was giving him a lot of attention at that young girl's funeral. Was he behind all this? Roger sat back, closed his eyes. Then;

"Boss!"

Roger's eyes snapped open as he heard Jeff shout from the bedroom, quickly standing, he raced upstairs. Jeff and Tom were standing side by side gazing out of the picture window at the front of the house. As Roger reached them Tom was pointing; two cars, driving fast, blue lights flashing. They had left the A2 and were now heading down the country lane towards the village of Cliffe. From their elevated position they could see that the cars were still around five or six minutes away.

Roger thought quickly; they could be going anywhere, there had been a young girl's body found in a nearby ditch a year earlier. Maybe there was some trouble with the locals having too much to drink in the Six Bells pub. Maybe, but Roger knew different. He shouted at the twins to get in the BMW and start the engine. Heading into the lounge he met Mrs.Cowens, she was about to say something, maybe offer him a cup of tea. Roger had often thought that she alone must keep most of the Chinese tea merchants in business. He shut her up with a wave of his hand. Mrs. Cowens then listened as Roger quickly explained that there had been an emergency and he had to take the twins to Gatwick Airport immediately.

Running outside he jumped into the back of the waiting

car. He ordered Jeff to drive to Chatham, not the direct route, go the back way through Cooling then towards Wainscott, through the tunnel and then find one of the car parks around the town centre. Roger had spent a lot of time in and around the Chatham area over the last couple of years. He had endured the boredom of escorting Sam around the Historic Dockyard and various other tourist traps. He had also seen the drugged up dropouts in the dirty pedestrian only high street, along with the countless illegal's begging in a more than threatening manner. Knowing they were desperate people Roger had decided to instruct the twins to leave the car unlocked and with the keys in the ignition. It would change hands several times as the police tried to find it. He doubted they ever would. As the car pulled out of the cobbled yard Roger looked back. He could see the blue lights through the hedgerows but not the cars that held them. Now after a series of bends and turns in the quiet country road he relaxed a little, happy in the knowledge that by the time the hapless coppers had spoken to Mrs. Cowens, and probably searched the house, he and the twin brothers would be many miles away.

***

"Where the fuck are we going?" Yvette shouted as Spike slammed the gearstick down scraping the tortured cogs into drive. Rear wheels spinning the car shot forward leaving behind a trail of smoke and burnt rubber. "Answer me!"

"We are getting out of here quick."

Yvette had heard Spike talking on the phone as she descended the stairs. He had sounded worried. As she had walked into the room he slammed the phone down and gave her what she thought was a guilty look. He then stormed over to where a petrified Meg was sitting in the low chair. Without speaking he had snatched the frightened child out of her relative safety and comfort before thrusting her into Yvette's arms. He then picked up the car keys along with a brown parcel and headed for the door with Yvette following him. Now as Spike slowed the car to a speed that would not cause unnecessary attention he spoke;

"That was that Lisa bitch from the social services. She told me that they were on their way here with the police. If they get into the house and find this stash we are in big trouble. So we are fucking off until they have gone."

Yvette shook her head;

"You idiot, that is not going to happen. Lisa does not work there anymore; she walked out last week, so why should she be ringing the house?"

"It was her you stupid cow, I recognised the voice. Maybe she has gone back there; maybe they asked her to go back, who knows, but we can't take any chances. We will wait a couple of hours then one of us will go back and take a look."

"If she had gone back to work there I would have known. Do you think I let that fat boss of hers do what he wants to me for my pleasure? No I don't. So turn the car round or next time I'll tell him he can cum in your fuckin' mouth!"

Outside of the two up two down terraced house on the edge of Brixton, Lisa put her phone back into her handbag before starting the car. She had a perfect video and maybe six still shots of Yvette and Spike carrying Meg, running from the house before throwing the screaming infant into the back of the car and screeching away. She selected first gear before slowly driving away. Twenty minutes later Lisa parked her car outside of Camberwell Police Station.

***

Mike Smith and Sam Scott sat in the lounge of the Novotel in Greenwich. After finishing several drinks in the Copper Tap and talking for a lot longer than they had planned, it had dawned on them that they hadn't any idea what they were going to do next. They had not expected the surprise meeting in Peckham or the long talk. Neither of them thought that after three years they would ever see each other again.

Now after maybe a little too much alcohol they appeared to have formed some kind of bond. Was it due to their previous relationship? Or maybe that they were both trying to run away from something, or maybe someone. Both Mike and Sam knew in the back of their minds that the reason they were there was due to a simple common denominator. Both of them thrown together in the same circumstances, or maybe because of the same person. Back talking like old friends; *because of one man*. Roger Scott.

Sam had insisted that it was too late for Mike to make his way to the rail station. She also realised that she herself had nowhere to stay; she certainly would not be going back to the London penthouse ever again. That bastard of a man was welcome to his soiled bed and the slag responsible for it. Sam had too many bad memories of the mansion near the village of Cliffe on the Hoo Peninsula. She had no wish to visit there again either. No, she had her own bank account and a company credit card, and would be able to manage for herself. Sam never wanted to see Roger again.

She reasoned that Mike and she could book separate rooms at the hotel and that she was happy to pay. Mike agreed, he was past caring; he had neither the physical means or the inclination to suggest anything more than

279

a good night's sleep, then to see what tomorrow would bring. He had watched Sam closely as they had chatted; yes she was still beautiful, even through her tears. Did he still love her or still have any kind of affection for her? No, well maybe a little. Sam had been his first love; she was different, not a bit of skirt to screw then bin, not a slapper to take out the back of the pub for a quick one.

Sam was maybe the first girl he had respected. He hadn't tried to seduce her, or suggest sex of any kind for the first few weeks they had been together. Indeed it was Sam herself that asked him to stay over in her flat, that led to them sharing her bed for the first time. Mike had thought at the time that they would be together forever, get married, have children, and grow old together. He had bought an engagement ring and arrived at her flat, intending to go down on one knee. Only to see her in a passionate embrace with Roger Scott, then watching as they entered her flat, continuing to watch the window as the light went out. He had never felt more hurt and disappointed in his life.

It was then, with the jealously tearing him apart that he attempted to go against Scott. Only to be caught and then punished in the most horrendous way possible. Now the thoughts and memories from three years ago and seeing Sam again, had rekindled his hatred for Roger Scott even more. He was about to disappear, hide from Scott, now his anger had changed all that.

"Mike, are you alright?"

He looked up at Sam, tried to smile. Then;

"Yes, sorry. I was miles away, well maybe only a few miles away. I was thinking about us, before we broke up. How happy I had been."

Sam hung her head; it was a conversation that she didn't

want. She knew it was all her fault. It was her who had been swept off her feet like some smitten fourteen year old, she hadn't given Mike a second thought at the time. She felt the tears appearing again as she looked back at him;

"Sorry." Was all she could come out with. Mike spoke;

"Not as sorry as I am or he is going to be. He has ruined my life, and it was him that condemned me to the rest of my life in this fuckin' wheelchair. It was him that took you away from me. I don't have a life now, I going to make sure he doesn't either. I'm going to kill him."

Sam looked over her glass at Mike. She didn't know how to answer him. He was in a wheelchair, crippled, hardly capable of anything. Sam knew it was anger. Mike spoke again;

"I was going to disappear. There are a family of Serbians who have being trying to hurt Roger, by now he will know that I was involved somewhere along the line. I saw the television news earlier, the Serbs' house was on fire, there was flames everywhere, anybody inside would be dead. If they are not he will find every last one of them and kill them, then he will do the same to me. I know what he is capable of. I can't hide, he will find me." Mike stopped to sip his drink. Then:

"I know some guys at the boxing club I used to train at. They know how to get their hands on a gun. No questions asked. Tomorrow I am going see them, borrow a gun, then maybe go to his snooker hall and shoot him. I don't know what will happen to me after that and I don't care. My life's not worth living now."

Sam looked at him as he spoke. She could see that he meant it. Could he do it? Maybe it was the wine she had consumed, or maybe she was still angry at finding Roger and Mina in the penthouse, but she didn't feel any hurt in

281

what Mike was suggesting. Quite the opposite, maybe she liked the idea of being a rich widow. Then maybe it was the alcohol that was talking and not Mike.

"Mike, we have both had a lot to drink, why don't we get some sleep and maybe talk in the morning." Mike nodded, she was right. He picked up his glass and finished the contents. Pressing the four way switch on the arm of the wheelchair he headed for the lift. Sam had booked him a room with disabled facilities. Upon entering the room he had managed to undress himself and use his fold up crutches to get into the bathroom, which contained a raised toilet and seated shower. Now as he lay in bed he thought about what Sam had said, maybe he had consumed too much alcohol;

"But it doesn't change anything. Scott was still going to die and he was going to have the pleasure of killing him!"

Sam had watched him go, a pathetic thin and weak figure in a wheelchair. She dabbed her eyes. Like Mike, she was thinking about herself and him before they broke up. He was a handsome strapping, well built guy. It hadn't gone unnoticed to Sam that on various nights out, many young girls and ladies would be looking at Mike, and then at her in an envious fashion. Sam knew that he had never cheated on her, and he probably never would have. *Unlike that bastard of a husband with his clapped out old slag.*

She thought of how it might have been if she hadn't got personally involved with Roger Scott. Maybe she and Mike would have been married by now; maybe she would have still been working for Roger, totally oblivious to being involved in the business of drugs, prostitution and even murder. Did she feel responsible for Mike's injuries? Maybe a little. Maybe she should have met him before he found out about her and Roger. Maybe explained the situation gently. Then maybe the revelation wouldn't have been so hard for him to take. The jealousy may not have set in. Sam took another sip of wine, tears streaming. *"Then maybe Mike would not have suffered the terrible injuries that had destined him to life in a wheelchair."*

Now feeling more sober than drunk Sam thought some more. Mike appeared to be serious about killing Roger, was she bothered or hurt or upset? At this moment, *no* she was not. She had caught him in the act, almost red handed and it was clearly not the first time it had happened. Who knows, he could have been seeing to her for the last three years. All the time that Sam was in the house in Kent and Roger had to stay in London because of *"work commitments"* he was no doubt screwing the ugly bitch.

Sam decided that while she wouldn't help Mike, she wouldn't try to stop him either. She would listen to what he had to say over breakfast the following morning. Maybe he wouldn't mention it; maybe he would have calmed down by then and changed his mind.

Lisa stood outside of the two up two down house on the edge of Brixton. She watched as Spike and Yvette were led out in handcuffs. Lisa waited impatiently for the two social workers from the neighbouring Social Services Department to appear. It had only been two weeks since she had last seen Meg this close but the sight that greeted her caused Lisa to cry out loud.

Meg appeared to be unconscious. Lisa could not believe it was the same healthy looking child that she had been instrumental in, and involved with, during the fostering process. The slightly chubby, well nourished infant was now thin, drawn out and almost skeletal looking. Her face and hands were filthy, as if she had never been washed in several days. Dark rings surrounded her eyes. Lisa looked on as an ambulance arrived and the frightened pathetic excuse for a toddler, was carried towards the now open back doors.

Standing to one side Lisa watched further as two uniformed police officers entered the house. She wanted to go in herself, have a look around, see if she could make any sense of what might have been going on since Spike and Yvette had taken Meg into their care. A third uniform, a female, kindly but firmly stopped her from entering. Lisa went back to her car, sitting inside she retrieved her phone, and against all previous rules she rang Sam.

Big Steve, as he was known in the small town near Durham, before he moved to London, sat on the lone chair in the scruffy bedsit on the edge of Peckham. After the police had searched the Pot Black Snooker Hall and found nothing, he was also searched before being briefly interviewed. He told them that he was there to play snooker, he had never heard of Roger Scott. The barman backed his story and the police freed him.

Now sitting back in the dirty bedsit, he was pondering his next move when his mobile rang. He listened as Johnny gave him instructions, before resisting the temptation to punch the air. The message was short and to the point, Johnny wanted Steve to go to *Sam's* nightclub and relieve Harry in keeping an eye on the place. He explained that every business that Roger owned had been raided by armed police, now Roger needed somewhere he could hide while he worked out his next move. The two nightclubs were the only premises that hadn't been raided, yet. Steve was to keep watch for any police activity and then ring Roger's private mobile immediately, he gave Steve the number.

Trying to remove the fixed smile, Steve packed the rest of his belongings before stuffing the 9mm pistol into his shoulder holster, he then left the filthy bedsit for the last time. He could hardly believe his luck; this was going to be far easier than he first anticipated.

***

Jamil Rashid had run for his life, his home in Syria shook to its foundations as yet another bomb exploded not fifty metres from what was left of his front door. It had been a nightly occurrence for the previous six months. He had lived in the forlorn hope that peace would come soon, that the futile war would be stopped. Jamil now realised that Syria, his home for the last ten years, was finished. He managed to grab a small rucksack and stuff what was left of his life inside it, before following many others in the same predicament out of the outskirts of Damascus.

Now three years later he was once again a happy man. Jamil had been in England for two years since travelling across Europe, he had being left disappointed after one or two countries refused to let him and his comrades across their borders. After finally reaching France he had been looked after in a refuge before giving the last of his money to a man, who knew a man, who could get him across the English Channel.

The journey had been horrendous and dangerous. After four hours of being thrown about in the small craft, as it was battered by rough seas, he was glad to be unceremoniously dumped on a beach of sharp shale. Jamil and the rest of the unfortunates hadn't been there long before the night filled with flashing blue lights. He happily gave himself up to the police and immigration officers as they arrived in force.

He successfully pleaded his case that Syria was too dangerous to return to, although he lied that one day he would like to. He followed the rules and worked hard at various jobs before finding, in his opinion his ideal role. Now as he sat in his taxi, in a long line of similar vehicles, outside of the Bluewater Shopping Centre in Kent, he pondered on how lucky he had been, although he had a twinge of sadness as he remembered his friends who had not made the journey to a new life.

Roger and the twin brothers sat in the fourth taxi in less than half an hour. After leaving the car in Chatham they had taken a taxi to Strood. Then after finding a second taxi and being dropped off at Gravesend, they had ordered the driver of the third one to take them to the Bluewater Shopping Centre. Now as they approached the M25, Jamil, the frightened driver of the fourth cab, was fruitlessly explaining that he wasn't allowed to take his fares to unknown destinations. He carried on driving after Tom had stuck the barrel of a small handgun into his ribs.

An hour later Roger, Tom and Jeff stood near the mouth of an alleyway, fifty metres from the still closed *Sam's* nightclub. They had left the shaken taxi driver with two hefty tips; one financial, the second sound advice, as to forget what had happened and who he had seen over the last hour. They knew who he was and who he worked for, one word to anybody and he would be dead.

Roger and the twins had now waited long enough; in the twenty minutes they had been there they had seen nothing untoward, they were convinced that the police were not watching the premises. Roger spoke;

"Jeff, tell Tom to stay here and keep watch, you come with me as far as the door, keep a few steps ahead, look out for anything unusual. When I'm inside I want you two to go to the snooker hall, I'm going to get the rest of the guys there, we need a new plan, the filth are getting too close."

Three miles away a taxi stopped in a lay-by on the approach to the M25. The driver spoke slowly and calmly to the lady who had answered his 999 call. Jamil explained how he had picked up a fare from Bluewater only to be threatened at gunpoint and made to drive to Peckham. The operator listened before transferring the call to Camberwell Police Station.

By now the whole of the nick was on alert for any information to do with Roger Scott. The desk Sergeant made notes before it dawned on him that the description fitted the wanted twins, and quite probably Roger Scott, who was now wanted in connection with the murder of two men in a massage parlour. He told Jamil to stay where he was and a patrol car would be there in a few minutes. The Sergeant then rushed the latest report to the office upstairs which housed the C.I.D. Three miles away Jamil selected first gear and drove away.

Sam had been lying on the hotel bed thinking about the previous night's conversation with Mike Smith. By now he would be sober, maybe calmed down a little. Getting out of bed she decided that she wouldn't mention the conversation. They would have breakfast together, talk a little more and then maybe go their separate ways.

Now towelling her hair dry she thought some more. *Don't get mad get even.* Sam couldn't remember where she had heard that before but she would try it. She would find the best female divorce lawyer around. She would take Roger and his finances to the cleaners, set herself up for life. Leave him and his slag Mina with nothing but each other, that's what they deserved.

Half an hour later Sam drank more coffee as she waited for Mike to arrive. An hour later she stood at the reception desk listening as the phone in his room rang out. After explaining that Mike was disabled and maybe needed some help, she stood as one of the hotel cleaners explained that the room was empty, Mike had left the hotel.

Sam picked up her phone to ring Mike; it rang before she had a chance:

"Mike, are you alright?"

"Sam, its Lisa from the social services."

Sam listened as Lisa the social worker quickly but precisely explained what had happened to little Meg. About the police and social workers arriving at the two up two down terraced house on the edge of Brixton. Sam listened in disbelief as Lisa described the pathetic state Meg was in.

Whether it was a build up of finding her husband with Mina, then discovering Mike Smith and hearing what had happened to him, or maybe that she expected something like this to happen to little Meg, but Sam burst into tears. She started screaming at Lisa that it was her fault, and that she had tried to warn her that there was something not right about those two scruffy looking people, who she handed Meg to. Lisa tried to calm Sam down, she realised she had said too much over the phone. She suggested that they should meet, talk face to face. Ten minutes later Sam was sitting in the back of a taxi; she was travelling to the social services office to meet Lisa.

It was an hour later that Sam had left the office. She was still very upset, Lisa and Sam sat impassive as a temporary Director explained that the previous boss had been suspended, and was under investigation, both internally and by the police. Yvette and Spike were still in police custody. Meg was undernourished but safe and she was being looked after in hospital prior to her going to a private residential nursery. There would also be a full enquiry as to what had gone so badly wrong.

Now standing in the street Sam was like a little girl lost. She badly wanted to see both Meg and Adie, but she knew it would not be possible any time soon. It was then that she pulled out her phone and rang Mike Smith.

In a street of terraced houses in Peckham Rye, Bojan Duric walked towards the remains of what was once his family home. He paused to look then stopped, taking in the devastation. Barriers had been erected to stop the looters and the ghouls with cameras getting too close. The four houses either side had been evacuated, the talk was that like Bojan's house they too would have to be demolished. As he looked through tearful eyes at what was once, where he and his now dead wife had spent many happy years, he came to a decision.

He stood awhile before making his way to the *Gowlett Arms*. Now sitting in the back room he sipped his drink. Bojan was in deep thought; he pondered on what was left of his life, a faint smile as he remembered the happy times, his beautiful wife, bringing up their three children. The smile faded as he remembered that one of them was now dead, killed in the most tragic of circumstances, the other two crippled for life. Mila, the only woman he had ever loved was gone. Why? Because his two sons had been fuckin' stupid? Maybe, but more so *because of one man;* Roger Scott.

Bojan glanced around the small room, he was on his own, the door closed, the barman was busy at the front of the pub. He slipped his hand inside his jacket and withdrew the 9mm pistol from his shoulder holster, another glance round as he checked the chamber, six bullets, more than enough. Retrieving his mobile phone he rang Aco, his eldest son.

It was twenty minutes later that Bojan, Aco and his youngest surviving son Dorde, stood in the burnt out ruin that was once their family home. The two sons had met Bojan at the back of the house as instructed. Bojan had kicked what was left of the flimsy back door, it fell in and the three of them entered the house. He had told them that the house was about to be demolished, and he wanted the three of them there for a last look before the cranes and bulldozers moved in.

Now as the remaining members of the Duric family stood in the blackened shell, that was once the kitchen and dining room they looked around in silence. Bojan pictured where the table used to be. He pictured the five of them enjoying many meals. Then to where the cooker had been, Mila happily cooking whilst singing to herself. The pictures faded as he turned to look at his two boys. Crippled and damaged, at fault for all this devastation before him. As Aco and Dorde stood side by side in silence Bojan walked behind them. The two young men were in deep thought, as if they were spell bound by the sight before them. The last voice they heard was their fathers;

"Good night boys."

The first bullet hit Aco in the back of the head at almost point blank range, as the front of his skull exploded across the charred room. Dorde stood in shock as his brother dropped to the floor. Bojan kept the gun raised as Dorde half turned towards his father. The pistol spat a second bullet that entered Dorde's head through his left ear. He joined Aco on the floor, dead before he reached it. Bojan looked down at his two sons' before taking a last look around the blackened room. Checking his gun once again, he replaced it in his shoulder holster and left the family home for the last time. He headed for the nightclub where all his troubles had begun; he wanted to try entering the premises that had been the cause of his family's demise. Bojan Duric would take a last look before he used his gun for the last time.

Assistant Chief Constable Ted Walton listened as Detective Inspector Terry Thompson explained that they had received a positive sighting of both the wanted twins and Roger Scott. He said that it looked like they may be holed up in the disused nightclub that was once known as *Sam's*. Ted thought about it, it seemed a reasonable assumption. He was aware that all of Scott's other premises had been raided with no result. It would an easy enough task to order an armed response unit to raid the nightclub and arrest Scott and the twins. He thought some more. Then what? An overpaid barrister would have him freed without charge in a matter of hours. *No!* This was not going to happen. He sat back in his chair as the D.I. watched him, Terry Thompson was waiting for the order to move in and arrest Roger Scott and the twins. Ted spoke;

"Ok Terry thanks. Leave it with me."

Thompson opened his mouth to speak, maybe protest. The Assistant Chief Constable continued;

"I want this doing right, no pointless cavalry charges like the last time. Give me an hour to organise the correct procedures and search warrants. I don't want some smart arsed lawyer getting him off on a technicality."

Terry Thompson walked out. Ted picked up his phone and ordered a car to pick him up in five minutes. He then stood and took a last look round the office. He doubted he would see it again. Leaving his desk he made his way to the basement and the evidence holding area. His plan was simple; he would arrive at the nightclub before the armed police. He would find Scott, show him his warrant card and then shoot him dead. Maybe he would then turn the gun on himself and squeeze the trigger. Ted knew he was a dead man walking, his time was limited, and he was now in constant pain. He was going to die, but he was going to make sure Roger Scott went first.

As instructed, big Steve, as he was known in the small town near Durham before he moved to London, now stood outside *Sam's* nightclub. According to Johnny, Roger Scott would be inside by himself. Johnny had told him to watch the place until another of Roger's guys turned up to relieve him; he was to then go to the Pot Black Snooker Hall where the rest of the guys would be in the back room. They needed to talk, work out and plan their next move.

Steve stood in an alleyway opposite the club; he pressed the bulge under his jacket, reassured that the gun was still there. Steve smiled to himself; of course the gun was still there, but it had been a habit over the years that he couldn't change.

With another glance along both directions of the street, he crossed the road and stood at the door of the building. Steve hadn't stayed alive in dangerous situations without being cautious. So when he noticed the door not only unlocked but slightly ajar he hesitated. He listened for any kind of noise inside, any movement, anything that could explain why the door wasn't locked. Nothing, no sounds at all. Patting his jacket again he slowly pushed the door open and stepped inside, he pulled the door behind him leaving it in the same position as he had found it. Big Steve stood for a full minute letting his eyes get accustomed the semi darkness, and also listening for any sounds. Hearing nothing he slowly made his way across the dance floor towards the flight of stairs at the back of the hall.

Bojan Duric stood looking at the nightclub. It was the first time he had been to *Sam's*. He had often been curious about the place. The place where all his problems began. The place where two of his three sons had been permanently damaged. As he had walked the short distance from where the taxi had dropped him, he contemplated his next move. All his family were dead, there was nothing left for him, nobody to love or care for. Nobody to look forward to being with each evening. Nobody to impress or cherish. Why? *Because of one man.*

Bojan had decided to track down Roger Scott and kill him, shoot him dead, and then maybe piss on his body before turning the gun on himself. He didn't care how long it would take him. He would make regular visits to all of Roger Scott's premises; it would only be a matter of time before he would find that *bastard* man. He wouldn't see it coming, by now Scott would think that Bojan was dead, murdered in a massage parlour. But before he killed Roger Scott he wanted to visit the shithole that had been the start of his life's ruination.

Now looking up at the boarded up window, he pictured in his mind the brick going through it, followed by the petrol container. Bojan smiled as imagined the scene inside, the fear, the panic, the screams. Burning flesh followed by painful death. He briefly thought about his youngest son Rodovan, who had been present to witness the full event. Now walking towards the door he stopped and turned away as he noticed an official looking car approach. Head down he crossed the road and pretended to look in a shop window. The shop was lit up with bright fluorescent lights, that made his attempts to use the reflection to see what was going on behind him almost impossible. Bojan waited a full minute before slowly turning around. He saw the car pulling away. What he hadn't seen was Assistant Chief Constable Ted Walton leave the car and enter the nightclub.

Now Bojan approached the door, his right hand moving up unintentionally to touch the bulge under the left side of his jacket, Bojan hesitated as noticed that the door was open. He stopped in his tracks; he hadn't survived the terrors of war and managed to build up an illegal business in south London without being aware and cautious. Slowly pushing open the door he peered inside the gloomy entrance. Bojan was thinking that maybe vandals or drug addicts or alcoholics or scrap thieves had broken in.

Moving further into the room the lingering smell of burnt wood and plastic hit him. Now pausing to look across the dark room he pictured once again the scene of tragic devastation the firebomb had caused. He could see where it had landed, a large round concentration of bare concrete, where the middle of the floor had once been. The bar was still intact where his youngest son would have been standing when it happened. He looked across the room to where there appeared to be a staircase, leading up to what looked like another lounge or maybe an office. He could see a glimmer of light coming from under a door. Bojan studied it for a few seconds. Was Scott up there? Had fortune smiled on him, if so this would make his job both easier and quicker. Still looking up he walked slowly across the ruined dance floor then approached the stairs. Taking the gun out of the holster Bojan slowly climbed the steps.

The Assistant Chief Constable, Ted Walton had told his driver to return to Camberwell, he said he had a private meeting to attend to, almost undercover. He would ring when he needed collecting. Entering the nightclub he was not surprised that the door had been unlocked. The report had said that Roger Scott and his minders were thought to be inside. Ted pictured the scene; the three of them getting out of the taxi, a furtive look around before quickly entering the night club. They would have kicked the door shut then moved away from it and to wherever they were now. Being in a hurry maybe they hadn't realised that the door had not fully closed.

Ted Walton stood in the foyer and looked across the dance floor. It was very clear where the fire that had killed his beloved goddaughter had started. He looked away quickly as he felt a tear start to form. He needed to have clear sight. Looking up, he saw the stairs at the back of the hall. Ted made his way towards them, more slowly now as an agonising sharp pain shot across his stomach. Reaching the bottom of the stairs he retrieved the confiscated gun, sliding off the safety catch he checked there was a bullet in the breach. Then he climbed the stairs.

Big Steve, as he was known in the small town near Durham ascended the dark gloomy stairs inside the boarded up *Sam's* nightclub. He took the stairs one at a time, as fast as he could. As he climbed he kept to the sides of each step to avoid any of the wood creaking. On reaching the top he noticed a room with glass doors on the left, and in front of him a dark wooden door that may have been some kind of private office. He stood for a moment listening for any noise that might give an idea where Scott was.

Steve saw the light shining from under the office door, then a shadow move across it; he silently opened one of the glass doors on the left and stepped inside what looked like a small bar, or maybe a private lounge. Quietly closing the door behind him he stood to one side and peered through the glass. He waited a full minute. Then slowly opening the door he moved quietly towards the office. The 9mm pistol was held steady in his right hand as he stood to one side of the door, and placed his left hand on the handle. Steve counted to three in his head then pressed the door handle down. He walked into to the office, right hand outstretched, gun first.

30 minutes earlier.

Mike Smith had been sitting in his wheelchair for over half an hour looking at the former *Sam's* nightclub. As he sipped some of the watery tepid coffee in the cafe opposite, he looked out of the grimy window. He cast his mind back to just over three years earlier; three years earlier he had been head of security at this same nightclub. In those days it was known as *The Pink Pussycat*. Mike had been fit and strong, he had trained other bouncers how to defend and attack if any trouble had started, although on most occasions it turned out to be more attack and attack. Mike had been happy then, it was the same nightclub where he had first chatted to Sam, his then boss's secretary. Their romance had blossomed until one man stepped in and took it away. The same one man who was responsible for changing his life forever.

Now Mike watched as Roger Scott entered *Sam's* nightclub. He had watched as Scott had closed the door behind him after looking furtively along both sides of the street. He noticed that Jeff and Tom, who he remembered from his time working for Roger, quickly turned and walked away. Mike had waited another few minutes. He knew he had a problem. While the front doors to the nightclub had disabled access via two concrete ramps, and the route to the dance floor and toilets were also wheelchair friendly, he knew that his target would be in the office upstairs. Up the stairs that were impossible for him to ascend. Mike took the keys from his pocket, Sam's keys, the same keys he had taken from her handbag, while they were drinking in the hotel the previous night. He looked at them before placing a five pound note on the table and leaving the cafe.

Outside Mike looked up and down the street as he waited at the crossing, then as the electronic bleeps indicated that it safe to cross, he pressed the four way switch on the right armrest and steered himself to the other side of the road, then up the concrete ramps to the front door of *Sam's*. Finding it difficult but not impossible, he managed to enter the key and unlock the door. Slowly wheeling himself in he stopped inside the doorway. He pushed the door closed as far as he could manage, but not enough to close it completely. Mike listened for any sound that he might have been heard. Nothing, he waited another thirty seconds. Still nothing. Taking the gun out of his inside pocket he checked it over. His friend at the boxing club had given some basic instruction on how to use it;

"Get as close as you can, do not rush, squeeze the trigger, don't pull it, aim for the body mass, centre of the chest, not a head shot, too difficult with a handgun, once he is down use a second shot to make sure."

Mike was ready. He would steer himself across the dance floor, he would then wait until Roger came down the stairs, which he reasoned at some point he would have to. Roger would see him, Mike would smile, ask him how he was. Roger would lose it and come tearing down the stairs. Mike would kill him at point blank range. First shot to the chest to drop him, second one to the head to make sure. Easy and straight forward. Mike smiled at the thought that he might even get away with it. There must be many people to have suffered, *because of one man*, that man; Roger Scott.

Now steadying himself in the wheelchair at the foot of the stairs, Mike waited.

Roger Scott sat in the upstairs office of *Sam's* nightclub. He was looking at the list of names in front of him. At the top was Bojan Duric. Picking up a pen Roger put a line through it. Bojan would be dead very soon. Once Roger got to the snooker hall his first priority would be to get every available man looking for him, even the youths, *the ones that wore similar hooded jackets.* Nobody had ever managed to escape Roger.

Next was the high ranking copper. Roger put a line through it. So they were trying to pin a murder on him that he didn't commit. He was innocent of that particular killing. It could be easily proved.

Next on the list was Mike Smith. Roger smiled as he put a line through it. He was convinced that the information Bojan, and the other Serbians had gained had come from Mike. How else would they have known about the call centre and the house in Kent? By now Mike would know that all the attempts and efforts to harm Roger had failed. He would be frightened, panicking. Mike would be long gone. *But he still wouldn't be safe, Roger would find him, and this time he would not be so lenient.*

The rest of the list was his inner circle, his most trusted allies. Johnny, Harry, Mary and Alan. Roger looked at it; he noted that he hadn't included the twins, Tom and Jeff. He shook his head thinking he was starting to get paranoid. Then something in the back of his mind jumped forward. He looked at the list again, picking up his pen he wrote down another name; Steve.

Now in deep thought he went over each name, crossing out each one as he went back through in his mind how long he had known the first four of them. Their loyalty over the years had been unquestionable. Several times each and every one of them had put their lives on the line for Roger. He also knew that if there had been a maverick among them one of the others would have told him. Four more names off the list. Roger looked at the final name; Steve. Clearly the guy was capable, he had proved that when Roger had ordered him to kill Jenkins in the snooker hall. He wouldn't have known that the gun was empty when he pulled the trigger.

Thinking again; Steve had followed his orders when he was told to help wreck the massage parlours. There was also the fact that he hadn't seen or heard of Steve since. Surely if the guy was involved with the recent events Roger would have heard his name mentioned by now. He put a line through Steve's name.

Now Roger sat back in his chair and smiled again. It was over, he was out of danger. All names deleted, list cleared. The next move would be to contact his barrister. Have a brief meeting with him, and then go to the police station voluntarily. See what flimsy evidence they had against him. Roger stood and stretched his body. The last few weeks had been both testing and strenuous; but now it was finished, time to get his life back together.

Roger realised that maybe now was the time to find his wife, maybe win her over. Rekindle the love and make up for the damage he had caused to their marriage due to the recent events. It had been an exciting few weeks which he had enjoyed. Back to the thrill of the chase, pitting his wits against the bad guys trying to damage him, and also the corrupt police. Despite all their best efforts Roger had won. It was never in doubt. Roger Scott *always* wins. Would he make an effort to find Sam and get his marriage back on track? Maybe, maybe not. Now standing, he walked towards the drinks cabinet at the back of the office. *Then stopped in his tracks.*

Was it a sixth sense? Or maybe a gut feeling? Roger felt the hair on the back of his neck move, a quiver, a feeling that he had experienced and then honed over the years. Part of being one step ahead, part of the reason he had always won and stayed alive while his enemies had perished.

Roger turned slowly to find himself looking down the barrel of a 9mm handgun.

***

Twenty minutes earlier Detective Inspector Terry Thompson stood with Detective Constable Farrell. They watched out of the office window as Ted Walton sat in the back of an unmarked police car, and then continued watching as the Assistant Chief Constable was driven away. Thompson spoke;

"What the fuck is he up to? He was supposed to be organising search warrants and an armed response unit."

As they watched the phone on Thompsons desk rang. He answered it, listened as the sergeant in the evidence holding area explained that Assistant Chief Constable

Ted Walton had just left there with a 9mm pistol. D.I. Thompson said a quick thanks before replacing the phone. Then looking at D.I. Farrell;

"Shit, I think I know where he is going."

Taking his eyes off the window he grabbed the phone again, hitting an internal button he shouted frantically.

Inside of the closed *Sam's* nightclub Mike had watched through the semi darkness as a man wearing black clothing came down the stairs. He readied himself; hand firmly around the butt of the gun. He would wait until Roger Scott got closer to him; close enough for him to get a clear aim on his target. Close enough for Mike not to miss. He waited then lowered the gun, as he realised that the man he was about to kill was not Roger Scott. The man saw Mike as he neared the bottom few steps. He glanced at Mike's gun, then walked around him and towards the emergency exit at the back of the dance floor. He stopped, then turned. Then, in a gravelly voice;

"Too late son, the job's done."

The man in black clothing aimed a sharp kick to the bar that held the emergency door shut, it flew open, and he was gone. Mike sat for a couple of minutes pondering his next move. What had happened up there? Who was the guy who had just left? He thought he recognised him but he didn't speak in a normal voice, and half his face was covered.

Mike thought quickly; *"Job done?"* and the guy had seen his gun, he must have known what Mike had intended. Then thinking again; *"Too late son."* Was Roger Scott already dead? Mike wasn't about to hang around and find out. Hitting the four way switch on the arm of his wheelchair, then pressing it forward he too headed for the emergency exit. As he cleared the door and set off along the back ally his phone rang. It was Sam.

***

Depending on the role they are required to perform, handguns are manufactured in various sizes of both calibre and velocity. One thing they do have in common is that upon the bullet leaving the gun barrel it travels at an average speed of around 1200 to 1500 feet per second. With the speed of sound being around 1125 feet per second, depending on the distance, the intended target would feel the bullet before he or she heard report of the gun being fired. On top of which this particular gun had been fitted with a sound suppressor. Which was why Roger Scott did not hear anything.

The small amount of noise the gun created was confined to the office. The gun had already been loaded, cocked and the safety off, no sounds, no metallic clicks. Roger had opened his mouth to speak, maybe to threaten the guy holding the gun. He clearly recognised him. He didn't get the chance. Scott felt a thud as the 9mm bullet entered his head just below his left eye, it smashed through his skull then exited at the rear. Not only did Roger fail to hear anything, he also failed to feel anything. The round did not go in a straight line, upon meeting the resistance of the bone below the eye socket, above the cheek bone, the trajectory changed, zig-zagging through his brain, scrambling all in its way, before leaving his instantly dead body.

The owner of the gun had leaned over Roger. He was clearly dead. He watched as the last of the heartbeats pumped blood onto an ever increasing pool beneath him. The gun owner knew Roger was no more, but that didn't stop the second bullet being fired from an even closer range into the dead man's right eye.

Placing the murder weapon back into the shoulder holster, the gunman took a last look round the upstairs office in *"Sam's"* nightclub, before descending the stairs and leaving through the back door and into the alleyway.

Detective Inspector Terry Thompson gripped the steering wheel until his knuckles were white, as the police car sped through the streets of south east London. Detective Constable Farrell sat next to him. They were being followed by a van full of armed police. D.I. Terry Thompson explained to D.C. Farrell that at first he had been slightly baffled by what looked like, and came across as the Assistant Chief Constables personal vendetta against Roger Scott. Farrell listened in silence as Thompson continued;

"That day we pulled Scott in on Ted Walton's orders, it was obvious to both us and Scott that we had nothing to go on. He made us look like a right pair of twats. Then, with Ted making us ignore other more important cases to concentrate on Scott, I thought for a while that it was personal. Remember the picture in the paper of the young girl's funeral, the one who was killed in the nightclub fire?"

Farrell nodded his head; "Yes, remember it well. Ted standing next to her parents in full dress uniform."

"Exactly, so I looked into it, it turns out that the girl, what was she called? Austen, yeah, Emily Austen, well it just so happens that she was his god daughter. He is clearly blaming Scott for her death, and then there was Nixon, the detective who was shot and killed in the nightclub. Ted Walton was best man at his parent's wedding and remained good friends with them. He is obviously blaming Scott for both deaths. Now he's got a fuckin' gun. It's too much of a coincidence for Ted not to be going to find Scott himself and take the law into his own hands."

Thompson hit the car horn as a small motorcycle carrying a Pizza container cut across in front of him.

"Then he sent that fuckin' idiot Jenkins to raid his call centre. All that achieved was to warn Scott that we were on to him."

The D.I. continued;

"Have you also noticed that he is in constant pain and the weight is dropping off him? Well I think he's got something terminal, I think he knows he's dying. He also knows we can't pin anything on Scott, so he is on his way to do something drastic."

The police car screeched to a halt outside of the now closed *"Sam's"* nightclub. The two detectives jumped out of the car as eight heavily armed police officers leapt out of the back of the van.

In the upstairs office in the building that was formally *"Sam's"* nightclub, the Assistant Chief Constable Ted Walton lowered the gun he was holding. He stared at a big guy who was staring at the dead body on the office floor. The big guy also had a gun, it had also been lowered. Ted was about to speak, about to say something official, when a noise behind him made both the big guy and himself turn their heads. Big Steve took in the sight before him. *Roger Scott clearly very dead on the floor.* A man who was very clearly a copper holding a gun. A big guy standing over the dead Scott with a gun in his hand. The three men looked at each other, none of them knowing what to say.

Then the silence was broken by the sound of police sirens, then brakes screeching, then car doors being opened then slammed. Bojan Duric was the first to react. Raising his gun before either big Steve or Ted did, he eyed them both as he moved to door; he stepped through backwards still looking at them. Two steps out then he turned and ran towards the stairs. Steve looked at the Assistant Chief Constable before following Bojan out of the office. Both of them still had the guns in their hands as they ran down the stairs. The entrance door crashed open as the first of the armed police burst into the disused nightclub.

Big Steve had served in the 2nd battalion of the Para's. He knew the drill, he knew what would come next. He dropped his weapon and put his hands in the air. What Steve didn't know was that Bojan either did not know the drill, or he was past caring.

Bojan looked down at the now increasing number of armed police filing through the door. By now the lead policeman was screaming for him to drop his weapon and put his hands where they could be seen. Bojan's mind flashed back to the reality of the situation he was in. His three sons were dead; his loving wife was dead, all *because of one man,* who was now also dead. Bojan was indeed past caring.

Turning sideways to present a smaller target as he had been trained, Bojan raised his gun and squeezed the trigger towards the leading armed policeman. The round exited the pistol in the general direction of the officer. The gun was an old well used weapon, out of date, and had not been accurately tried or tested by Bojan. He hadn't bothered to clean it or oil it or check it over. Also it had been a long time since his Serbian Army days; he was out of practice in the use of handguns. The bullet slammed harmlessly into the wall to the side of where the police were standing.

By now all of the armed police had entered the room. All highly trained, and all carrying Glock 9mm self loading pistols. The men behind the guns regularly attended the Police Firearms Academy near the Kent town of Gravesend. Practising for hour after hour, each one fully trained to handle situations of this kind. After hearing the gunshot and recognising the danger, each one of them aimed and fired their 17 round pistols. With the Glock having a trigger safety mechanism that negates the need for an external safety selector, the rounds were fast and accurate. Bojan had fired first; it was a self-defence situation.

Both Bojan Duric and big Steve, *as he would no longer be known in the small town near Durham,* fell to floor as a hail of well aimed bullets penetrated their chests and other parts of their torsos. They were both dead before their lifeless bodies hit the stairs and tumbled to the bottom. The armed police stood their ground as Detectives Thompson and Farrell entered the dancehall. Through the smoke and cordite they took in the scene before them. Two men down, clearly dead. The police covering every part of the room with their guns.

Then as the smoke started to lift, they looked towards the top of the stairs, to see a thin withered man standing with his arms outstretched. The man shouted;

"Assistant Chief Constable Ted Walton. Unarmed." Immediately eight guns trained upon him before Detective Inspector Thompson shouted for them to lower their weapons. Ted slowly walked down the stairs stopping briefly to look at the two dead men strewn across the floor.

***

"Mike, where are you?"

"Near your nightclub."

Sam was pleased to hear his voice. She had a lot on her mind with the Meg situation, but she was still worried about what Mike was going to do, even though what he had said the previous night was after alcohol, and she now cared little about her husband.

"Are you alright?"

"Yeah I'm fine, but I'm not sure your husband is."

"Why what's happened?" Mike answered, he lied;

"I'm not sure, but I saw him go inside the nightclub a while ago, he hasn't come out yet and now there are police everywhere."

Sam thought for a minute then saw a taxi approaching, a light showing that it was available. She flagged it down.

"Stay where you are Mike, I am on my way, maybe ten minutes." She ended the call.

Detective Inspector Terry Thompson examined the scene around him. Roger Scott was dead along with two unknown people, both of whom were or had been armed. The armed police had searched the rest of the premises, and now they stood waiting for their next order. D.I. Thompson gave it;

"Detective Farrell, stay here until the uniforms and further back up arrive, then do what you need to do." Then turning to the lead armed policeman;

"I want all of you to follow me to Scott's snooker hall on New Cross Road; the report was that the two brothers we are looking for were here. Clearly they are not. He must have told them to go somewhere. It can't have been either his flat or house, my guess is the Pot Black. Kill the sirens before we get there, we go straight in, the back room first."

He walked out of the nightclub then waited as the armed police got back into their van.

The three brothers from Liverpool sat in a stolen taxi

two streets away from the Pot Black Snooker Hall. They had driven the damaged Lexus to a multi-storey car park and left it there. Maybe they would report it stolen later, maybe not.

The two younger siblings had argued with their elder brother that their feud with Roger Scott was over. It had gone far enough. Clearly the police were onto him, why else would they raid his snooker hall so heavily armed? The elder brother argued that they would have heard if Roger Scott had been arrested or shot in the last raid. He wanted to be sure that Scott was either dead or in jail. He wanted one more visit to the snooker hall, no violence just a visit, somebody in there would know what had happened. Then they would go back to Liverpool and forget all about Roger Scott.

Reluctantly the two younger brothers agreed. The elder brother smiled inwardly, he was lying. What he wanted was access the hall, in the hope that the man who had put him in his wheelchair was there. He would shoot him in cold blood regardless of the consequences. He knew that his two younger siblings weren't happy, but by now he was past caring.

Leaving the keys in the taxi with engine running, the man in the wheelchair sat back as one of his brothers pushed him across the road to the entrance of the Pot Black. The other one held the door open as they then led him inside.

Sam stood next to the seated Mike Smith; they were maybe twenty metres from the front door of what was once *Sam's* nightclub. They were among many other people standing behind a police cordon, while watching the various policemen and women. Some were armed, some were in plain clothes, most of them were in uniform. They had been there around ten minutes when an ambulance arrived and reversed towards the double doors.

Mike had told Sam that he intended to kill Roger Scott; the previous night was not bravado or drink. He lied to her saying that when he arrived at the nightclub the police were already there. He said he had heard people saying that somebody had been shot inside the club.

Sam looked on as the ambulance paramedics carried a stretcher through the doors. Was her husband dead? Maybe it was just some drug addict who had been squatting in there, maybe taken an overdose, or maybe an alcoholic choking on his own vomit. Still watching the proceedings Sam noticed Detective Constable Farrell standing near the ambulance, she recognised him from her visit to Camberwell Police Station, before she had gone to Spain. Moving away from Mike she pushed through the people in front her and managed to get within a few feet of the detective. She shouted his name. Farrell saw her and walked towards her. Sam saw his face change as he recognised her. She spoke;

"Do you remember me? I'm Sam Scott. Is my husband in there?"

Half an hour later Sam stepped out of the back seat of a police car, a police woman had got out first and now she held the door open for Sam. D.C. Farrell remained in the car. Mike watched her, maybe waiting for her to burst into tears or maybe collapse to the floor, or maybe show some kind of emotion. What he saw was Sam calmly walk back to him and suggest they left the scene

***

The three brothers from Liverpool sat together. One in

309

wheelchair, the other two either side of him. They looked around the room at the five men and one woman who were glaring back at them.

It had seemed straight forward enough, enter the snooker hall, then look and listen to glean any information they could about Roger Scott. Get what they wanted and leave. What the three brothers didn't know was that they had been recognised as soon as they had entered the building.

Johnny leaned over the eldest one, clearly the leader.

"So, what brings you pieces of shit back to London?" The guy looked up at Johnny, defiant. He didn't answer. Johnny continued;

"Roger warned the three of you three years ago in this same room, that if you showed your faces here again you would be dead." Still no answer.

Johnny glanced at the rest then pulled out his phone. He dialled Roger's number, then waited. It rang several times before eventually connecting to the answer phone, he tried again. Same thing. He tried a different number, Roger's personal phone. Still nothing. Johnny looked over to Jeff;

"Get back round to the nightclub, see what's happening, something isn't right." Jeff looked at Tom, a slight nod of his head and they stood as one. Then stopped as the barman put his head through the serving hatch;

"Johnny, the police are on their way in, looks serious, same pricks as last time."

Jeff turned back to Johnny; he looked at him waiting for some kind of instruction. Johnny opened his mouth to speak as the doors crashed open, and the armed police rushed in. The lead guy shouting for everyone to get on the floor.

It had been many years earlier when Tom and Jeff were working in a car wash as sixteen year olds, that a fight had started with the manager. In the ensuing battle Tom had been knocked unconscious, after being struck with a tyre iron just above his ear. After many weeks in hospital he was discharged, not only 90 per cent deaf, but due to some brain damage, he had turned into a more dangerous psychopath than he had been before he had been admitted. He was totally fearless in any situation, and also had a hatred of police in any shape or form.

His slow brain didn't register the seriousness of the situation; all he saw was intruders looking dangerous. Standing his ground he reached inside his jacket. There were no shouts, no warnings, just two loud bangs, as a double tap from the lead policeman's Glock self loading pistol halted Tom in his tracks. Jeff looked at his twin brother as two holes appeared in his chest, just left of centre. Jeff watched as his twin brother died. He then shouted;

"Murdering bastards!" He wasn't carrying a gun but it didn't stop him launching himself towards the armed policeman. It was the last thing he did before receiving the same fate as Tom.

Johnny, Harry, Mary and Alan slowly raised their hands as did two of the brothers from Liverpool. The armed policeman screamed at the elder brother to do the same. He shrugged, said he couldn't, he was paralysed. His hands stayed where they were on the chair arms. The man in the wheelchair and the policeman staring at each other. The policeman lowered his weapon;

"Keep him covered." He turned to look at the other men and one lady in the room.

The wheelchair bound brother from Liverpool listened as Johnny spoke, telling the police that they were wasting their time. Roger Scott wasn't here, they had killed Tom and Jeff for nothing. The armed officer smiled at him;

"We know he isn't here. He is in his night club, on the floor. Dead."

At that point Detective Inspector Terry Thompson stepped through the doorway; he looked around the room then quickly assessed the situation; two more dead bodies, the twins who he had been trying to find and arrest. He spoke;

Ok. I will take it from here."

The man in the wheelchair took in what was being said. *Roger Scott dead.* All the pain he had endured. *Because of one man,* and now he was not going to get the chance, or have the pleasure of killing him. He looked again at the leader of the armed police. He was still smirking like he was taking some kind of inane thrill out of the situation. The crippled man had his mind set on the murder of the man who had been responsible for his three years of pain and misery. The man responsible for his life sentence in a wheelchair. The man responsible for the end of his life as he knew it. Now he was dead, clearly he had been killed by this uniformed, arrogant prick.

He felt cheated, for three years he had dreamt of the day when he would get his revenge on Roger Scott, now it had been taken away from him. He looked at his two brothers, a slight smile, if they kept their hands in the air they would be fine, no problem. Moving quickly he thrust his one good arm inside of his jacket and pulled out the gun he had checked before concealing earlier. His finger was on the trigger before it left the inside of his jacket. Maybe because he was in a wheelchair the other armed police were not taking much notice of him. Maybe because the menacing looks they were receiving from Johnny and the rest of Roger's crew they were more focussed on them.

Whatever the reasons it gave the man in the wheelchair a vital second to squeeze the trigger and put a bullet between the eyes of the lead armed policeman. He dropped to the floor, dead before he got there. The crippled man smiled as he watched his victim die, then turning his gun towards his own head he attempted to take a second shot. The room filled with sound of rapid gunfire, as around six Glock self loading pistols spat their deadly load into the eldest brother from Liverpool. He slumped down into the wheelchair as he died instantly.

D.I. Terry Thompson surveyed the carnage before him. Now four dead, including an armed policeman. He looked at what remained of Roger Scott's empire. All but one of the Scott's gang glared back at him.

Johnny was looking down at Tom and Jeff. He had known them for many years. They had always been inseparable. Born within ten minutes of each other, they had stuck together without the need for other friends during their time at infant and junior schools. It was then in the senior school that they had finally taken enough of the taunts and ridicule, that was shouted at them on a daily basis, due to their lack of academic skills and their unusual size. It was then that their violent cruel streak was first demonstrated to devastating effect. Five boys, all older and bigger than them finishing up a bloodied heap on the floor of the school toilets. They were never picked on again. Soon after leaving school they met Roger and their vicious ways were used to good effect.

Now as Johnny continued to look they were still locked together. Tom had fallen first, sprawled on his back. Blood seeping from the two holes in his chest. Jeff had stepped forward as the bullets hit him. As he fell he had landed on top of his brother. Now it was as if their arms had somehow locked together. They were clinging to each other like some kind of Siamese twins, as if they were still in their mother's womb. They had lived together and now they had died together.

Johnny was a murderer, and a killer, and Roger Scott's chief henchman. It didn't stop him shedding a tear as he continued to stare at the pathetic sight before him.

Detective Inspector Terry Thompson gave the order for the remaining members of Roger Scott's gang and the two brothers from Liverpool to be handcuffed and led away.

Outside of the snooker hall, on the opposite side of the road five or six guys, maybe late teens or early twenties, *all wearing similar hooded jackets,* watched as the police led what was left of Roger Scott's gang out of the door and into the waiting police vans. They stood as one until the biggest of them; maybe the leader spoke, quietly but firmly;

"Hoodies up, walk slowly, don't attract any attention, we are getting out of here." They slouched away, unnoticed, attracting no attention, melting in with the crowds who had stopped to observe what was going on outside the snooker hall.

***

In the evidence holding area beneath Camberwell Police Station, Assistant Chief Constable Ted Walton held on the wall with one hand as he thanked the sergeant who was manning the room. Ted handed over the 9mm handgun that he had requested two days earlier, as part of the proof against two would be armed robbers. As it was still in an evidence bag the sergeant didn't bother to check the weapon before locking it in the cage behind him. Ted Walton slowly and painfully made his way back up the stairs to his office.

Ted had explained to Detective Inspector Terry Thompson, that he didn't want to scare Roger Scott into disappearing again by organising an "all guns blazing" style arrest. He thought the quiet approach would be more successful. His plan had been to corner Scott in his office, one on one, chat to him behind closed doors, try to get him to admit some of his crimes, before Ted would produce the gun and call for back up. Ted Walton went on to explain that Roger Scott was already dead when he had got there, that one of the guys the armed police had shot dead was probably responsible. He was about to arrest both men when they heard the sirens and attempted to make a run for it.

D.I. Thompson had listened patiently. He didn't believe a word of what his superior was saying.

Sitting down at the desk Ted Walton allowed himself a rare smile, he hadn't found much to be happy about in recent weeks. He knew his condition was deteriorating rapidly, much quicker than both he and the specialist at the hospital had anticipated. How long would he have left to live? Clearly he didn't know, but now it crossed his mind that he didn't care. Roger Scott was dead. He was sad that it was not himself that had sent the fatal bullet that did the damage, he was sad that he hadn't been there to witness the event.

After Ted had entered the now closed *Sam's* nightclub with the gun in his hand, cocked and ready, he had seen the body sprawled on the floor, with two clear holes in the face, and part of the back of the head missing. Ted stood for a little while gazing at Scott, taking pleasure in what was in front of him; the man responsible for the death of his beautiful god-daughter, but more so the *bastard* responsible for the death of his son, *his secret son*. It was only then that the Assistant Chief Constable had looked at the man standing over Scott with the gun in his hand. Was he the man who killed Roger Scott? Then the other guy had walked in also carrying a gun. Was he going to kill Roger Scott?

Ted Walton pushed his hands into his stomach as an agonising pain shot through his body. Opening his desk drawer he moved some papers to one side and picked out a small bottle. He looked at the contents through the glass. Slowly removing the top he tipped four tablets into the palm of his hand. He looked around the office, then looked at the pills again before throwing them into his mouth, and quickly swallowing all four.

Ted sat back and closed eyes, he forced a smile as he thought to himself;

"If I had known there was going to be a queue to kill the bastard I would have got there earlier."

The smile disappeared. His body went limp. Assistant Chief Constable Ted Walton was dead. He had died a happy man.

***

November 2012.

Sam stood outside the imposing building that was the Kings College Hospital; she was taking a guess that Adie may be able to receive visitors. Dr. Ahmed had returned her call after her third time of pestering, and now he appeared to be happy to talk to her. A few minutes later Sam sat opposite the doctor as he explained Adie's injuries. He went on to describe that although she had received various head wounds they had been treated and they had healed satisfactorily. The main problem was the recurring psychological issues from her injuries three years prior. Sam remembered what had happened, how when Adie had come out of the induced coma she could not talk or walk or do anything for herself. Then how she had slowly started to recover, before she incurred a further self inflicted head trauma. It was the shock of seeing the person who was partly responsible for her injuries and incarceration, that had made her fling her arms and fists around erratically. It was her own blow to the head that had miraculously aided her recovery.

Sam listened intently. She vividly remembered Adie panicking and causing the damage. Although at the time both Sam and Dr. Ahmed had feared the worst, it was not for the first time in medical history, that it proved to have the opposite effect.

Now Dr. Ahmed went on to explain that in his opinion the recent psychiatric hospital that Adie had been treated in, had caused her more harm than good. He was going to do his utmost to have their methods fully investigated. He also said that he thought the place should be closed for good. They chatted and discussed Adie a little more, and then ten minutes later;

"Adie, how are you?"

Adie allowed a sad smile, she recognised her cousin as she approached the bed. To Sam's joy Adie appeared to recognise her;

"Hello Sam, I've had better days. How are you?"

"Er... fine." Sam sat down next to the bed;

Fine, she thought, fine, never been fuckin' finer, if you consider that I have recently been widowed by a two faced lying cheat, who I now know was also a murderer."

"But never mind me; it is you we are concerned about."

Sam left the hospital an hour later feeling a little better. Adie looked well considering what she had been through. Dr. Ahmed was very pleased with her progress.

***

August 2012 Present day.

It was a day or two later, after hearing about the demise of Roger Scott, that the five or six guys, maybe in their late teens or early twenties, *all wearing similar hooded jackets,* resumed their position on the corner of Peckham Road and Bellenden Road. Near the Burger King, near the array of scruffy shops, some of them boarded up. Near the *Vegas Slots.* Making a nuisance of themselves. Bragging to each other and anybody who would listen, how they had worked for Roger Scott, and had been on his payroll. Elaborating on how they had been involved in various crimes, maybe even murder, and how the police couldn't touch them.

With Roger gone and most of his gang locked up, the pavements were now theirs. They were more than happy that their street cred would be cemented forever in local folklore. Untouchable and invincible.

Only now they were one less.

Mike had asked Sam to help him get to the boxing club where he used to train before his injuries. He said he had something that he needed to deliver. Sam left him there then caught a passing taxi and asked to be taken to the Novotel in Greenwich. She had left what few possessions she still owned there. Sitting in the taxi she was in deep thought, her mind in turmoil. Maybe it was the delayed shock of what she had been through during the past few weeks, maybe it

318

was the fact that so much had happened to keep her mind occupied, that she hadn't really had time to stop and think about her own problems, and the cause of them.

Now it appeared to be over, not any kind of closure to her problems, but a strange sense of relief that Adie was going to recover, that Mike hadn't killed anybody, and under the circumstances he was going to be fine. The thoughts she harboured were about her future, and what to do now the problem of her husband's infidelity had been taken away from her. It now dawned on Sam that she felt little or no sadness at the fact that Roger Scott was dead. It was as if a huge weight had been lifted from her shoulders, a strange sense of relief. Then as suddenly as she had started to enjoy these almost comforting thoughts they disappeared. Now maybe the shock was starting to get to her.

A sudden twinge of sadness, of what might have been. Was it her own fault that her husband had strayed with an ugly well used old woman? Did she not do enough in the bedroom to keep him from straying? In her own opinion, she considered herself to be a lot fun in bed. She would never refuse any request he made, and she considered that after he left her body he was always satisfied.

Looking out of the window as the taxi crawled its way through the London traffic, Sam realised the utter confusion that her thoughts had played on her. Head spinning she ignored the friendly driver as he attempted to start a conversation, or even a little chat. On reaching the hotel Sam paid the man before running to her room, slamming the door shut behind her, before throwing herself onto the bed, and weeping uncontrollably.

***

Yvette had made a full confession as to how she and Spike had hatched the plan to have themselves registered on the list of temporary carers. She found out the name of the guy in charge, a name she knew, a name she had remembered from her youth. One of the many visitors to her mother's house. One of the many men who would enter the small semi in Brixton. One of the tens per week that would disappear upstairs with her mother, and then return half an hour later wearing a satisfied smile.

Yvette had remembered this particular visitor very well. Maybe too well. It had been a Friday night when she had answered the door to a smartly dressed man wearing a suit, and a greasy perverted smile. Her mother had been out of her mind on heroin for most of the day. Although Yvette was only fifteen she knew the situation; that her mother was nothing more than a drugged up whore. She had been explaining to the suit at the door that her mother was in no fit state to accept any visitors. The guy didn't listen; he roughly pushed her to one side and entered the house. Climbing the stairs he called out her mother's name, before entering the bedroom that he knew to be hers.

Upon seeing the unconscious woman as she lay fully clothed on the filthy bed, he shouted to Yvette, telling her to come upstairs quickly, that her mother looked like she was in some sort of trouble, that she needed her daughters help. Yvette ran up the stairs and into the room to find the sad looking sight that she had seen many times before. Only this time there was something different, something that didn't look right. It was then that she felt the sweaty hand on her shoulder; it was then that her mother suddenly opened her eyes and stared at her, a slight smile, maybe a sly smile. Yvette stood shaking as the woman who had

320

given birth to her fifteen years earlier sat up in the filthy bed, and addressed the slobbering visitor;

"Money now! Before you go any further I want to see the cash."

It was at this point that Yvette, at the tender virginal age of fifteen realised what was happening. She began to cry and shake with fear. She pleaded with her mother that she had done her best to look after her over the years. She pleaded more that she was under the lawful age of consent, and still a virgin. Her mother looked on impassively as she counted the money that the fat drooling pervert had handed over. Then she suddenly stopped and looked up. Yvette thought that she had changed her mind, that she had realised what she was doing was wrong. Her mother spoke;

"You are what? Did you say you are still a fuckin' virgin?"

Yvette tearfully nodded. "Yes I am mum. Please, don't let him do this to me." Her mother ignored her; then;

"Did you hear that you perv? Still a virgin, so get your fuckin' wallet back out now, if you want to take her I want more money."

Yvette cried out loud as the guy reached into his inside pocket.

Now as she pleaded guilty to all the charges of child cruelty, child neglect, lying and deceiving in order to procure herself onto the list of foster carers, she suddenly felt sad. Not for herself, who had been warned by her solicitor to expect a custodial sentence. Not for the former head of temporary care, who had earlier been jailed for ten years, for the historic rape of Yvette. Not for her waste of space husband who would be incarcerated for the next five years. Yvette felt sad that she had been instrumental in almost bringing another child up in the same way she had been. Yvette accepted her punishment with the vow to change her life forever upon her release.

***

Silence descended as the man walked into the back room of the Club Cabana in Brixton. It reminded him of old cowboy films he had watched as a child, when the bad guy who usually wore a black hat, entered the saloon and everybody stopped what they were doing to stare at him. The man looked through the fowl smelling, illegal smoke and spotted who he was looking for. Slowly making his way across the room, having to manoeuvre himself around the dozen or so men who refused to move, he finally stood silent in front of the giant of a guy who was clearly feared by all around him. Without speaking the man slowly unzipped his jacket and produced a brown canvass bag. He placed it on the table then stood with his hands by his sides. The big guy spoke;

"According to the word on the pavement you used it."
The man slowly nodded, then:

"Yeah, twice, two bullets." The seated guy replied;

"You know the deal dude, that piece was new, and the silencer, never used; now it's traceable."

The man nodded in agreement; the deal had been to hire the gun for £1000. Plus another £1000 deposit which would only be returned if the gun hadn't been used. Maybe if it had only been hired for use as a threat, or maybe a frightener or maybe something to carry for security. The man answered;

"Not a problem, you can keep the money, all of it. It was worth every penny."

He turned as if to walk away, he then stopped. He

looked at the big guy. Then;

"It isn't a silencer; it still made a noise, that's why it's called a sound suppressor."

With that he walked away with a little more confidence, almost a swagger, back through the crowd, who this time separated to allow him to pass. Leaving the drug filled premises he made his way along Jebb Avenue towards Brixton Hill, then turning left he disappeared through Rush Common and into the maze of terraced streets that pack the surrounding area. The man noticed that the people who he was passing as he walked were giving him strange looks. It dawned on him that he must have looked like the village idiot as he strolled along grinning like the proverbial Cheshire cat.

An hour later sitting on the Gatwick Express as it left London Victoria Station he was still smiling. Replaying over in his mind the way he had set up Roger Scott. The odd anonymous phone call to Camberwell nick. The odd letter with details of Scott's various addresses of his homes and businesses to the Assistant Chief Constable. Over the last few weeks he had unwittingly acquired more time than he might have earlier anticipated. To work on the finer details that would ultimately lead to Roger Scott's demise.

It hadn't been difficult. He knew that the Assistant Chief Constable wanted Scott so badly that he would look at any tip off that came his way. Then it was a case of being patient and watching until Scott made an appearance at his disused nightclub. The man had spent many days sitting in the cafes and bars around *Sam's* It was only a matter of time before Scott would show up.

Glancing out of the window as the countryside sped by, he thought he had probably taken his greatest pleasure in the way the arrogant Scott had smirked at him when he walked into the office in *Sam's* nightclub. How the bravado had disappeared when he noticed the gun pointing at him. Then the smile returning as he opened his mouth to speak. Maybe to say *"You wouldn't dare."* Or maybe *"You're a dead man."* Or maybe some other comment. He never got the chance to say anything. He had died on his feet. The first bullet taking the back of his head out as it exited. The second bullet to the eye was purely for pleasure, three years of pent up anger and frustration being released with a squeeze of the trigger. Was he smiling as he did it? Maybe, he couldn't remember. If not on the outside he certainly was on the inside.

The man now glanced down at boarding pass that would allow him to escape the memory of not only Roger Scott, but more so the misery of his wife. It dawned on him that this was maybe the happiest he had been in many years. *Ironic* he thought; the guy he had just murdered had not only helped, but had also been responsible for freeing him of that bitch of a wife. His sad life had been turned around.

"Because of one man."

The ex P.C. John Jenkins leaned back on the headrest and closed his eyes.

***

Three months later.

Sam sat back in the leather armchair. From behind her desk on the fourth floor of the office block, she could see across many of London's landmarks. Looking away from the window she smiled at Sol Hindmarsh. Sol had been Roger Scott's accountant for many years. He smiled back then spoke:

"I have done everything you asked already Sam. All the

gaming salons have now been transferred into your name. New accounts have been set up so that every penny will be accounted for and the correct amount of tax and VAT paid. Every one of them is now a legitimate business.

I have also found buyers for both of the nightclubs. In a matter of months they will be modern apartments, unrecognisable from what was they were previously." Sam answered;

"Have you made it clear to the buyers that there is a clause in the contract that stops them changing their mind? I want all memory of both those buildings wiping away completely."

"Yes, very clear Sam. They are not interested in clubs of any kind; they see both sites as prime development for modern flats."

Sam smiled;

"All good Sol, I want every part of this business legal and above board. I know we deal with a lot of cash, I also know how good you are at laundering it. Those days are gone; from now on we keep within the law."

Sol slowly shook his head;

"Holy poly. I don't know what Roger would have made of all this." Sam's smile immediately disappeared;

"Mr. Hindmarsh! The name you just mentioned does not exist anymore, and as far as I am concerned it never did. So if you want to continue working for me you will not mention it again!"

Sol was taken aback. He knew Roger Scott was dead, the whole of south London knew Roger Scott was dead. It had been widely reported that one of the two gunmen, who the police had shot dead in the former *Sam's* nightclub, had been responsible for his demise. Sol had realised that something was wrong when there were no official funeral announcements forthcoming. Roger's body had remained in the hospital mortuary for weeks. Nobody had come forward make any arrangements. Eventually he was disposed of without any formal arrangements.

Sol Hindmarsh composed himself. Then;

"I have received a firm offer of three million pounds for your house in Kent, which I have accepted on your behalf. The people involved with purchase are happy to retain the services of Mrs. Cowens as you requested." Sam nodded her head in approval.

Sol continued;

"The contracts for the sale of the London penthouse and the office in Peckham that was used as a call centre, will be signed and exchanged this week. Again on your behalf I have accepted two million pounds and three hundred thousand pounds respectively."

Sam allowed a slight smile, another part of her previous life that could soon be forgotten. She nodded her head again.

"Now before I go any further with transfer of ownership of the flats that Roger owned, er… sorry that were previously owned, are you sure that you want me to give them away?"

Sam answered;

"Yes, very sure, never been so sure. Well all but one. The poor girls who were forced to work in them deserve something, each of them can have the flats free of charge, they have earned them."

Sol scribbled a note. Then;

"And the one in question?"

Sam smiled, an almost evil smile, or maybe a satisfied smile;

"The one in question was occupied by a slag named Mina. She tried to convince me that she was forced to shag my bastard ex-husband. I don't believe a word. She is currently being held in an immigration centre, apparently she has been under the radar for many years, but now it looks like she is going to be deported. I am having the flat fully adapted to cater for a disabled man. He will be moving in as soon as the alterations are complete."

"No problem Sam. That just leaves the snooker hall. Have you thought about what you want to do with it? It returns a decent profit. Enough for somebody to live on" Sam answered, smiling broadly;

"Yes, I have given it a lot of thought. The snooker hall will be wiped out, thrown away like all the other bad memories. I going to have all the snooker tables and the bar removed, I want the two downstairs rooms made into one. It will be a fully adapted a day centre for both physically and mentally disabled people."

"A lift will be installed for access to the upstairs. It will be a place where disabled people can meet safely, have somewhere to go, and be made welcome. I will take advice as to what is required to both entertain and educate the people who attend."

"I want it set up as a charity, so that it will be available for anybody and everybody who wants to go there. I shall be sponsoring that charity personally."

Sol slowly nodded his head as he made more notes; finally he looked up at Sam;

"You are going to be a busy lady, have you thought of enlisting any help already?"

"Yes, after it has been officially opened, by a special guest, a guest so special that the centre will be named after her, the new manger will take over."

"Good, good, anybody I know?"

Sam pressed a button on the phone on her desk. Then;

"Mike, can you come in here please."

Sol turned to look as the door opened and a man in a wheelchair entered the office.

"Meet my new business partner, and the manager of Adie's Day Centre."

***

Epilogue

December 2012.

Dr. Ahmed sat in the background of the comfortable room in the large house that was once a privately owned stately home. It had been in the same family for many generations, before rising costs and the need for refurbishment took its toll. After the resulting auction, it had been converted into a convalescent home, which acted as a go between for psychiatric patients to further their recovery, before being allowed back into society and to fend for themselves.

Adie looked around the room. She had been here for two weeks now. It was a world apart from the first horrible hospital that she had been confined to for many weeks. After going through an assessment period in the Kings College Hospital, in which she had been well looked after and treated as more of a human being, Adie had finally been moved here. The nurses who looked after her here smiled, they said nice things, encouraged her. Now she was allowed to wear normal clothes and shower by herself, and retain a degree of dignity.

Dr. Ahmed had been instrumental in Adie's recent progress. In his opinion the so called hospital that had housed her in recent weeks should have been closed down years ago.

Now he smiled as the door opened and two young ladies entered the room. They walked with bounce whilst giggling and laughing with the toddler that was holding both of their hands, swinging merrily as they advanced further into the room. The happy commotion caused Adie to look round from her chair.

She squealed in delight, as did the small child. Releasing her grip on the two nurses Meg ran across the room shouting *"Mummy"* as she went. Adie turned, arms open as her daughter advanced, leaping into her arms, they melted together as one. Tears ran down the faces of both nurses as they took in the joyous sight before them. Both Adie and Meg cried their own tears of joy as they clung to each other. Dr. Ahmed remained in his chair, watching, taking in the happy scene. He had taken more than a professional interest in Adie. It was three years ago that he had saved her life, only for her to be back in his care in the most tragic of circumstances.

Adie would remain in the home for the foreseeable future, until Dr. Ahmed and the staff were satisfied she could manage on her own. Then she would be monitored as well as cared for, before being allowed back into the house that had been her home for the last three years. Meanwhile the room in which she and Adie would be housed whilst convalescing, contained two single beds. One was a standard size, the other smaller, an ideal fit for a child. *Meg, her child.*

The End.

Author's note

I hope you have enjoyed reading *"Because of one Man"*. Whilst it could be seen as a sequel to the previous story of Roger Scott, *"Destined for the Top"*, it was written in the hope that the book could also be enjoyed as a standalone novel.

This book could not have been written and published without the invaluable help of three very good friends:

Patricia Taylor, Jo Hudson and Trish Farrell. Proof readers extraordinaire.

Also the expert guidance and advice from Mark and Anne Webb of Paragon Publishing.

I, like the thousands of other budding authors, rely on their work being visible. It would be greatly appreciated if you could find the time to leave a review on Amazon.

The competition is fierce, I thank you in advance.

***

My next book is due for publication 2020. It will be a completely different subject to the Roger Scott series.

String vests and catapults.

Is the true story of a man I met by chance while propping up a bar, in a pub in Darlington, Co. Durham.

What started as a *"hello"* turned into a three hour, and mainly one-sided conversation with the guy who said his name was Peter. He told me in a soft spoken, laid back voice that he had served almost twenty five years in the army. Eighteen of them spent in the 2nd battalion of the parachute regiment.

As our conversation developed three guys decided to start a fight in the corner of the room. As I glanced across at the mayhem, Peter put a hand on my shoulder telling me to not get involved. I explained that I had no intention of getting involved, that I had never been involved in a fight in my life and that I would have no idea what to do if approached. He slowly nodded his head in some kind of agreement. Then to my surprise he said that he also did not know how to fight. I looked at him quizzically - an ex Para who couldn't fight????

Peter went on to explain that he would have no problem at all in killing the three of them, but he would not know how to fight them!

I very quickly became both captivated and enthralled at his life's experiences, from childhood through to puberty and into adulthood. As the night wore on I began to realise that Peter had not come through these experiences unscathed. At times he became bitter, as he relayed some of the treatment that life had dealt him. Also, after leaving the Paras he found that he was suffering from Post

Traumatic Stress Disorder. He made it very clear that he did not blame the Army in any way for this condition.

At Peter's request, and with his permission, I have put together his story. The vast amount of what is written is true; most of the rest is based on the truth.

**

Also by Barry Waters

When Adie is discovered in a disused WW2 bunker, traumatised and barely breathing, a number of people take a chilling interest. Why are her injuries self-inflicted?

Detective Sergeant Bill Nixon is determined to expose the violent gangs which thrive in London's corrupt, drug-fuelled underbelly...but is he a match for the ruthless Roger Scott – a man you'd rather not know?

Barry Waters 2019

Still living in Puerto de la Duquesa, Southern Spain. Still working the summer months as a licensed power boat skipper, still enjoying writing and living life to the full. (And the odd glass of wine!)

Lightning Source UK Ltd.
Milton Keynes UK
UKHW020622110320
360160UK00015B/1128